"*It Was Something I'll Always Remember. . . .*"

"I won't apologize for the other night, Erin. I want you to know that. It was something I'll always remember. . . . "

"Sure, Matt. Put another notch on your gun and stash it along with all your other *memories*." She shook his hand off.

"Damn you, you little red-haired vixen! Can't I get through to you?" He spun her around easily. She saw the anger in his face, *real* anger. His blue eyes darkened, shooting cold fire at her, and she began to feel afraid.

"Damn you!" he repeated hoarsely. Then he bent his head and buried it in the soft hollow of her throat, his lips brushing her skin.

"No, no, please," she begged, her fierce courage gone now. She tried to push him away, but her strength was no match for his.

His mouth found hers, and he crushed her to him.

Dear Reader:

We trust you will enjoy this Richard Gallen romance. We plan to bring you more of the best in both contemporary and historical romantic fiction with four exciting new titles each month.

We'd like your help.

We value your suggestions and opinions. They will help us to publish the kind of romances you want to read. Please send us your comments, or just let us know which Richard Gallen romances you have especially enjoyed. Write to the address below. We're looking forward to hearing from you!

Happy reading!

Judy Sullivan
Richard Gallen Books
8-10 West 36th St.
New York, N.Y. 10018

The Silver Kiss

LYNN ERICKSON

PUBLISHED BY RICHARD GALLEN BOOKS
Distributed by POCKET BOOKS

Books by Lynn Erickson

This Raging Flower
Sweet Nemesis
The Silver Kiss

Also published by RICHARD GALLEN BOOKS

Fortune's Choice
  by Eleanor Howard

The Perfect Couple
  by Paula Moore

The Sudden Summer
  by Muriel Bradley

 A RICHARD GALLEN BOOKS *Original* publication

Distributed By
POCKET BOOKS, a Simon & Schuster division of
GULF & WESTERN CORPORATION
1230 Avenue of the Americas, New York, N.Y. 10020

ISBN: 0-671-43348-2

First Pocket Books printing July, 1981

10 9 8 7 6 5 4 3 2 1

RICHARD GALLEN and colophon are trademarks
of Simon & Schuster and Richard Gallen & Co., Inc.

Printed in the U.S.A.

This book is dedicated
to the people of Aspen

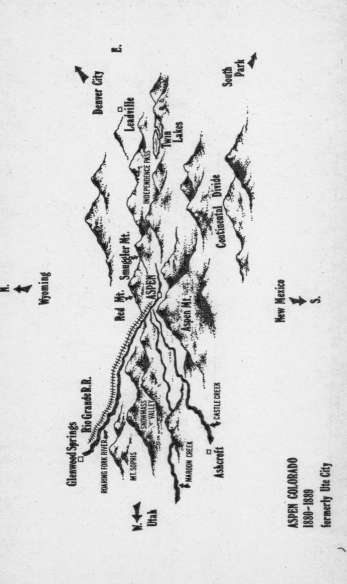

ASPEN COLORADO
1880–1889
formerly Ute City

Author's Note

I have tried to give the flavor and atmosphere of Aspen as I know it now and as it was in the years between 1880 and 1889. Some modern place names have been used to minimize confusion for the many readers familiar with the area.

B. Clark Wheeler had been closely involved in the growth of Aspen; he chose the name of the town and traveled the country to promote its bounties.

The infamous Doc Holiday lived in Glenwood Springs during the last years of his life, dying there in 1887.

It is true that the White River Utes were bodily removed from the western slopes of Colorado and sent to a reservation in Utah in 1881, following their unsuccessful uprising in Meeker, Colorado, in 1879. A small skirmish broke out there in 1887, initiated by a group of white men against a weak band of Indians who had strayed off their reservation.

The railroad moguls were as determined and conniving as depicted. Charles F. Adams was president of the Union Pacific, and General William Jackson Palmer was president of the Rio Grande. The race between the standard-gauge Colorado Midland and the narrow-gauge Rio Grande to reach Aspen is factual, with the Rio Grande arriving in Aspen in November 1888, three months before its rival. Although history does not single out any particular individual in charge of the race in behalf of the Rio Grande, I have created such a character.

LYNN ERICKSON

The Silver Kiss

PART I

Chapter 1

Erin Conner felt the September sun scorch her fair cheeks and sweat bead her brow as she stooped to collect a handful of twigs for the evening fire. Placing the precious wood in the bowl formed by the bunched-up skirt of her yellow dress, she walked along the dry riverbed wishing she were anywhere but here, on a barren Nebraska prairie. She turned around momentarily to reassure herself that her family's wagon was still in sight, then moved up through the waving wine-colored grass and hard, cracked earth to finish her chore.

Although her father had smiled and promised his wife and their two children that everything would turn out fine, Erin could not help but recall his fierce argument that very morning with the wagon master. In spite of the shimmering heat radiating from the tall prairie grass, Erin felt a chill run along her spine; never had she heard her father use such abusive language nor seen his face so etched and drawn. And it had all been so sudden, she remembered—the abrupt, sickening lurch as they hit a prairie-dog hole, the sharp sound of the axle as it broke, and the decision that the wagon train would continue into North Platte without them.

And then they had been alone, the four of them standing helplessly by their crippled wagon and watching the convoy grow smaller and smaller. The wagons had become only a line of dust, then had finally disappeared into the sun-streaked western horizon.

As she bent over now, her skirt catching on the brightly colored wildflowers, Erin remembered the unearthly silence that had hung in the air between her family this morning. But then her father had laughed nervously and broke the ill-boded spell, reassuring everyone that the wagon master would send help as soon as he reached North Platte.

3

Erin smiled hopefully; her father was seldom wrong about anything, so all they had to do was sit tight and wait. Before they knew it, they'd be back with the main party.

She pushed her springing mass of golden-red curls back over her shoulders and began retracing her steps along the sun-splashed hillside toward the camp. She could see her mother bent over the iron cookpot; her older brother, Perry, leaning idly against the wagon wheel, talking with her father. It felt good, somehow warm and safe, to see the family together, seemingly unafraid in spite of this temporary setback. If they weren't worried, she wouldn't be either. In a few days they could catch up with the others and head west through the tall grass again, across the barrier mountains to the California gold fields, where a man could realize his wildest dreams, where they would settle and build a new, rich life.

Suddenly Erin stopped dead in her tracks, the breath snatching in her throat, her hands dropping her gathered skirt and the twigs tumbling around her feet. On a flower-spangled, sloping bluff not far from the wagon she saw an unmoving figure silhouetted incongruously against the bright sky. Quickly she blinked, shading the glare from her eyes with her hand, her heart thudding uncontrollably in her chest. It couldn't be—not in this tranquil setting of amber and gold and green grass undulating in the sunlight. But the Indian *was* there, the sun streaming across his bronzed, painted body, his ebony hair falling down his back. He belonged to this scene as much as the wild geese winging their timeless way overhead, as the antelope that bounded so lightly, as the humped bison grazing serenely in the waist-high grass. Yes, he belonged here, too.

The mounted Indian remained statuesque against the blue, cloudless Nebraska sky; even his black and white spotted pony stood frozen atop the grassy bluff.

Erin's mouth opened to cry out to her family, but no sound emerged through her dry, constricted throat. It was as if she, too, were suspended in time against the soft breeze stirring the ever-moving landscape, and her large, gray-blue eyes could not tear themselves away from the painted brave.

And then abruptly, as if she had contrived the image in her mind, the figure vanished, and all was as it had been only moments before.

4

A sudden nausea rose from her stomach, and her feet moved again, lamely at first, then finally breaking into a terrified run toward the wagon. Incoherent words of fright emerged from her lips as she raced, stumbling, into her father's arms.

"Papa! Papa!"

"There, now, lass! What's all this?" came Patrick Conner's concerned voice. And then, "Come, now, Erin . . . sure and you look as if you'd seen a spirit."

She let her tears flow, lifting her face from his broad chest and looking into his eyes. "I saw—an Indian—up there!" She pointed a shaky finger toward the empty bluff.

For a fleeting instant, Patrick Conner's face grew taut before it relaxed suddenly into a warm, familiar smile. "Coulda been a vision, lass. You've had many of 'em before . . ."

"No!" Erin cried half hysterically. "No—I saw him! I did!" She spun around and faced her mother and Perry. Their faces were reassuring, their smiles condescending. "Oh, please! You must listen . . . I *did* see him!"

"Look, Sis," Perry said, "there's no hostiles 'round here, the wagon master told us that." Perry returned to whittling on a stick, unconcerned.

Her heart contracting in frustration, she realized that they simply didn't believe her. It hadn't been one of her so-called visions—those visions that flitted through her consciousness like fairies' feet, touching her mind's eye with a feather-soft breath, leaving her cold and shaken as if someone had stepped on her grave. This had been real; the painted heathen had sat on his pony and looked silently down on their lone wagon.

Again Erin faced her father. "I *did* see him!"

"If you did, girl, then there's not much we can be doin' 'bout it, now, is there?" He led her over to his wife, Claire. "Now, you sit here with your mama and I'll walk on up there and have a look, if it'll make you feel better. All right?" He gave Claire a sidelong glance that made Erin aware that he only sought to pacify her.

As she sat next to her mother, who quietly resumed peeling potatoes, Erin watched her father check his rifle and then trudge up the dry wash toward the gently sloping bluff. She glanced over at her brother and back to her mother; they

5

acted as if nothing had happened to dispel the peaceful afternoon, as if she were merely a silly fifteen-year-old with overblown fancies.

Resentfully, and a little shakily, Erin picked up a paring knife and began to scrape the skin from a withered potato, her heart still pounding rapidly.

She didn't even look up when her father's warm hand fell on her shoulder and he announced that the prairie was empty save for a rabbit and a couple of hawks. Instead, she bit her full lower lip and gnashed her teeth, wondering in spite of herself whether what she had seen earlier had truly been real or only one of her visions. A tear escaped her eye and fell hotly onto her hand while she ardently prayed that her family was correct and that she was merely beset by an overactive imagination.

The September day would be cloudless. The first frail rays of sun reached across the prairie and touched the yellow-tipped grass in promise of a splendid morning. The peacefulness on the wide expanse of plain was complete: prairie dogs darted from mound to mound, an occasional hawk spiraled toward earth, rabbits bounded cautiously from grass cover to arid stream bed, and deer grazed silently with watchful eyes.

Abruptly, the prairie solitude was pierced by a shrill cry. A single doe raised her head sharply, her ears twitching nervously. Another cry and a muffled sob echoed through the bluffs and dry stream beds. An eagle banked sharply to the left, catching an ascending shaft of air and soaring high above the disturbance. Finally the cries subsided into long, agonizing moans.

Erin sat bolt upright from her sleep, realizing that the dreadful cries had come from her. Her father's hands were on her shoulders, his voice low and soothing. She buried her sweat-dampened head in his chest, unable to voice aloud the vivid nightmare that had awakened her in utter terror. Her chest heaved with her labored breathing.

". . . it was only a dream, girl . . . there, now." He held her tight while his hand stroked her coppery curls.

Long moments later, in the dim, weak light of the wagon interior, Erin finally took a deep breath and dared a look into her father's eyes. "I . . . I saw . . . oh, God! It was so horrible," she wept.

"You had a bad dream," he soothed. "It'll be all right in a minute . . ."

"No!" she wailed. "It won't be! The Indians . . . they . . . they came on horses and they . . . they attacked! Oh, Papa, I'm so scared! I saw it all!"

Again her brow broke out in a cold sweat of fear while her body shook uncontrollably. And all the while Patrick Conner attempted to calm her, Erin could not stop the intense flow of mental images from her nightmare: the garrishly painted faces, the arrows whizzing through the air, the deafening sound of gunfire echoing off the surrounding bluffs.

When her father's efforts to quiet her seemed to have no effect, she felt her mother's gentle touch on her shoulder. "Erin, darling . . . we know you're frightened, but you've had bad dreams before and they don't always come true, now, do they, dear?"

Erin emitted a weak, tearful sigh. "No. But sometimes they do, Mama! You know they do! And even *you* said I could see things!"

"I know I did, dear. But this time you're mistaken. Why, we're perfectly safe, and I'm sure the dream came only from thinking you saw that Indian yesterday and—"

Whatever Erin's mother had been about to say was lost in the eruption of another shrill cry—this one from the crest of the bluff overlooking the Conner wagon.

Erin froze in her mother's arms while she watched her father grab his Sharps rifle and tear aside the canvas flap. She could feel the fear emanating from her mother's body, and an icy chill swept over her. Glancing at her brother, she found no help there, either; Perry was sitting upright, clad in his long underwear, a look of abject horror crossing his youthful features.

A pregnant silence filled the air until the shrieking wail was repeated, followed this time by more bloodcurdling howls.

"Claire!" her father's voice called. "Get the children out and under the wagon—hurry!"

Erin's mother tugged on her arms but could not budge her.

"You heard your father! Hurry! Out, and under the wagon!"

Watching mutely as Perry scrambled off his makeshift bed and through the canvas opening, Erin finally found her strength and quickly followed his example.

The dawn light was pale, and she could only vaguely discern the crouched figure of her father as he took cover by a rock pile.

From her position next to Perry under the wagon, the dry grass prickling her tender skin, Erin closed her eyes tightly. She was afraid to look out, afraid the piercing war cries would begin anew, to slash through her mind and drive her mad.

Minutes seemed to pass like unending hours as they awaited the moment when the heathens would swoop down on them. Erin could feel her heart threatening to burst through her chest, and her ears rang from the pounding of her blood. Why didn't they attack? she wondered, then prayed, Oh, God, please help us, please!

The sudden, awesome sound of hoofbeats filled the air and shook the ground under Erin's stomach; closer and closer it came, until it mingled in her brain with the whoops and cries of the renegades who charged down from the bluff into the tiny camp.

Her eyes flew open and she screamed when she saw the clouds of dust, the relentless hoofs, and her mother's skirts billowing as Claire Conner ran from the wagon's protective shield to her husband's side. Rapid rifle fire split across the hideous roars that poured from the Indians' mouths. Erin lay perfectly motionless, paralyzed with fear.

Then, abruptly, the bedlam ceased. An unhealthy stillness settled over the camp, broken only moments later by Erin's piercing shriek. Before her eyes, under the wagon, appeared a face out of a demonic dream, painted red and yellow, the features twisted and the mouth grinning insanely. The Indian grabbed her chemise and began dragging her out from her hiding place, ignoring her frantic attempts to thwart him.

Then she was standing next to Perry, her chemise and petticoat ripped and tattered. Perry looked on helplessly as Erin continued to struggle against her tormentor. The spotted war ponies danced and skittered nervously around them, then scattered suddenly. When the dust had settled, Erin saw something whose horror she could not avoid: the broken, sprawled bodies of her parents. She immediately bent over and retched, again and again, until it took every ounce of her strength to raise her head and face the painful reality of what had happened.

Like a protective blanket, a numbness enveloped her mind

while her eyes fixed on the lifeless figures of her mother and father. Oddly, it was then that she remembered having seen it all before, in her agonizing nightmare of only minutes ago. Then she had wept until no more tears would come, but now she felt only a slight pricking sensation beneath her eyelids.

Erin slowly became aware of Perry's presence next to her, of his crying and his incoherent pleas to their captors. Seeing her strapping seventeen-year-old brother with his shoulders hunched, his expression of pitiful weakness, made her stiffen involuntarily. My God, she thought, we mustn't show our fright! We must be brave—they mustn't see we are afraid!

Sudden anger overcame her reason. She twisted and fought; she wouldn't grovel at their feet like Perry; she'd fight them with her dying breath.

While four of the Indian renegades sacked the wagon, Erin's captor laughed gruffly at her fruitless struggles. Finally, he became so consumed with amusement that he shoved her roughly to the ground and stood over her, legs spread apart, glaring at her in both triumph and bewilderment.

"Go to hell, you heathen murderer!" Erin spat.

Perry fell to his knees. "No, Sis! They'll kill us!"

"They'll kill us anyway, Perry. Can't you see that?" she retorted sharply, observing the smile fade from the Indian's grotesquely painted face.

For a fleeting moment, as her eyes refused to show her fear and would not leave his countenance, she thought she saw a look of begrudging admiration play across his features. But then it was gone, replaced by his former savage amusement.

Finished with their pillage, the others jumped down from the wagon. All but one remounted the waiting ponies. Approaching Erin's captor, the young, wild-eyed brave pulled his knife and began speaking in deep, guttural tones.

"They're going to kill us," Perry screamed. He turned to the impassive men. "Why don't you take us with you? You could sell us!" he pleaded.

Seeing that Perry was hysterical, Erin said, "We'd slow them down—that's why they won't take us. But if we both act brave, maybe they won't kill us after all."

But her hope fled quickly when the wild-eyed Indian reached down and grabbed a handful of her hair. She squeezed her eyes shut tight, fighting back the overwhelming urge to strike out against him. Oh, dear Lord, she prayed, let him get it over with . . . I'm not strong enough . . . I'm too weak to bear the waiting . . .

Voices reached her consciousness; she opened her eyes. The two Indians appeared to be fighting over her, deciding her destiny in intonations that made her knees quiver and her lips tremble.

Then, abruptly, her hair was released and she saw the young brave stride angrily over to his pony. For an endless moment the frightful face of her captor loomed over her; finally he spoke softly, as if by smoothing his tone she could understand his words.

She remained frozen in her sprawled position while she waited for his next move. Perhaps he wanted to kill her himself—after all, she had fought against him, almost taunting him into vengeful action. She had heard many stories of Indian brutality around the campfires. Weren't the lifeless, mangled bodies of her parents enough to convince her of their bestiality?

She recoiled tightly and flicked her eyes away when he snaked his hand toward her face. And then strangely, amazingly, she felt his fingers on her cheek, not biting into her soft flesh, but stroking her sunburned skin as if he had never touched a white woman before.

Turning her head back slowly, Erin met his gaze and was shocked to see an apparent softening on the painted features. For an instant the brave remained motionless, then he snatched his hand away, moved quickly toward his pony, and mounted.

Then they were gone, the dust from the ponies' hoofs hanging in puffs in the cool morning air, until that, too, disappeared, settling on the earth and covering Erin and her brother in a red, powdery blanket.

"Sis?" Perry's voice reached her stunned mind. "Sis? My God! Can't you answer?"

With great difficulty she directed her attention to Perry, meeting his confused stare. "I . . . I can't believe it . . . they left us—just like that. Why? Why didn't they kill us, too?"

"How in hell do I know?" He got to his knees, his face white and pinched. "My God, Erin! Papa and—"

"I can see them!" she cried suddenly. "Get hold of yourself, Perry—we must!"

"We'll die out here," he sobbed. "They're dead! We'll die for sure!"

Rising to her feet, Erin tried to ignore Perry's outburst, telling herself to gather her wits, not to let herself become like Perry, or they both would die out here.

Suddenly Erin knew what she had to do. The tears, the mourning, would come later, after she had buried her parents and had time to let the horror seep in and take its black hold.

Don't think about that now, she told herself; do what must be done and stay calm. They're dead, and nothing can bring them back now. They must be buried, but I surely can't do it alone.

"Perry?" She faced him again, his eyes a purposeful shade of deep gray now. "You'll have to pull yourself together and help me . . . We've got to bury . . . Mama and Papa."

His mouth fell open. "No! I can't! I can't stand to touch them! You're crazy, Erin—you're heartless!"

"Very well, Perry," she said tiredly. "If you won't help, I'll do it myself."

And in the end, she nearly did—with her hands bleeding and her stomach rising in her gorge. She managed to dig a grave in the hard earth while Perry shoveled only two spadefuls of dirt and fell to sobbing again. When the shallow hole was finished, she dragged her parents' bodies to the edge and quietly talked Perry into lifting them into their final resting place.

Kneeling next to the rough mound of earth, Erin whispered a silent prayer, then rose to her feet and bade her brother carve a cross out of planking from the wagon.

It was late afternoon when the marker was finally completed. Golden shafts of light caressed Erin's shoulders as she took the cross from Perry and pounded it into the mound, her fingers and knuckles bleeding freely over the rock in her hand. She then straightened her stance and viewed the crude handiwork.

"Patrick Conner, 1838 to 1880—Claire Conner, 1842 to 1880," she whispered. It was the best she and Perry could do for them in this lonely, desolate prairie. And only a day before, her parents had held such hope for the future, had done little else but talk about the sparkling new life awaiting them, a life abounding with promise.

Trancelike, Erin walked back to the wagon; she leaned

against the wheel, finally sagging to the ground with her face in her hands. Gradually, inevitably, her shoulders began to shake and her body was racked with sobs, the tears streaming down her dirt-smudged cheeks and wetting her hands hotly.

While the hurt and terror of the day poured from her soul and drained what little strength she had left, she could not help but wish they had never left their poor but secure home in Killarney, Ireland. As her young heart was being torn with pain, she began to curse her uncle—Edward Conner, cold, merciless, and arrogant—the man who had so coveted his brother's wife that he had literally robbed Patrick of his inheritance and ousted him from his lands into a world of poverty and misery. But even while Erin's parents had been all but penniless, they had had an undaunted hope for the future and had made the decision to come to America. Now they were dead—dead and buried on a barren Nebraska prairie without a decent prayer over their grave. Yes, Erin cried mutely, yes . . . it was Uncle Edward's fault! And now he was ensconced in his warm Killarney home, while her parents lay beneath the ground.

"Erin . . ." Perry's voice jolted her back to the present. "Erin, I'm . . . sorry about your having to . . . to dig the grave. I don't know what came over me."

"It doesn't matter," she said with effort, wiping her eyes roughly with trembling fingers.

"Anyway, Sis, what're we going to do now? We haven't much food . . . those dirty savages took everything!"

"No," she whispered faintly. "No . . . they left us alive. That's something, isn't it?"

She felt his eyes on her and knew that Perry didn't really understand; knew that he was weak, insecure, as he had always been. She was the strong one. Hadn't her father said that she was as tough as nails?

And yet now, alone on a foreign plain thousands of miles from home, she didn't feel strong any more. Instead, she felt helpless, unable to cope for another minute, and almost wished that the renegades had killed her, too. What would she and Perry do? Why now, when she most needed a glimpse into the future, couldn't she have one of her visions, anything, even a small hint of what would become of them?

As if he read her thoughts, Perry said, "Come on, Erin, you always know everything. What are we gonna do?"

"I—I'm not sure," she murmured. "I can't see clearly right

now . . . Tomorrow, tomorrow we'll decide . . . For now, we'd best rest . . . it's been a long day . . ."

Ignoring Perry's mumbling, Erin stretched herself out on the rocky ground. There was no hunger or fear now, only a deep emptiness that threatened to swallow her, to spin and plummet her down into its black, bottomless well of despair.

That night, even as the stars arched brightly overhead in glistening splendor, Erin did not sleep, nor did she find peace. Instead, she fought silently against the bleak horror of her present situation, longing miserably for a shoulder to lean on, a friendly face to bring her out of the darkness. There was none. When the thought of her future left her weak and shaken, she desperately forced her mind back to the past—to better days of lush, green Irish leas and soft, loving arms welcoming her.

As the faint, spindly rays of dawn illuminated the tall prairie grass, Erin vividly remembered another dawn, a new, promising morning when their crowded steamship had docked in New York harbor. She sat up slowly in the chill air and looked over at the darkly shadowed grave. Was it only three months ago that she and her family had stood on the dock, happiness swelling their chests, smiles lighting their faces? Was that possible?

She glanced at Perry's sleeping form, then wrapped her thin arms around her chest, suddenly intensely aware of the cold. What would become of them now? Oh, dear God! Why couldn't she see into tomorrow? Why? And oh, God, how she missed her mother and father! Was there ever a greater pain than the one she suffered now?

Tears filled her swollen eyes and spilled down her cheeks. She bit her lower lip and tasted the salt of her misery.

"Oh, God! Please help us . . . please . . ." She hung her head and wept in lonely fear, feeling very small and insignificant in the immensity of the brightening prairie.

Chapter 2

Later that morning, Erin lit a small fire and attempted to cook a few of the staples left by the renegades. We won't starve to death for a little while, anyway, she thought bitterly.

After the poor excuse for a meal, she purposefully tried to put the physical remnants of their life in order: mending their torn clothes, gathering wood, straightening the wagon interior as best she could. But even as her capable hands worked, she could not entirely quell the flow of thoughts threatening to crumble her temporary facade of calm—images of her parents, alive and cheerful; the painted face of the savage who had, strangely, spared her life. But foremost in her mind was the empty loneliness that lay so heavily within her.

Putting the finishing touches on the torn bodice of her yellow dress, she realized that she and her brother had to find a way out of the prairie, for there was no guarantee that help would be sent back from North Platte. Why should she put trust in the word of a wagon master who had left them defenseless in the first place? If they were to survive at all, it would be through their own efforts and because of a plan formed out of sheer desperation.

Suddenly Erin's hand froze in the middle of a stitch. "Perry!" she cried. "The mules! Where are the mules!" Why on earth hadn't she thought of them before? Of course, they would ride out . . .

She watched Perry continue to whittle on his stick, his fair head still bent over his work. When he finally spoke, it was as if from a great distance, and she had to strain her ears to hear him.

"They're gone . . . Indians took them. God, Sis, don't you realize we're stranded? We're going to die out here; might as

14

well face facts." When he fell silent, she looked across at him in amazement, wondering at the ease with which he seemed to slide into helpless despair, to succumb to the situation.

She came to her feet and pulled the remnants of her dress over her head, a stubborn tilt to her chin. *"I'm* not going to die out here! I'm going to walk out—right now—and if you've any good sense, you'll do the same."

Realizing she would need some supplies, Erin climbed into the rear of the wagon and began gathering up handfuls of spilled beans, the water canteen, and finally her flowered bonnet, into which she tucked her mass of coppery curls.

"You're not serious!" she heard Perry call from outside.

"I've never been more serious," she answered, stuffing the pitiful supplies into a leather satchel. Then she straightened her yellow dress, a look of defiance narrowing her changeable eyes, her wide mouth pursed in determination.

But the moment of strength passed, for she realized she couldn't leave without Perry—she would have to convince him to come with her. Perry! How typical of him to hunch his shoulders in defeat and let someone else do all the worrying! Even though he was her older brother, Erin sometimes despised his weak, simpering ways.

She climbed out of the wagon, clenching her teeth in a flash of anger, and approached Perry. "Get your things together," she told him curtly. "We're leaving. I mean it, Perry."

As he opened his mouth to whine out his fear, Erin suddenly cocked her head slightly and widened her eyes in confusion.

"Sis . . . I'm not going anywhere—" Perry began.

"Be quiet, Perry!" She placed a slim finger to her lips. "I thought I heard something."

The far-off sound reached her ears again as she stood motionless, listening, aware of her own pounding heart and the faint sound of rumbling wheels rolling through the prairie grass.

"Someone's coming," she whispered expectantly, an electric shock of hope coursing through her as she turned and fixed her eyes on the blue, eastern horizon.

As the sound grew louder and stronger in the still air, hope began to swell her chest, and her breathing became quick and dry in the agony of waiting.

"You're right!" Perry jumped to his feet, shading his eyes. "It's a wagon! No—it's a whole train! I can see them now!"

Letting her breath out slowly, a smile playing on her pretty lips, Erin thought she had never viewed a sight so lovely, so welcome, as the small band of wagons that inched closer, emerging more distinctly with each moment.

"We're saved, Sis! My God! We're saved!" She felt Perry's arms surround her waist and then was lifted in the air and spun around. Finally he let her go and began waving wildly at the caravan.

"Yes," she breathed in relief, "we *are* saved. It's a miracle."

A soft prairie breeze stirred the tall grass as the young girl watched the wagons in mute disbelief, her blue-gray eyes riveted on the spectacle. And as the figures of the people drew near enough so that she could make out their features, she thought her heart would burst with joy.

And yet, in spite of the enormous relief she felt, a sudden dark, unwanted cloud of despair began to settle over her. As the lead wagon pulled up to their ruined campsite, Erin found herself turning away from it and walking slowly, trancelike, toward the rocky mound that was her parents' grave.

She knelt down on the dusty ground, her hands folded before her. "I . . . I guess we're going now," she whispered. "I only wanted to say goodbye . . . I shouldn't think I'll be back this way . . . I love you still."

Hot, mournful tears welled in her half-closed eyes, then spilled onto the arid earth, leaving tiny wet balls in their wake.

"Sioux, I'd say they was . . . Yeah, them renegades get loose sometimes and don't stop a-killin' till they're all tuckered out, then they skedaddles back to their tribe as if they'd never left."

Erin listened quietly to Joe Ferguson's lurid tales of Indian attacks on the tall-grass plains: the hate the redskin harbored for the white man; the brutal, bloodthirsty search for scalps; the tribal significance of the war paint and the battle cries. And all the while she sat alongside Joe on his wagon, she could not help but wish he would keep his mouth shut—as if *she* needed an education on this hideous subject!

"They lift yer folks' hair, girl?" he asked flatly.

Now Erin fought back tears and the growing urge to scream at him to stop. "Yes, sir . . ."

Her face grew pallid at the memory of her parents' disfigured bodies. However, it wouldn't do to have Joe Ferguson angry with her, for it was only his kindness that had kept them from dying on the Nebraska prairie. What if he should decide to leave them behind? No, she must keep her sharp tongue under tight control; their very lives might depend on it.

"You know, girl, never did figure out what makes these redskins think they got any rights at all to this here land. Did the U.S. government give it to 'em? No, sir! I say, drive 'em all west—right into the Pacific Ocean!"

"Oh . . . my," she replied hesitatingly. "That would be . . . well, awful. Maybe because they were here first . . . well, maybe they resent the settlers and—"

"You been listenin' to them flat-landers back East, girl?" He turned his seamed face to her.

"No, sir. We've only been in America for a few months. I'm afraid I don't know very much about the Indians."

Joe watched her pretty face grow distant, then heard her say, "I was only thinking about home—Ireland, that is. You see, sir, my parents were sort of driven off their lands by my uncle, and . . . well, maybe it's the same with the Indians. I'm sure I don't know . . ."

"You bet you don't, girl. And I'll tell ya another thing— better not go 'round feelin' sorry for these savages. People'll think yer plum crazy, they will."

Of course, Joe thought slyly to himself, girl that looks like her, people ain't gonna care if she's nuttier than a wild mustang. No, sir, it's been a cold day in hell since I've seen a filly as slick and pretty as this little Erin Conner, even if she is a bit young.

Joe glanced sideways at her. It had been nearly a week since he had picked the two of them up and brought them along with his small wagon train, and his urge to reach out and touch those burgeoning mounds on her chest hadn't grown any less—in fact, he guessed it was getting stronger every day.

Wondering just how far she would let him go, he moved his bony leg over and let his upper thigh graze her hip, a lopsided grin pulling at one corner of his mouth. Damn! he thought. Here I am, forty years old and gettin' gray, and anxious as hell to get a feel of a fifteen-year-old! Must be pretty hard up.

Well, shit, she's as nice to look on as a fresh summer peach, all rosy and golden like she is, sittin' by my side.

From under his gray, bushy brows, Joe let his eyes feast on Erin's face. Again he wondered if a little smooth talking might not make her look in his direction. After all, he wasn't so bad-looking himself. His hand reached up to the peppery stubble on his chin and he rubbed the bristles thoughtfully.

"Yer from Ireland, ya say?" His smile revealed his yellowed teeth.

"Yes, sir."

"And ya ain't got no kin out West?"

"No, nowhere in America," she replied grimly. "Mr. Ferguson?"

"Yeah . . ."

"I was wondering, sir, if you've any idea what Perry and I can do in Denver City."

Joe was wondering how on earth her eyes could change color like that. Sometimes they were gray pools; other times a blue or green shade with an odd yellow ring around the pupil.

"Listen, girl, you just let Joe, here, worry 'bout finding you a place. There's lotsa work in Denver City—real booming town it is."

Yeah, he mused silently, real booming, all right, full o' whorehouses and saloons. A few nice places, too, but no way would I get her a job at one of them fancy establishments. No, I only knew a few of the madams, but that'll have to do; least she'll be fed. Pretty as she is, she'll end up in a whorehouse sooner or later anyway. Why not do a favor for my favorite madam, 'fore someone else sells her into a house? Too damn bad, though, she seems a nice enough kid . . .

"You mean you can find us work? A place to live?"

"Sure. Got a lotta friends in Denver City, so, like I said, you must stick with Joe, here." He patted her on the shoulder, feeling the firm young flesh under the thin yellow cotton. Joe's heart began to beat rapidly, and a flood of desire spread through his groin. Then he recalled her brother, lying asleep in the rear of the wagon. The brother might be a problem, but the more Joe thought about it, the more he doubted that Perry would raise a finger to help his sister. The boy seemed yellow-bellied, a real greenhorn. Yep, Joe cackled to himself, if old Joe plays his cards right, he may just have Erin eatin' out of his hand 'fore we get to Denver City.

For the rest of the afternoon Joe fell silent, driving his mule team west along the well-traveled trail. But if his mouth was still, his brain was not. He imagined his hands tangled in Erin's golden curls, the way her bosom would look with the firelight dancing over the small tips, the soft hair between her legs, the feel of her rosy skin in his arms, how she would cry out when he penetrated her, and how she would cry out later, when he had taught her a few things.

For two full weeks Erin had been all but forced to tolerate Ferguson's attentions; if she dared voice her loathing for him, she was certain he would leave them stranded. At least she believed he would, and that kept her humbly silent whenever he leaned closer to her ear or just happened to brush against her breasts. And each time he made a move toward her, Erin's fear of him grew stronger, so that finally she felt it necessary to speak with Perry. Surely her own brother could help her in this delicate matter.

Erin and Perry were walking behind the wagons with some of the other people when she broached the subject. "Perry . . . there's something I've been meaning to ask you," she began hesitantly.

"Yeah? What, Sis?"

"Well . . . it's about Mr. Ferguson." She felt her heart beat more rapidly; the words were difficult to form. "He . . . he touches me a lot, and I hate it."

"He touches you? You mean . . . well, in a private place? Is that what you're trying to say?" Perry stopped walking and turned to face her.

She felt ashamed now, cheeks flaming scarlet and eyes averted from her brother's. "Yes . . . and I'm afraid to say anything. You know how it is . . . ."

"You bet I do, Erin. And I'll tell you something else, just in case you've forgotten. We're here, alive, because Ferguson was good enough to take us in." She thought Perry's tone sounded strained, as if he were about to say something unpleasant. He continued slowly. "Look, Sis, you don't appear to be harmed, so it can't be all *that* bad, now, can it? It sure would be a lot easier on all of us if you'd just humor him—"

"What? Are you actually telling me to let him shame me? Oh, God, Perry, I can't believe it! I thought you'd stand up for me!" Sudden tears sprang into her eyes as she whirled away from him. A rush of hatred filled her, hatred for her own flesh and blood. And what was she supposed to do now? Let Ferguson grow bolder and bolder until he did something unspeakable to her? No! Never! She'd die first!

At dinner that night, while they sat around the crackling fire, Erin had a chance to prove her vows of that afternoon, for Joe inadvertently brushed against her backside while she measured out the coffee.

Spinning around abruptly, hands on hips, she spat, "I'll thank you, sir, to—to keep your hands to yourself!"

She saw the lines in his craggy face deepen, his hooded eyes narrow perceptibly. When he spoke, Erin nearly stumbled backward at the harshness of his voice. "Better be gettin' used to it, girl . . . where yer goin', they'll do a lot more than touch ya!"

And then she heard him laugh, deeply and thoroughly, until the sound of his mirth crashed in her ears and she felt a chill run up her spine.

"What . . . what are you talking about?" she breathed in confusion, afraid to look him in the eye.

"You'll see, girl—you'll be seein' real soon. Mark my words!" He reached for her then, almost knocking her into the fire pit when she reacted to his sudden movement.

But in spite of her instinctive recoil, she was unable to avoid his embrace.

"Stop it! Stop!" she wailed as his hand closed over her bosom and squeezed it.

And all the while she was forced to endure his crude attack, his breath making her gag, she knew there was no help in sight: Perry had disappeared quietly into the night shadows.

"All right—all right," Ferguson said. "I ain't got no use fer a kid, anyways. I'll be gettin' me a real woman when I get to Denver City. The hell with you."

Erin felt herself shoved backward. Her foot caught on the hem of her dress, and she stumbled and landed on her backside in the dust. An all-encompassing weakness coursed through her body, leaving her unable to move.

When her head cleared at last and she realized she was alone by the fire, sprawled like a rag doll on the cold ground, an odd, bitter thought sprang into her mind: Is that what it is like? A man's rough hands on your cringing flesh, his hot breath making your skin crawl? My God, she realized, it's horrible, a nightmare!

And then Ferguson's words echoed in her brain: *Better be gettin' used to it . . .* What had he meant? Was he going to attack her again? Abuse her horribly? And Perry, her own brother—would he forever fail her, like a weak strand of yarn that gives way at the least strain?

For days she went about her camp chores with dark circles under her usually bright eyes, and jumped every time Ferguson came in sight. The fear that he wasn't yet done with her would not lessen, even though he seemed to pay her no mind. The thought that she would soon be in Denver City and have a real job did little to assuage her. For hadn't Joe hinted that something terrible awaited her there? Perhaps, she told herself often, he was just threatening me because I wouldn't give in to his vile attack.

Time and time again, as she trudged slowly behind the wagons, she prayed for one of her visions, for even a clue to what lay in store for her in Denver City. But none came.

With the prairie now behind them, the land swelled ceaselessly to the west, rolling at times, split occasionally by dry riverbeds; but something now banked the western horizon. She could see it when they topped the crest of a hill or when a deep valley stretched its wine-tipped, waving grass across the expanse. It was the rising of the majestic Rocky Mountains, reaching upward mightily to touch the clouds, puncturing and delineating the azure Colorado sky like a stage backdrop.

The spectacle lifted Erin's spirits; just to see the famed barrier of giant rock made her breath catch in her throat and her eyes turn a deep blue. She knew they must be near Denver City, for her father had told her it sat at the base of the snow-capped peaks, where the plains halted abruptly before the lowering immensity of the mountains. There she would find security, that much, she promised herself. No matter what destiny Joe Ferguson planned for her, it couldn't be as bad as what she had just lived through. And she would work hard and save money, enough money to see her and Perry through.

The day before they reached the raw and growing settlement of Denver City, Erin decided to put the past from her mind and cease skittering around like a scared rabbit.

Ferguson had not touched her since that night by the fire, and even Perry seemed somehow more alive, more vital. She would dismiss her anxieties, too. A new life lay ahead, one that she would strive to perfect. Her hands were skilled and she was willing to work diligently at any trade. In America, as her father had said so often, a dream could become a reality overnight; all she had to do was decide what her dream would be. Suddenly, everything seemed so simple.

With cheerful thoughts on her mind, Erin moved quickly to catch up with Perry. "Wait up for me—I want to talk," she called ahead, breathless with excitement.

He stopped and turned around. "Well, you sure look happier now, Sis."

"Oh, I am! I really am! I was just thinking about our future, and suddenly I remembered Papa's dream. It can be ours, too . . ."

"Now, hold up there, Erin," he said, half-laughing. "I've got plans of my own—thought I told you."

"I—what do you mean, plans of your own?" Her eyes widened in surprise.

"I'm going prospecting with Joe—he asked me to. Said he was sick of leading all these greenhorns 'cross the prairie from St. Louis and was going to get rich now. Come on, Sis, don't look like that. I was sure I told you."

"Liar!" she accused. "You know you never said a word!" Tears traced down her cheeks as the bottom fell out of her world.

"Erin, what'd you think I was going to do? Get some filthy job for ten cents an hour?"

"You're just stupid, Perry," she retaliated in a flash of fury. "Joe Ferguson is a nothing! He only wants you around to slave for him! Why—why, he's using you! Can't you see that?"

Why, just when she was finally accepting the fact of her parents' death, did everything have to turn sour again? Her eyes grew red and swollen as she stood facing Perry; the yellow-brown prairie seemed to sway and undulate sickeningly all around her.

"Look, Sis, I talked to Joe about you. He's already got in mind a place for you to live and work. You'll be all right. And besides, I'll only be gone for a while, and then I'll come back for you."

"You . . . you promise?" she heard herself say, a frail, newborn ray of hope lighting the dark void she felt.

"Sure. You didn't think I was going forever, did you?"

They began walking again while Erin tested the idea of Perry's leaving her for a time. She attempted to examine all aspects of it, but she was frightened; images crowded her mind. What if Perry didn't return—what if he were injured or killed? She felt that gnawing loneliness in the pit of her stomach again, reminding her of the day her parents had been killed.

"You can see it's the best, Erin," he said slowly as they trudged on. "Maybe I'll be rich when I come back for you."

"Maybe," she mumbled, still in shock.

"Erin? There's . . . ah . . . something I've been meaning to ask you. Seeing how Joe said you'd be fed and kept, even paid probably, well . . . I was wondering if you'd lend me those dollars you've got sewn in your hem." He placed a fist in his mouth and coughed nervously.

"My silver dollars?" She turned her gray-blue eyes on him. "Mama gave them to me. They're all I have."

"Just a loan, Sis . . . I'll pay you back."

What did it matter now? she wondered. She had no use for them anyway. Perry was the only family she had left. She couldn't bear to quibble about such trifles when her last link to her former life was to be severed so rudely. Let Perry have them. Maybe if she lent them to him, he'd feel more obligated to return. Again, a tear escaped her eye.

"Well, I guess it would be all right." She picked up the hems of her dress, fumbling with the torn material because her hands were trembling. "But you promise you'll be back?"

"I said I would, didn't I?"

Joe Ferguson's wagon rolled down the rutted streets of Denver City, bouncing and jostling Erin until she thought she would be sick. She kept her eyes fixed ahead, her hands clasped tightly before her.

It was truly autumn now. Yellow leaves rushed down the streets and swirled around the mules' legs as the wagon plodded west toward Larimer Street. Ahead, the brown plain washed against the foothills of the mountains, frothed with foamlike white, the peaks meeting the crystal sky. But this time the marvelous sight did nothing to lift Erin's spirits. Like the crisp, dry leaves around them, she felt dead, brittle, crushed under the weight of her unknown future.

Suddenly the wagon lurched, then halted. She looked nervously sideways at the freshly painted, turreted edifice that sat nestled in a hard-baked plot of dirt. So this was to be her new home, her future. It lay mysterious and frightening behind the empty-looking facade, behind the tightly drawn, green damask shades that hid the inside world from view.

"Wish ya had a better dress, girl," Joe boomed gruffly as he eased himself from the driver's board onto the street.

Erin glanced at the house again and then down at Joe's brown-splotched hands, which were reaching up for her, beckoning her forward, into a new life.

Chapter 3

Erin could feel Ferguson's rough hand on her arm as they climbed the steps to the house. Her heart pounded dully in her chest. Where was he taking her? What awaited her behind those closed doors and drawn shades?

"Who lives here?" she asked, trying to keep her voice calm. "What will I be doing here?"

She twisted her head around and saw her brother sitting on the wagon, staring straight ahead, seemingly unconscious of her plight. Tears blinded her eyes and a pang of anguish gripped her heart as she stumbled up the last step.

"This place b'longs to a . . . friend o' mine. She'll take care of you, kid. I just can't be saddled with a greenhorn girl where I'm headed." Ferguson's bony fingers released her arm, and he knocked on the varnished wood door.

A small window slid aside in a dark panel, and Joe straightened involuntarily. The door opened, gliding silently and smoothly back, giving Erin the quick impression of a dimly lit but richly furnished entryway hung with too much fringe, too much opulent drapery.

Joe guided her into the vestibule, and the door clicked as it settled back into its frame, shutting off the outside light.

Erin blinked several times in the sudden dimness, trying to make out the details of the figure that had allowed them entrance.

A husky feminine voice broke the hushed stillness, penetrating Erin's fear. "What's this, Mr. Ferguson? Bringing along your own entertainment these days?"

Joe shuffled, embarrassed, on the plush Persian carpet. "Heck, no, Hattie. This here's a girl I found out on the prairie. Orphan. Injuns got her ma and pa. There's not a soul to see to her, so I thought . . ."

"Oh, the poor child! How terrible!" The sympathy in the woman's voice caused a crack in Erin's tight control. Was there such a thing left in the world as a person who could really care, who could really feel something for her?

At the touch of a soft hand on her shoulder, Erin turned toward its owner as a storm-tossed ship turns toward a welcome beacon of light on the shore. She saw a slim, attractive woman who wore her red hair fluffed high on her head; a blue satin wrapper covered her frame and was tied carelessly with a fringed sash. She was perhaps thirty-five, and her pale face was powdered and rouged just short of tastelessness. Erin even thought her perfume was rather strong and musky. But as Hattie's arm came around her shoulders with no trace of condescension and their eyes met, Erin sensed that she might possess a measure of human compassion.

"What's your name, my dear?" the woman asked. "Mine's Hattie Nelson."

"Erin Conner, ma'am."

"Well, Erin Conner, I'm certain we can find a place for you here. You sure there's no one at all you can go to? Relatives? Friends?"

"No one, ma'am. There's not a soul . . . no one." Erin felt her eyes begin to fill with tears again; the mere voicing of her terrible loneliness brought all the anguish back and filled her with dark imaginings. She tried hard to swallow her tears, not wanting to break down in front of a total stranger, even one who she thought would understand her plight.

Joe Ferguson's voice rasped across her consciousness, giving her time to compose herself. "Then I kin go, Hattie? You'll see to her? Introduce her to Lucille and all?"

It struck Erin that Joe sounded oddly relieved. He's glad to get rid of me, wash his hands of me, she realized bitterly.

"I'm sort of in a hurry," he continued. "Gotta find me a spot for the winter. Headin' for the gold camps 'fore the snow breaks loose. I'm through babyin' flat-landers 'cross these here mountains."

"Sure, Mr. Ferguson, you and a few thousand others. Well, good luck to you."

"Thanks, Hattie." Joe turned to Erin and regarded her from under his bushy brows, almost wistfully, she thought. "Bye, kid."

"Goodbye, Mr. Ferguson." Suddenly she felt both relief at his leaving and a desire to hang on to the only person she knew in this raw new world full of strangers. She steeled herself against the latter, reminding herself that Joe Ferguson was a dreadful old lecher and she was well rid of him.

"Tell Perry not to forget his promise—and tell him goodbye again for me. I'll . . . I'll miss him."

"Sure, kid. I'll tell him."

The door opened, the light streamed in, brightening the colorful pattern in the carpet for a second, then the door closed and the hall was dark again. Erin heaved a wavering sigh of sadness, and of acceptance of the future, and turned to Hattie.

"Is this your house?" she asked shyly.

Hattie laughed harshly. "My house? No. But don't I just wish it were! Come on, Erin. Let's fix you up some before you meet Madame Lucille, make you a bit more presentable. Lucille—she's the one that owns the house. I just work here."

"What do you do, then? Are you a housekeeper, a governess?"

Hattie stopped short, and Erin thought that her eyes narrowed slightly. "So he didn't tell you what goes on here?"

"Who, Mr. Ferguson? No, he never said anything—just that you'd take care of me . . ." Erin felt as if the words they were speaking were at cross-purposes, leading to bramble thickets of confusion.

Hattie seemed embarrassed, her pale face flushing under the rouge. "Well, kid, it's like this. We . . . ah . . . entertain menfolk here. You know—champagne, cigars, music . . . and women."

Suddenly Erin felt the blood drain from her face. Her brain whirled feverishly. How stupid she had been, how unutterably innocent! But naturally, who else would Joe Ferguson think to leave her with? She was in a house of ill repute! A brothel!

Through the fog of confusion and shock that surrounded her, she sensed a cool hand on her arm; and a husky voice reached her ears.

"Hey, Erin, it's not as bad as all that. Lucille treats us pretty decent, most of the time. And besides, you're too young. Most likely you'll just work in the kitchen. It's sort of like a big bunch of sisters here. You'll get along just fine."

As Hattie prattled on, Erin's mind seethed with unanswered questions. What would this Madame Lucille really make her do? Would she actually be working in the kitchen, or would she be forced to flee into the unfamiliar streets of Denver City? She tried desperately to quiet her fears, telling herself that she should wait and see what happened before she panicked and spoiled her only chance for survival.

Hattie led her down a hall, up a narrow flight of stairs, down another hall, and into a cheerful, feminine-looking room.

"This here's my room. We'll give you a bath, and I'll get a new dress for you. That one's sure seen better days." Hattie cocked her head to one side, hands on hips, and pursed her lips in thought. "Luisa's about your size. Those Mexicans are little skinny ones like you. I'll get one of her dresses—she won't mind."

Later, when Erin was soaking in the hot tub, she felt the weeks of horror fade for the first time. Hattie bustled about, gossiping incessantly and hardly giving Erin a chance to talk. The girl merely lay back in the steaming water, closed her eyes, and relaxed, determined to live only in the present and not worry about tomorrow, or the tomorrows beyond.

She was alive, she was warm, she even was clean now. This place couldn't be too bad, she mused, listening idly to Hattie. It could certainly be worse.

A picture of the Indian attack rose unbidden before her, and for a fleeting moment it was as if the savage shrieks and rank animal smells were there in the same room with her.

She shuddered involuntarily in the cooling water and opened her eyes, drinking in the reassuring yellow roses on the beige wallpaper, the bright green quilt on Hattie's bed.

"Let's wash your hair now, Erin. My, it's as dusty and tangled as an old bearskin!" Hattie poured fresh water on Erin's head, lathered it, and began scrubbing with thin, strong fingers, talking all the while. "You'll see Lucille when we're done here, but make sure you call her Madame—Madame Lucille." Hattie leaned closer to Erin's ear and spoke in an exaggerated whisper as she toweled the girl's red-gold curls dry. "Says she's a countess—from France, no less." Hattie winked. "Like hell she is! She's an octoroon from New Orleans, and one with hoity-toity airs at that. Countess, ha! The closest she ever got to being a countess was in bed with the count!"

Erin smiled weakly, shocked but also amused by Hattie's indelicate chatter. Mama would be turning in her grave if she saw me now, Erin thought to herself, being bathed and pampered by a—well, a woman of ill repute. Mama, I'm sorry, but I'm here, and it's better than being out on that prairie, alone, starving, or worse. I'll just stay here until Perry comes back for me, or until I find another job in a more respectable place.

"There," Hattie said. "That's better. Now, put this dress on. It's the plainest one I could find in Luisa's closet."

With Hattie's help, Erin succeeded in getting into the dress. It was a vivid turquoise, a harsh color, but oddly flattering to her complexion. It fit well enough, although it was somewhat loose in the bosom and hips.

"It'll do," said Hattie, her head to one side. "Not bad at all. Now I'll take you downstairs to Madame. She's a crusty old harridan, but if you act respectful to her, you'll get along. That's what she wants—respect." Hattie gave Erin an apologetic grin. "It's a failing in our profession."

Erin felt a flush rise to her cheeks at Hattie's words, which made her think of what went on, what was perhaps going on at this very moment, behind the closed doors they passed. And this Lucille, what would she do with her? Cast her out again? Send her into one of those rooms? God, please, Erin prayed, don't let her do that.

Suddenly she wanted to turn and run back down the corridor to Hattie's cheerful room, never to leave it again. It was safe. What lay ahead was so uncertain, so fearful, and she felt so alone. But Hattie led her relentlessly down the carpeted stairs to the front of the house, then knocked lightly on another closed door.

"*Entrez.*"

Hattie straightened up and smoothed her hair, the unconscious gesture frightening Erin more than anything Hattie had said. Who was this madame who had total control over her life now? What could she hope for in the hands of a complete stranger? The impossibility of her position struck her once again, and she felt weighted down with the burden of her grief and apprehension. Her limbs were cold, leaden, and she hardly had the strength to follow Hattie into the room.

A tall, imperious woman dressed in black stood posed against the red satin draperies that covered a high window. The snapping black eyes regarded Erin openly, disdainfully, as if she were an insect. Gracefully, the woman approached them, seeming to glide across the floor as if she were on wheels.

"And who is this . . . this urchin, may I ask?" The woman's head turned slowly on the long stalk of a neck, the eyes finally resting on Hattie.

"This is Erin Conner, a poor orphan. She's been traveling from Nebraska, madame. Joe Ferguson brought her here, not knowing what else to do with her."

Erin noticed that Hattie's voice had become thin, almost quavering. What power did this woman hold over her?

The small head, with petal-like curves of black hair piled stylishly on top, moved on its stem, a prolonged turning, the large, darkly liquid eyes fixed speculatively on Erin. Erin felt a chill crease her spine, as if a deadly snake had riveted its poisonous gaze upon her.

The full lips pursed, then were still for what seemed an endless time. A cold sweat broke out on Erin's forehead. The tension in the opulent room was palpable. Hattie was deathly pale.

"No mother or father, you say?" Lucille asked Erin sharply.

"No, madame." The words were whispered, barely audible. "They were killed by the Sioux." Erin's eyes threatened to fill with tears in spite of her profound effort to control herself.

"None of that, *s'il vous plaît, chérie.*" Madame shook a long finger at her. "We're all cheerful in this house, and we don't look back at anything, *comprends-toi?*"

"Yes, madame," Erin said, terrified of the flashing black eyes and the imperious tone of voice.

Then Lucille looked at Erin closely, turning her around, her hands cool and talonlike on Erin's skin. She even lifted the girl's skirt to view her ankles.

"She will do quite well, *n'est-ce pas?*" Madame Lucille spoke half to herself as she stood back and put a ruby-tipped finger to her lips.

Do quite well at what? Erin's mind screamed the question mutely, but she kept her eyes downcast and said nothing, too afraid to ask the question, too afraid even to try her voice.

"*Assieds-toi, chérie.*" The hard voice broke into Erin's thoughts, and she looked up to see Madame Lucille seated like a dark flower behind an ornate desk, pointing to a chair.

The head turned to Hattie. "You may go, Hattie. Wait outside. You have done well."

The words fell like a dirge of funeral bells on Erin's ears. *You have done well.* In God's name, what had Hattie done well? Trapped another innocent victim? Oh, God, what did she mean?

Erin sank into the proffered chair, her knees suddenly so weak that she was grateful for its comfort, and hid her clenched hands in the folds of her dress.

Lucille sat back in her chair and put the tips of her jewel-laden fingers together in front of her as she fixed her intimidating gaze upon Erin. The full, sculpted lips moved, tearing Erin's eyes away from the blood-red tips of those long fingers.

"You are a bit young yet, *chérie,* although there are those who like that. But I will save you for a while. *Oui,* in a few years you will be quite *magnifique.*"

Erin stared at the woman, mesmerized, hardly hearing her. She waited for the words that would seal her doom and send her off into one of those closed rooms, where a man would be waiting to do unspeakable, private things to her. She shuddered, thinking of a strange man's hands on her body, not at all clear about what would happen, but very fearful. She couldn't go through with it—she couldn't! If only her knees weren't so weak, she'd get up and run out of this house, away from the black-garbed, aloof woman who emanated a strong aura of danger.

But somehow her legs did not move, and she sat as still as a statue under the frightening stare of Madame Lucille. She knew that a girl alone would not get far in the rough frontier settlement of Denver City, and that she would end up no better off—worse, more than likely—than she was here in this house. A small voice of reason fought against her overwhelming disgust of Madame Lucille, of all that she stood for, and told her to put up with the situation until she could gather her wits and escape.

Lucille was speaking again. "You will help my cook in the kitchen for now, and do laundry for the girls. Then, when I feel that you are ready, you will be asked to undertake . . . other duties. You must work very hard, for I will not allow laziness here, do you understand? A girl alone on the streets is quickly done in, so you will want to remain in my good graces."

"Yes, madame," Erin said, feeling as if an icy breeze had brushed her body, even though the room was warm and stuffy.

"You may go, *chérie.* Hattie will show you to your quarters. Do not disappoint me, *petite.*" The black eyes locked with Erin's wide gray-blue ones and sent their message to her: obey or leave, live or die, it is all in my hands.

Somehow Erin found the strength to rise and walk to the door; she opened it and stepped out into the hallway, gulping in deep breaths of the cooler air as if she were strangling. Then she noticed Hattie sitting on a settee, a pinched look of unease on her face.

"Well?" Hattie asked nervously.

"She said I am to help in the kitchen . . . for a while," Erin replied weakly.

"That's a start, and not a bad one at that. Come on, we'll get you all fixed up." Hattie smiled, obviously relieved.

Erin followed the redheaded woman down the hall, feeling like a lamb that had been led to slaughter, only to be reprieved from the butcher's knife for a brief spell.

"You'll see," Hattie said, laying a hand on Erin's arm, "it's quite nice here, really. And you'll be in the kitchen, so you won't even have to see any of the gentlemen."

Erin's heart lurched at Hattie's mention of "the gentlemen." How had this happened to her? How long would it go on? Until Perry came back? And when would that be? She stifled a frightened gasp with her hand, hoping Hattie had not heard it.

The walls seemed to close in on her, their gold damask pattern whirling and twisting before her tear-blurred eyes; the draped velvet hanging over the archway appeared to undulate and reach out; the fringes suddenly swayed and pointed at her, reminding her of Madame's long fingers.

There was no escape.

Chapter 4

Erin moved her stool as near as she dared to the radiating heat of the wood stove; the warmth flushed her cheeks, but the back of her neck still felt a draft from the window. She shivered as her body began to respond to the fingers of heat reaching out for her, enveloping her in a pleasant cocoon of comfort.

It was gray and blustery outside, and an early snowstorm was whipping precocious flakes down the town's muddy, rutted streets. Erin craned her neck to look out the window at the October storm, then resumed polishing the huge silver service that was Madame Lucille's pride and joy. She rubbed the metal vigorously, watching the tarnish disappear and the mellow glow of old silver take its place. Her face appeared in the round platter, fuzzy and blurred, and she stopped for a moment to contemplate her reflection. She could see the pale oval of her face, the springing halo of reddish-gold curls surrounding it, the large, shadowed hollows of her eyes, the too-wide mouth and small nose.

Suddenly she froze in stunned fright. The reflection dissolved for an instant and she saw instead two dark horses, their sharp hoofs raised menacingly above her; then the surrealistic sight was dispelled as swiftly as it had appeared. Goose bumps rose on her flesh; she felt cold, weak, dizzy, as if she had been through a terrible ordeal.

It will pass, she told herself, closing her eyes and gripping the silver tray tightly. It will pass; it always does. But for a moment her surroundings seemed very distant, while the image of the horses rising above her was acutely tangible, terrifyingly real.

A vision now, when she least expected it! And where had her "sight" been when she was stranded on the prairie? She drew in a deep, calming breath and shook her head as reality crept back into her mind again, leaving her shaken but glad to view the kitchen clearly once more. Horses' hoofs indeed! Why, she hadn't seen a horse in weeks! She would dismiss the vision as absurd!

The kitchen door flew open and Madame Lucille swept in on an aura of perfume, expensive cigars, and brandy. She walked quickly over to Erin and tapped her on the shoulder. As always, Lucille made her feel anxious, as if the butcher's knife might fall at any moment. She could not fathom what went on behind those dark, fluid eyes; they were unreadable.

"Erin"—Lucille rolled the "r" expertly—"go to the red room with a carafe of wine for Mr. Mortimer. He wishes some refreshment." She seemed to notice the startled expression on Erin's face, the pallid cheeks and frightened eyes. *"Qu'est-ce que c'est?* What is this? You must look more cheerful. What will the customers say—that I beat you? Smile, *petite,* and hurry, hurry. This man does not like to wait." Her expert hands fluffed Erin's hair, smoothed her patterned dress, pinched her waxen cheeks. She found a crystal carafe, filled it with wine, and put it on a silver tray. *"Voilà!* Now go, *ma petite,* and be polite to Mr. Mortimer— he is a fine, rich gentleman."

Erin rose and walked as quickly as she could while balancing the silver tray. For the moment she wanted only to escape Madame's sharp scrutiny. As she left the warm, sweet-smelling kitchen, she heard Lucille call after her, "Be quick now, *vite.* The red room, and don't spill a drop!"

Erin walked carefully up the stairs toward the red room, then paused at its door. She had not been sent on such an errand before. Why now? And why not one of the other girls? But suddenly she realized that so far she had been treated most fairly, and this was probably nothing more than a simple chore that the other girls were too busy to take care of. She shook off her fleeting suspicions and decided she had best attend to the task at hand or she would bring Madame's wrath down on her.

When she received no immediate answer to her knock, she rapped louder. A deep, throaty voice bade her enter. Turning the doorknob, she looked at the tray and saw the ruby liquid slosh up the sides of the crystal decanter. She prayed the wine would not spill.

The single oil-burning lamp did little to light the elegant bed chamber, and her eyes adjusted slowly. Doing her best to appear capable, Erin moved slowly to where a large man sat engulfed in a circle of floating blue cigar smoke.

"Good evening, sir." She smiled weakly. "Madame has asked me to bring this to you." She placed the tray on a side table. The man merely nodded his head but did not speak. "Will there be anything else, sir?" she asked, stepping slowly away from him. There was something distasteful in his intent perusal of her, and she began to wonder if she had done something wrong. Perhaps it was something she had said. She glanced at the decanter; not a drop had spilled.

"What is your name, child?" Mortimer placed the cigar in a leather-bound ashtray, shifting his great weight as he did so.

"Erin, sir . . . Erin Conner." Her eyes tore themselves away from his gaze and traveled uncertainly around the richly decorated chamber.

"An Irish lass. You've got that look about you, girl. I like that."

With seeming effort, he rose to his full height and approached her. She did not move, but was intensely aware of his massive bulk. When his hand came up and brushed her cheek, then pushed her curls away from her face, she flinched and involuntarily stepped back.

"Come, girl." He motioned toward a chair. "I wanna talk to you."

Talk to me? What on earth does this man want to talk to me about? Erin wondered confusedly. Madame said only to bring the wine . . . surely there is nothing more to the errand . . .

Nevertheless, as Erin seated herself in the leather chair, she could not tamp down her mounting suspicions. A tenacious prick of fear tingled at the back of her neck, and she sat rigidly, her hands clasped tightly in her lap.

"Name's Ben, girl. Lucille told me you just lost both parents. How sad for such a pretty, young thing."

Erin looked quizzically across at him as he took the seat opposite her and poured wine into two crystal glasses. He's the biggest man I've ever seen! she thought. And his clothes must be bursting at the seams. He's nearly bald, and his head looks like a huge, unhatched egg.

"Would you like to stay a spell with me, Erin girl?" he asked, handing her a glass of wine.

A cold, iron fist of panic seized her, and she shivered in the warm room. "I—uh—must finish my chores." A lump rose in her throat as his small eyes narrowed slowly. She placed the untouched glass back on the table and began to get up.

"Nobody told you to go, Erin. Sit down." He seemed to be thinking for a moment, a smile gathering at the corner of his lips. "Madame Lucille is concerned for your welfare. I'm here to see that you're taken care of, girl."

"But . . ." She rose this time and made for the door in an agony of nervousness.

"Get back here and sit down!" Mortimer thundered. "Would you like me to tell Lucille that you wouldn't cooperate?"

Her body froze. "I was only to deliver the wine," she whispered, turning slowly around, her heart pounding dully in her chest.

"And so you have." His voice softened quickly. "You've done a fine job, too. There's nothing to fear, girl," he added with a slow display of small, even teeth.

Erin shuffled her feet and came a little closer to him. "I'll . . . I'll be in trouble if I don't get back to the kitchen."

"Ridiculous! Why, Lucille wants me to look after you, that's all. Now, here"—he reached over and patted her chair—"sit down and be a good girl."

She obeyed, very slowly. "I really . . . don't need taking care of, sir. I'm fine just doing my chores and—"

"That isn't what Lucille wanted for you, Erin." His brow furrowed momentarily. "Lucille is concerned about you. Yes, she's afraid you might ail or something."

"Ail? But I'm fine, really I am." Abruptly, her eyes widened. "Are you a doctor? I don't understand."

"A doctor . . . yes, that's what I am, a doctor, lass." The leather strained and creaked as he sat back in his seat and

35

drained his glass of wine. "Now, we must find out all about you—that is, what ills you may have."

She saw a slow grin spread across his face, his eyes seeming to disappear in folds of flesh.

"But I don't have any—I'm perfectly healthy!"

"Don't be naughty and rude!" He bent forward. "Lucille has gone to a great deal of trouble for you, and so, I might add, have I."

"Oh," she replied weakly, not knowing quite what she should do or say.

"Now, Erin, you must behave and do as I tell you. Is that clear?"

"Yes, yes, sir," she murmured.

"Stand up and remove that rag."

A chill touched her body. "My . . . *my dress?*"

"Now! Before I'm forced to call Lucille!" His tone was no longer friendly; but it had become strangely impatient.

Her breath snatched in her throat and a surge of fear swept through her; she hesitated, then remembered how the overbearing Madame Lucille could make her quake with a single, imperious glance from those snapping black eyes. Afraid to do otherwise, afraid to be shut out in the cold, Erin stood meekly and turned her back to Mortimer.

As she began to unfasten the tiny buttons on her flowered bodice, she tried desperately to recall the doctor in Ireland who had come to their home when she was a small girl. She had not been afraid or embarrassed then, so why were her fingers shaking now, her head dizzy with fear?

She lifted the print dress slowly until she had shrugged out of it, then held it in front of her.

"The chemise, too." She sensed his presence at her back, then felt his hands come to rest on her hips. "Here, I'll help you."

"Must I?" Her voice was barely above a whisper.

"If I am to . . . examine you."

He pulled the scanty chemise over her head, his eyes narrowing as her body—except for that part covered by her pantaloons—was revealed to his hot stare: the way her waist curved in at the point where her youthful, firm hips flowed out; the long, slim limbs that gave her an air of grace; the peachy, glowing skin.

"Turn around." His voice was low and hoarse; he was so near she could smell the foul cigar on his breath.

Erin was certain that she would faint; her brow was perspiring and she felt like screaming, running, *anything* to drive away her mounting panic.

His hands were on her shoulders then, turning her slowly around to face him. She shut her eyes tightly; it seemed an eternity before he spoke.

"Over to the bed, girl . . . I'll begin the examination there."

An arm came around her shoulders, his fingers lightly touching her soft, curling hair, then moving lower, to the hollow at the base of her throat. He led her toward the large, garrishly ornate bed and helped her to lie down. She braved a look at his face; her heart skipped a beat when she found his eyes fixed oddly, terrifyingly, on her naked breasts. I'm not sick! I'm not! she wanted to cry aloud.

"Just budding . . . like tender round berries." With his index finger he smoothed a nipple; she bit her lower lip in mortification. The walls felt as if they were closing in on her, crushing her.

His finger began a slow, circular motion on her breast, around and around, tracing an endless path over her shrinking flesh. Occasionally, he would cup and squeeze her skin, making her close her eyes in shame as she suppressed the urge to cry. Surely he won't harm me, she wept mutely. He is a doctor . . .

"There, now, you're perfect here, girl . . . Now, let's see about other places."

His hands moved under her bottom and eased her pantaloons down; finally, he discarded them altogether. The air in the room caused goose bumps to raise on her flesh, and she desperately wanted to pull up the covers around her. Then she felt his fingers again, only this time they were prying her legs apart, almost urgently. Terror mingled with her shame.

"Oh, please, sir! I'm honestly not ill—please!" Her entire body began to shiver uncontrollably. Tears spilled over now and ran down her red-splotched cheeks. She longed to escape, but to where would she run? What would Madame do? Oh, God, someone, help me! she cried inwardly.

"Spread your legs apart, Erin . . . yes, that's better now . . . maybe a little further . . ." His finger touched the soft inner folds of her flesh and instinctively she closed her legs, but his hands forced them open while he muttered in annoyance. Then, abruptly, his fingers were on her again, prodding, searching, pressing into her skin. Moaning aloud in fear and panic, Erin tried to roll away from the assault but was halted by a firm, stinging slap on her face and then another, until her skin burned and she could taste the blood welling on her lips.

"Hold still! I just have a little more checking to do . . ."

Through her pain-filled eyes she saw him rise and undress quickly; now she knew for a certainty that he meant to do some crude, fiendish thing to her. The slapping had only been a prelude to something much, much worse.

"Oh, no! No!" she shrieked, then felt a hard blow to the side of her head. The room spun wildly around—the blood-red walls, the ceiling, and Mortimer's face all fusing into a spinning, hellish, demonic nightmare.

In her tortured consciousness, Erin sensed an oppressive weight crush her body. She fought helplessly, desperately, to catch her breath; and when she had almost blacked out, she felt his hands again, probing deeply, and she gagged in terror.

Low, throaty groans and filthy words escaped Mortimer's lips before his mouth came down over hers in a smothering, brutal kiss. And then Erin became aware of a new, larger object tearing at her flesh—a sudden pushing sensation and a sharp, piercing stab deep inside her that racked her body cruelly.

With all her strength she cried out, uselessly, as the massive man plundered her body while his mouth, tongue, and teeth explored her, biting into her skin until she was red and swollen, crushing her abused torso down into the mattress to stick to her sickeningly virgin blood.

Sweating profusely, pumping his immense weight into her body, Mortimer remained heedless of her suffering. Minutes, hours, an eternity, went by for Erin before she felt his bulk lift from her and heard his chortling threat to keep her on her back for a week.

"A fiery little bitch you are—and that hair of Irish copper!" He threw one leg over her hips and almost immediately began to snore.

Tears of horror and shame streamed down Erin's cheeks and into her hair as the immensity of the situation struck her; through her sobs came the pain and the utter degradation of her predicament. And finally, after a long time, the aching, stabbing agony subsided, replaced by a dullness in her limbs, a sickness in her stomach.

And when her mind began to function again, she wondered what she would do now. She couldn't stay in this place—she couldn't! There was no one to help her here, not even Hattie. The red-headed woman was too cowed by Madame; she could do nothing.

Erin felt Mortimer's hot, revolting breath on her face, the bristling hairs on his legs scratching her skin. A knot of disgust began to form in her stomach; slowly, it built into a strong feeling of hatred that forged itself into her very soul. He would pay! She had done nothing more than treat him fairly and respectfully, and he had nearly killed her! Yes, he would pay!

This new, unaccustomed emotion of hatred was somehow strengthening, gratifying, to her young spirit. A glimmer of sanity made her realize that she still had a brain, a will to help herself.

Erin slowly moved her sore, numb limbs until she could no longer feel Mortimer's touch; mercifully, he still slept, snoring loudly. With infinite care, she took advantage of his oblivion to ease herself off the bed and inch backward in the lamp's dim light to where her garments lay discarded on the floor. Her heart thudded wildly.

"Ahh . . ." Mortimer groaned as he rolled onto his side, his hand reaching across the bed, searching unconsciously for her.

Erin held her breath for a long moment before pulling the thin petticoat over her head. In a frantic rush to escape, she snatched up her dress and headed toward the door, fumbling with the material.

"And where are you going, girl?" Mortimer yawned widely. "Get back here!"

Her heart stopped. She gritted her teeth and looked hopelessly at the door, then trembled when she heard him say, "Now! Or I'll tie and whip you!"

Slowly, in agony, hating him all the more for his sadistic cruelty, she began to approach the bed. Her arms and legs shook with fear and her teeth chattered uncontrollably.

"You'll be damn sorry you tried to sneak away from Ben, here! Now, get back in this bed and hurry it up!"

"No . . . please, mister." She stood frozen.

"Why you stupid bitch!" He reached out toward her, but in his ire he inadvertently knocked over the lamp. Immediately, the oil spill flared on the red carpet. Erin grabbed for the lamp bowl with her dress in an automatic effort to smother the flames. But when she held the scorching metal in her hands, a sudden flash, an instinctive act of self-preservation, overcame her, and without hesitation she flung the bowl at Mortimer's encroaching figure.

The lamp struck his head with a sharp thud. The flames grew anew on the bedcover, but Erin did not wait to see if he lived or died. Instead, she raced for the door, flung it open, and rushed down the hall toward the stairs.

I must escape! she thought desperately. I've got to get out of here—away from him!

Voices wafted up from the front parlor; laughing, sickeningly sweet tones of pleasure echoed through her mind as she fled down the stairs, still unnoticed. She heard Madame Lucille's low voice nearby, and her bare feet seemed to move in slow motion toward the front door. At last she succeeded in unbolting the lock, to be greeted by a blast of biting-cold wind and sleet. She barely felt the freezing wetness on her exposed flesh; she did not care that she was shoeless and that the thin petticoat afforded little protection.

Down the four steps she raced, into the half-frozen, ankle-deep mud, until she thought her heart would burst. Yet in spite of her personal agony, her bruised face and aching limbs, she saw only one image: Ben Mortimer's huge, unconscious body being consumed in the leaping flames.

He deserved it! her mind screamed. I hope he's dead! And then suddenly, her body numb with cold, the fabric molded wetly to her frame, she knew for certain that she would never allow a man to come near her again. If any man tried to touch her, she vowed to kill him, too.

Chapter 5

Erin had no idea where her icy feet were taking her. What mattered was that she get as far away from that house, from the image of the nefarious Mortimer, as possible.

She lurched into the middle of the road, hardly aware of the mud or the driven snow that buffeted her. Then she stopped and looked frantically around, seeing nothing but a few lighted buildings that appeared to be saloons from the noise within, and one or two dark-fronted stores. No one was visible on this stormy evening, no one to whom she could plead for help. She wouldn't dare venture into one of the saloons, and she couldn't retrace her footsteps. But where could she go? Perhaps there was a church nearby, she thought. At home in Killarney the parson always offered help to someone in distress. Surely here, too, it would be the same.

Brushing aside the wet hair that was plastered to her face, she whirled ahead and began to walk swiftly, not knowing what lay before her, but determined to find shelter.

Her head was lowered against the storm when she heard the jingle of a harness in front of her. She lifted her head to see where it was, and was momentarily blinded. After her vision had cleared, she gasped in fear as she saw two horses hitched to a wagon standing directly in her path, their huge heads bearing down on her.

"No!" she cried, terrified, unconsciously throwing up her hands as if to ward off the sight. "No! Stop!" But her scream was lost in the wind.

Again she shrieked, a long wail of terror that startled the horses and caused them to rear up, their eyes rolling whitely. Erin saw their powerful legs pawing the air above her head, exactly as in the vision she had so recently dismissed. It seemed as if time were frozen for an agonizing eternity, and the slow-motion scene was burned into her brain. Her last coherent thought before she was struck by a hoof was that of stunned surprise that her vision had come to pass with such unerring precision.

Later, not knowing or caring how much time had passed, she was aware that an excruciating pain was shooting through her temples, leaving her weak and dizzy, her sight blinded by its intensity. In her confusion, she vaguely heard an unfamiliar male voice speaking somewhere near her. A low moan inadvertently escaped her lips, and she tried to raise a hand to her head to touch the swollen area; it felt like a knife thrust, splitting her head in two.

"I think she's coming to, Dad," the voice said.

Where am I? Erin wondered, fear suddenly overcoming the pain. Was she back in that house? Had they found her?

"Thank God. I thought she was gone, Matt. Thank the Lord we didn't kill her," another voice said.

With great effort, Erin opened her eyes and blinked into a lantern's weak light.

She was *not* in that house! Oh, thank God! She was not back there. But where was she, then?

Her eyes finally focused on a face leaning over her. The man's mouth moved, but his words kept fading away, frustrating her. She squeezed her eyes shut tightly, then opened them again; this time she could hear his rush of words.

"Are you able to speak? What's your name, girl?"

She saw his face more clearly: the weathered features, the wide mouth, the deep-set blue eyes. She licked her dry lips and tried to speak, but found that her voice was only a hoarse whisper. "My name is Erin Conner." Her head pounded with the sound of her words.

"Well, Erin Conner, you had us scared there for a time. Let me tell you, you were knocked out cold! What the devil was a young girl doing out in the middle of the street at night, and with barely any clothes on?" the man asked in a surprisingly gentle tone.

"I was . . . I was running away from someone." Her eyes began to brim with tears while fear twisted her features. "You won't . . . you won't take me back there . . . promise! Please

42

promise you won't take me back!" she cried, her fingers pressing against her temples to quell the throbbing ache.

"Easy, child. I don't know where you were runnin' from, but if it was that bad, I sure won't take you back. Rest assured."

The man sounded sincere, and she was too weak and too full of pain to question him further.

She looked around and realized she was inside a wagon, its brown, canvas-covered top showing dancing shadows from the single lantern. "Where am I?" she asked faintly.

"You're in our wagon, not far from the spot where you ran into us—or we ran into you—whichever it was," he said with forced humor. "How do you feel now?"

"My head hurts, but I think I'm all right."

"Can you move your arms and legs? Anything broken?"

Erin dutifully tried to move her limbs; they still worked, it seemed, but the movement brought back the other pain—the ache between her legs, the bruises on her hips and arms. She remembered, then, all that had transpired in the blood-red room.

Was Mortimer dead? Had she murdered him in her frantic effort to escape? The flood of hideous recollection made Erin moan again; she rolled over onto her side and drew her legs up to her chest as if to make herself small, and her tears began to flow anew, monotonously, steadily.

"What is it? Are you in pain? Tell me," the man urged, upset now.

"Yes . . . no . . ." Her voice was muffled, the words emerging with difficulty.

She felt a rough, warm hand on her shoulder; then another, younger voice broke scornfully into her consciousness. "She's just having female hysterics, Dad. Ignore her."

The deep tone of this voice penetrated her mind. How dare he speak like that! If anyone in the world had reason to cry, she certainly did! What worse could happen to her? How much agony was she to bear? And this stranger had the gall to mock her tears!

Erin tried to rise, but dizziness overcame her and she fell back onto the rough blanket, sweat beading on her upper lip from the sudden effort.

In the eerie flickering light, she searched for the owner of that voice; he seemed a young man in his twenties, slim, and apparently tall from the way he crouched over in the wagon's interior. His hair appeared thick and dark, his eyes mere shadowed hollows in the lamplight. His nose threw a sharp shadow across his cheek, and his mouth was thin-lipped and tense. It was difficult to see clearly in the dimness, but she could make out his cleft chin, and the muscles working under the skin of his square jaw. When he turned his head toward her, he appeared diabolical in this light, frightening in the wake of her recent experience.

Although Erin's body would not obey her will, her power of speech had not left her. "What do you know of it?" she tossed out bitterly. "I've reason to cry—and it's not hysterics!"

"There, there, child. Calm yourself. Matt didn't mean anything by it. He has a hasty tongue." The older man patted her shoulder. "Now, what are we going to do with you? Where are your parents, Erin?"

"They're dead." She spoke flatly, unemotionally. She refused to dissolve into tears again and have that crude Matt jeer at her, but her heart, nonetheless, felt as if it would burst with pain.

At last she broke the strained silence by murmuring, "I have an older brother, Perry, but he's gone to the gold fields and I don't know where to find him." She swallowed several times to keep her voice from cracking.

"Hmm, that's hard, girl. It must be a terrible lonely thing. I truly am sorry."

Erin lowered her gaze, unable to bear the pity she saw in the older man's blue eyes.

"Where'd you come from, then?" He sounded genuinely puzzled.

"Ireland. We were going to California, but I don't know a soul there either. My father said . . ." But she could not go on; her throat closed up tight with a lump of misery.

"Lord, Erin, you're quite alone, then . . . a mere girl . . . And what were you running from?"

She turned her eyes up to him, and they shone huge and silver in the lantern light as she wondered whether to tell this seemingly kind man the truth. But no, she couldn't. It was too horrible.

"I . . . I'd rather not speak of it, Mr. . . . Mr.—" She looked away quickly lest he see the shame and degradation in her eyes.

"I'll not press you, Erin. And my name is Steele, Llewellyn Steele. But everybody calls me Lew. This is my son, Matthew."

His voice was soft, and she was glad he had not asked her more questions. She could not bear to think about it, much less speak of it. She closed her eyes tiredly as the conversation eddied around her.

"Poor girl, she's all done in. Matt, we'll have to find a room. We can't stay here tonight with her like this, and we sure can't go on. The poor thing needs rest and care and a good washin'—she's covered with mud."

"Dad, do you expect to take care of her? Why, she's a girl—a kid. She can't go with us! What are you going to do with her?"

"Matthew, this girl has no one to turn to, not a soul, it seems. It's our fault she got hurt, so we've got to look after her, at least until she's better."

"Our fault!" the young man snorted, and Erin wished she had the strength to give him a piece of her mind. "The crazy gal ran smack into our team—and look at the way she's dressed—or undressed! There's more to her story than meets the eye."

"Nevertheless, we will look after her for now. Where's your Christian charity?" Lew chided his son. Erin forced herself to remain silent, hating the arrogant tone of Matt's voice.

Matt subsided into mutters, climbed angrily out to the driver's seat, released the brake, and started the team down the rutted street. Erin felt the movement jostle her sore body and she groaned.

"You'll be fine, girl, just fine. We'll find a room for you tonight. It's an evil night to be out for either man or beast. Now, you rest."

Once Matt had gone, Lew's voice lulled her into a fitful doze. When he saw that Erin was resting more easily, Lew climbed out onto the driver's board to join his son.

"Can't see much in this storm." Lew hunched his shoulders against the wind. "If you see anything resembling a hotel, pull over. I'm just praying that after a night's rest the girl will be fine."

"You heard her, Dad. She might be fine in the morning, but what're you going to do with her? She admitted she's got no one."

Lew glanced sideways at his son. "I'll worry about that when we come to it, Matt."

His son was right, of course. What would he do with her? And Lord, surely there *was* more to her than met the eye. She was running, all right, but from whom or from what? Judging by her almost naked state, whatever it was must have been pretty terrible.

The front wheel sank into a deep rut; the horses skittered and pulled until the wagon bounced free of the mud-filled pit. Lew drew aside the canvas and checked on Erin; she appeared to be sleeping still, rolled up into a scared, timid ball on the makeshift bed.

Gesturing toward a hopeful-looking, wood-frame building, Lew said, "Try that, Matt—looks like a hotel or boarding house."

"This is crazy, Dad. We ought to take her to the sheriff, or to someplace where they could help her. It's not our responsibility."

"Damn it, Matt! The girl's not more than fifteen, I'd guess, and you just want to dump her! Why, she wouldn't stand a chance!"

"Okay, okay . . . you're probably right. But I don't like it. There's one thing for sure, though. If you won't get her to tell us more, then I sure as hell am going to find out what she's hiding."

Lew saw the familiar look of determination furrow his son's brow. It was like Matt to question everything, to ferret out the facts like a pulp-magazine detective. Maybe it was all that highbrow education he had gotten back East. At any rate, Lew realized, Matt was a good man—a damn good son. If he sounded harsh on the outside, well, his bark was always worse than his bite. Underneath it all, Matt wasn't so different from himself; he only chose to keep his sensitivities on the inside and present a hard facade to the world. Yes, in the end Matt would have taken the girl to a shelter himself. Like his dad, he had a soft spot inside him, hidden now in his bitterness over his mother, but there just the same.

"You stay here," Lew said, climbing down into the frozen slush. "I'll check and see if they've got a room for the night."

Drowsily, emerging from her restive darkness, Erin heard a snapping sound and opened her eyes to see Lew Steele bent over a potbellied stove in a small room. Then she heard him speak, as if from a great distance. "We're going to have to clean her up, Matt. I'll help you lift her off that muddy blanket."

She felt a pair of gentle hands raise her body slightly, pulling the rough blanket away. It was when she felt her soaked petticoat being removed that she froze in sudden fear, recalling other hands on her flesh. But then Lew's kindly face and tender smile reassured her. In any case, she was so weak, so tired, so full of wretched misery, that it hardly mattered what he did to her; she had no strength for feelings of modesty.

Matt's face hung over her, his deep blue eyes averted as he helped his father. In her exhaustion, his face became indistinct, seemingly to drift away from her, and a strange vision clouded her perception. As reality slipped away, the figure of a man approached and loomed over her—tan, virile-looking, his chest half bared. Somehow the strange form was not frightening, but oddly familiar. A rough silver pendant hung suspended in front of the man's body, and Erin's eye was drawn irresistibly, willingly, toward it. The silver became brighter and brighter, hypnotizing her, until it dissolved into a brilliant starburst of light and then complete darkness.

She must have passed out, she realized later, for the voices around her seemed worried, calling her name insistently. For a moment she forgot where she was or to whom the voices belonged. Then it all flooded back, and she remembered the image of the man with the compelling silver pendant. What had that been? One of her visions? Or merely a delirious dream? But it had been so distinct! She sighed deeply and closed her eyes, feeling confused and weary beyond endurance.

"Erin! Are you all right, girl?" Lew's voice reached her finally.

"Yes," she whispered, "yes."

Lew turned to his son. "Matt, perhaps you'd best get our bedrolls ready while I get Erin cleaned up. We could all use a good night's rest." Then he turned back to her and looked at her with reassurance.

She tried hard to smile at him, but her lips were cut and bruised. She let herself lapse into semiconsciousness—that was easier. Distantly, she felt the rough washcloth stroking her sore flesh. She winced at times when it touched a tender spot, and then the movement would stop, only to resume more gently.

Suddenly she heard a muffled oath as the cloth reached her thigh. "Good Lord! What's this?"

Erin's eyes flew open and she saw Lew staring openly at her, a shocked expression on his face. She twisted her head and lifted it enough to see what he was looking at. On the inside of her thighs were dried streaks of blood and dark bruises from Mortimer's assault.

She whimpered and turned her face away from Lew in shame, nausea rising in her throat.

A pregnant silence filled the room, broken only by the crackling flames in the stove.

"Who did this to you?" His voice was low, vehement.

Oh, God! He knew! She couldn't tell him—she simply couldn't! There were no words with which to give him an answer; her mortification made her faint and queasy. She wished she could be swallowed up by the earth—buried, forgotten, her tainted body returned to the soil from which it came.

"Who did this, Erin?" Lew's hand forced her face around to confront his white, angry countenance. *"Who did it?"* What kind of an animal—" He did not finish the sentence, but kept looking at her, fixing her with his intense regard.

"A . . . a man . . . in the place I ran from . . . he forced me . . ." A sob escaped her. "It wasn't my fault!" She felt hot crimson stain her cheeks, and the nausea choked her.

Lew swore under his breath. "Who was it? Tell me, Erin. I'll kill the—he deserves to die, the filthy swine!"

"No!" she wailed, suddenly frightened. "No, you can't go there! The man . . . I hit him and ran. I think I killed him—I don't know! But they'll find me! I'll go to prison! They'll hang me!" Her voice rose in terror. She tugged impotently at his arm, trying desperately to convince him. She saw the anger on his face turn to confusion, and then finally, with seeming effort, the lines around his mouth relaxed.

"There, there, don't get yourself all riled up. What's done is done. I won't go if it means so much to you, and I'll not ask you more about it, child. It'll be all right."

He turned away to hide his anger, then hit one fist into the palm of his other hand, uttering a low curse as he did so.

A long moment later, he faced her again, his voice under

control. "Erin, my son and I are headed for Leadville. It's a boom town up in the mountains. We're looking for a place to settle. I'm a miner, you know." He gave a short laugh. "All of us Welshmen are miners. Anyway, we're just passing through Denver City . . . and what I mean to say is . . . I think you should come with us. There's nothing for you here, apart from some bad memories that best be forgotten anyway. And besides, child, we need someone to cook and mend. Though I can put my hand to it if I'm forced, I'm not likin' it much. What do you say?"

She searched the man's face; he looked sincere. Could she trust him? Did she have a choice? So far he had treated her quite decently, and if she went with him, she wouldn't be alone any more. Suddenly it occurred to her that the authorities might already be looking for her—she would have to leave! And if she didn't like him after a time, she would take off on her own and perhaps find Perry. It was better to go—in fact, she had no other alternative.

"Yes, Mr. Steele, I'd like to come along . . . that is, if I'm not in your way," she said, smiling tremulously up at him.

"Good Lord, child! You'll be a help to us, you won't be in the way at all." His face broke out in a smile, the first genuine, warm smile she'd seen since her parents were killed. "Now, you get some rest, and Matt and I will turn in, too. And don't you worry, Erin, you're safe with us. In the morning, we'll get you some clothes and be on our way."

"Thank you, Mr. Steele."

"Aw, never mind that. Why, we almost ran you over! The Chinese have a saying, you know: if you save a man's life, you are forever responsible for it. And I'm guessing they're not too far wrong. Now, sleep, child." He patted her on the head, pulled up the covers to her chin, checked the stove, and stretched out on his bedroll, next to his son, at the other end of the room.

As her eyes fixed on the patterned light dancing on the ceiling, Erin realized that running into Mr. Steele's wagon had been a heaven-sent blessing. And now this apparently good-hearted man was going to take care of her.

But a dark cloud quickly descended over her calm as she thought of her son. She wished he hadn't been in the room when Lew had discovered her shameful secret. The low drawl of Matt's voice came to her mind, and the way his sapphire eyes had looked mockingly down at her, as if he had no use for her at all. Never mind him anyway, she tried to convince herself. I don't have to depend on him. His father will see to my welfare whether or not Matt likes it.

But Matthew Steele's image would not be so easily dismissed. As she lay exhausted, trying to clear her head of fresh doubts, his face kept floating in her mind's eye. What really bothered her, she finally had to admit, was the simple fact that Matt had been there when his father had discovered the blood on her thighs. And where, exactly, had he been then? She tried to remember, to concentrate. Lew had been bent over her with the wash cloth, but where had that son of his been? Had he been bent over her, too? Had his eyes been fixed on her abused body?

And then she remembered how the lamplight had cast the room in semi-shadow, how she had averted her gaze from Lew's face. Matthew Steele had been standing by the far wall, the bedrolls tucked under one arm, his shoulder resting casually against the door frame.

What had his expression been like? she wondered against her better judgment. Unreadable. That was the only word she could think of to describe his face then, his eyes a hollow blue, carved without feeling into his handsome features.

Handsome, she thought—yes, but touched by an extreme masculine arrogance that intimidated her. Matthew Steele was a man bent on having his way at all costs.

It had been a mistake to say she would go with them, a decision made in fear and haste. Oh, Lew Steele seemed kind enough. In fact, she could almost say she liked him, but his son—the very thought of Matt made her feel weak and inadequate in the face of his aura of self-assurance; a very few minutes with him had taught her that much.

What should I do? she asked herself mutely, again and again, until the question filled her brain with panic-stricken confusion. Go with them? Or stay in Denver City? Hide out from the authorities? Maybe she should go to them and confess the whole sordid story. But no! They'd never believe a penniless orphan—and wasn't that what she was now?

I should stop thinking about it, she realized. I must rest now. I'll decide tomorrow morning.

Yet all the effort she put into trying to sleep was for nothing as the question swarmed in her mind, forcing her to make a final decision so that she could rest at last. And in the end she carefully disciplined herself to weigh all the possibilities open to her.

She dismissed going to the authorities—if they didn't believe her, which they probably wouldn't, she would wind up in jail, or worse. She couldn't stay in Denver City—she had no money, not even clothes on her back. So what choice did she have? To find Perry? That was impossible without money.

The answer was obvious. She had told Lew yes, and she would stick with that decision; she would go with him in spite of Matt and the aversion she felt toward him. Furthermore, Matthew Steele did not run his father's life, that much she had already seen. So if Lew wanted her to come along, and if Lew would see to her welfare, then so be it. She would trust him; for the time being she had to. There really was no other choice.

The tension ebbed slowly from her body. Now that her immediate future was somewhat settled, she let herself relax. The fact that the sheriff was probably already searching for her entered her mind again, but she pushed away the idea, at least for this night. She also dismissed from her mind the reality of her lost virginity; she had already vowed never to let a man near her again. Not *that* way!

Erin yawned widely and rolled slowly onto her side, tucking her hands under the rough pillow ticking. The day's memories receded into a dark blur of jumbled thoughts, less painful, best forgotten for now. Tomorrow she would start anew, would travel to the boom town in the mountains, the fabled land of gold and silver.

Her father's face came into her half-awake consciousness, and she remembered his telling her she was as stubborn as the soil of Kerry. For her father, she would try to be. He was somewhere, she was sure, watching her, and he would understand her decision to go with Mr. Steele . . .

Her eyes closed, she floated on a soft cloud, then the cloud dissolved, fell away, and there was nothing, blessed nothingness.

Chapter 6

In the rear of the jouncing wagon, Erin folded up her new sheepskin jacket, smoothing its suede surface absent-mindedly. The rising sun was getting stronger, and she had almost hated to take off the attractive garment.

It would be several days before they reached Leadville, but already the excitement of the boom town had her in its grip. It would be a new start, far from the dreadful memories that still clouded her mind. Thank God, she whispered fervently to herself, thank God Lew Steele came along when he did. Without him . . .

She crawled to the front of the wagon and climbed onto the driver's seat, next to Lew. Tilting her head back, she drank in the shimmering heat of the Indian summer day that caressed her face and neck; the bright, intensely blue Colorado sky above them; the brown-gold plains of waving grass that spread to the base of the snow-capped peaks.

"It's so beautiful here, Mr. Steele. I had no idea!" Her eyes fixed on the clouds that lay snugly against the northern mountainsides. "I only wish my family could have seen this, too. Papa looked forward to it so much."

"I know, Erin. Losing your loved ones is hard, very hard. It's something we all have to face sooner or later, but it's never easy."

The compassion in his voice soothed Erin; just knowing there was someone else she could talk to, someone who cared, lifted her spirits immeasurably. Lew never spoke of the nightmarish circumstances of their meeting, never seemed to belittle her. He was unfailingly kind, generous, and fair.

"Feels like summer," he said. "I sure like that. But we'll be near Fairplay tonight, and they say it gets powerful cold up at that altitude. We'll be camping above ten thousand feet."

Nodding in response, Erin searched ahead to find Matthew, who was now riding alongside the other wagon accompanying them. Of course, she told herself, he *would* be riding near that other wagon—because in that other wagon was Minny Williams, a sly-faced, black-haired, petite female who literally threw herself at the handsome Matthew Steele. It's disgraceful, Erin continued silently, the way she makes up to him—smiling, batting her lashes, smirking, brushing up against him—not so accidentally!

Erin tried to put Minny out of her thoughts as they rolled ponderously across South Park toward the mountains, but she couldn't. It had only been a day since they met up with the Williamses' wagon at the far end of South Park, but it seemed to Erin that she had been bouncing forever across the high grasslands, uncomfortable and edgy in the face of Matt's sudden interest in young Minny.

Well, at least he won't be stalking around rudely, glaring at me with those angry blue eyes of his, Erin thought with a toss of her copper curls, not for a while anyway. He's too busy with that Minny creature. And so what if he is? she asked herself. So what if he pays a lot of attention to her? What do I care? Matt Steele can do anything he wants—it's no business of mine!

Lew's voice broke into her thoughts. "They call these wide open spaces a park here, Erin. We think of them as plains or meadows, but to the mountain men they're parks."

"It *is* huge—so huge it almost seems as if the mountains are getting further away. I wonder if we'll be able to breathe up there." She pointed a slim finger to the distant peak and the pass they would cross.

"Day after tomorrow, we'll find out!" he laughed. "We'll cross Weston Pass, then Leadville's only a few miles."

Erin and Lew sat quietly alongside each other then. She continued to watch the lead wagon cut a seemingly unending path through the grass; then a breeze would come up, and the grass would close over the wheel tracks as if they had never existed. She looked over to the beaten road running alongside them to the north and remembered Lew's telling her that it was nearly impassable now, with deep mud-filled ruts from the recent snowstorm. Erin could see patches of white dotting the row of peaks surrounding the plain; she shivered involuntarily and was thankful the sun was so accommodating this day.

"The bruise on your forehead seems mostly healed now, Erin. A few more days of fresh air and sun will have you looking back to normal."

Instinctively, her hand went up to her brow. "Do you really think so?"

He chuckled. "Yep, sure do."

Erin felt the bump on her forehead with careful fingers; it did seem smaller today, and her headaches had practically disappeared. She actually felt quite well these days, better than she would have thought a short time ago. Lowering her hand, she became aware of the hot sun on the dark blue denim of her pants and smiled to herself, recalling Lew's arguments against her purchases: the britches, the blue denim shirt, the sheepskin coat, the spanking new leather boots.

Well, she thought, I had to wear *something*. And I made it quite clear that I'll work extra hard to pay Lew back. That ripped-up old petticoat was useless, and the rest of her clothes were at Madame Lucille's. She felt more comfortable—safer, somehow—in her boy's get-up. No one would ever need know she was a girl as long as she kept her springing curls tucked up under her soft, wide-brimmed hat. She had even wanted to cut her hair short, but Lew had put his foot down at that notion and forbidden her to do it. She remembered that Matt had stood off to one side while the argument had raged, smiling in his cocksure way. She had given in to Lew on that last point, but only to put an end to the amusement in Matt's thin-lipped smile.

And if she hollered her chest a little, instead of standing up real straight like Mama had always told her to, no one would notice the slightly rounded contour of her chest. She was lanky enough to pass as a boy otherwise. And who would ever want to be feminine anyway? There was no place for girls in this new world of hers, so she would not be a girl. It was that simple.

Minny Williams's high-pitched giggle drifted downwind to Erin, disrupting her tranquility. There was Minny, sure enough, her trim legs dangling out of the back of the wagon, her black stockings showing to her knees. She laughed vivaciously at something Matt was saying to her as he leaned down from his horse, humor gathering at the corners of his mouth.

A few minutes later Matt rode up to their wagon. Erin hated the way he seemed to do everything so effortlessly. He looked as if he had been born on a horse, and his Western clothes fitted him perfectly. Even the way his Stetson tilted so casually to the back of his head angered her strangely. But in spite of herself, she could not help but appreciate the handsome picture he presented.

She recalled the scene that morning, when she had risen early to start the fire, only to fail miserably. Matt had appeared, and with a few quick motions he had had the flames leaping high into the cool air. Then he had turned to her. "Quit trying to please Dad so damn hard, kid. You always manage to make a mess of things." He had spun around and left her standing mutely.

"Dad, why not ride the mare for a spell? It's my turn to drive the wagon," she heard Matt say now, bringing her back from her flustered musings.

"Yeah, I guess I am getting a little stiff at that. Thanks, Matt." Lew's strong arms worked to rein in the team.

"I'll walk for a while," Erin muttered suddenly, her hand tucking a stray curl under her wide-brimmed hat.

"Oh, no, you don't, Erin," Lew said hastily. "Maybe tomorrow. Today you still need your rest."

"But I'm fine, sir!" She blushed hotly as she looked down from her perch and caught the intent regard in Matt's mocking blue eyes.

"Let her walk, Dad. The kid could use some exercise."

The kid indeed! she fumed, then began to climb down, but Lew ushered her straight back onto the wagon, where she was forced to sit next to Matt or start a childish argument.

The Williamses' wagon was stopped ahead, waiting for them. Erin knew they would travel together over Western Pass, for Lew had told her that it took two teams just to haul one wagon over the steeper parts. She saw Minny then, peeping out of the open canvas top of her wagon, a wide, toothy grin covering her face as she winked at Matt.

She's pretty, Erin thought abruptly, feeling very small and insignificant sitting next to Matt while he expertly handled the team.

And then, as if he read her mind, he said, "You really do look ridiculous in those pants, kid."

She could think of no quick reply; instead, to her immense surprise, she felt like crying. But she wouldn't give him that satisfaction.

"Cat got your tongue?"

She kept her eyes averted from him. "No. I was just enjoying the nice afternoon . . . and besides, Matt, I don't have to keep you entertained!"

He chuckled. "That's true, kid. But you seem to talk enough to Dad."

"I like your dad! He's kind and—"

"And safe?" Matt turned his head and saw a look of humiliation mask her features.

Suddenly her eyes filled with moisture, but she swallowed hard and tried to keep her emotions under control. Of course! He was referring to the rape! That was why he had just taunted her—no wonder he treated her like a tainted thing!

"Why don't you mind your own business, Matt?"

"Look, Erin, we're saddled for a time with each other—thanks to Dad's big heart—"

"And no thanks to you! If it hadn't been for your dad, I might be dead!" she retorted sharply.

"You think I'd have left you there? In the street?"

"Yes, I do." That should put him in his place.

She glanced at him sideways, to see a muscle working in his jaw, his hand jerking the brim of his Stetson over his brow.

"Look, Erin," he finally said, "I know you've suffered a great deal, but still, this is wilderness here. It's not always safe for a girl where we're going. That's all I meant."

"Oh?" Erin arched her brow. "And I suppose little Miss Williams up there is more the pioneer than I?"

Matt threw Erin a crooked smile that told her he saw through her jealous observation. Well, let him smirk at me! Erin scoffed inwardly. I'm as capable as that creature in the lead wagon—more capable, in fact.

"Maybe," Matt said evenly, "you might make a good pioneer. How in hell would I know? But one thing's for sure, kid. You better stop cowering around like a scared rabbit every time a . . . a man gets too near." Then, much to her humiliation, he added, "At least Minny Williams knows how to handle herself out here."

Erin's fury rose to its full height, but when she clenched her fists to give him a good piece of her mind, she stopped short, her breath catching in her throat. Matt was staring at her intently, but not at her face. Instead, his eyes were fixed on her heaving chest. Looking down self-consciously, she saw that one of her shirt buttons had come undone, revealing a "V" of pale skin. His glance traveled up to her reddening cheeks, over her hair, which had fallen loose in golden disarray, and then rested on her eyes.

Erin was speechless. Matt was actually looking at her as if he were envisioning what had happened to her at Madame Lucille's! The look in his eyes was extremely disconcerting. And it was all her fault for having tried to compare herself with Minny. Why couldn't she have kept her mouth shut?

Erin turned away from his close perusal and pressed her lips together. The silence hung heavily around her.

"So you think I'm afraid . . . of men," Erin said with exaggerated control, "that I'm incapable of handling myself as well as your girlfriend seems to do."

She forced her eyes around to meet his. But Matt was not looking at her now; his gaze was ahead, on the Williamses' wagon. A casual smile tilted the corners of his mouth.

"Well? That's what you said, isn't it?" she goaded. "You think I'm beneath you—not strong enough?"

"Look, kid," he replied tightly, "I don't want to argue. You're here at any rate, capable or not."

"That's right," she spat, "and I'm tied around your neck like a chain right now. But when we get to Leadville, you'll see." Sudden tears sprang to her eyes. "I'll be out of your way then. I'll get a job!"

Abruptly, Matt lost his temper and riveted his blue gaze on her. "Where do you plan to work, Erin? But wait, I forgot," he said slowly, his tone sending a chill through her. "You already have experience, don't you? You could leave our protection and get a job any time you want!"

He couldn't really mean . . . ? But yes, that was exactly what he meant.

When Erin flung herself down from the driver's seat to walk behind the wagon, she barely noticed Matt's effort to stop her. Nor did she hear him curse himself for being such a bastard—and she could not have known that this was the first time Matthew Steele had admonished himself for belittling a girl.

Damn him! Oh, damn him! The silent words screamed in

her mind, words she would never have dared use before, let alone think. She bit her lip until it nearly bled, trying to stop the tears from flowing; she'd never give him the satisfaction of seeing her cry. Why was he so unkind to her? She had never done anything to him. For God's sake, she had only known him a week or so! Why did he seem to resent her? Yet he was friendly, more than friendly, to someone like Minny Williams.

If Perry were here, Erin found herself thinking, he wouldn't let Matt Steele treat me like this! But then she sighed, knowing that her brother would do nothing at all. He hadn't protected her from Joe Ferguson, and he wouldn't have the guts to stand up to Matt either.

Erin continued walking behind the wagon as the afternoon waned, her legs growing heavier, the new boots chafing her tender feet. Her head ached abominably where the horse's hoof had struck her.

The sun dipped behind the distant peaks and suddenly she was cold; the temperature had dropped rapidly. She noticed that the wagon was moving farther away and she tried to quicken her pace, but it was painful and she grew breathless. Where was Lew? Oh, yes, she remembered, he had ridden on ahead to Fairplay, promising to have a campsite and a fire ready.

As she twisted her ankles over the stony path, a faint panic stirred in her breast that she would be left out here on the prairie again, alone. She tried to push her tired muscles, but they refused to obey her.

Even when dusk had settled over the high plain, she did not call to Matt for help, so that when she sank down onto a rounded boulder, cradling her head in her hands, the wagon was nearly gone from sight. Shivering uncontrollably in the near-freezing air, she refused to admit she was defeated—that her defiant little walk had backfired on her. As pain and fear began to overcome her, she gave a low moan, then jerked her head up at the sound of a voice next to her.

"Erin! You should have yelled for me!" Matt's voice was so full of concern, she could not stop her tears from overflowing. He put his warm jacket snugly around her shoulders, lifted her easily into his arms, and carried her back to the wagon. Erin was so cold that her body shivered inadvertently against him; he felt so warm, so strong, that for a moment she forgot his earlier remarks and melted against him, putting her arm around his neck and laying her head against his broad chest, thankful to be spared a cold, lonely death on the plateau. He placed her carefully on the makeshift bed and stared down at her. "Damn! You sure are stubborn! Lucky I looked back when I did, or I'd never have found you after nightfall."

As he stood crouched over her, hands on hips, his gaze suddenly shifted to her boots. "It's your feet, isn't it?" Before she could reply, he had reached down and was tugging off her boots as gently as he could.

Erin remained silent, biting her lower lip to keep from crying out. A low whistle escaped Matt's lips when the boots and socks were removed.

"Walking all that way in new boots was just about as dumb as running around the streets in a petticoat, kid." He poured water from the canteen over her feet and then rubbed a cooling ointment into the sores. "It's camphor—helps take away the pain. You sure won't be wearing these boots for a while."

"Mr. Steele will be so mad at me," she sighed. "I always seem to get into trouble . . . my father used to tell me that."

"He sure was right on that count!" Matt eased back on his lean haunches. "Now, curl up here and get some shut-eye. We'll be at the camp soon. I can see the glow of the fires ahead."

Erin dozed until they reached the cozy spot among the pines, near a small mountain stream, that Lew had found. There were several other wagons in the area, including those of the Williamses' and three young brothers heading to Leadville to seek their fortune. Lew had ready a pot of coffee and an iron skillet of beans and salt pork, which Erin could have devoured single-handedly. Matt produced a pair of heavy wool socks that she grudgingly put on to fend off the chill. Thankfully, when Lew noticed her limp, he kept silent, and Erin was certain it was only because he hoped she would learn by her mistakes.

That night she was careful to keep her long curls tucked securely under her hat: men were gathering around the fire, drinking coffee or enjoying long swallows from the whiskey bottle being passed around. She didn't want to be noticed by them, and felt apprehensive just at the sound of their loud boasts and rough voices.

The three brothers were there, too, she noticed, and Lew was engaged in a deep conversation with Mr. Williams, so she kept to herself in the shadows near the Steele's wagon. Finally, she felt the weariness of the long day and decided to retire, but thought she would first scrub the dishes in the stream.

She walked over to where Matt and Minny Williams were sitting near the orange flames and gathered up the black-charred pots and plates.

Matt looked up. "I'll get those later, kid." He seemed irked to be interrupted. Minny giggled, and Erin thought the sound was like a horse's whinny. It grated on her nerves.

"I'm capable of doing them myself, Matt. I've only got blisters, not a broken leg."

"Oh, Erin?" came Minny's honeyed voice. "It's none of my business, but why do you wear britches? Aren't they terribly awkward?"

Erin's cheeks burned. She was angry, too, that Minny's voice was so loud, for one of the brothers sitting nearby had looked up and was staring at her intently.

"It's easier for travel, Minny—guess I better get these dishes done—" she stammered and fled, crossing the meadow to the stream.

The moon offered enough light to see by, and she quickly tackled the dishes, scrubbing the char from the skillet with sand from the stream bottom. She had done a lot of dishes this way, since her family had often camped by the banks of rivers and creeks.

Erin sat back on her heels and looked up at the satiny black sky; the stars appeared so close that she thought she could reach out and touch them. They were like a blanket of diamonds, shimmering in the chill night air.

"Pretty, ain't it?"

She gasped. "Oh! You—you scared me!" she managed to mutter, grabbing the stack of clean dishes and rising.

"Name's Ken, girl. Ken Rafferty. What's yours?"

He looked to be about Matt's age, maybe younger, tall and heavyset, with curling blond hair and a narrow look around the eyes that Erin instantly distrusted.

"Erin . . . Erin Conner. I better get back now, it's late." But when she turned to leave, his hand barred her way, then gripped her arm tightly.

"How old are ya, Erin? Sixteen, seventeen?"

"No, I'm not that old. Now I really must go."

But he would not release her so easily. "You're real pretty anyway," he said in a low tone. "Let's see ya without that hat." His other hand snaked up quickly, snatching the hat off, letting her shining curls fall free down her back and shoulders.

"Look, mister, I'll scream if you don't let me be!" Her panic mounted as she tried to keep her voice calm.

"I ain't hurtin' ya," he laughed.

"And you're not going to."

Erin let out a gasp at the sound of Matt's voice slicing through the night air, freezing her with its cold, biting sound before she felt a rush of relief.

"What's it to you?" Ken retorted angrily. "She your sister or somethin'?"

Matt's gaze remained locked on Erin; even as he spoke to Ken his eyes never left her face. "Just let go of her arm if you don't want your teeth rearranged."

She could detect a barely suppressed tone of fury in his low voice. Was he angry at her, or at this oaf holding her arm?

"It's all right, Matt, let's just go back to camp." She wondered briefly at the high, brittle tone of her own voice—and why did her heart thud so oddly?

Ken held her a moment longer, then finally let go. "It don't matter . . . I'll see ya in Leadville." Giving her a quick, twisted smile, he turned on his heel and strode off.

Matt broke into her wonderment at the man's parting words. "Don't worry, kid. He's just talking through his hat."

"You didn't need to bother doing that . . . he would have let me go in a minute anyway." She suddenly felt completely unnerved, standing there by the stream with Matt towering over her, regarding her as if this were the first time he had seen her.

She braved a timid glance at him, and for an instant their eyes met and held. She barely heard his next words.

"Don't ever underestimate his kind, kid. It might be a bad mistake on your part."

"What do you mean?" she mumbled.

"You know what I mean, Erin. Don't act dumb."

Matt's eyes were shadowed in the darkness but burned through her, nevertheless, making her want to flee. But she stood as if paralyzed by his gaze, shivering, her will to escape dissipated by his presence.

What does he want? she wondered in sudden confusion.

"Look, kid," he said as if reading her thoughts, "I don't want anything from you, but there are some—like that Ken—who might think differently. Watch yourself. No need goin' off in the dark alone . . . you understand? I can't keep an eye on you every second, and neither can Dad."

Erin was suddenly embarrassed. She felt a flush steal up her cheeks and was glad that the night hid it from him. She looked down at the ground, unable to think of any reply. Matt stood unmoving, so close that she could hear the sound of his soft breathing.

The seconds ticked by silently, the tension making her skin crawl. Not a word came to her mind, nor a graceful way to make her exit. And she could do nothing to stop her rapid heartbeat.

Then, just as she felt herself ready to crumple to the ground, Matt said, in a strangely gentle tone of voice, "Take it easy, kid. No harm done. Go back to the wagon now."

His strong fingers brushed her arm—or did she imagine it?—in a feather-light touch, so fleeting that it could have been the night breeze.

The spell had broken. Erin backed involuntarily away from him and scurried off toward the welcome glow of the campfire, her skin aflame where she had felt his touch.

Chapter 7

Weston Pass was totally unlike anything in Erin's experience. It was extremely high, the road winding upward beyond her sight and snaking its way into the clouds, and in her wildest imagination she could not picture how they would be able to lead the team up the side of those rocky cliffs. It seemed as if they would ascend the mountain and disappear forever in a blue expanse of nothingness.

Trying to convince herself that her fear was unfounded, a childish display of ignorance, she drew in a deep breath of the thin, crisp air and said, "Mr. Steele . . . perhaps I should walk from here." Her sea-colored eyes gazed upward toward the first narrow switchback.

"Now, Erin, how can you possibly walk with those blisters? Maybe later, when we have to hitch the teams together." He laughed, and worked the long brake lever.

"I—well, if you can ride on the wagon, I guess I can, too." Lew thinks I'm being silly, Erin realized, chuckling half-heartedly along with him.

As the team rounded the first narrow turn, almost pulling sideways, she squeezed her eyes shut and held her breath, her hands white from gripping the seat.

"Not a bit like Ireland, I bet," Lew remarked. "But back in Pennsylvania we had steep roads, too. The mines were always in the hardest spots to reach, so don't worry too much, we'll make it."

She opened her eyes to see that they had, amazingly, made the turn. The horses' heads bobbed up and down from the enormous effort of the uphill pull. In the rare, cool atmosphere their breathing was labored, and great billows of white emerged from their mouths. Erin braved a timid glance over the side of the steep hill; below was a small band of wagons inching up to the approach of the pass. They resembled a tiny line of ants, and again she felt a tug of fear.

A sudden, biting breeze came up and swirled sheets of dust around the wagon, causing Lew to slow their pace even more. When the air cleared, Erin noticed that everything was covered with a fine, powdery red dust. Her handsome new sheepskin jacket was smudged and dirty now, and she wondered dismally if she would ever have clean clothes again. For a time when she was small, back in Killarney, she had had beautiful clothes, but that had been before Uncle Edward had ruined it all, she thought with a flash of anger.

As the horses lugged their heavy burden farther and farther up the mountainside, she could not help but compare these great craggy mountains with the soft, rolling green hills of her home in Ireland. They had had much to be thankful for there; even when others had been starving, they had had land and livestock. Then her grandfather had died, and her father's older brother, Edward—tall, red-haired, and cruel—had inherited the estate. How well Erin recalled the day he had cast them off their beloved land without mercy or regard for their plight. Her mother and father had fought bitterly then, for a long time, but Erin had known little of the arguments until the crowded steamship had docked in New York harbor and her mother confessed to her that she felt responsible for the family's misfortunes.

Erin looked over at Lew Steele, measuring his comfortable, lined face against the memory of her father, then glanced ahead to where Matthew rode alongside the Williamses' wagon. How odd that two Welshmen were all the family she had now. And how long would that last? Oh, yes, Lew would take care of her, but Matt did not seem to share his father's good nature.

Would any man take her as his wife, she wondered, a girl with no mother or father, and robbed of her virginity? Then, abruptly, she remembered that it didn't really matter, because she hated men—all of them except Mr. Steele—and would never marry.

Another switchback appeared, then another; still the wagon creaked its way toward the summit, toward the billowing white clouds that obscured the top of the surrounding peaks. And as the afternoon proceeded, the sky seemed to grow bluer, the mountains more purple, like a brilliant day frock her mother had once owned back in County Kerry.

"You look a little white there, Erin," said Lew, breaking into her reverie.

"It's just the cool air. I'm not scared any more." Then she shared her thoughts with him. "I was just thinking about home—Ireland, that is."

"Tell me, Erin, how did your family come to leave there?"

"I guess it doesn't really matter if I speak of it now, Mr. Steele, what with my mother and father dead . . ." She went on to tell him about her detestable uncle and how he had robbed them of their land; about the years afterward in Killarney, where they had lived on the brink of poverty in a thatched-roof cottage.

Finally, she confided to Lew the terrible thing her mother had confessed to her when they had first arrived in America. "It was a sort of feud, my mother told me, between my father and my uncle. Mother said it had started over her when she was a poor village girl in Killarney and Uncle Edward asked her to marry him. But it was my father she loved, and when she married him, Uncle Edward swore to ruin them. Everything was all right, though—that is, until my grandfather died and Uncle Edward inherited. The first thing he did was to banish us from the manor; even though Grandfather had provided for my father in his will, Uncle Edward convinced the courts to see things his way. Father said it must have cost him a pretty penny." She looked over at Lew, who was nodding in an understanding way, and went on to reminisce about how beautiful her mother had been. Then thinking to turn the subject from herself, she asked, "How did you come to leave Pennsylvania?"

"I'm sorry," he said in an odd voice, "but that I cannot speak of, Erin. Maybe some other time . . ." His face became different, Erin saw to her surprise, hard and remote.

The Williamses' wagon had stopped ahead; they had reached the steep incline that led to the summit of Weston Pass, and now they would double up the teams to haul one wagon at a time.

"The going will be slow, Erin, so if you want to stretch your legs, now's the time to do it."

She walked up slowly, limping slightly, to where Minny stood waiting for the men to unharness Lew's team.

"Oh, hello," the Williams girl said, looking over Erin's shoulder to see where Matt was. "The menfolk seem busy . . . want to walk ahead with me?"

"I suppose so. Looks like they'll be a while."

Erin fell into step with Minny, who was wearing a pretty blue dress that showed her petite figure to advantage. The girls made their way up the narrow, rutted trail. Twice they stopped to look over the edge at remnants of wagons that had never reached Leadville, a sad reminder of lost dreams.

As they trudged along, the dust gritting in their teeth, Minny took the opportunity to question Erin casually about Matthew Steele.

The girl's questions were beginning to grate on Erin's nerves—and all this talk about Matt and how handsome and powerfully built he was. To Erin, he was an arrogant bore, a conceited lout who took a perverse pleasure in hurting her feelings.

"Look, Minny, what you do with Matt is your business. But

I'd appreciate it if you'd quit asking me about him. Why, I really don't even like him!" Erin found herself delighted with Minny's indignant reaction.

"Well, if that's the way you feel, I'm sorry I confided in you!" Minny tossed her head angrily, turned around, and began to walk back down the steep incline. "You're just jealous! Go on by yourself!" she called over her shoulder.

And so Erin did, gladly, mounting the grooved road with a childish smile upturning her lips. After a short time she grew breathless and stopped by the edge of the road, where she could look down and see the Williamses' wagon with two teams hauling it around a treacherous switchback. While she was standing there, she saw Minny, a patch of bright blue, race toward Matt and point up the trail. Erin knew that at that moment Minny was telling Matt what a rotten little girl Erin Conner was; she chuckled aloud at the notion, like a naughty child caught in the act of mischief.

Abruptly, Erin's amusement came to a halt. The loose gravel at the road's edge was giving way to an increasing downhill movement. Her feet began to lose their leverage, and she was swept along with the boiling tide of dirt and rock that formed a granite rivulet down the cliff's side. With her arms flailing, Erin tried to dig her heels into something solid but succeeded only in landing on her bottom. She glided downward even more rapidly, and before she could scream or scramble aside to safety, the rock slide had catapulted her into a horrifying spin.

The blue sky, the road far below, the mountains, tumbled and rolled in a never-ending circle, until suddenly she was halted by a hard, breath-stopping slam against a stationary rock.

The flying earth had all but covered her completely, and she ached everywhere. Her vision was blurry, her mind dulled with shock and terror, as she lay semiconscious in the shelter of the boulder now supporting her.

An indeterminate time later—was it only minutes?—she heard a voice from below. It called her name over and over, echoing off the surrounding rocks, but she was unable to reply. Her lips formed words, but they were inaudible, and she trembled violently with reaction. The weight of the earth felt like a heavy, unbearable blanket atop her body.

She heard the voice again, not really registering its

significance. "Erin! Erin! For God's sake, if you can hear me, answer!"

"I'm here," came her faint, whispered reply. "Over here." Oh, Lord! Thinking she was dead, he'd leave her in this cold tomb of a rock!

"Oh, help me, please!" she cried, forcing strength into her voice.

"Erin, is that you?" The male voice was closer now.

"Over here," she called, her heart suddenly beginning to beat wildly.

"Hold on! I think I see you!"

The sound of loose gravel reached her; footsteps climbing closer; labored breathing. And then a static, brushing sensation as hands worked feverishly to uncover her.

Suddenly she felt herself being dragged up through the blanket of dirt into arms that were strong and welcome, hands that tenderly brushed her dusty hair from her face.

"My God, can you hear me?"

It was Matt . . . and only then did she realize that she wasn't going to die. She had been saved—by Matt!

"Erin, are you okay, kid? Can you talk?"

She could not speak, but managed to nod her head as tears of relief and joy slid down her bruised cheeks. Never in her life had she been so glad to see anyone!

"Dammit, Erin, stop crying. I've got you now, but if you don't help I'll never get you off this cliff."

Still she clung tightly to him, but he succeeded finally in breaking her shaking hold; then she heard him draw in his breath and mutter a string of oaths when he saw the extent of her injuries.

"Look, Erin, you're pretty banged up, but we can't do much about it here. Can you walk?"

She looked at him through tear-blurred eyes; she ached so badly, felt so faint, she doubted that she could stand alone, much less walk. Yet his crystal-blue eyes seemed to urge her on, and this made her try even harder, knowing she would have to depend solely on Matt to get her down. Oh, how he would mock her later!

"Okay, then." He stood up. "I'll have to carry you. You got any broken bones?" Now his tone turned impatient. "Come on, kid, you can say something."

"I . . . I don't know . . . I'll try to walk," she whispered through trembling, cut lips. But when she made the effort to stand, she found herself doubling over in sharp pain, her hand pressing into her side.

"What's wrong?" He steadied her carefully.

"My side . . . it hurts . . ."

"Here, lean up against me and I'll have a look." He began to pull aside the torn shirt and raise the thin chemise.

"No . . . *please* . . ."

"For God's sake, kid! What do you think I'm gonna do?" His grip tightened around her shoulder and he pulled her chemise up, whistling through his teeth as he saw the ugly red slash under her arm.

"Ouch!" she cried as his fingers searched for a sign of a break.

"I think you'll be pretty sore for a spell, but as far as I can tell, there's nothing broken." As deftly as he could, Matt lowered the scanty chemise, but in the process, she felt his hand brush accidentally against her breast.

Her tear-filled eyes met his suddenly, her sobs stopping as if a spigot had been turned off; she stiffened with a gasp of indrawn breath. Matt's eyes were fixed on hers, blue, so blue, and deep as a pool of still water. A slight frown clouded his brow as he gazed at her intently.

Erin felt as if all the air in her lungs had evaporated. Her heart hammered frantically when Matt put his hand on her chin and lifted her head until her lips met his. The kiss was burning, thrilling, terrifying; then it was over, before she could protest, scream, or push him away.

Her wide gray-blue eyes, bright with unshed tears, stared at him with a wild animal's desperation.

"Sorry, kid," he said brusquely, a smile twisting one corner of his thin-lipped mouth. "You don't have to look like that—I certainly didn't hurt you."

But Erin could think of nothing to say as she stared at him, unconsciously rubbing her lips with the back of one dusty, scratched hand where they still burned from the force of his kiss. How could he have done such a thing? Her mind whirled in confusion, shock, disgust at her thralldom to his spell. And she had sworn never to let another man touch her! How could she have let herself—let him kiss her? She felt that she no longer understood herself, her promises to herself, her innermost wants. *He* had made her break her word to herself, had touched her against her will. Oh, God, how could she bear to be near him ever again, to look him in the eye?

But all her torturous thoughts went for naught, because just then Matt leaned over and swept her into his arms. "Now listen, you better hold on tight—it's a steep drop-off for a while."

She buried her head in his shirt and clung tightly to his neck—in spite of her fear of his nearness, in spite of her still-pounding heart.

For the first few steps she was certain they would slip and fall, but his powerful arms held her securely and his feet took to the trail with seeming ease. Once, when they had reached the gentler slope, Matt tightened his hold on her, hoisting her up to a more comfortable position.

"You okay?"

"Yes," she whispered, her head still buried in his chest so that he couldn't see the confusion in her eyes.

The sun had dipped redly down over the western mountains and the two wagons had made camp on the far side of Weston Pass when Erin awoke. Her first recollection was of the accident and the concerned faces hovering above her after Matt had brought her to safety. But for all the fuss everyone had made, it was Lew who had taken command and quickly cleaned her injuries, washing the grime from her body. Matt, of course, had immediately sought out Minny's company. Erin recalled her ambiguous feeling of relief and regret when Matt had gone, leaving her alone with Lew. But she had been glad to see him go—she *had* been!

As she climbed stiffly from the wagon into the cloudless night, she saw that Lew was by himself and still awake. She seated herself next to him, talking for a time about the long day that was indelibly etched in her memory. Then a shared silence fell easily between them, and Erin allowed herself to recall the kiss—the terrible, thrilling warmth of Matt's lips on hers—the way his strong arm had pressed against her bosom; his eyes, so very blue, so incredibly deep and unreadable.

Under the perfect ebony blanket of night, she went over the strange encounter again and again, remaining sleepless from both confusion and exhaustion. She was still lost in contemplation when Matt strolled up through the dark shadows.

From under the veil of her lashes she watched him run a hand through his unruly hair. "Glad to see you up and about, kid. But listen, try not to get into so much trouble in the future, will ya?"

"It wasn't my fault! You talk as if I did it on purpose!" she cried in sudden anger, surprised at her own vehemence. But he made no further comment, shaking out his blanket near the wagon, and seemed to fall asleep within moments, leaving her shaken and furious by the fire.

He's been with that Minny, she thought in a blaze of unwelcome jealousy, remembering his unconscious effort to smooth his dark hair. Oh, that conceited Matthew Steele with his tall frame and piercing blue eyes! Never mind that he was the most arrogantly handsome man of her young experience, he was still a man. Abruptly, she again recalled the touch of his lips on hers, and even now her cheeks grew crimson, a strange, unfamiliar feeling causing a queasiness in her stomach. In the future, she would simply have to stay away from Matthew Steele—and, most definitely, out of trouble.

She glanced quickly to her side, as if someone could read her thoughts, but Lew was asleep, snoring lightly, his head propped uncomfortably on a knotty log. She rose stiffly and pulled his blanket up around his neck, then made her slow way back to the wagon.

She turned around suddenly, an odd feeling at her back. Matt's eyes were open and watching her.

"Good . . . good night . . . Matt," she said, fumbling over the simple words.

"Yeah. Sleep well, kid."

Chapter 8

One late afternoon the two weary but grateful parties drove their wagons into Leadville, the infamous boom town of overnight millionaires, of glorious hotels and restaurants, of carefree women abounding in every saloon.

Erin was excited beyond measure to have arrived at last; she was eager to begin her duties as cook and housekeeper for Lew. Maybe here she could reshape her life, heal her shattered nerves and wounded heart.

The wagon wheels oozed and sucked their way through the muddy streets until Lew pulled suddenly on the reins to avoid hitting a crowd of men and women heedlessly blocking the road.

"What the devil!" he grunted, trying to control the nervous team.

Then Erin saw Matt ride up from the direction of the horde; he appeared casual, but was evidently trying to get his father's attention. "Better take a detour, Dad. Looks like these people aren't going to move so easily." His expression was grim.

"What is it?" she asked, piqued by curiosity.

"They're . . . they're punishing someone, Erin," Matt replied, tugging impatiently at the brim of his Stetson.

He glanced across her at Lew. Their faces showed concern. She quickly stood up on her seat, straining to see whatever was causing the throng to cheer and holler so boisterously now.

"Get the hell down," Matt commanded.

Too late. Erin had just witnessed her first hanging. The involuntary spasms of a man's body, the freakish twist of his noosed head, burned themselves into her brain. She felt as if she had been scorched by a hot piece of iron. Her stomach rebelled while her hands reached out, unconsciously seeking support.

"Oh, my God . . ." Her mouth formed the words as she sank down next to Lew, shivering from an unearthly chill.

"Christ," Matt said, as if from a remote distance. "You should've listened to me." His annoyed tone was only a murmur in her ears.

Slowly, silently, the crowd dispersed, picking its way through the mud, and then disappeared.

Erin became aware of the ensuing silence and realized it was far worse than the noise that had preceded it. Her eyes were still drawn unwillingly to the limp, distorted figure hanging in an alleyway between two buildings; an oblique ray of amber sun fell mutely on the man's body.

An odd, frightening thing happened then. She had a quick, debilitating wave of dizziness that narrowed her vision but enabled her to glimpse something she had seen before. Where the sunlight struck the body's torso, she saw a man's chest, his buckskin shirt open to the waist; a strange brightness gleaming against his skin; but this time a shadow fell across the silvery object, casting a portion of it into semidarkness. Then, as abruptly as it had come, the scene dissipated. Meaningless, familiar, yet somehow important. The corpse once again hung before her wide gaze.

"Erin! Answer me!"

"What? What, Mr. Steele?" she whispered, making an effort to regain control of her senses.

"I said, are you all right?" came his concerned reply.

"I . . . I think so, sir." But her stomach churned sickeningly, and she was certain she would vomit.

"That sure was no thing for a fifteen-year-old to see," Lew said in disgust. "Are you really all right?"

She felt the sweat break out on her brow, the saliva gather in her mouth, the blood drain from her cheeks, yet still she nodded her head.

He smiled reassuringly at her. "Well, then, I'll go into that saloon over there and find out where we can set up camp around here."

"Sounds fine," she forced herself to reply, fighting back the mounting nausea.

As soon as Lew had disappeared through the swinging doors, Erin eased herself off the wagon and made her unsteady way into an alley, her arms wrapped around her middle. That Matt was following her, was aware of her plight, escaped her attention completely, so great was her malaise.

Bracing herself against a rough wodden wall, Erin let the nausea have its way. In the throes of retching, she felt a warm arm encircle her waist, a hand touch her forehead. She forced herself to look up for an instant, to see Matt there, his face cloaked in compassion.

Again her stomach churned and her body heaved. Matt's powerful arms held her weak form while the sickness came and went. When at last she was spent, Matt unfastened the red kerchief from his neck and put it to her trembling lips.

"Just lean against me. It'll be all right, kid," he said in a low, soothing tone.

She turned her moist eyes up to meet his blue, fathomless gaze. "I . . . I'm much better now . . . thank you," she murmured.

"Dad'll be back in a minute and we'll make camp. You need a night's rest. That was a hell of a greeting, wasn't it?" He laughed tightly.

"I've never seen a . . . hanging before." She tried to gather her strength and stand on her own feet.

Matt allowed her to pull away, and she was grateful that he made no more of her attack. But still his hand gripped her arm, steadying her as they walked slowly back to the wagon.

Erin stopped short, caught up by a sudden thought. "You—you won't tell your father, will you?"

"Tell him what?"

The blood rushed back into her cheeks. "That I was sick," she fumbled. "He'll think . . . he'll think I'm not strong enough."

"Will you quit worrying about what he thinks?" Matt pulled her around to him, his hand tilting her face to meet his. "This is no place for a young girl. I tried to tell Dad that back in Denver City. But he doesn't care whether you're weak or strong, a boy or a girl. He's stubborn enough never to turn you out, Erin. Not when he feels beholdin'."

Unshed tears brimmed in her eyes. Matt was right, of course. Lew Steele would not turn her out, ever, so why was she so afraid? Was the death of her parents the reason? Was it the . . . ? Oh, God! Why was she so afraid all the time? Afraid to be alone, afraid to look in a mirror, afraid beyond all reason, beyond her former good sense.

Out of the corner of her eye she saw Lew leave the saloon and head toward them. Immediately her heart pounded. She was standing in the entrance of an alleyway, with Matt holding her arm, his other hand forcing her chin up to his face! It looked like—like— Dear Lord! What would Lew think? Like a fine, delicately brushed painting, her face displayed all her hopes and fears, her confusion and embarrassment.

"You don't need to help me any more, Matt." Her voice shook with emotion while she twisted slowly away from him.

Nonetheless, Lew seemed to take no heed of her dilemma. He walked straight toward the wagon and motioned up the street.

"We'll camp up the hill there," he said, pointing, "so let's get moving before dusk."

Erin, seated next to Lew on the wagon, kept her eyes trained forward, unable to look at him for fear she would betray herself.

As the vehicle lurched forward, she could not help but question the strange, involuntary insanity that overtook her whenever Matthew Steele came near her. She truly believed she disliked him. Why, then, did her knees weaken and her heart flutter at the mere thought of him?

It didn't take Erin long to form a negative opinion of Leadville, the much-publicized Colorado boom town. This wasn't merely because of the zany, live-for-today attitude of its inhabitants; the overall, transitory atmosphere caused her to dislike the place almost immediately. She was accustomed to the quieter, age-old habits of the Irish, not to the bawdy, compulsive display of wealth by get-rich-quick opportunists.

Lew held the same opinion. He had checked with the claims office and found that most of the promising sites were already staked. Also, the prospects of opening a business seemed slim indeed, for already there were a number of stores just scraping by. Even Matt agreed that Leadville was nearly peaked out as far as they were concerned.

So when Lew confided to her that they might look

elsewhere for a new start, she was relieved, if not outright happy, to hear it.

They had set up camp, risen early the next morning, and explored Leadville thoroughly. Later, when Lew and Matt went off to one of the many local saloons, Erin returned to their campsite and heated the washtub. Carefully she scrubbed the grime from their soiled clothes and hung them in the cool November sun to dry. She then made an effort to prepare a hearty meal, but since their supplies were low, supper consisted of beans laced with thick molasses, a hunk of hard bread, bacon, and strong coffee that she was certain resembled thick, dark mud.

Long after sunset, Lew and Matt returned to camp, with Lew the worse for the evening's frivolity. He was overly apologetic to Erin for his inebriated state, explaining that such might be the habit on many a Welsh miner but was a rare occurrence for him. Matt, on the other hand, was relaxed and teasing, leaving her confused as to how she should react to the pair.

"I saw Ken Rafferty tonight, kid." Matt displayed his perfect white teeth in a smile. "He asked about you."

Erin stiffened at the mention of the young man who had accosted her back at the Fairplay stream. "So? He doesn't bother me."

"That'll do, Matthew." Lew slurred the words.

"Look, Dad." Matt's voice took on a serious note. "You'd better get used to it. Erin's growing up. And this is one hell of a place to bring a young girl."

Lew mumbled something, scraped the remaining beans from his plate, and then sought his bedroll next to the fire.

Erin silently washed the dishes and tidied up the canvas tent, but Matt still lingered behind, seemingly reluctant to follow his father's example and retire. Erin felt unnerved; she already accepted the fact that Matt's presence could alter her normal behavior and make her feel as if she were walking on eggshells.

"Matt, I'll sleep outside tonight if you want," she offered, to break the silence, hoping he would take the hint.

"No, I'll go. Guess it's getting late, anyway." He unfolded his lean body and joined his father next to the warm orange glow from the fire.

Erin unrolled her blankets in the tent, shed her clothes, and curled up snugly next to the small iron stove.

The following morning Lew handed her twenty dollars to buy supplies for the next few days. "I hesitate to buy more," he said, "since we may be leaving."

"It's all right, Mr. Steele. Something will turn up."

"For today, Erin, I've asked Matt to keep an eye on you. I'm going to be out talking with people to see if we can come up with a plan. Okay?"

"Oh, Matt doesn't have to bother with me. I'm almost sixteen now. Besides, I'm certain he'd rather visit with Minny Williams."

"Matt was right last night. It's not safe here for a young girl. So do as I say and if he wants to visit with the girl, you tag along." Lew departed, leaving Matt standing by the tent, his arms folded, a frown creasing his brow.

A sudden gust of wind whirled down the dusty street. The canvas of the tent strained against its pegs, and the horses skittered nervously.

"Storm's comin' up. We'd best get down to the store, kid," Matt said impatiently, then added, "Bring your jacket."

"I can see the clouds, too, Matt," she retorted.

The oddly matched pair—Erin with her coppery curls shoved under her hat, Matt with his Stetson tilted downward against the wind—made their way past hastily erected tents and through the streets of three-room, wood-frame houses.

The biting wind grew stronger as they turned into Main Street. Huge dark clouds were descending from the distant peaks and promised to unload their heavy burden on the town. Main Street was still muddy, thanks to the heavy traffic. Luckily, there were a few wooden sidewalks in front of the finer hotels and stores.

They were entering the warmth of Smitty's Dry Goods when shots rang out, slicing through the cold air.

"What's that?" Erin jumped.

"Probably two miners fighting over a claim. Happens every day here, so they say."

"Oh," she replied casually, trying to avoid Matt's knowing grin.

Smitty soon filled a wooden crate with flour, sugar, molasses, and beans—the staples that were running low. Just then Minny Williams and her father came into the store.

"Hi, Matt." The girl swayed up to him, her dark eyes lit with obvious pleasure. Erin thought her behavior was positively brazen.

"Oh, hello, Minny . . . Mr. Williams." Matt tipped his Stetson.

"Can you come for dinner tonight, Matt?" Minny's dark eyelashes batted wildly.

"Ah . . . not tonight, Minny. I've—uh—promised to help Dad with a few things."

Erin's heart skipped a beat. Matt was lying to her! But why would he . . . had he tired of the girl already? Erin was confused by her own reaction to the interchange and pursed her lips in thought.

"Are you ready, Erin?" Matt said a quick goodbye to the Williamses and lifted the heavy box of expensive goods.

They walked outside into the icy wind and saw that snow was falling lightly. Erin could feel the dry flakes melt on her cheeks and tickle her long lashes. She giggled and looked up at Matt as he strode alongside her; his profile was strong, powerfully handsome. No man had a right to look that attractive, she mused; no wonder he treated her as a mere dalliance and could so easily cast all the Minny Williamses from his life. He could have his pick of any woman. If only I were older, or prettier, she sighed silently, then remembered that men were dangerous, with dark, frightening needs, and that she had no use for them.

Suddenly, as they neared their camp, Erin recalled that she had left Lew's change on the store's counter. Why hadn't she minded her own business instead of eavesdropping on Matt! And how would she ever repay Mr. Steele?

"Matt," she said hurriedly, "I forgot something." His low curse reached her ears as she turned away from him, but before he could chase after her, she had disappeared down the narrow street and into the now-blinding snow.

Luckily, Smitty was an honest man; he handed Erin her change and reminded her to be more careful in the future. She thanked him profusely, thinking that maybe there were a few nice people in this town of glitter and mud and wealth.

She rushed out, to discover that the snow was coming down more heavily, driving in sheets at an acute angle to the buildings.

"A real blizzard," she heard a familiar voice say behind her.

Turning abruptly, she saw Ken Rafferty. A shiver ran through her and she quickened her pace, rounding a corner that led away from Main Street.

"Hey! Hold on!" Ken's hand brought her to a complete stop.

"Let go of me, Ken Rafferty! You've no right to—" She was afraid now and looked around the deserted street for help; there was no one about.

"Christ, girl, you act as if I wanted to hurt ya." Although it was early in the day, his breath reeked of whiskey and cigar smoke. She shuddered involuntarily.

"You *are* hurting me! Please, I just want to get out of the storm . . ."

"In a minute . . ." His tone was challenging. "You know, you're a pretty girl, Miss Erin, a real nice looker. If ya come back to my tent, we could git to know each other. It's pretty lonely here."

"Are you crazy?" she cried in shock.

Ken was not to be so easily put off. With sly determination in his eyes, he backed her up against the red brick side of a building, forcing her head up to his, his hand biting into her flesh.

"Give me a kiss, Erin, that's all I ask."

"Let me go—you—you bloody pig!" She twisted desperately against him.

But her struggle was useless; Ken brought his harsh lips down onto her trembling mouth, causing her to choke from the assault. Her hat fell off and her long hair spread wildly over her shoulders. Pressed tightly up against the cold wall, there was nothing she could do to stop him. All she could do was endure his revolting kiss and pray he would let her go with no more abuse—that what had happened to her in Denver City would not be repeated.

Suddenly Ken tore his mouth from her bruised and swollen lips. But her reprieve was fleeting, for he quickly sought her neck and bit into her skin. She cried aloud, succeeding only in infuriating him, and he clamped his hand roughly over her mouth.

"You little bitch!" he swore. "I only wanted to be friendly!"

Moaning miserably against his hand, she sank her teeth into the soft palm, which he snatched away, uttering a low curse.

"You monster! Let me go!" she screamed as she brought up her fists to shove against him.

"Why, you little tart!" He grabbed her wrists. "You bit me!" And then, as if by hurting her he could display his power over her, Ken wrenched Erin's arm around to her back and forced it upward toward her shoulder blade, immobilizing her.

Pain shot down her arm. From her shoulder to her wrist she was in such agony that white spots danced before her eyes and she nearly passed out.

"Stop it! Oh, please—stop!" she cried between clenched teeth, certain her arm would snap.

As abruptly as he had grabbed her arm, Ken released it and let Erin sag weakly against the wall, her heart pounding.

"I got no use for you. You're a little tease, little Miss Hoity-Toity Erin Conner," he muttered gruffly. "Think I'll just go over to the hotel and get me a real woman. Yeah, that's what I'll do. Better to shell out a few bucks than stand here lettin' you rip me apart with them teeth!"

Then, as if nothing had happened, with no words of apology, Ken Rafferty turned and disappeared from sight, leaving Erin white and shaken, her arm and shoulder aching insistently.

She stood against the building, rubbing her sore shoulder and blinking against the slanting snow, hardly believing her good fortune to be rid of him. Then she gave a great, wavering sigh, bent slowly down to retrieve her hat, and set off toward the tent, walking faster and faster, then running as if the devil himself were chasing her.

With her head lowered to protect her face from the storm, Erin was too preoccupied and in too much haste to keep from running straight into Matthew Steele.

She drew in her breath quickly, not knowing at first whom she had careened into, and then looked up into Matt's stern face.

The last thing on earth she wanted now was a confrontation with him! Not when Ken Rafferty's touch still caused her to tremble with disgust. She wanted only to reach the shelter of the tent and bury her head in a pillow and weep out her misery.

But that was not to be.

"Damn it, Erin! I've been waitin' out in this storm, worryin' my head off about you! Where've you been?"

Erin said nothing; instead, she tried to push her way past him.

"You been cryin'?" came his low drawl.

"No! Don't be ridiculous!" she lied lamely. "Now, let me by. I'm freezing cold, that's all."

Matt raised a dark brow but offered no argument. Erin ducked down through the tent flap, tossing her jacket aside and smoothing her hair, her face averted from him as she began to unload the box of supplies. But out of the corner of her eye she noticed that Matt stood inside the doorway with his hands on his hips, seemingly appraising her. Doggedly, she kept stacking the supplies, moving awkwardly because of the pain in her arm.

"Something's wrong—what is it?" he asked, not surprisingly.

"Nothing," she replied with a muffled sob.

"Look, kid, I may not be old enough to be your father, but I'm sure strong enough to put you over my knee and give your bottom a good tanning. Now, what happened out there?"

She gave him a quick sidelong glance. Why couldn't he just let her be? She felt her cheeks flush with humiliation, knowing that if she told him, he would either laugh at her or—worse still—say it was her own fault.

Suddenly she felt herself spun around, Matt's fingers biting into her wrenched shoulder under the thin denim shirt. Her heart gave a sick lurch and she stifled a moan of pain.

"I—I won't tell you!" she cried. "Leave me alone!"

"Did someone hurt you?" She shook her head. "Damn it, was it that bastard Rafferty?" Still she kept silent, shaking her head, her eyes wide and glistening with pent-up tears. "All right, then, I guess you want that spanking . . ."

He grabbed her arm and pulled her toward him; she tried to struggle, but her efforts only tore at her throbbing shoulder, causing a sharp spasm of pain that set spots to dancing in front of her eyes again. Unable to fight him, she collapsed across his lap in a limp heap, sobbing, hiding her head behind the thick veil of copper curls.

"Erin?" His voice was oddly gentle, but with a blade of steel underneath that dissolved her will to defy him. "Tell me what happened. Did he . . . touch you?"

"He . . . he twisted my arm." She could hardly force this partial truth from her constricted throat; the words came out so softly that Matt had to lean closer to hear them.

A quick, indrawn breath revealed Matt's sudden anger. "That no good—" Then he gently lifted her up to face him, pushing back her tangled curls. In spite of his care, she winced.

"Where exactly does it hurt?" he asked, his precise, demanding tone making her raise her eyes to his, startled. Was he angry at her?

"My shoulder. It's really nothing . . . he just wrenched it a little. I'll be fine, honestly."

"You sure he didn't do anything else?" That accusing, stern voice again. Those bottomless blue eyes under frowning dark brows.

"No," she lied. "He only hurt my arm."

"Well, then, is anything broken?"

"No, really. See?" Erin moved her arm around, a weak smile on her face to hide the stabs of pain. She couldn't allow him to undress her for an examination!

It was then that the memory of his kiss came back to her in great clarity: the confusion, the shock, the thrill of his nearness. She could not forget the roughness of his cheek against hers; the clean, pungent smell of man-sweat; the burning of his lips on hers. The flash of memory flooded her brain, making her intensely nervous. Surely he wouldn't do it again! He couldn't! Her teeth began to worry her lower lip, and she edged away from him with an unreasoning fear of his proximity.

Finally, unable to bear the strained silence a moment longer, Erin glanced timidly up at him, catching his odd, penetrating gaze. She lowered her eyes immediately, feeling a hot surge of panic and embarrassment; it was almost as if she had been caught chatting with friends by a teacher back in Ireland and was about to be caned. But this was no black-frocked, skinny-shanked teacher who leaned toward her; this was the hard-muscled and handsome Matt Steele, whose warm breath on her skin made her tremble with a delicious, forbidden tingling.

Is he going to kiss me again? she wondered breathlessly. Oh, God, please, no. Make him stop—I can't bear it! But somewhere, concealed so deeply that it seemed not a part of her at all, a small, secret voice urged her to experience what he had to offer her, to drown in his warm male flesh, to taste the mystery of him.

And then she felt her face raised up toward Matt's, his

hands cupping her cheeks softly. She could not help but meet his eyes. They looked somewhat puzzled now, such a dark blue that they were almost black in the shadows of the tent.

Erin waited endless minutes for him to do something, anything. She felt frozen, torn between her desires and her fears. Neither could prevail. She was unable to move. Only a tiny, relenting motion was necessary, she felt instinctively, but she was helpless to act.

Yet Matt still did not kiss her, and a part of her heaved a sigh of relief. He continued to hold her face, looking at her searchingly until she couldn't bear his grave perusal another moment, nor the heat of her face where his hands touched her skin.

Then suddenly, roughly, he dropped his hands and turned away. She was certain she heard him mutter something like "Damn women!" under his breath, and the spell was broken, her shoulder still ached, and Matthew Steele had reverted to his unpleasant, rude self once more.

He pulled on his coat and strode to the tent flap.

"Matt, where are you going?" Erin was surprised at the panic in her voice.

"I'm going to teach that Rafferty a lesson!"

"Oh, please, don't start any more trouble on my account! Please!"

He whirled on her, angry now. But at whom? Her? Ken Rafferty? Himself?

"Listen, kid, I just can't let that guy get away with it. I'll only bust him up a bit."

A wicked grin curved his thin lips and she felt a stab of fear. For whom? she asked herself, agonized, as she clutched at his sleeve, trying to hold him back. But he put her from him easily and disappeared into the worsening storm.

"What in God's name happened to your face, Matthew?" Lew asked later in apparent bewilderment as he entered the tent.

Matt was sitting cross-legged near the stove, a ball of fresh snow pressed to his bruised cheek, while Erin stirred the stew, unable to face her mentor.

"Just a minor disagreement, Dad. It was nothing."

Erin's heart leaped. He wasn't going to tell Lew! He wasn't going to shame her! And when Lew said only, "I hope the other lad looks worse," she thanked the Lord that Lew had let it go so easily, and then wondered at the many sides of Matthew.

"He's got a toothless smile now." Matt grinned widely, giving Erin a conspiratorial wink, then changed the subject. "Any good news?"

"I think so." Lew shed his snow-covered sheepskin. "Met a man named B. Clark Wheeler, just back from Ute City, over Independence Pass. He's selling land there cheap, but says the town is ready to boom. Silver is rumored to be in several of the surrounding mountains."

Erin's face brightened and she forgot her confusion about Matt. Lew was definitely thinking of leaving Leadville!

He went on to say, "Anyway, most of the fellows in the saloon backed his story up—seems the town is just taking off. But I gotta warn you, only a few people are there now, and there's not likely to be more this year, what with winter coming and all. Might be a bit . . . primitive."

Erin listened intently while Lew and Matt discussed the possibilities and then decided it was worth a try: there was no store yet in Ute City, and there were men with money burning holes in their pockets.

"What do you think, Erin?" Lew asked kindly.

She felt a thrill of pride that Lew would ask her opinion, and she was about to respond enthusiastically when a dreadful thought flashed through her mind. She was almost afraid to voice it. "Would there be any . . . Indians? I mean, is there any chance of Indians attacking?" The blood drained from her face.

"It's true there was a threat of an uprising last year, but that's all over now, Erin. The Indians are peaceful and the government is taking care of everything—even talking of sending them to a reservation in Utah."

Lew's work-hardened hand patted her shoulder. Her face took on its natural color, then became animated. "Well, then, I guess it sounds like a good idea. I'd love to help out in a store. Father always said I had a good head for figures."

Lew smiled warmly. "Then we all seem to be in agreement."

At ten o'clock the next morning Lew Steele, along with Erin and his son, met B. Clark Wheeler and purchased two town lots in the barely established settlement of Ute City,

Colorado. For a Welshman who had traveled from Pennsylvania with limited funds, this cold, bright day in November 1880 was an exciting one indeed.

And for Erin, an orphan whose very existence depended on the good judgment of a man she had known only for a short time, it was a monumental happening. A new life, a new town, a town called Ute City, where they would settle. Why, Lew would be like a founding father! A landowner! Her heart pounded with pride and an equal measure of apprehension.

There was, however, a dark cloud dimming her bright horizon. She had begun to wish that the new adventure would include her and Lew alone, that Matt would remain in Leadville or go elsewhere. Even though the notion was absurd, was it so very wrong of her to want it? After all, she hated Matt . . . didn't she?

Chapter 9

As it turned out, the purchasing of Lew Steele's land had been the easiest part of the planned move to Ute City. It took a full eight days more in Leadville to sell the wagon and horses, put together a small train of mules, buy the supplies for the upcoming winter, and dismantle their camp.

But Erin loved every minute of the preparations, for Matt had been sent on ahead to Ute City to scout out the land and, hopefully, to begin felling trees for their new home. In place of his critical eye, his infuriating manner, his arrogant good looks, was Lew's warm smile and unfailing optimism. Erin reveled in their hours together, clung to Lew's every word. He became the perfect replacement for her own family, the sun that illuminated her clouded horizon. She began to smile more often, laughing merrily out loud at times, and discovered a newfound happiness in her everyday chores.

It hadn't been that way before, she realized on the morning they were to depart Leadville. Before, when Matt had been there, she had felt strangely inadequate, unable to deal with the tiniest of problems or tasks. She had attributed her apparent clumsiness and depression to the death of her parents, to Perry's leaving her alone in Denver City, and, of course, to what happened at Madame's.

But those hideous memories were not the entire reason for her discontent. A large part, she knew now, had to do with the mere presence of Matthew Steele—hovering over her, watching to see if she made a false move, waiting to drop a sly word about her inability to cope, causing her to tremble like a frightened rabbit.

As she and Lew secured the last sacks onto a mule, Erin could not help but remember the many times Matt had pointed out that the Colorado wilderness was no place for a young girl. And each time he had casually mentioned it, she had invariably, almost on cue, burned her hand on a cookpot or forgotten to dress warmly enough in the chill air, making so many small mistakes it was as if *he* had willed her to.

She glanced across the mule's back at Lew; how relaxed and at ease she felt with him. This past week they had gotten along splendidly, enjoying each other's company while working hard to make ready for the journey.

An abrupt, selfish thought flew into her mind again—what if Matthew Steele were no longer around? Wouldn't it be grand if he'd just disappear?

"Got that rope fastened secure, Erin?" Lew broke into her faraway musings.

"Oh—why, yes. We're all ready now, I think." She forced her mind back to the task at hand and looked over her shoulder to where their camp had stood. Only a few wooden planks remained, scattered on the frozen ground.

"What about the flooring, Mr. Steele?"

"We won't be taking it. I hear tell that the Ute City valley is as lush and green as any, covered with fir and pines and aspen—enough trees to build a city the size of Philadelphia and then a few more!" He laughed. "Now let's be off. I wanna make Twin Lakes by tomorrow night, and it's a good thirty miles."

And so they left Leadville, slowly, on foot, with Erin pulling and tugging on the lead mule's rope until she thought her arm would come off. Only once did she stop to look back at the wild mountain community she had so quickly come to dislike. Yes, she was truly glad to be going.

Ahead lay an unknown future, a virgin valley with a new town of only a few people who must believe in the land, or why else would they be there? In a week she and Lew would be there, too, building, working, and striving toward a better existence. And, of course, she remembered, Matt would also be there. He was already in Ute City, waiting somewhere in the heart of the Rocky Mountains, on the land his father had purchased, the land on which their dreams would be built.

Erin looked toward the mountain pass, where the azure sky collided with the craggy peaks, the deep blue meshing perfectly with the frozen white—the same flawless, icy hue as Matt's eyes—crystal cool, precise, somehow threatening.

While she trudged along, occasionally admonishing the mules, Erin began to experience a gnawing sensation in the pit of her stomach. The more she tried to ignore its roots, the more her mind turned to its source.

It was Matthew Steele, *his* damnable memory, that disquieted her. She recalled so clearly the morning he had left for Ute City: the cocksure manner in which he had tipped his hat to her, the silly wink he'd given her, the way he'd swung his body so lithely onto the horse.

Snow had been falling lightly that crisp morning, yet she vividly remembered that the sun had shone through the clouds and struck the flakes, lighting them like sharp-edged, sparkling diamonds. And Matt had been silhouetted against the blinding background of sun and snow, his thin, sculpted lips voicing the words of farewell, his drawling tone teasing her ears. Then he had wound his way down the narrow streets and disappeared into the throng of other riders.

What was it she had felt then? Relief—an exhalation of her breath, as if she'd been holding it for months. Yet there had also been a strange wrenching, a feeling of loss.

It's just not fair, she thought to herself now; the conceited oaf gives me a little brotherly kiss, and for weeks I can't get him out of my mind. Why, he's much older than I am . . . he thinks because I'm young that he can play with me, tease me like he did that horrible little flirt Minny Williams. Well, I'm not stupid! Nor am I a silly romantic. I'm not going to let him bother me again—ever—and all I have to do is remember that I don't even like him.

"Were you talking to me, Erin?"

Oh, Lord! Lew's been listening to me—I've been thinking aloud! "I—uh—no, Mr. Steele, I was talking to this stubborn mule."

He took the rope from her hand. "I'll lead them a spell and you walk on ahead." Then he noticed something. "You feeling all right? You look a little flushed."

"Oh, I'm fine, Mr. Steele," she fibbed. But no matter how hard she tried to forget about Matthew, his haunting image would not leave her mind that day.

Erin and Lew traveled four days before they reached the base of Independence Pass, the tall barrier they had to cross before descending into the Roaring Fork Valley, which was home to Ute City.

If Erin had found Weston Pass insurmountable, she thought Independence to be doubly so. It was part of the Continental Divide, Lew told her, the massive wall of rock that stretched from Canada into Mexico, the rugged backbone of North America.

"Let me put it this way, Erin," he said. "If a drop of water were to fall on the Divide, half would flow to the Atlantic and half would flow to the Pacific."

And so they walked deeper and higher through the rough-hewn vertebrae of America; with each footstep Erin felt a sense of exhilaration. They were drawing closer to Ute City, and already she had formed a picture of the town in her mind's eye. Not one of her visions this time, but instead, a hopeful fantasy of what her new life would be like.

As the miles passed behind her, so did the memories of Ireland and Denver City and Leadville—difficult miles, difficult steps in her life, but taken nonetheless, each one different from the last and bringing her closer to her destiny and a welcome maturity. Like the towering mountains around her, she was reaching ever upward, groping toward the heights.

They reached the summit of Independence Pass late one cold, windy afternoon. It had been a long, hard climb and Erin's legs ached. Lew complained of sore muscles, too, but never stopped smiling or encouraging her with words of optimism.

Atop the flat summit, they breathed heavily in the thin,

frigid air, where the stunted firs met the high-country tundra. The steep foot trail they had ascended was obscured now, for the shoulder of a peak hid that view from them; ahead was only a gorge, winding and descending darkly. The sun sat splendidly on the peaks to the west, a great orange orb casting giant shadows toward them. Patches of snow filled the hollows and clung to each shadowed northern face; dark stands of trees nestled far below.

Erin gratefully plumped herself down to rest against a cool boulder and gazed over at Lew's strong, relaxed profile etched against the granite peaks. Was there ever such a fine man as Lew? Was it possible that he had come to take the place of her father? And if he had, what did it matter? She needed to lean on him, wanted his kind protection.

"Come on," Lew said after several minutes had passed. "It's only a few miles to Independence, and we gotta make it by dark. It's bound to drop below freezing tonight."

He shouldered his newly purchased Sharps rifle and began to follow the rough path across the flat turf. Finally she drew in a deep breath, pulled on the rope of the lead mule, whom she had christened Napoleon because of his stubborn, imperious nature, and tracked Lew's lead into the growing shadows.

An hour later they reached the small, bustling gold camp of Independence, its lantern-lit windows beckoning them through the oppressive darkness and cold. Lew knocked on the first door they came to and inquired about a place for the night.

"Sure," replied the grizzled oldster who had answered Lew's knock. Fumes of whiskey wafted to Erin through the thin air. "Over to Old Man Steiner's—he's got a shed he rents out cheap to travelers. He's just over there." He pointed a grubby finger down the sloping meadow to a dark shadow lit from within by a blurry square.

They thanked him, followed his directions to Steiner's, and soon found themselves in possession, for the night, of a small, musty shed without windows, but with an inviting squat iron stove in one corner.

"It'll do," Lew said with a sigh. "You start a fire in the stove and I'll see to the mules."

Even though each and every muscle in Erin's body ached unbearably from the day's hard walk, she nevertheless followed Lew's instructions, and soon the shed was warm, the iron stove giving off life-preserving heat.

Shortly after dawn the following morning, they left Steiner's shed and descended through the tall spruce and fir, the great stands of bare-branched aspen, to wind their way around boulder fields in which huge jagged rocks loomed above them, seemingly ready to plunge down and crush them like ants. The path was precarious; smooth round stones from an ancient riverbed rolled perilously underfoot, and they had to watch the mules carefully to keep them from breaking a leg. On the left side of the rough trail the ground plummeted down to the river that glinted below. Erin remembered her ordeal on Weston Pass and stayed as far away from the edge as possible.

By midday they had reached much wider grass- and tree-covered meadow, the mountains around them farther away and less menacing. Then the river flattened out and began to meander, winding itself lazily and forming several miles of marshland. Myriad birds flew up at their passage; browsing deer started and leaped away in front of them.

A series of hastily constructed bridges spanned the many river channels here, and they had to pay a toll at each crossing.

Then the valley narrowed slightly again, the humped and heavily wooded mountains encroaching on the grassland. They rounded a bulge of hills and the land widened in front of them, the tree-lined route of the river easily discernible until it disappeared in the gray-brown distance.

"The Roaring Fork Valley," Lew breathed. "We made it."

"I see a few buildings, Mr. Steele—it must be Ute City."

"Yes," Lew said slowly. "Just picture it as a great city, the land teeming with people, mines covering the hillsides, neat little houses with picket fences all over. That's what Wheeler said it'd be soon—hard to imagine."

Erin stood there pensively, looking at the brown, winter-tinted valley, the mountains rolling away to the west, the sky gray and threatening.

Abruptly, the scene faded; a mist obscured her vision for a moment, and then she saw the valley floor: full of people, coaches, horses, brick buildings; also a train depot and the ugly, rising structures of mines. The noise of the crowds grew and grew, blocking her ears, and an empty, desolate fear chilled her heart. She closed her eyes to block out the apocalyptic vision.

"Erin! Erin! You haven't heard a thing I said! What's wrong, girl?" Lew's voice brought her back to reality. She turned to look at him, white faced and shaken.

"Mr. Steele . . ," She found it difficult to talk for a moment. "This place will be a city, and there will be mines here . . ." Her voice faded as she realized how ridiculous her words must sound.

"Why, Erin, you say that with such assurance, I'm bound to take your word for it. But you scared me there for a second. You looked as if you'd seen a ghost!"

She lowered her head, embarrassed, but somehow wanting to confide in him. "I—I see things sometimes, and they usually come true. My mother used to say I had a 'gift.'"

She was about to tell Lew what she had seen when she noticed the worried look on his face. Oh, Lord, she thought, this will not do! He'll think I'm a witch or something—or quite unbalanced. I can't possibly tell him now, and besides, he'd probably never believe a word of it!

So she swallowed her words and was relieved when Lew began talking.

"I'm anxious to see Matthew again. It should be easy to find him. Looks like there're precious few inhabitants of our new home." He patted her on the shoulder, and she felt the warmth and solidness of his affection for her. "Let's go, my dear, and find Matt—and my land!"

Let's find Matt. The words echoed in her mind while the clarity of the vision faded, and she realized that in a few minutes she would see *him* again.

Unconsciously, she tucked her shirt into her pants and smoothed her hair, replacing her hat more tidily on her head.

They walked across the crunchy brown grass to the few tents and log cabins in evidence, and Lew began digging in his pocket for the map that Wheeler had given him in Leadville.

They could see a few people now, mostly men, several mules and donkeys, a horse or two, and dogs that ran toward them, yapping. There were no pigs, chickens, or cows, but the homey sight of wash on a line and smoke from tin stovepipes was reassuring.

Erin's attention was drawn to the rapid approach of several people who were obviously pricked by curiosity at the arrival of new settlers so late in the year.

"Much snow yet on the pass?" asked a weathered old prospector.

"Bring any whiskey with you? Ammunition? See any Indians?" another inquired.

"How's Leadville doin'?" a third wanted to know.

The questions flew at them, until each in turn was answered to the best of their ability. Lew introduced himself and Erin, speaking of her as his adopted daughter; he had told her earlier that this would avoid any problems over her status in his family. They were then informed that only about thirty-five pioneers lived in the valley, most of the others having gone back to Leadville at the first hint of snow. Yes, there were good signs of silver ore in the mountains, several claims were already staked, and yes, they were desperately in need of a store in town, supplies were short, and although game was plentiful, flour and coffee and sugar were worth their weight in gold—or silver, rather, chortled one man.

Lew finally managed to break into the nonstop flow of words. "My son, Matthew, is here already, perhaps you know him. Matthew Steele?"

The men most definitely did. It seemed that Lew's son had become a popular figure around Ute City. In the week he had been there, Matt had obviously made friends of these men, for they spoke of him warmly, even praising his tireless effort to have enough logs ready to start building before winter took its icy hold.

Well, of course Matt would win their words of praise, Erin surmised quickly; he always made it a habit to befriend everyone—especially the women, she thought hotly, the very notion unsettling her.

"Come on, I'll take you to the corner of Mill and Main streets," a young man offered enthusiastically. "Your land's there, right near the corner—nice lots, located real good, too. Bet your son's there right now."

Erin and Lew followed the young man across the leaf-strewn meadow.

"Just past this stand of aspens," their guide said, "and you'll be at your new home."

Just past the trees—Erin's heart beat more rapidly—and she'd see Lew's land for the first time. And there, too, Matt would probably be, swinging a long ax, his shirt sleeves rolled up, his dark hair glinting in the weak November sun, his infernal, mocking grin . . .

It hadn't been a vision this time, just a hunch, but nonetheless, Erin was correct. Matt stood tall and straight over a felled pine with an ax in one hand, the other hand sweeping his unruly hair from his brow; the sleeves on his green and black plaid shirt were rolled above his elbows, his arms suntanned and strong.

"Dad!"

She heard his familiar voice cut across the short distance, and she stopped in her tracks when she saw him drop the tool and run toward them. No, not toward *them*, she thought suddenly, but toward his father.

Just as her heart was sinking miserably, unaccountably, Erin realized that she had been wrong. For Matt reached his father, embraced him, and grabbed her hand, drawing her into the warm cradle of his arm.

Matthew Steele was happy to see her! His blue eyes were smiling down at her in genuine delight to see her! Why had she thought he would look at her with his taunting smile that could freeze her very soul? Her skin under her clothing tingled oddly where his arm pressed against her flesh.

"It looks perfect, Son!" Lew said breathlessly. "And you've worked so hard!"

"The work was nothing—but I'm damn glad to see the tent. It's cold up here at night!" Matt laughed.

"I'll bet it is," Lew agreed. "I think we just made it over the pass in time. Have you got the lots staked off?"

Matt took his arm away from his father but still rested a casual hand on Erin's shoulder. She kept her eyes downcast, averted from his face.

"It's staked off, all right—first thing I did. The southeast corner is there"—Matt pointed a finger—"over behind that first tall aspen."

While Lew walked slowly around the perimeter of his land, Matt questioned Erin about her trip over Independence Pass. He still did not remove his hand from her shoulder, so that each time she tried to reply to his questions, her voice emerged almost as a whisper.

Finally, unable to bear his touch a moment longer, she laughed nervously and said, "I . . . I think I should look around the land, too. Don't you think so?"

"Sure, kid. Look to your heart's content."

Was his smile genuine? Or was he making fun of her

discomfort? She could never tell with Matt. Did he realize why she was suddenly so nervous, or was he unaware of all her whirling, bewildering, contradictory feelings?

Before she could free herself from his oh-so-casual grasp, Lew walked back to them and pointed a gnarled finger. "This is where the cabin will go, and the store, but we'll have to put up the tent for now. Then we'll be in business." A grin split his handsome, seamed face. "Look at it, will you! My own land! And no more mining for me, or you either, Son! We're to be gentlefolk now—storekeepers! No more grubbing in dark, grimy tunnels underground. We'll be in the sun all day and we'll make our own silver—right out of bags of flour, and from cans of coffee and condensed milk!" He laughed and slapped the tarpaulin-covered sacks on Napoleon's back, causing the mule to jump and to twitch his long ears.

Erin smiled broadly now, sharing Lew's enthusiasm and happiness. Matt, in a completely out-of-character gesture, threw his hat into the air, whooping loudly, then grabbed Erin by the waist and swung her around in an impromptu jig.

There was nothing she could do to stop his sudden attack. Her hat fell off and her coppery curls cascaded down her back and bounced merrily. Matt whirled her around and around through the fallen aspen leaves. Her cheeks flushed pink, her eyes sparkled. They finally collapsed together on the ground, breathless, and grinned at each other like children.

Lew's voice called them back from their celebration. "Hey! We better put this tent up, or we'll be freezing our fannies all night! Let's unload those mules. Erin, get the rope and stakes."

They labored until dusk, then consumed a hasty supper of corn bread spread with thick condensed milk and washed it down with cold, clear water from the Ute City spring. Lew devised a curtain to partition off part of the tent for Erin, after which he and Matt built a campfire. The graceful cone of Mount Sopris, many miles away, was silhouetted against the darkening sky.

Lew filled his old briar pipe and leaned back against one of the flour sacks, sighing with contentment. "This is the life, isn't it, Matt? Sittin' here on our own land, in a beautiful valley, no ugly black smoke against the sky. It's worth everything, isn't it, lad?"

Matt appeared to be thinking for a minute, his blue eyes

reflecting the firelight, his brows drawn together in a frown. "Yeah, Dad, I guess so. But heck, it's almost December, and we've got lots to do yet."

"And an extra pair of willing hands to help us do it." Lew smiled, patting Erin's shoulder. "Well, I'm all done in. You youngsters must have more energy than I do. I'm goin' to my bed. See to the fire before you come in." He knocked out the pipe's ashes on the ground and entered the tent.

Erin looked over at Matt, who was staring at the fire, seemingly mesmerized by the leaping flames. She was aching and exhausted, too, but not quite ready to retire. Her mind raced with excitement at having reached this untamed valley. Like Matthew, she sat cross-legged, her eyes closed lightly, listening to the logs crackle. The valley itself was quiet, the silence echoing back from the surrounding mountains. Suddenly the stillness was broken by a coyote's mournful howl, which was repeated twice before halting abruptly.

A chill ran through her as she remembered that the wilderness held violence and danger as well as beauty. She shivered and hugged her arms around herself, edging closer to the fire.

"Cold?" Matt's voice emerged lazily from the darkness.

"No . . . just thinking . . . wondering where my brother is, for one thing."

"It's a big country. He could be anywhere, kid. Quit worrying about him and get some sleep."

"Yes, I suppose so." She glanced across at him, then said, "But sometimes I can't stop myself from worrying, from wondering."

"Well, you've been through a lot—more than most, I'd say. Maybe it just takes time to forget."

She stared intently at him for a long moment, wondering what he was thinking. Did he pity her for what she had suffered? She hoped not. His pity would be unbearable. Yet he seemed completely immersed in thought right now. Was his mind on something to do with her? Did he remember, ever, the time he'd kissed her? Probably not, she thought. He must have kissed dozens of girls, and forgotten each one in turn. She felt her temper rising, but was unsure as to what had angered her.

"There's something that has to be said," he announced, breaking into her musings. "It's about that brother of yours, Perry."

What was he talking about? Did he know something about where Perry was? "What do you know about him?" she half cried.

"It's hard to say this to you, Erin, but he can't be a very—a very good sort to have left you alone like he did—in that place."

"He . . . well, he—he had to go," she replied defensively, tears glistening in her eyes. And then, in her hurt confusion, she blurted, "You're not any better—the way you took advantage of me!"

"Took what?" he said in bewilderment.

"You know very well what I mean! You—you kissed me—"

Matt laughed suddenly, slapping his knee as he did so. "Little Erin Conner . . . so that's why you've been so skittish lately! You've got a lot to learn, kid. That kiss was only a gesture to reassure a little girl when she'd been hurt and crying." Then he leaned forward, the smile fading from his lips. "You didn't actually think that I . . ." His voice trailed away.

"No!" she insisted too loudly. "Of course not!"

Embarrassment overcame her and she became speechless. Why had she brought it up? Her cheeks flamed, she leaped to her feet and rushed into the tent, a weight of humiliation suffocating her in its intensity.

Oh, how could I! she screamed silently. I betrayed myself and he threw my words in my face! And what's far worse, he laughed at me!

The tears that had threatened earlier flowed now, rolling hotly down her cheeks. She threw herself onto her blanket and sobbed quietly into the rough wool.

She had thought that all her misery was in the past, but now she knew better. She would have to face him again, in the morning, in the afternoon, every morning and afternoon. It wasn't fair! Oh, how she hated him for laughing at her with that perfect white smile of his!

Sleep was impossibly slow in arriving for Erin that night; her brain spun with confused mental images. Even after the tears had dried and the moon had risen above the dark mountains, she still could not stop thinking about her future, spoiled so quickly by the younger Mr. Steele. Before tonight she'd deeply believed that Ute City held some sort of magic for her. But as the night hours slowly fell away and she tossed restlessly on her makeshift bed, she felt less positive about tomorrow, or any of her tomorrows.

And the reason why her future seemed so clouded, so fragile, was as always: that smug young man still lounging outside, still laughing by the fire.

Tiredly, her eyes closed. In the tender morning hours, exhaustion had its way and carried her down, ever downward, into its blessed release. Her last thoughts before she drifted into oblivion were hazy but tenacious. She could forget about Matt Steele, could act as if he didn't exist; he would not be a part of her new life. Here, in this valley of blue sky and towering mountains and white river, she would grow and thrive on her own. And someday she would awaken to find herself rich and happy, from her own doing, without *him*. Here, in the Roaring Fork Valley, she could be anything she pleased . . .

Chapter 10

Erin straightened up slowly, feeling every taut muscle in her slim back. She had never worked so hard in her life, but somehow that gave her a feeling of security and self-confidence. She knew she was a big help to Lew, even if Matt scoffed at her efforts and refused to acknowledge her contributions more often than not. Why is he so unkind of late? she asked herself. Why can't he just accept me as a human being, with a mind and feelings of my own? But to him she was just a kid, for whom he alternately felt pity or irritation. And that hurt, she had to admit in a moment of clarity.

She bent over again, to chink the irregular spaces between the logs with mud dug up from the riverbed. When she finished the bottom row, she stood back to view her handiwork. The sturdy logs fit together beautifully, and her rows of mud between them made symmetrical lines. What a handsome, cozy cabin they had built! Lew with his new, shiny ax, and Matt with the long saw, had done a good job, she thought. And even Napoleon had helped, dragging the logs to the building site, with only a few episodes of prideful stubbornness when a log was particularly heavy.

The day was warm and sunny, surprisingly so for late November, and Erin wiped the sweat from her forehead with the tail of her plaid flannel shirt. There had been several days like this one, but the weather could change abruptly here. Thick black clouds would come rolling in from the west, obscuring Mount Sopris, then would advance rapidly in a line to push the wind forward with angry gusts. Then the snow would come; they had already had one snowstorm since their arrival, but the ground covering had melted in the next day's sun, leaving only white caps on the mountain peaks. The few men who had spent last winter in the valley warned them of the severity of the cold and the snow, but even they had to admit that 1879 had seen a particularly bad winter.

Erin heard voices shouting to the mules. They must have got it, then, she thought, and ran to meet Lew and Matt. Sure enough, the mules, hitched to an improvised sledge, were dragging a squat, black iron stove toward her.

"Oh! You managed it! How wonderful!"

"Yes, we managed it, all right," Lew said wryly, "but it cost an arm and a leg. We're just lucky Fallon was leaving and wanted to sell it. Now, how are we going to get it inside?"

After much grunting and a few colorful expletives from the Steeles, the heavy item stood in a corner of the cabin, a stovepipe attached, and with a flat top on which to cook.

Erin cooked dinner that evening on the new stove, burning the biscuits slightly, but to her credit the rabbit stew was delicious. Matt kept them well stocked with small game, deer, elk, and even speckled trout from the river, but they had to be careful of their supplies. Most of the extra flour, sugar, coffee, and beans would be sold to the valley's inhabitants, for once winter struck, there would be no way to traverse the pass for goods from Leadville. They would be totally isolated until spring.

Erin had met the women of Ute City—the wives, sisters, or daughters of the men settled there—but she knew they looked upon her with bewilderment and a measure of distrust because she always wore men's denims and a shirt, stuck her hair up under a hat, and rode her mule astride, like a man. Erin, on her part, was slightly contemptuous of these women, knowing most of them had come to Ute City on the easier wagon road over Taylor Pass and down through Ashcroft. Mrs. Gillespie even spoke of starting a literary society to while away the winter days! A literary society, indeed!

Erin hated the way Matt behaved around them, taking off his Stetson with a flourish, asking about their health—as if he really cared! His blue eyes would light up and crinkles would form at the corners; his white teeth would show in a broad smile. Erin was revolted.

To her, Matt acted the same, sometimes softening and thanking her for a particularly good meal or a nicely stitched patch on the elbow of his shirt, but mostly ignoring her, or taking her for granted. At least Lew appreciated her hard work, she thought again, comforting herself with that knowledge.

The next morning dawned bright and clear; a white frost silvered every blade of grass, every bare branch, but soon evaporated as the sun touched the valley. Erin set about her chore for the day—washing their clothes in the river with strong lye soap. It took a long time, for the water was cold and the heavy denim pants, flannel shirts, long johns, and thick wool socks were difficult to squeeze out. By the time she had finished the job and carried the heavy load back to the cabin, clouds were building up and the air was nipped with chill. The wind kicked up leaves and dust into her eyes, covering the wet clothes with a fine coat of grime.

The first flakes of snow eddied around her as she began to hang the clothes on the improvised line, but her fingers, now red and stiff, were hard to bend. After a few minutes they would not move at all, and ached so much that she sank down to the ground and put her hands between her knees to try to warm them. Tears of anger and frustration filled her eyes and spilled over. How would she ever get this job done? And if she couldn't perform this simple task, how on earth would she cope with all the chores during the long winter months? For the first time, she wondered if she was strong enough to live up to the image of a pioneer woman.

"Hey, now, kid, what's this?"

Erin realized with a sense of unreality that it was Matt's voice reaching her ears, but it sounded kind and worried, quite unlike his usual tone of impatience. He grasped her shoulders firmly and pulled her up, but she could not meet his eye and hung her head, trying to wipe the tears with the back of her hand. He cupped her chin in his fingers and raised her face to his, noting her brimming eyes, tear-streaked face, and trembling lips.

"What's the matter? Are you hurt? And what are you doin' out here in the storm with no jacket on?"

"I . . . I was washing the clothes . . . and it got cold. My hands . . . my hands got so cold!" She looked at him, her shoulders shaking with suppressed sobs. "I tried so hard to hang them up—but it was cold!"

Matt took her hands in his and rubbed them while she looked away in pain and humiliation. "Listen, kid, you shouldn't have stayed out in this weather. The laundry can wait."

"But I wanted to do it myself and surprise you! Oh, I know I'll never be any help to you this winter! I'll ruin everything! Why, we'll have to leave, and it'll be all my fault!" Erin sounded so much like a small child that Matt drew her into his arms and let her cry herself out against his chest. Finally he led her inside the cabin and quickly restoked the fire. Erin's sobs subsided and she tried to wipe her eyes, suddenly becoming very self-conscious of her loss of control. And to have Matt see her like that! She felt a hot flush of shame burn her cheeks and hoped he wouldn't notice.

Matt finished feeding the fire and turned back to her. "Better now, kid? Here, hold your hands near the stove." He went to the cabin door and opened it, disappearing outside for a moment. He reappeared quickly, carrying a wild turkey by the legs. "D'you know what, kid? Today, I do believe, is Thanksgiving—give or take a few days." He smiled at her. "Think you can do something with this bird? What d'you say?"

Erin sniffed, then smiled through her embarrassed tears. "Oh, yes, Matt, I'm sure I can do something with it—but just what is Thanksgiving? Is it a holiday or some such thing?"

"Honestly, kid, you've got a lot to learn." Matt sat down next to her on the bench and explained the meaning of Thanksgiving: the pilgrims, the Indians, the celebration of the newcomers' survival in a strange land.

"I see," Erin said slowly, thinking hard. "So we're like the pilgrims, then. If they prevailed in a new land, we can do it, too." She smiled confidently. "This will be our first Thanksgiving, won't it?"

"Sure, kid, but don't burn the biscuits this time!"

"Oh, Matt, can't you ever be nice and not throw things in my face? I do try so hard."

His expression sobered. "I know you do, but I guess it's just my way, kid. Never mind." He put a hand on her shoulder, and Erin could feel its warmth and hardness through her flannel shirt. Then he snatched it away quickly, as if he had touched something hot. She looked up at him, puzzled, her brows curving like the graceful wings of a bird.

"It's too bad your mother can't be here with us, isn't it?" she said suddenly, not quite knowing why. "How did she die, Matt?"

His face grew white and hard, his blue eyes turning cold and remote. "Never mind what happened to her," he replied curtly. "She's dead, all right, dead to us. Let it be, kid."

Erin drew back from his caustic tone, sorry now that she had brought up the subject. Was his mother really dead? Perhaps she had been wrong to assume that. And now she had broken the truce that had existed temporarily between them, and Matt was angry with her again. Tears threatened to spill, but she clenched her teeth and moved away from him to prepare the turkey for dinner.

Thankfully, Lew entered the cabin soon after, and his arrival dispelled the air of tension. Erin breathed a silent prayer that Lew was there, his seamed face familiar and reassuring, but she could not forget the feel of Matt's strong arms or the unique male smell of him.

Winter officially arrived in Ute City on December third. The storm left two feet of snow on their roof and threatened to collapse the tent, which still stood attached to the back of the cabin for storage. When the storm ended, the clouds disappeared and the sky was as deeply blue and serene as on a midsummer day. But the surface of the valley was covered with a sparkling blanket of snow that rounded and softened the contours of the land; the terrain seemed unfamiliar, and the air was bitterly cold.

Erin pushed open the cabin door and cleared a path. She had never seen so much snow, in Ireland it rarely snowed, and never like this! She just might like winter here, she mused as she trudged through the powdery fluff to see how Napoleon and his friends had fared in their lean-to. The few cabins and tents in the valley sent up their lonely plumes of smoke, the only sign of human habitation, but she noticed that several dogs were already romping and cavorting in the fresh, untracked mounds.

Erin reentered the cabin and stamped her boots, her cheeks red from the cold.

"Have you ever seen so much snow?" she asked the men.

"Hell, kid, it storms harder than this in Pennsylvania sometimes. This is nothing!" Matt said, squelching her excitement.

She tossed her red-gold curls and began to make breakfast. It was the same every day: cornmeal mush, coffee, and some leftovers.

Matt had shot a bull elk a week ago, and the quartered animal was snugly stored in the tent; it would last most of the winter, but they all craved something fresh—fruit, vegetables, anything at all. Even a sour crab apple would have been welcome. They had a bag of dried fruit, which Erin guarded jealously, saving it to make fruit pies for Christmas, which was only three weeks away.

The ladies of Ute City, few as they were, had decided to hold a Christmas dinner for everyone in the settlement, and even the prospectors from Castle Creek or Maroon Creek were invited. It was to be a gala affair; everyone was going to pool his resources for the feast, and Erin had promised to provide several pies.

Christmas Eve saw her busily rolling out dough and struggling to make the oven draw properly. She had prepared an elk roast and some dumplings for the men, and was concentrating hard on her pie crust, an empty flour sack tied around her waist as an apron, when Lew and Matt entered, blowing on their fingers, stamping their feet, crimson-faced from the cold. They carried a load of split logs and dumped it next to the stove.

"I'm starved, kid. When's supper?"

"You'll have to wait till I put the pies in the oven," Erin snapped. "They've got to be done first!"

"Hey, calm down, kid. We'll wait."

Lew sighed; he was growing used to the quibbling between

Matt and Erin. Sometimes he could see a softening in Matt and was glad for Erin's presence, but then his son would revert to his former bitterness and resentment.

Damn my wife! he thought angrily, as he had so many times before. It's not bad enough she had to hurt me, but she's wounded the very soul of our son by her indecent behavior. Maybe Erin will have an effect on him yet. She's a sweet girl, hard-working and smart. Just like the daughter I always wanted, but Amanda refused to have any more children. Lew shook his head to rid himself of these unwelcome thoughts and took the lantern with him back into the tent. He emerged soon with a package wrapped in brown paper and tied with a string.

"There!" Erin said, sliding the last pie into the oven. She stood back, her hands on her hips, a smudge of flour on her cheek, her face flushed from the heat of the iron stove. "Now we can eat."

"I have something for you, Erin," Lew said shyly. "It's a present—it's Christmas, you know. I got it in Leadville before we left."

"Oh, Lew, you shouldn't have. And I never even thought . . . I have nothing for you . . ."

"No need, child. You've done enough here, workin' so hard to take care of us and all." He handed her the package, catching the quick blush rising on her cheeks. A spurt of warmth shot through him, and he wished he could do more for her than merely give her a simple Christmas gift.

He looked across at his son for a moment and saw an expression of vague surprise on Matt's face. Matt couldn't be jealous, could he? No, it looked as if Matt were thinking along the same lines as he had, that Erin deserved all they could give her. Fleetingly, Lew wondered if Matt recalled his own childhood: the games of mumblety peg with his friends at school, the chocolate cookies Amanda had baked for those special times, the carefree hours spent building tree forts. How different Erin's and Matt's childhood experiences had been!

Lew glanced back at Erin now, and a smile crossed his lips as he saw her face light up with the prospect of the package's contents. She wiped her floury hands on her apron, then unwrapped the present eagerly. She gasped in surprise, then quickly looked up at him, her eyes a smoky blue now.

"It's to wear to the party tomorrow," Lew said. "I thought

102

you should have something besides that boy's get-up. Hope it fits."

"Oh, Lew," Erin breathed, shaken by the generosity of his gift but suddenly afraid to put it on. She hadn't worn a dress in so long, had sworn never to wear one again. But she'd have to wear it, for Lew simply would not understand her aversion to femininity.

She shook it out of the box and smoothed the flowered fabric: green posies, a high, frilled neck, a tucked bodice, sweeping skirt with a flounce at the bottom. A beautiful dress! Her skin tingled both in fear and in pleasure at the thought of putting it on. The last time she'd worn a dress had been that hideous night; she remembered Madame Lucille's hands smoothing her dress in the kitchen before sending her up to Ben Mortimer. She suppressed an involuntary shudder.

"I'll wear it tomorrow—oh, thank you, Lew. It's beautiful!" She moved quickly to the stove to hide her confusion, and began to serve the roast and dumplings.

Lew ate heartily, not noticing that Erin was unusually silent. Matt, too, was uncharacteristically quiet, and he often looked up from his tin plate to glance quizzically at Erin.

Even as she cleared off the table and started to wash the dishes, her nerves were still unsettled. *A dress.* She'd simply have to wear it tomorrow or Lew would think her ungrateful and selfish. But what if it didn't fit? What if it was too big and she looked foolish? Or worse still, what if it was too small and fit too tightly across the bodice? Again, for the hundredth time since she had received the present, her cheeks turned scarlet with inner confusion.

Coming silently up behind her, Matt took hold of the coffee pot and poured himself a cup. "Nice dress. Dad knows pretty things."

Erin jumped, dropping the plate into the dishwater and splashing the front of her shirt.

"Sure are nervous tonight, kid," came Matt's unwanted observation. "Couldn't be that you're afraid to put on a dress, now, could it?"

"That's ridiculous, Matthew Steele." She retrieved the plate from the pan with trembling fingers.

As he turned away, he said simply, "There's nothing wrong with being a girl, Erin. Besides, there's not much you can do about it anyway."

Perhaps, she told herself, Matt was absolutely correct in his observation. There isn't anything wrong with being a girl, and certainly there is nothing I can do to alter the fact. I'll have to wear the dress tomorrow, like it or not, whether or not it fits properly. After all, it's not the end of the world, and I need wear it only for a few hours.

Christmas Day of 1880 came and went so rapidly for Erin that when she finally went to bed late that night her fears about wearing the dress seemed like a forgotten dream. She sighed with deep relief that the day had actually gone so well. The townsfolk had made some comments on her attire, but their words had been pleasant enough, and she had managed to murmur a reply to everyone.

Suddenly Erin's heart leaped; she had remembered Matt's face when he'd first seen her in the pretty frock. His eyes had held hers for a long, agonizing moment and then traveled slowly over her form, as if taking in each button, each pleat at her waist. Then had come one of his smart-aleck remarks. And how had she felt then? Like a rabbit in a snare, she recalled. Almost the same way she had felt when Ben Mortimer's gaze had bruised her so thoroughly.

Go to sleep, she told herself now, and forget crude Matthew Steele with his bold stare. Tomorrow's a new day, and soon it will be 1881, a new year, in a new and marvelous town.

Chapter 11

It was a dismal time of year, this spring of 1881, in the Colorado Rockies. Erin looked out of the store window and saw another storm in the offing; the thick clouds hung low in the gulches and ravines of Aspen Mountain, and the sun was obscured by a suffocating blanket of gray. There were no buds yet on the aspens and cottonwoods; even the green of the pines seemed faded, waiting impatiently for the tender warmth of spring.

She sighed and turned her attention back to Lew. "Do you suppose it will ever stop snowing?"

Lew chuckled at her frown. "Oh, I imagine so, Erin. In fact, I'm given to understand there is no place prettier than this valley once June rolls around."

"I certainly hope you're right!" Indeed, Lew was usually correct on almost every count. He had a definite way of cheering Erin's low spirits or calming her when she became rattled. He was becoming more and more important in her young life, yet Erin was not afraid of her dependence on him; for some reason, she knew he would not let her down.

"Now, where do you suppose Matt is?" Lew asked offhandedly, wondering if his son had had any success with fishing that day. A few trout would be just the perfect supper; even Lew was growing tired of their staple diet of venison, elk or rabbit, cornmeal, and precious dried fruit. He hoped Erin would learn to grow vegetables this spring and can them in the fall. Maybe they could start a small garden soon.

On the sparse days of sunshine in April, Matt and Lew had built the first addition to their tiny shop; a few more favorable days would see the completion of their efforts. Happily, a single wagon had made it over Taylor Pass in mid-April, bringing a load of expensive supplies. Lew had bought everything in sight and still had managed to show a profit.

Several townspeople visited the newly erected Steele's Emporium that afternoon; more than usual, Erin realized. And, like herself, they grumbled about the May storm and were eager to see summer come. Erin sold Mrs. Blanchard the last bolt of printed cotton for a new spring dress, and a chew of tobacco for her husband. She sighed to see how low the supplies were getting.

The afternoon lengthened into evening, cold and stormy, before the front door banged open, setting off the tinkling of the new bell, and Matt strode in covered with wet snow. Erin's heart thudded with a familiar unease. She was glad that Matt had been gone most of the day; she grew weary of fighting her confused emotions where he was concerned.

"Just tell me there's fresh fish," Lew said, his mouth obviously watering.

Matt laughed, but seemed ill at ease. "Five nice ones," he answered, shifting his weight from one foot to the other.

"Praise the Lord," Lew intoned with an exaggerated Welsh lilt. "I swear, Son, I'd have sent you back out into the snow! I'm starved!"

Erin thought that Matt was behaving oddly indeed, as if something were itching at him under the wet sheepskin jacket. "Matt, what on earth are you doing, wiggling like that?" she asked.

"Well, I was going to look for a ribbon first, but this damn thing's tickling me to death!" His hand went inside his jacket and quickly produced a fluffy ball of fur, the exact color of Erin's coppery hair. The ball finally emitted a soft "meow."

"Oh, Matt!" Erin cried. "It's a kitten!"

"Yeah, thought you'd like him."

She rushed over to Matt, took the tiny kitten in her arms, and nuzzled it with her cheek.

"Oh, Lew! Did you see him?" She walked over to Lew. "He'll be a grand mouser for the store!"

"What are you going to call him?" Matt asked, his blue eyes regarding her warmly.

"I don't know. Perhaps I'll call him Abraham, after your—our—late, great president!"

"First Napoleon for the mule, and now Abraham for a cat!" Matt laughed. "What an imagination!"

Erin giggled and went to find a box for Abraham, then carefully deposited him in the shallow wood frame. The kitten hopped straight out and followed her with a disgruntled "meow."

"He's so cute—thank you, Matt. But why the gift? It's not my birthday."

Matt looked over at Lew for a brief instant, then back to Erin. "It's a going-away gift, Erin. I'm off to St. Louis for a while."

"But—but why?" Erin's surprise, and something else, too, clearly played in her light-voiced query.

"Matt's not going to be a miner, Erin," Lew said. "In Pennsylvania he had a good education, and now he's looked into the possibility of working for a railroad—surveying, you know. He's had a letter from the Union Pacific in St. Louis."

"Oh," was all Erin could reply. She felt confused, disappointed, and yet happy for Matt—relieved and sad all at once.

Lew explained that as soon as all the rooms in the store were completed, they would accompany Matt to Leadville, see him off, and return with a supply of goods for their expanded emporium.

That night, after the trout dinner, Erin retired, with Abraham to keep her company. She held the tiny fur ball nestled in her arms; this gift from Matt she would cherish always. Yet, in a way, Erin knew she would be content to run the store alone with Lew, without Matt's acid tone and disapproving glares.

And so the days before Matt's departure sped by. The snow melted in rivulets running off the mountains and down the rough streets of Ute City. Like that in Leadville, the main street was soon a deep mud puddle and promised to remain that way until all the high snows had disappeared.

Late in May, Lew and Matt completed the work on the store, and the townspeople grew eager for the Steeles to restock their supplies. Erin, too, was anxious these days, but not from the building or the oncoming summer, nor from the long days spent working in the store. Instead, her anxiety was related to the nearing of Matt's departure. Time after time, Erin convinced herself that the strange, unsettling feelings she harbored for him were merely the growing pangs of a young girl toward an extremely attractive older man whom she happened to be thrown together with constantly. A crush, a simple crush, that's all it was. And when he was gone, she doubted that she would even remember what he looked like.

To reconfirm her belief that Matt was a conceited oaf, Erin often goaded him into arguments these last days. When he gritted his teeth in frustration over her biting tongue, Erin was secretly pleased. She, too, could be hard and rude.

One morning in early June, the day they were leaving Ute City, Lew tapped on Erin's door.

"Are you ready, Erin?"

"Yes. I'll be in directly," she replied, hurriedly stuffing her few belongings into a saddlebag.

"Bring along your dress—we'll be havin' a farewell dinner in Leadville," he added.

She nearly dropped the bag; her face grew hot and her heart pounded. Did she have to wear it again? She bit her lip, remembering Matt's cruel taunt when she had been forced to wear the dress on Christmas. She had not forgotten it. "Maybe you should stick to pants, kid," he had said with his mocking grin, his blue gaze raking her.

She quickly folded the green print dress and packed it in

the saddlebag, closing her mind to the idea of having to wear it again.

They reached Leadville five days later, grateful for the mild June weather and tired from the long trek over Independence Pass. Lew took two rooms in one of the more sedate hotels for the time they would remain there.

It was decided that Erin should not go about unescorted, and she ended up spending most of her time reading in her room while the men bought and stored the supplies to be hauled by mule back to Ute City.

Finally, the eve of Matt's departure arrived. At first Erin had thought to plead illness and avoid the dinner altogether, but Matt would see through her game and no doubt humiliate her. So grudgingly, reluctantly, she dressed for the evening.

Yet she found herself taking great care with her bath, scrubbing her skin until it glowed with health. She spent a lengthy time on her hair, brushing the springy curls until they shone like Irish copper and then tying them back with a green ribbon. Her eyes showed a gray-green this night, she noticed in the mirror, remembering that her mother had once told her it was from excitement. But she did not feel excited; rather, she felt a little apprehensive about showing herself in public in a dress. She wished she were a man! And undoubtedly, Matt would still scoff at her attire!

Erin closed and locked her door, wishing she had a shawl; the dress Lew had given her fit perfectly in December, but now the fabric was beginning to look strained around her bosom. She cursed her womanhood. And wearing a dress could only remind her of that horrible night in Denver City.

She quieted her nerves as best she could and went below to her appointed meeting with Lew and Matt, but when she reached the hotel lobby, they were nowhere in sight. Self-consciously she took a seat and waited, feeling gawky and dreadfully edgy in the velvet-draped, dark lobby filled with men smoking fat cigars and staring curiously at her.

At last, when she was ready to flee upstairs, Matt appeared before her.

"Lord! I barely recognized you, kid!" His eyes examined her appraisingly for a moment.

She felt hot splotches of red stain her cheeks. "Where's Lew?" she murmured to break the awkward silence.

"Upstairs. Says he'll join us if he can, but I'm afraid he's got the grippe, so I guess we're stuck with each other." Matt held out his arm in a rare gesture of manners. "You know he'd be awfully disappointed if we, at least, didn't have that farewell dinner."

Erin hardly noticed what he said; she was thinking wildly what a joke this was—*she* had been ready to plead sickness!

Suddenly she looked up into Matt's face. "I'm . . . I'm not hungry. Let's just skip it if Lew can't be here. I'll go to him." But when she rose and turned toward the stairs, Matt placed a hand on her arm.

"Come on, kid . . . Erin. We'll be out of each other's hair soon enough. Let's call a night's truce."

There was no one in the world with a voice like Matt's, she thought suddenly; he could melt an ice block with that infuriating drawl of his.

"Well," she said in a moment of indecision, "I guess it wouldn't hurt."

He led her, his hand touching her elbow lightly, into the plush red velvet dining room. It wasn't until they were seated that Erin remembered why she hated red velvet. That room in Madame Lucille's had been done in blood-red velvet! The room where . . .

"Erin, you look pale." Matt leaned close to her, his warm breath touching her hair.

"Oh . . . I'm . . . It's this room. All the . . . red."

"You don't like it?"

"No, I hate it!" Sudden tears sprang into her eyes and she felt queasy, even a little dizzy.

"What is it, Erin? What's bothering you?" His soft, deep voice tugged at her, confusing her, forcing the words out.

"That room . . . in Denver . . . was red velvet. It was so red!" Reluctant tears slid down through her dark lashes. She shouldn't have told Matt. He would laugh at her—or worse—pity her again!

But Matt did neither. Instead, he watched intently while she struggled to control herself. "Do you want to talk about it?" he asked quietly, amazingly.

"No."

The waiter came and took their order, Matt easily replying for Erin.

"He's gone now. Listen, kid, it's none of my business, but maybe if you'd quit hiding all that . . . the thing in Denver inside you . . ." He took her chin in his hand. "You're growing up now, Erin. It's time you looked at yourself in the mirror."

"I . . . *do* look at my mirror! But sometimes what I see scares me." She turned her head away from his hand. "I'm not going to talk about it, Matt. And least of all with you!"

They ate the meal in silence; thankfully, Matt let the subject drop. But Erin's mind whirled with his words of a moment ago—he *had* noticed that she was growing up. Somehow it was important that he did so; contrarily, she longed only to hide behind her cloak of imaginary, innocent childhood. The conflicting emotions made her feel torn and confused.

Well, she told herself over and over, tomorrow he'll be gone. I won't have to think about him ever again.

Matt paid the check and led Erin up to Lew's room. For the first time that evening, she began to relax a little. Lew's mere presence had, in itself, a calming effect.

"Don't fuss over me, Erin. I feel much better already. Sorry about dinner, though."

"That's all right, Lew. Just so long as you're better." She looked over at Matt for an instant, wishing he would disappear. But after all, he was leaving tomorrow and probably wanted to be with his father.

"I guess I'll leave you two now—it's getting late. Good night, Lew, Matt."

"Good night, Erin. I'll see you in the morning." Lew smiled warmly.

"Wait. I'll see you to your room." Matt opened the door for Erin and walked her down the short corridor.

"Look, kid, I'm sorry if I upset you earlier. Honestly I am."

"It's all right, Matt. Well . . . good night." Why did he seem to hesitate? Or was it just her imagination? Suddenly she felt strange indeed, standing alone in the dimly lit hall with Matt Steele hovering over her.

"Erin," he said quietly, "you really *do* look pretty in a dress." And then, before she could think of a tart reply, he bent over and planted a light kiss, a quick brush of his lips, on her flushed cheek.

When Erin was finally inside her door, safely locked away from the outside world, she could not even remember if she had said good night to Matt. All she could recall was his odd chuckle as he had ushered her inside and turned away.

Instinctively, as she let out her breath and relaxed against the door, her hand went up to her cheek. Why did it burn so where Matt's lips had barely touched her? What in heaven's name had come over her now? Why did she harbor such secret, deep feelings for him? Was it more than the silly crush she'd already admitted to herself?

Still, no matter how hard she tried to tear her mind away from his kiss, no matter how hard she attempted to move away from the door, she could not. It was as if his warm breath still lingered on her skin: soft, tingling, thrilling.

When at last she had regained a measure of control, she abruptly recalled that he was leaving. To think, even for an instant, about his touch was a waste of her time. She would probably never see him again.

Chapter 12

June was all that the local townsfolk had promised. The sun shone gloriously in the azure sky; day in and day out the weather remained flawless, and Erin reveled in the dry mountain warmth. The quaking aspens were green now, their tiny leaves tinkling and shining like emerald droplets. Yes, Erin thought, she would grow to love this valley and call it home.

Now that Matt had been gone for two weeks, she felt that her relationship with Lew Steele was strengthening each day. Without Matt she could be herself around Lew, and if she made a silly mistake, Lew would laugh or help her correct the error.

The early summer weeks had seen an influx of people to Ute City—now known as Aspen. Erin remembered that B.

Clark Wheeler thought that name more apt, and more likely to bring in the speculators than the old name with its insinuation of Indians. Each day she would look out the store window and see more growth. The wood-frame houses were popping up overnight, dotting the narrow valley with their stovepipes and picket fences. The roughly delineated dirt streets were lined with staked-off lots that sold as fast as the surveyors could pound in the sticks—streets that already had names like Gillespie, Bleeker, Durant, Hopkins. Erin thought whimsically at times that Aspen Mountain, the majestic lady looming over the new town, must look with dismay, or even anger, at the interruption of its age-old peace.

The business boomed, and Lew was already planning a July trip to Leadville for more goods to sell. Erin heard of small silver strikes almost daily now in the surrounding mountains, strikes bearing names that would become famous—the Durant, the Spar, the Smuggler. There was even a little town, complete with a school, on a rolling hillside two miles up the mountain, called Tourtelotte Park.

Lew and Erin worked hard in the store, often from dawn until dusk; tirelessly they sold their wares and restocked the shelves with more goods. There were now two bedrooms upstairs over the store, a storage shed out back, and a storefront with a large glass window proclaiming STEELE'S EMPORIUM in rounded gold lettering. Erin remembered the long days spent hammering, sawing, and nailing that spring; Lew could not have done it without his son's help. But now they didn't need Matt, she often realized. They were doing just fine without him.

The local population had grown from thirty-five to around five hundred, most of them men, but there were several women in Aspen, and Erin was grateful for their presence. As long as there were skirts swishing down the streets, no one ever paid her much mind. She was just Lew Steele's slightly odd, adopted daughter, who wore men's trousers.

Abraham grew enormous, much to Erin's delight, for he, too, put in long hours gobbling up the pesky field mice around the emporium. Sometimes at night, after a long stroll up Hunter Creek, Erin would fall asleep with Abraham snuggled warmly against her, reminding her always of Matt's uncharacteristic thoughtfulness.

Erin stayed busy, often working more than she had to, and she seldom had time to think of her past. She grew two inches in height that summer and rounded out nicely, yet she still refused to acknowledge her femininity. She did, however, discard her hat, following Lew's suggestion that her hair would look just fine done up in braids on top of her head. He rarely pressed Erin on her manner of dress but hoped she would begin to act more like a lady than a tomboy.

And so Erin and Aspen grew apace; young, vulnerable, and proud, they developed their uniqueness and separate personalities that summer of 1881. And so, too, did Steele's Emporium. By mid-August, Lew was able to ride up to Independence, walk proudly into that town's bank, and deposit nearly ten thousand dollars in cash.

Aspen now had its own post office, to which Erin walked twice weekly for Lew to see if there was word from Matt. At first, the letters had come regularly, but as the warm weeks sped by, Matt wrote less frequently. When a letter did arrive, Erin and Lew would sit on the wooden steps after dinner and Lew would read it. It seemed that Matt was happy. He had a well-paying job with the railroad, yet he said little of what his work involved. Once he had mentioned a pretty young seamstress who lived at his boardinghouse. Erin recalled having felt oddly undone by this. But why should she have? Unless, of course, she was afraid Matt would bring a girl home and upstage her place in the little family. But it was silly to think about it at all, for Matt would be gone for years, and a lot could happen in that time.

It was on a gilded September afternoon, when Erin was closing up, that a young man came hurrying down Mill Street to the store.

"I'm sorry—are you closing?" he asked, breathless.

"Well, if you'll hurry, I guess we're still open."

The man slid inside past Erin and began collecting a few staple food items. As he bent and stood effortlessly, she realized there was something naggingly familiar about him, even though he was a total stranger to her. Suddenly it came to her: the easy way he carried his tall frame brought Matt to mind. Her smoky eyes fixed on his broad back, his lean flanks, the way the muscles worked in his forearms.

"Guess this is all I need, Miss . . . Miss . . ."

"Erin Conner, sir. That'll be twenty-two fifty." As he

113

handed her the money she noticed that his face was kind-looking, yet not particularly handsome. Not at all like Matt's. It was silly even to compare this ordinary-looking young man with Matt . . .

Erin closed the door behind the stranger and watched him depart down the street. Her mind raced back to that warm June day in Leadville, the day Matt had gone. She could almost hear the slow chug of the engine, and the first turn of its huge wheels; could almost see Matt's lazy smile at the open window.

The sun had shone through the white, billowing clouds, Matt's eyes reflecting the pellucid Colorado sky and his happy expectations for the future, a future far away from Aspen, and from her. Erin had found it very hard to tear her gaze away from his. Her mood had been the opposite of the sun-drenched day: cold and heavy, gray. Why? she had asked herself. Why should I feel this way when I really want Matt as far away as possible? I don't need his disapproval or his sudden, patronizing spells. He doesn't like me at all. I know that.

But the tight knot in her stomach would not go away. For Lew's sake, she had tried to smile, to be cheerful, for she had known that for him to part with his only son would be extremely painful.

If only it was over and he was gone! Erin had thought frantically as they had stood on the wooden platform waiting for the train to leave. But at the same time, she had desperately wanted the minutes to stretch out indefinitely before the train would actually move, taking Matt away from them, from her.

She recalled the unbearable tension of those last few minutes, the silence that fell among them so heavily. And then Matt had climbed the three steps into the train and disappeared momentarily inside the car, causing her heart to clutch and lurch inside her breast. He had taken a seat, unlatched the window, and held Lew's hand affectionately through the opening.

Erin had looked up to see him leaning half out the window, talking quietly to his father, but the sun had slanted into her eyes, making them tear, and she had looked down again.

His voice had startled her then, even though it had been soft and gentle.

"Hey, kid."

She had glanced up quickly, to see his wide mouth stretched into a grin, his head tilted to one side, his dark hair glinting where the sun hit it, his blue eyes crinkled with humor.

"Aren't you going to say goodbye?" His voice had been low, teasing.

"Of course, Matt. I was just waiting until you were . . . through talking to Lew."

"Well, I'm through now."

Her voice had been stronger and steadier than she would have believed possible, feeling as she had the sick hammer-like beat of her heart. "Goodbye, Matt. I wish you luck."

"Thanks. And take care of Dad for me, will you?"

"Of course. You know I will . . ." Her voice had lowered and threatened to break, so she had said no more.

"Don't look so down, Dad," Matt had told his father. "We decided this together. It won't seem long—you'll be busy—and you have Erin to take care of you. And I'll write."

"I'll miss you, Son. I'll write, too."

"If you need me for anything, I'll catch the first train back."

The wheels had started to turn; Lew and Erin had walked slowly alongside, prolonging the moment.

"Goodbye, Matt. Thank you again for the kitten . . ." A loud hiss of escaping steam had startled her; it had momentarily obscured Matt's face, while the sick knot in her stomach had grown, almost gagging her.

Now, in the store, Erin could feel again that terrifying emptiness in her stomach. She carefully extinguished the oil lamps, her confused emotions of that day over three months ago still vivid. As she climbed the steps to her room, she wondered if it was possible that she cared how Matt spent his time in St. Louis. No, she told herself firmly, quite the contrary. I couldn't care less, any more than he cares how I spend my time. That is, if he remembers me at all!

Erin turned down her patchwork quilt and adjusted the lamplight so that she could read herself to sleep. But though she scanned the pages of the silly Western magazine, she could not concentrate on the words; instead, she again vowed to herself that she would never marry, would never let a man use her. But at the same time, her young body was beset by strange, restless yearnings, perplexing hungers of the flesh and of the spirit, that she would not admit even to herself. That night Erin went to sleep racked with doubts and bewilderment at the thought of Matt. But in the morning, with the fragile rays of the sun streaming through the window onto her, she awoke with a growing sense of confidence, a nurturing of her spirit, and she threw off the mystifying disquiet of the night.

The leaves began to turn a bright, unusual golden color as September gave way to October. Still the newcomers climbed the pass and ventured into the Roaring Fork Valley. There was gold in the color of the leaves, but there was silver in the cool mountains, silver beyond reckoning. Aspen held a promise, and strong men came to toil unflinchingly for their hopes and dreams: a wealth beyond imagination.

As the mountain air took on a briskness and the autumn leaves spread, brittle-brown, over the earth, Erin often walked among the faded leaves of the aspens. Already there were memories here for her, those of the past summer and also of the previous harsh winter. She found it hard to remember what it had been like when the emporium was a single-room cabin—when Matt had been there with them.

In truth, she could barely remember what Matt looked like. It was just as she had promised herself: his image grew blurry and undefined, fading as time passed. Even when she consciously tried to conjure up his face in her mind's eye, she could see only bits and pieces—his flashing smile when something pleased him, his angry frown, the square line of his jaw. In truth, there was much to see and learn in Aspen, and she had little time to think about the past.

On a cold, blustery day in November, Erin and Lew closed the store early and walked up Mill Street toward Aspen Mountain. As they passed a hotel, Lew commented, "Looks like snow, Erin. Won't be many more people over the pass this year."

But Erin barely heard him; a small, fragile snowflake had fallen on her hand. She looked down at the crystalline speck and wondered idly if winter would always remind her of Matt

Steele, and how many winters it would take until she no longer could recall the low, easy embrace of his voice. When would his very name sound unfamiliar? And would he return someday, years hence, with a pretty wife on his arm?

Damn! she thought. How many winters must pass before his memory is erased?

PART II

Chapter 13

The bell over the door tinkled and Erin muttered to herself, irritated. She would have to leave all the new cans as they were and wait on the customers. She put a polite smile on her face and went to meet them.

Oh, no, she thought, not *him* again! It was Nick Evans, a middle-aged prospector who had, fortuitously, struck it rich last year, and on his arm was the latest "soiled dove" in his flamboyant love life. This one was tall, black-haired, and dressed in garb from the latest catalog out of Chicago. Her magenta shot-silk dress was bustled in back, the leg-of-mutton sleeves were tight to her wrist, and the bodice was crisscrossed with mauve velvet stripes; her hat floated with ostrich plumes, and she carried a ruffled parasol. She must be hot as the devil, Erin thought, wearing that get-up on this warm June afternoon!

Erin settled herself for another long episode of indecision and ridiculous airs from the couple.

"Honeybun," Nick Evans said to his paramour, "what did you want to see today?" Then noticing Erin, he doffed his pearl-gray fedora. "Afternoon, Miss Erin."

"I wish to look at the perfumes," the apparition in magenta replied.

Consequently, Erin had to spend half an hour showing the different vials of perfume to the woman. She sighed inwardly, knowing the toiletry articles she had persuaded Lew to stock sold well, but hating to help silly females ooh and aah over the dainty items. *She* would never use the stuff: soap and cold water usually did for Erin; her skin glowed and her eyes sparkled. Her red-gold hair hung down her back today, carelessly knotted with a blue ribbon.

Her slim, straight figure, tall now that she had reached her full growth at twenty, was flattered by the red and black plaid shirt and denims she wore so comfortably. But no one could mistake Erin Conner for a boy; her firm breasts pushed against the shirt front, and her hips curved suggestively under the rough fabric of the pants. She looked at her image in the mirror sometimes, seeing a tall, spare body, very unlike the pinched-in waists and bustles of 1885 fashions. Her face was attractive, but also unfashionable—her cheekbones were too high, her mouth too wide, her nose too small. Only her eyes pleased her, for they were large, darkly lashed, and a smoky blue-gray color that changed tints with her emotions.

Finally Nick Evans and his friend left the shop, pleased with the precious vial of French perfume that Erin had ordered from Denver City. It was so expensive that she had been embarrassed to tell Evans the price, but he hadn't blinked an eyelash, pulled a fat roll out of his pocket, and peeled off bills as if he had wanted to get rid of them.

Erin went back to the shelf she had been working on and began to arrange the jars of preserves. Mrs. O'Leary made delicious jams from wild chokecherries and serviceberries, and sold them through the store; this gave her pocket money, even though her husband made a fair living working in the Molly Gibson Mine.

The bell tinkled again, and Erin sighed. She'd never get the shelves done! Lew was upstairs resting; his cough had come back and he tired easily, so she hated to ask him to help right now.

As she approached the front of the shop she could see the silhouette of a man, but the light from the plate-glass window was behind him and his features were shadowed. The man's wide-brimmed hat was pushed to the back of his head in a way that teased pleasantly at her memory for an instant. His jacket was slung casually over one shoulder. Erin could see the dust motes dancing in the shaft of light that streamed through the big window; the wide, rough planks of the floor creaked as the man took a step forward. Oh, blast! Erin thought. It's some rude miner, wanting a grubstake and a free pinch into the bargain. She suddenly wished Lew were with her; there was something portentous about this tall figure standing so nonchalantly in front of her.

"Yes, sir, what can I do for—" Erin's stock greeting froze on her lips as she drew closer and saw the man's face. She felt all the blood leave her head, and she swayed slightly, holding on to the counter top for support. Suddenly the blood rushed back, flushing her cheeks hotly, and she threw herself wildly on the figure before she could even think.

"Matt! Oh, Matt! You're back! And you didn't let us know! We've had no letter, nothing! Where have you been? Oh, Matt! It's so good to see you again!"

Then her voice failed her completely and she could only nestle her face in his broad chest, inhale the vaguely smoky, male scent of him. Her knees immediately felt weak, as if they would collapse under her if she weren't clinging to him. Not for an instant did she realize how tightly she was pressed to him, nor had she noticed the slight tensing of his muscles when she had flung herself at him. She knew only an extraordinary and immense joy as she continued to hold him.

Finally, when he became too aware of her body curved against his, he said, "Wait up, kid. You're gonna break my ribs! You're stronger than you used to be—and taller, too." Then he held her out at arm's length and looked at her for a moment. It was Erin, all right, but Lord, had she changed! She was tall and slim, almost statuesque, and definitely all female. But he saw that she still insisted on wearing men's duds. Nevertheless, she was not bad-looking at all. Her eyes were the same, and her wide, mobile mouth was familiar but somehow different, more sensuous, more lovely, with the four years that had passed.

"Where's Dad?" he asked, looking in amazement around the large room filled with rows of gleaming cans and jars, sacks of stapes and bolts of cloth, piles of clothing, kegs of nails, and saddles. "Wow! This place *has* changed! I wouldn't have recognized it except for the sign outside!"

"Lew is upstairs—he's resting. That cough of his is bothersome, but I can handle the store by myself. Oh, come up and see him—he'll be so happy!" Erin flipped over the sign in the door. "There! We're closed for now—it's a holiday!"

She took his arm self-consciously, blushing, and led him upstairs to their living quarters. "Where have you been? What are you planning to do? Will you stay with us long? How'd you get here? Oh, Matt, it's been a long time . . ." Suddenly she stopped, realizing her rush of words was unanswerable. She stole a look at him from the corner of her eye and saw his familiar, mocking smile.

"Slow down. I'll answer all your questions, kid, but one at a time, and Dad may as well hear the answers, too."

Erin paused at the top of the stairs, put her hands on her hips, and frowned slightly. "Matt, I've one favor to ask of you—please, don't call me 'kid' any more. I am not a kid. I'm twenty years old and have been running the store for a long time now—just ask Lew." Then she broke into a grin. "But, gee, I *am* glad you're back. You won't believe Aspen—it's changed so!"

"Yes, I can see that . . . a lot of things have changed around here," he said lightly.

As she turned and led him to Lew's room, he could not help but notice the way her hips moved or how her back narrowed gracefully down to her small waist. He tore his eyes from her form quickly, ashamed of his surge of feeling. Why, she's practically a sister, he told himself.

Erin flung open Lew's door with a flourish and ushered Matt in, grinning broadly and bursting with excitement.

"Lew! Look who's here!" she cried.

Lew put down the book he was reading and slowly took his old pipe out of his mouth, cradling it carefully. One hand froze above Abraham's yellow fur. The expression on his face was almost comical, but the emotion beneath was pure and open.

"Matt." The wonder in his voice said it all. He rose from the bed, where he had propped himself, and crossed the room to embrace his son. Then he stood back and looked at Matt carefully, studying him from head to toe.

"Hmmm. You've grown some and put on weight." He embraced him again, pounding him on the shoulder, then stood back and put a reproachful expression on his face. "Precious few letters we've had from you lately, Matthew. Did you forget to write while you were so busy with the railroad?"

"Sorry, Dad. I got busy, and, well . . . you know how it is."

"Yeah, I guess I do, Son." Lew smiled, shaking his head slowly. "You've sure surprised us. Tell me what you're up to."

"First, Dad, what is this cough Erin mentioned? Are you sick?"

"Lord, no, Matt. What's she been sayin'? I've just got a touch of rheum, that's all."

"I'm glad to hear it. I must say, you've changed this place

124

beyond belief. The store, the whole house." Matt walked around the cozy room, noticing the simple but tasteful furniture, the warm rugs and round table of mellowed wood. "I can hardly believe it."

"Yes," Lew said proudly. "Erin's done most of the furnishin' and decoratin' up here. And she takes good care of this old Welshman, too. The store's bringin' in a good living. Now, if you want to stay, we could expand. I've been thinkin' of carryin' more building tools—hardware, you know. That sort of thing. The town's growin' so fast, buildings goin' up all over the place . . ."

"Hold it! Hold it, Dad," Matt laughed. "Don't start ordering yet. You sent me to school when I was a kid to be a surveyor. Now, I can't be puttin' all that to waste, can I?"

"No, no, of course not, Matt. I'm sorry, I forgot. I get carried away sometimes, don't I, Erin?"

"Only a little, Lew," Erin said earnestly. "But I know this will be the biggest, fanciest store in Aspen before you're through!"

"Well, what are your plans, Son? Be with us long?"

"Not really. My job with the Union Pacific involves a lot of traveling." Matt hesitated. "Actually, I've been on the road for them for a year or so now, and they've sent me out here to do some . . . exploratory work."

"Why, that's wonderful! You'll be closer to home! What kind of job is it, Matt? Sounds interesting." Lew was enthusiastic.

"Oh, you know. The usual. Surveying right of ways and things like that." Matt seemed anxious to finish the subject of his job and turned to Erin. "And what have you been doin' with yourself, kid? Any beaus?"

Erin felt herself grow hot and awkward. "Beaus! I should hope not! The only males around here are either still in school or prospecting up in the mountains. I've no use for them. I keep busy in the store and I help Lew do the accounts. He wanted me to go back to school, but I wouldn't—I know enough already. What do I need that for? He was mad at me for a whole week over that!" She giggled, remembering Lew's dire threats.

Lew was silent for a moment, thinking. "Look, why don't you let Erin show you around Aspen? You'll need a street map to find your way now, it's grown so. I'll watch the store and you take your time. Show him the Clarendon Hotel, Erin, and go have an ice cream at the soda fountain. This town has everything now, Matt. You'll love it here."

"Oh, yes! I'll take you around—there's so much to see!" Erin grew excited, wanting to share the glories of her adopted home with Matt.

"Okay, kid—oops—Erin. Let me get my bag from the stagecoach office, then we'll be off."

Erin felt surprisingly shy, walking next to Matt down the hollow-sounding wooden sidewalks of Mill Street. She stole a look at him as they strolled along; his profile was sharply handsome and his hat sat on the back of his head as usual. Suddenly he turned and smiled at her, and she looked away uncomfortably. His eyes were still the same piercing blue; the cleft in his chin was as deep; his square jawline was slightly heavier, more mature. He seemed so familiar to her; how absurd to think that she could ever forget his face!

She pointed out some of the landmarks of the town: the Court House, the Durant Block, the Congregational Church, and the new ore smelter. The streets were dry, it being June, but in the spring and fall they became a veritable quagmire of mud. Now they spewed out an unending cloud of dust that settled on every available surface. Horses, mules, wagons of all descriptions, were everywhere. Well-dressed gentlemen with spats, pinstriped trousers, and finely brushed hats mingled with grime-covered miners and fine ladies attired in the latest fashion. Children, out of school for the summer, ran and played in the alleys and under the parked carriages in front of the Clarendon, infuriating the Negro doorman. An old Indian squatted under a dirty blanket, upending a bottle to his lips from time to time; a few Chinese people with pigtails and wearing loose pants scurried along, intent upon their own business.

The whine of a sawmill could occasionally be heard over the street noises and the sounds of pianos and laughter from the crowded saloons. As Erin and Matt approached a popular drinking establishment, a man was thrown bodily through the swinging doors and landed in front of them on the dusty street. He picked himself up and shook a fist at the imperturbable bartender, who stood with arms folded, blocking the doorway. The man wandered off, muttering to himself.

Erin and Matt looked at each other, then burst out laughing at the same time. He took her hand, almost unconsciously amid their laughter, and they rounded the corner.

"Here it is!" Erin proclaimed, still chuckling. "The one and only soda fountain west of Denver City and east of San Francisco!" They entered, and Erin sat at a small round table while Matt went up to the long counter to order. He returned with a strawberry soda for himself and a chocolate sundae for her.

"Oh, yum! I adore chocolate, Matt. You remembered."

"Well, I reckoned you'd like one or the other, Erin. We could always trade." He pushed back the bentwood chair and stretched his legs out, took a sip of his soda, then set it down and watched Erin's obvious enjoyment of her ice cream. She seemed such a child right now, but he already knew that she could suddenly switch into a woman, beguilingly familiar to the kid Erin, but infinitely more interesting. Her very movements held a fascination for him, and he watched her while she devoured her sundae. She looked up once, meeting his eyes, but seemed embarrassed and quickly looked down again.

A young man, blond, smiling, and obviously shy, approached their table. "Hi, Miss Erin. How are you?"

"Oh, Bobby! I didn't see you. I'm fine. Is your dad in town for supplies?" Erin's question was guileless, but the young man shuffled and stammered as though she had asked him to marry her.

"Oh—Dad? Yes . . . yes, Dad's over at your store, as a matter of fact," Bobby replied.

"Good. He's buying us out again." She smiled at him and he blushed profusely. "I'm sorry, I haven't introduced you. Bobby Fairchild, this is Matthew Steele, my—uh—a friend of mine. You know his father, of course, Lew."

"How d'you do, Mr. Steele," Bobby said, his face suddenly paling. "Nice to meet you." His expression belied his words.

Matt stood, unfolding his tall frame from the chair, and shook hands with the youth, returning his greetings. He had the usual mocking smile on his face, but a quick, unaccountable stab of jealousy had shot through him at Erin's casual way with the lad. Just how well did she know him? Matt wondered. The silly, red-faced kid—why, Erin had been more mature than that at fifteen!

Bobby Fairchild took his reluctant departure, and Erin finished her sundae. She raised questioning eyes to Matt, noticing his untouched soda, and, laughing, he pushed it toward her. She seemed to be oblivious of Fairchild's evident crush on her. Was she really so naive? Matt mused. Or did she actually care so little for men? She intrigued him, he had to admit it; her aura of uncaring but ripe sensuality tugged at his manhood, challenging it.

"Now I've spoiled my appetite," Erin sighed, licking her long-handled spoon. "I'm ready to burst." She turned her darkly fringed eyes up to his. "I haven't time to prepare much for supper tonight, Matt, but tomorrow I'll cook all day. I promise I'll fix you the best meal you've ever had!"

He had to laugh at her serious tone. "Hell, I'm not fussy. I've eaten in some pretty poor dives in my time."

"Well, not tomorrow night! I'm going to put the Tabor House to shame! You'll see. Now, we'd better be getting back. Lew may need some help, and I bet you'd like to get settled and cleaned up."

"I wouldn't mind it. That stagecoach beats walkin' over Independence Pass. But there's not a dustier ride west of St. Louis." His tone became far away, almost sad. "Things sure have changed, Erin, since we walked that trail back in '80. It's hard to keep up, you know."

"I know." Her voice was soft. She extended her hand and grasped his. "But it's only because you've been away so long. You'll see. Aspen is a wonderful place to live. I know you'll appreciate it if you can just stay a while."

Suddenly Erin realized she was holding his hand. She snatched hers away as if she had been burned, then reached for her napkin and fumbled with it awkwardly. Her innocent joy of the afternoon was withering slightly, a small but creeping dark cloud obscuring her happiness.

Chapter 14

At first Erin had thought to invite several of their friends and make the dinner a festive affair. But after pondering the matter all morning as she bustled around the kitchen, she decided it would be more fun to have a family meal, just the three of them, the way they had started out in Aspen. She planned to serve an elk roast—for beef was still scarce in the valley—locally grown potatoes and carrots, and her specialty, a rum-flavored cake, for dessert. She even had a bottle of good burgundy she had saved out of the last case shipped from Leadville, destined for the cellars of a rich mine owner.

She took lunch downstairs to Lew and Matt and added a couple of bottles of cold beer from the root cellar—once the original small log cabin they had built—to keep them happy. Then she sat down at the table in the kitchen and began to consider her most pressing problem: what to wear. For the first time, Erin was beset by a dilemma common to women and as old as time, but it perplexed her sorely, since she had never had to deal with it before. She pictured in her mind's eye the candlelit, white-clothed table, sparkling with silver, crystal, and the good china. The men wore their frock coats which would be appropriate, but, to save her life, she could not see herself in a shirt and trousers, drinking French wine. Oh, this was ridiculous! She had never concerned herself with clothes before—why now? What difference would it make? Lew was used to what she wore, and Matt—why would he notice, anyway?

But the problem would not fade from her mind, and finally she threw down her apron in exasperation, grabbed her old hat, and strode purposefully down the back stairs. She knew exactly where to go, having passed it often enough. Fanny's

Ladies' Apparel was just around the corner, on Galena Street.

Taking a deep breath, Erin pushed open the door to the shop and walked in, looking around defiantly at the racks of dresses, blouses, and evening gowns, and at the piles of frothy unmentionables that caused her cheeks to redden.

"May I help you, mademoiselle?" asked a cultured voice from behind her.

Erin whirled around. "Yes." She swallowed nervously. "I . . . I would like to buy a dress—no, a skirt, I think."

"Of course. This way, please." The petite woman, her hair done up in a fashionable pompadour, led Erin to a rack of skirts. "What size do you wear?"

"Size? Why, I don't know," Erin answered, feeling like a fool. She realized that the woman could see her confusion and probably pitied her. She bit her lower lip in embarrassment as the saleswoman studied her, head to one side.

Then the woman put her hand on Erin's arm. "My dear, this is not a visit to the dentist. Now relax, and we'll have you all gussied up in a jiffy." She took out her measuring tape and soon had Erin's size.

"Do you like this?" She swished a tightly hobbled, bustle-backed skirt of deep pink with a candy-striped ruffle around the hem.

"Oh, I don't think I would feel exactly . . . right in that one. Have you something a bit less frilly?" Erin asked, full of consternation. Lew would choke on his food if she appeared in that skirt, and Matt—Matt would probably laugh.

"Here, I've just the thing!" The woman pulled out a stunning red and green plaid taffeta skirt. It had a small bustle in the back, and a big plaid bow nestled on top of the bustle. It reminded Erin of one of her plaid shirts, but the fabric rustled and shimmered quite unlike the flannel of her shirt.

Then a lacy white blouse was produced from somewhere, and Erin found herself dressed in the garments and staring at herself in the octagonal floor mirror. A stranger stared back at her, looking tall and elegant, but a little frightened. The high, lace-frilled collar of the blouse accentuated her long, graceful neck; the tiny, lace-edged tucks on the yoke of the blouse rounded provocatively over her firm young breasts. The skirt cinched in her waist and curved out over her hips, the large plaid making her appear statuesque. She could hardly believe that the elegant young woman in the mirror was Erin Conner.

"Yes, lovely!" the saleslady was saying. "Not many women could carry off that skirt, but on you it's just right. Your figure is good, you know, my dear, not as full as fashion might dictate, but the bone structure is there. And now you need undergarments. First a corset, although perhaps that won't be necessary, a chemise, petticoats . . ."

And so Erin was outfitted, from the inside out. She walked back to the emporium, carrying a large, red-and-white-striped box containing her purchases, and climbed the back stairs quietly, somehow afraid to face the men downstairs. Once in her room, she hung the clothes in the wardrobe, next to her men's shirts. They looked out of place, as if a new girl were moving into Erin's quarters.

Erin purposefully avoided Lew and Matt the rest of the afternoon, feeling slightly ashamed, as if she had somehow betrayed herself, and finished her dinner preparations. When the table was set and succulent aromas rose from the oven, she prepared for her bath. She heated the water on the kitchen stove and filled the old wooden tub in her room, mixing it with cold water until the temperature was just right. Then she eased down into the tub and began to scrub until her skin glowed. She washed her hair with scented soap from the store, and wrapped a towel around it while she soaked in the water. She asked herself more than once why she was going to such a bother; it was only Lew and Matt, and both of them had seen her as a young girl, in all conditions, sometimes at her very worst. Why did she feel the need to impress them now? But she had washed and scrubbed anyway, then, after drying herself, had even put on a dab of that ridiculous French perfume, also from the store.

She sat in front of the small mirror in her new chemise, pantaloons, and frilled petticoats, feeling foolish but glamorous, and reveled in the brand-new sensations that encompassed her. She had decided to put her hair up in a pompadour, like the saleslady's, and had even bought herself a packet of pins. Now she sat and looked at her hair, newly washed and dried, and wondered how on earth to fix it.

After an hour of fruitless attempts, she finally managed to tuck all the curling ends under and pin them in place. The final result was not bad, not as perfectly done as some, perhaps, but passable. The style flattered her prominent cheekbones and long neck. She was afraid to move her head in case the stubborn curls would fall out of their imprisonment, and she felt every sharp-ended pin sticking into her scalp. Then came the new blouse and skirt. She did not have a long mirror, but had to be satisfied with a blurry reflection in her window.

Finally, she went to the door and put her hand on the latch. Her feet would not carry her into the hall; they were frozen, and her hand on the latch began to tremble. What if Lew and Matt laughed? She squeezed her eyes shut, took a deep breath, and sallied forth to do battle. Let them laugh! This was how ladies dressed, and they could damn well get used to it!

Lew rose from the easy chair in his room as if an invisible hand had plucked him up, causing Abraham to spill to the floor with an irritated "meow"; his pipe almost fell out of his mouth before he remembered to grab it. "Erin!" was all he could say. "My lord, girl! You look . . . beautiful!" His amazement was so evident that Erin had to laugh in spite of herself.

"What a surprise—why, it's enough to give a man nervous fits, the way you youngsters will shock a body!" Lew went on. "First Matt comes home, then you dress up . . . like a lady . . . a right pretty lady, too." He walked around her and viewed her from all sides. "What do you think, Matt? Isn't she a beauty? A real thoroughbred?"

"She sure is, Dad." Matt's voice was uninflected, well controlled.

Erin turned to him, fearing to see derision in his expression, or worse, mockery. She searched his brilliant blue eyes but could not read his expression; his countenance was closed, betraying no opinion.

He thinks I'm quite ordinary, she thought, one of many women he's seen in his life. I should have expected it of him. She felt deflated, as if her efforts had all been for naught. The clothes made her feel awkward and self-conscious; the skirt kept tripping her up, and she could not take her usual long strides around the kitchen. She was afraid of splashing grease on the blouse and almost burned her hand trying to lift a heavy pan from too far away.

The meal was excellent; at least she had the satisfaction of knowing that. The roast was done to perfection, and the potatoes, even though last year's, were delicious. Erin could not eat much, however. Usually her appetite was quite healthy, but tonight, somehow, the food repelled her. Matt and Lew ate heartily, enjoying the fare and talking lengthily between courses.

Matt spoke of St. Louis, then went on to tell his father more about the railroad and its intricate workings.

"It needs surveyors and engineers, especially men who aren't afraid to go into new country to explore proposed routes—Indians, blizzards, you know. They're hired by the Union Pacific, but actually, they work under a contract company that does all the real work. The railroad only has the land grants from Congress, but has to pay the contract company to do everything else. Railroading is big business these days—it's profitable and quite socially acceptable, if you care about that sort of thing."

"Yes, I know. We're working on getting a line here to Aspen. We're putting out feelers to the Rio Grande and the Colorado Midland, and they're both interested," Lew said. "Then you'll see growth and riches in this valley! Our problem is that it's too damn hard to get the ore out and the supplies in."

"That'd be something, wouldn't it? A train to Aspen! And remember how we first got here? But I'm sure it'll happen, and not too far off."

"Then we'll be able to expand the store. I'll be able to order things from Chicago, New York even, and they'll be here in a few days. I'll build a new store, even bigger, like Macy's in New York . . ."

Matt listened while Lew elaborated on his plans for growth. It was pleasant to be sitting here in this comfortable room filled with friendship and warm aromas. He dangled a small piece of meat above Abraham's nose; the cat was begging by Lew's chair, obviously used to being fed scraps. Matt glanced at Erin; she was very quiet, her eyes downcast, a coppery curl escaping from her pompadour and twisting down her neck. She looked serene, lovely, devastatingly feminine. He hadn't been able to say much when he first saw her dressed this way, and he wondered if he had hurt her feelings, for she had become rather silent afterward. But Lord, what could he have said? That she was far and away the most beautiful creature he had ever seen? That she overshadowed any woman he had escorted about St. Louis, or Denver

City, or anywhere else? He'd be damned if he'd give her the satisfaction! She knew, she *must* know, the effect of her looks on men. She couldn't be that innocent, not with those eyes and curving hips and long, white throat. What a shock, to come home and find little Erin grown into a raving beauty, a sensuous woman. He felt a hardening in his groin, and then realized that his father had asked him a question.

"Hey, don't fall asleep over the dinner, Matt. You're not listening. I asked when you'd be leaving."

"Oh, sorry, Dad. Just daydreaming. I've got to be on the job by July first. We're to explore some new land in Utah for the railroad—pretty wild stuff, I've heard."

"So you'll be here a while, anyway. Good. Ah, here comes Erin's specialty. It's my favorite, I'll tell you."

Matt watched Erin lean over to cut the rum cake, then heap freshly whipped cream on each serving. He could not help but notice the shadow along the line of her jaw and the habit she had of biting her full lower lip. Each one of her motions became exaggerated and isolated, like the movements of a ballet, and each was agonizingly, exquisitely, sweet to his eye.

My God, Matt thought, what's come over me? She's like a kid sister—

"A toast," Lew announced just then. "A toast to my son's return and to Erin's splendid meal." He raised his glass of wine and clinked the other glasses.

Erin was embarrassed. She busied herself by clearing the table and serving coffee. The conversation ebbed, and half an hour later Lew gave a mighty yawn and shooed the somnolent Abraham off his lap.

"I'm off to bed. Too much French wine for me." He kissed Erin on the cheek, patted Matt's shoulder, and disappeared down the hall to his room.

Chapter 15

Lew's cough could be heard from time to time, echoing down the short hall; the only other sound was that of Erin wiping dry the blue willow china.

Holding a cup of strong coffee in one hand and a pipe in the other, Matt rested his feet on a wooden footstool, pensively watching Erin Conner tidy up after the excellent meal. Each time she reached an arm over her head to replace a dried plate on the shelf, Matt was reminded of and somewhat amazed at how much she had filled out.

His mind drifted back to his last lady friend, dark-eyed Elizabeth, with her short stature and large chest. How totally unlike her Erin was! He almost chuckled aloud at the idea that Erin probably thought her usual men's attire completely hid her femininity. This, he knew, was far from the truth.

"More coffee, Matt?"

"Ah . . . yeah, sure." Matt rose to help her with the pot. "You've learned to cook—and better than most, I'd say."

"I'm sure you've had a lot of good, home-cooked meals, Matt." Erin bit her lip, wishing she had phrased it differently.

"I've had my share." He grinned widely. "Does that bother you, Erin Conner?"

"Of course not!" she snapped, then narrowed her eyes. "I'll not be baited any more by you. You seem to forget, I'm older now and won't fall prey to your taunts so easily." But in her confusion, she nearly spilled the hot brew.

"Erin, I have eyes in my head. I can see you've grown."

That damn, irritating, low drawl of his! It scraped across her taut nerves just as it had four years before. Obviously he's used it on others—to his advantage, of course, she fumed. Well, other girls might find him charming, and he certainly thinks he is, but I'll not smile coyly back at him. Never! It's what he expects.

"Don't try to charm me, Matt. You forget that I know you all too well. I'm not interested in you." Now, why had she gone and said that? "I'm turning in now—good night, Matt," she finished hastily, a pink glow on her cheeks.

"Since you brought the subject up," he said teasingly, barring her exit, "maybe *I* am interested. Want to talk about it?"

"No, I most definitely do not!"

But when Matt smiled knowingly at her, Erin clenched her teeth and turned back into the room. She knew he was just playing a silly game with her, and it would be better to set him straight right now than to let him think she was fair game.

She poured herself another cup of coffee and drew a deep breath. As she turned to face him again, it suddenly occurred to her that Matt had said *he* was interested! Her hand began to tremble.

"Matt," she said as she seated herself, "in the time you've been gone, I've been . . . well, I've been approached by a few men." She put every ounce of strength in her voice, for surely it would fail her at any moment. "The answer has always been no—emphatically. Men have no place in my life."

Matt did not reply at once; instead, he sat down and stared at her intently. She looked about to cry, and something told him that he had pushed her too far. The game he so often played was somehow less satisfying with her. In the past, he had enjoyed wooing the ladies with a quiet word and a teasing look, then had watched them literally talk themselves into the bedroom. But with Erin, this strategy seemed unfair, because she could not possibly know how vulnerable she really was.

"Erin," he said at last, "I'm sure you've never given in, and I didn't mean to embarrass you. I meant only to compliment you—you've turned into quite a pretty woman."

"Thank—thank you, Matt. Perhaps I, ah, misunderstood. I'm awfully sorry." But she knew that she had not misunderstood—*he had said he was interested!*

"No need to apologize, Erin. There was no misunderstanding." He leaned forward, "I guess I was truly surprised to see what four years have done—that is, you're so different now. A woman, and I forgot for a moment that you were just Erin, the kid."

Her eyes flashed at him. "Oh! I see! And I'm not good enough for the great, handsome Matt Steele!" She rose, unable to bear his nearness.

A firm hand grasped her arm. "For God's sake, kid—Erin. We always seem to argue . . ."

"You've never, never liked me!" she hissed. "You've blamed me, ever since Denver! Well, it wasn't my fault, but in your eyes I'll always pay dearly!"

He didn't mean to touch her—but damn! it wasn't true . . . or maybe he *was* making her pay, in a way.

He suddenly spun her around, holding her at arm's length, staring strangely into her smoky eyes for a long moment. His fingers tightened unconsciously on the flesh of her upper arms. Her lips trembled so deliciously . . . In spite of his better judgment, he brought his lips down onto hers in a hard, demanding kiss.

For a split second Erin melted into his strong grip, inhaling the smell of pipe tobacco that clung to him, feeling the rough stubble on his chin. Then, abruptly, she twisted and fought against him, but Matt would not relent. He was positive, always had been, that underneath her air of purity there was a hot-blooded Irish girl. Hadn't his own mother's behavior taught him about shy, smiling women with words of protest dripping from their lips while their bodies reacted with heated passion? Women! They were all the same! And Erin, too; he had felt her involuntary surrender a moment ago . . . He kissed her more fiercely, but she continued to struggle.

"No . . . please," came her strangled cry against his unrelenting lips.

Had he gone a little farther, he would not have been able to stop. But hearing her muffled cries and sensing her mounting panic, he realized what he was doing and released her. After all, this was still Erin, not some hotel tramp.

Her hand went instinctively to her lips, and she backed away from him in fear and confusion. "You're . . . you're all alike," she sobbed, then quickly turned and raced out the door.

But instead of going directly to her room, she rushed down the creaking steps and through the back door of the emporium. The fresh night air greeted her coolly but could not halt her heedless flight down along the rutted streets and into the trees. She ran until her breath was gone, and then fell in a sobbing heap on a secluded path far from the throb of Aspen.

137

The sound of the Roaring Fork River was close by, but she didn't care how far she had run—just as long as she'd never have to face him again. Her young mind screamed against his attack and she longed to claw his eyes out. Yet deep inside her, Erin felt the same dreadful tightening in her stomach that occurred whenever she told a fib or tried to fool herself.

When her sobs had finally lessened, she slowly realized that Matt's unwelcome embrace had not been like that of the incident in Denver City. This one had been frightening, certainly, but not at all revolting.

"Lord! I thought I'd never find you! Are you crazy, runnin' away from me like that?"

Her heart leaped. How had Matt found her? Why had he followed? "Go away!"

"Are you hurt?"

"No—leave me alone!"

He knelt down beside her, feeling suddenly like an utter cad. "This is all my fault—damn! I'm sorry, Erin. What can I do?" He reached out slowly and laid his hand gently on her trembling shoulder. She instinctively recoiled. "Erin, please . . . I was wrong to kiss you that way. Lord, girl, it should be different."

"I—I hate you, Matt Steele!" Again the tightening in her stomach, the inner knowledge that she had secretly thrilled at his touch and had run as much from her own reaction as from him. However, fear was in control of her emotions, and she knew she was not thinking rationally.

"You don't hate me, Erin." With great tenderness, he eased her quivering body into his arms. "No, my pretty Irish lass, you definitely don't hate me."

She felt his mouth on her hair, his warm embrace enfold her with understanding. She wanted to flee again, but to leave those arms . . . "Please, I'm scared . . . You frightened me."

"I know." His tone was a low whisper. "You had every right to be." And then, in that mesmerizing voice that she no longer had the strength to fight, "Listen to me. It doesn't have to be bad, Erin. It can be beautiful with a man and a woman . . ."

"No . . . no . . ." Yet it felt so natural, almost safe, when his lips brushed her neck.

"Trust me. I want you, kid. If you'll just let me show you . . ."

"I . . . have been shown," she murmured sadly, almost wearily.

Matt laughed lightly in her ear. "Oh, no! No, far from it. Maybe I'm wrong, but I think it's time you forgot about the past and learned to be a woman."

"No . . . I can't, Matt." Her voice was shaky, not because she was frightened now, but because she wanted to believe him.

"Let me show you." Again his lips grazed her neck, her ear. "If you tell me to stop, I promise I will." His hand squeezed her upper arm slightly, sending an odd, tingling sensation along her spine.

He could still feel her resistance and took great care to go slowly with her frail trust. Only for an instant did he consider stopping, for back in the kitchen, Erin had been correct in a way: he could not help but think of her having been abused in Denver City, and if he could, he would erase her past. The deed had been done to her child's body, and now he felt an almost compulsive need to purge that memory from her. And true, he admitted, he was conceited enough to believe that he alone could show her the way to forgetfulness.

Matt's lips caressed her cheeks and eyes, the tip of her nose, as he held her gently in his embrace. Then, when her body ceased its trembling, he kissed her lips. This time, however, he was careful not to panic her.

For a long time they held each other like that. Erin found herself placing her arms around his neck, and eventually her fingers coiled in his thick dark hair.

"Now . . . I haven't hurt you, have I?" he murmured against her cheek.

"No . . . but we should go now, Matt."

He stiffened slightly for an instant; his eyes looked down into hers, shadowed as they were by the darkness. Was it possible that she thought he meant only to kiss her out here? No woman was *that* naive.

"I'm afraid, my little girl, we have gone too far just to walk away." While his eyes held hers transfixed, his hand began to undo the tiny buttons at her throat, slowly. "I want you, Erin, the way a man wants a beautiful woman."

"Please . . . please, Matt! It's not you—don't you see? I made a vow to myself, long ago . . ."

"I'm sure you did, but that was when you'd been hurt. Face

it, Erin, you were raped. And I don't mean to rape you. I think you want me as much as I want you."

"I don't," she protested as his fingers adeptly unfastened the ribbon holding together her chemise.

"Erin, you are beautiful." He freed her firm, ripe breasts and stroked them gently. "Really exquisite."

Erin's mind whirled and fought against the sudden sensations coursing through her. His touch, his words, were wildly thrilling. Yet she was so afraid that when she told him to stop, he wouldn't. She was nearly gasping for air from his expert arousal, and she knew only that she didn't want him to stop. Not yet. Not quite yet . . .

Matt sensed her timid submission and eased off her blouse and chemise top, discarding them. Even in the cool June evening his hands were warming, almost hot where he stroked and kneaded her creamy flesh. All the while he whispered to her in his deep, hypnotic voice.

The bright moon moved slowly overhead as the two lay side by side. Eventually, when Matt did no more than caress her bosom, Erin relaxed completely in his arms. She even admitted to herself that this was what she had always wanted from him, not words of kindness, but his hands on her naked skin, his gentle words of pleasure.

Erin's breath was coming faster now, and she began to long for some unknown release. When Matt felt her breasts heaving, he moved his hands under the material of her bunched-up skirt to caress her hips and thighs. He pressed his hard, bursting manhood against her hips and crushed her to him.

It was then that she panicked, fear washing freely over her. "No, Matt! We must stop!"

For a split second he nearly gave in, but he had gone too far, and the moment of indecision passed as quickly as the night breeze. His mouth took hers in a fierce kiss while she struggled against him in earnest.

"Please! No, Matt!" Oh, God! He was shedding his pants, and his free arm was pinning her while she fought to escape.

"You promised!" she cried futilely.

Matt nearly tore her skirt away. "You want me, Erin—I know you do!"

"No, I . . . not *this* way! Please . . ."

"Dammit, woman! You don't mean that!" But he grasped her arms and held them over her head.

"God! No! You wouldn't do this to me! No, Matt!" The thundering river drowned her sobs.

With his glazed eyes riveted on her tear-stained face, he forced her legs apart and posed himself above her. "Give in, Erin." His tone was hoarse. "I don't want to hurt you . . ."

She twisted and arched herself uselessly against him, until she thought she heard him whisper, "I'm sorry." And then, abruptly, she felt a stabbing pain deep inside her belly.

"Relax, Erin. I won't let you go until you've felt it, too." He moved within her until she finally lay submissive under him, her energy spent.

She was not disgusted, nor did she feel shame; rather, she had a growing need to have him do this to her. Her mind rebelled against what was happening, but her body responded quite shockingly, with a will of its own.

"No . . . oh, no," she moaned.

"Let it happen . . . it was always meant . . . between us."

"No . . ." she protested more weakly.

With each passing moment, a desperate ache built up inside her, an ache that impelled her to draw Matt ever nearer, until they were one. And then suddenly her senses spiraled upward, her eyes flew open and fixed unseeingly on the blanket of stars above, and she moaned incoherently through trembling lips. The pulsating desire to be fulfilled rocketed again and again, until she felt a sharp peak and shook helplessly, digging her fingers into Matt's broad back and crying aloud with abandoned release.

"Oh, God, Matt," she breathed weakly. His response was a series of groans, then he shuddered against her convulsively and held her close.

Later, a very long time later, Matt murmured, "Kid . . . you surprised even me."

"What?" Her voice was very small.

Matt slowly eased himself away and touched her disheveled hair. "I said, you were wonderful." He meant it, too. He couldn't recall ever feeling that kind of incredible explosion with any other woman.

Erin reached for her blouse. "I suppose I should thank the *great* Matt Steele." Her voice dripped with venom as reality precipitously washed back.

"Come on, Erin. It wasn't like that. We both wanted it. And, dammit, it was great!" He stood and dressed quickly. "You should be glad you know what it's all about now."

"Oh, yes, I should be glad!" She pulled her skirt on roughly. "I should be kissing your feet for raping me!"

He took her chin in his hand. "*That,* my dear, was *not* rape. What happened to you in Denver City was."

"Oh! So you're different from Ben Mortimer!"

"I see you remember his name."

"And yours now, too, Matt Steele! The only difference between you and Mortimer is that he took my virginity and you couldn't!" She swatted his hand away. "I'm going back now. Maybe if you search the streets you'll find another innocent girl—"

He spun around, nearly knocking Erin off her feet. "What the hell do you want, Erin? Undying protestations of love and loyalty? Do you want me to marry you?"

"I'd sooner die first!"

"Then what?"

"I want you to leave here—leave Aspen. You're no damn good, Matt. Oh, yes, for years, I admit, I thought you were the sun and the moon. But now I know differently." His eyes narrowed in anger, but she continued. "Now I can see that your only attribute is extraordinary good looks. Inside, you're just another man who can't keep his pants on!"

She might as well have slapped him in the face, for what she said had nearly the same effect. But with her it *had* been different! And in spite of her acid tongue, the amazing thing was that he still wanted her.

"Erin." He tried to reach for her. "Maybe I was wrong about what you wanted . . . It just happened. But I meant what I said. I'll marry you, if that's what you want."

Even though her heart was beating wildly, she believed he was lying. Therefore, she wouldn't let him see any weakness in her. "And *I* still mean what *I* said. I'd rather die than be married to you—or, for that matter, any man!"

This time Matt let her go. The thought uppermost in his mind was that Erin Conner, little Erin Conner, was the first woman he had ever proposed to, and she had the gall to spit hatred back at him. He should never have bothered with her in the first place. Never mind that he had always wondered about her, from the first time he'd seen her in Denver City in that blizzard, with barely a stitch on. He shrugged and tried to convince himself that she was like all women, full of protests but wanton at heart.

Chapter 16

Erin's eyes were fixed on the rising needle of the scale as she measured and weighed Mr. Sullivan's coffee, but her mind was far from the task at hand, and she had to shake her head to clear her glassy-eyed focus.

"Comes to four pounds, nine ounces, Mr. Sullivan," she finally said.

He paid her, thinking Miss Conner was acting a bit strange this day, and left without a word.

Erin went back to unloading another crate of apricot jelly, but her mind refused to stop dwelling on Matt and what had occurred between them.

Well, he manages to walk about as if nothing happened—must be from long practice, she thought bitterly. Why should I feel guilty, as if it were my fault? I don't need him. I have the store and Lew—that's all I want. Ever.

Erin thought back to yesterday, when she had gone about her business with a hot face and tears near the surface every time Matt, or even Lew, had spoken to her. She had been drained all day, not having slept a wink the previous night, torn by disgust for Matt and also for herself. Her body had ached, but not unpleasantly, and she had taken a long, hot bath the next morning to try to wash away the very touch of him. But his presence reminded her of everything that had passed between them, every sensation. Mechanically, Erin went about wiping the dust from the glass jelly jars. The job done, she tossed the rag halfheartedly aside.

It was then that Matt sauntered in. "Erin, at least let me help with the chores."

"No. Go away."

"Well, then, I think we better plan to meet later, away from Dad, and talk this out."

"Talk?" She laughed weakly. "There's nothing to say—and besides, I wouldn't meet with *you* anywhere!"

Matt gave a short chuckle, causing her taut nerves to leap. "I've tried to be considerate, Erin, but if this is the way you want it, then I'll leave you be."

"That's how it's going to be, Matt. It's the way I want it." She turned away from his intent, blue-eyed gaze, that gaze she could drown in if she let herself; she couldn't abide the way his look bore through the very clothes on her back and left her skin tingling.

Matt shrugged his broad shoulders and headed toward the door. "Just one thing . . . you can't hide away from men forever—there'll be plenty in your life, kid. I'm only the first," he added, sounding almost jealous to her ears. But that, of course, was impossible.

"Still, Matt, that's my business and not yours."

The door closed roughly behind him.

Her eyes filled once again with confused tears and she leaned back against the pinewood counter, her fingers pressing on her temples. She recalled that Jenny Perkins had come into the store late yesterday, and nearly seduced Matt with her sweet, honeyed ways. What woman wouldn't want him? He was flawless, and he knew it! No, she'd never give in to him again. Let him leave a trail of broken hearts all over the West; she had better things to do with her time.

And that, she was certain, was what bothered Matt Steele—the fact that she was not begging him to marry her, begging to have his strong arms hold her. An unbidden image of Matt's matchless grace flew into her tortured mind: his powerful muscles, his tall frame, the clean, sculpted lines of his body.

Shaking her head to clear away the picture, she continued her work. Thank the Lord he'll be gone soon, she consoled herself.

As the day wore on, a slow change came over her; she began to feel odd, almost excited. It was as if facing the facts about Matt had cleansed her mind of doubts, purged him from her very soul. Suddenly Erin found herself humming a cheery tune, and the worry lines left her brow. She tried not to analyze this strange lightheartedness. Just enjoy it, she told herself.

The customers came and went; it was almost closing time.

By now, Erin was feeling remotely giddy and beginning to wonder what had come over her. It was like a prelude to a marvelous adventure, and it had absolutely nothing to do with Matthew Steele, she was certain.

The emporium bell tinkled. It was lecherous, wrinkled Fred Zimmerman, no doubt drunk on Taos lightning.

"G'day to ya, Miss Erin." He slurred the greeting as always.

"What will it be today—we're almost closed," she said impatiently.

"Been down on m'luck, pretty lassy. Jus' came by to bid ya farewell. Leavin' this valley fer good!"

"What? You're just abandoning the mine?" Erin was incredulous.

"Ain't got no woman to keep me here, an' only took a hundred dollars this spring from that black, filthy hole!"

"Well, I'm—I'm truly sorry, Mr. Zimmerman, really I am. Why don't you sell the claim? There's people who'll buy it, I'm sure."

"Gonna do jus' that—but in Denver City, where they's too dumb to know better." He sidled over to Erin, half stumbling with the effort. "How's 'bout a goodbye kiss for ol' Fred? You sure is the prettiest thin' this side o' the Divide!"

Erin drew back and quickly sought the other side of the counter. "I think you should leave."

"Aw, c'mon. Jus' a lil' kiss?"

"No, really, Mr. Zimmerman."

"C'mon. I'll flip ya fer it—feel lucky today."

Erin could not help but laugh aloud. Old Fred Zimmerman lucky? Not a chance!

"Mr. Zimmerman, I think you *really* should leave." Then she added, a twinkle in her eye, "And besides, what would I get if I won the toss?"

"Now that there's a good question, Miss Erin." He grinned from his dark-toothed mouth. "Tell ya what. I win the toss, I get a kiss . . . you win, the Silver Lady's yers! How 'bout that?"

The Silver Lady? His mine? What would she do with a worthless silver mine? She began to giggle behind her hand at the notion, but stopped abruptly as a chill swept over her body. The room went gray and she swayed slightly against the counter. She had not had a vision for a long time, and what was happening now was so overwhelming that she shook visibly in reaction to it.

Before her eyes was an elegant drawing room, done in shimmering green velvet with handsome, dark wood furniture. In the middle of this extraordinary room, under a gleaming crystal chandelier, stood a beautiful woman wearing a rich, red velvet dressing gown trimmed with floating white feathers. The woman, obviously very wealthy, had Erin's face.

"Ya sick or somethin', Miss Erin?" came Zimmerman's gruff voice.

"I . . . I'm fine now." His seamed face once again filled her eyes; the vision was gone. She whispered slowly, "Are you certain you want to toss for the mine?" He nodded his head with anticipation. "Do you have the deed?"

Again the nod was affirmative. Fred Zimmerman produced a silver dollar from his pocket. "I sure am lookin' forward to that kiss, Miss Erin!"

Not for an instant was there any doubt in Erin's mind who would win the toss. Somehow she did not question this; it had been preordained. Her entire twenty years had been building to this one moment, this toss of a fated coin. And somehow, some way, the toss would be hers. On the side of Aspen Mountain, amid the jagged rocks and aspens, in a dark, musty cave, lay the fulfillment of her destiny.

"Flip it, Mr. Zimmerman."

"Sure ya don' wanna?"

Erin's eyes took on a faraway look. "Mr. Zimmerman, it wouldn't matter who tossed the coin. I'll take tails. Go ahead."

High into the air the gleaming dollar spun; it was like a slow-motion dream to Erin, watching the heavy coin whirl and dance, reach its height, then slowly, inevitably, fall back to earth with a glorious clink as it struck the hardwood planking.

"By God! It's tails, it is!" the miner cried in utter amazement, his intoxicated grin fading.

"Of course it is," Erin said matter-of-factly. "Now, if you'll sign over the deed, Mr. Zimmerman." She hurriedly produced a pen and inkwell from the accounts desk. For a brief moment she thought he hesitated, but then he extracted a folded piece of paper from his pocket, laid it on the counter top, and made his mark.

"Don' know what yer gonna do with it, but ya won it fair an' square."

Erin smiled warmly at the down-on-his-luck old-timer. She then walked him to the door, her feet seeming to float as if she were above the ground. This couldn't be happening—it just couldn't—but it was!

"Guess I ought to give you this, too," he said while swaying in the open door, the golden, late-afternoon light striking his wizened form. He reached into his shirt pocket again and withdrew an odd-shaped, gleaming mass that dangled on the end of a thin silver chain. Erin's eyes fixed hypnotically on the necklace. The shafted sunlight struck the object on the chain, causing it to glow and sparkle. "What . . . what is it?" The words were wrenched from her throat.

"Why, it's m' first nugget outa the mine! Had it put on this here chain."

He handed her the silver nugget.

She clasped it tightly in her hand and quickly allowed him to bestow a sloppy kiss on her cheek. It didn't hurt at all, she thought briefly.

She locked the door behind him and held the chain on her finger in the column of light streaming through the window. Now she had the nugget! It spun slowly around as she gazed at it in mute fascination—hadn't she seen it before? Of course! Several times before! Somehow, by some mysterious quirk of fate, the vision of a lifetime was slowly, miraculously, unfolding before her eyes. This very chunk of silver, as well as the thin, intricate chain, was the same as that in her visions—the strange object that had always hung around a man's bared chest, his buckskin shirt open to the waist.

As the nugget finally stopped its mesmerizing motion, Erin came back to reality. What did it mean, this necklace? Where was the connection? She had always felt that the man in her visions, faceless though he was, was the one who would forge and share her life. Yet certainly there was no man attached to this necklace! Not old Fred Zimmerman!

Erin held the nugget in her hand for a moment before slipping it into her pocket, vowing to think more about it later. Now she had other things to do—she was going to be rich!

"The Silver Lady," she whispered aloud. This would be the tool that would set her on the path to personal freedom. For a brief instant she thought about her parents, their decomposed bodies lying in a cold grave; about her brother, Perry, gone now for years, maybe even dead. And then there was Uncle Edward, snugly ensconced in his Killarney manor, satisfied to have cast out his only relatives.

She shook her head to dispel these thoughts. She was Erin Conner, the proud new owner of the Silver Lady in Aspen, Colorado. Perry, Uncle Edward—they belonged to a past life.

A smile gathered at the corners of her mouth; she felt her heart beat furiously; she threw her arms out and twirled around and around until she was dizzy with overwhelming happiness.

"Erin! What in heaven's name . . ." Lew's incredulous voice reached her.

"Oh, Lew!" She threw herself at him. "Oh, it's too marvelous—I don't know how to tell you—but we're going to be rich!"

"What!" He managed to extricate himself from her tight clasp and sat her down on top of a beer keg. "Now, slowly, girl. What are you talking about?"

She took a deep breath and began. "It was a bet with Fred Zimmerman—" Suddenly she noticed Matt standing at the bottom of the steps. How long had he been there? Well, it didn't matter. She went on in a rush to tell Lew about the Silver Lady and produced the deed to prove her wild statements.

"My God, Erin!" He looked the document over. "This is all fine, I'm sure, but the mine's worthless. You know that—everybody knows old Fred picked a poor spot."

"Oh, but you're wrong! I *saw* it, Lew, in my vision—I saw it all!"

"Not those damn sights again?" Matt folded his arms in disgust. "I thought you gave that stuff up years ago!"

"It's not stuff, Matthew Steele! You'll see!" She faced Lew again. "You believe me, don't you?" Her wide eyes pleaded to him.

Lew was pensive for a moment. "Well, Erin, I remember once, when we first came to Ute City, you *did* see how it would be. Maybe you really have a gift—I don't know."

"Not you, too, Dad!" Matt groaned. "You're both plumb crazy!"

"Oh, be quiet, Matt! You don't know the first thing about it. Why, I've seen a lot of things that have come true!"

"And now you're telling us that you—a woman—are going to work a mine." Matt regarded her sarcastically. "And strike it rich!" he added, laughing.

"Matt," Lew said sternly, "I owe Erin more than I can ever repay. If she wants to try this thing, well, I'll grubstake her myself. I trust Erin's good judgment."

Matt grimaced at his father. "Yeah, just like you trusted that wife of yours! Gave her the money for her so-called shop, and she left with Judd—"

"That's enough, Matt! I won't allow you to speak of it!"

"I'll speak of *her* any way and any time I choose!" Matt's tone was scathing.

"Please," Erin intervened. "I didn't mean to start an argument . . . I can get the money somehow . . ." She was thinking frantically. How would she get a grubstake? At the same time, she realized why Matt treated women so badly. And all these years she had thought his mother was dead! She suddenly recalled his saying only that his mother was dead to *them*.

"Erin, are you listening?"

"Yes, Lew."

"I said, pay Matt no mind. I insist that you let me help. Of course, I hope your dream comes true, but if the mine's a loss, we'll go on like before. We've done just fine, anyway."

Erin threw her arms around Lew's neck. From the corner of her eye she saw Matt storm upstairs, but she vowed that not even he could spoil her happiness.

She was standing at the window in her room, dressed in her nightshift, when she heard a creaking sound at her door. She turned to see what it was.

"How dare you!" she cried, shocked.

Matt's frame filled her doorway. "Just came to say good night," he drawled. He had obviously visited one of the local saloons.

"Get out of here! You're drunk!" she flared.

"I will, Erin." He quirked a dark eyebrow. "I'll go . . . but I just wish you'd listen to reason."

She pulled on a robe to hide her thinly clothed body. "Nothing you say will change my mind." Then she added, as he started to close the door, "Matt? I know you don't believe me, but I've seen it come true—the mine, that is."

He hesitated, a hard look on his face. "And what else have

you seen, Erin? Me? Or a life without a man? Are there any children?"

"I . . . I don't know about that." She bit her lower lip. "But I do know that there's a man, Matt Steele, and he's—he's not you!"

"I think, Miss Conner, that either your visions are lying to you or you are lying to yourself."

The door closed gently; Matt was gone. Erin stood motionless for a time in the silent room, staring blankly at the wooden door. He was wrong! Her life would be filled with . . . but what would it be filled with? Men, a husband, children . . . or emptiness?

She turned and looked back out the window; the lights of Aspen could be seen clearly in the thin mountain air. They dotted the valley with their warmth and welcome. Above the glow of the town stood Aspen Mountain, reaching mightily toward the stars. Up there was the answer to Erin's hopes and dreams, the key to her unknown but predestined future. Gradually her mind drifted back to Matt's parting words. *Somehow* she would find happiness. It might not be with a man, but at that moment she knew that her path, although rocky thus far, would smooth itself out in the end. It had to.

Chapter 17

The sun was high overhead when Erin finally reached the Silver Lady. Napoleon had been stubborn, the climb hot and tiring. Sweat stood out on her upper lip, trickled down between her breasts, and dampened the curling tendrils of hair around her face. But the thrill she felt when she stood before the mine transcended her discomfort. It was hers alone, and somewhere within its black, yawning mouth lay a rich vein of ore, immensely rich; she knew this as if it had already been discovered. She had only to search it out, to coax it into the open as if it were a reluctant child.

The strength of her ambition and her desire for wealth surprised Erin with its vehemence; she would not rest until she had everything money could buy: a beautiful house, clothes, servants, carriages, travel if she wanted it. She could go back to Killarney and toss her wealth into her uncle's face—and then stand back and laugh at his miserable expression. She would never again be at anyone's mercy, especially not a man's—no more Ben Mortimers, and no more of Matthew Steele. She would be rich, secure, far above their lusting ways, and, she thought fiercely, she would never have to marry anyone.

Erin unloaded the saddlebags from Napoleon's back and tied him to an aspen tree. The packs were filled with the paraphernalia of mining: picks, shovels, lanterns, a candle in a perforated can, ropes, and pulleys. She had also brought Lew's old Sharps rifle; there might be claim jumpers or drunks around, and she was taking no chances. She leaned the long rifle against the inside wall of the mine tunnel and gave it a pat, then turned to the heavy bags and pulled out a canteen of water, which she gratefully tipped to her parched lips. It certainly was hot on the unprotected flank of Aspen Mountain, Erin thought as she sat by the mine's entrance and looked down on the town of Aspen. Across the valley loomed two mountains, Smuggler and Red; they were already half denuded of trees because of the constant need for lumber for mine shoring, construction, and firewood. They had been heavily forested when Erin had arrived in the valley in late November 1880.

The bustle of Aspen seemed remote, even though she could see the horses and wagons and could occasionally hear the high whine of the sawmill. Up here the air smelled of grass and trees and wildflowers; the sounds here were only the rustle of aspen leaves when they were touched by a breeze, the chattering of squirrels, and the sporadic call of a bird.

She took another drink from the canteen and wiped her mouth with the tail of her shirt, an old habit. Then she rose, slapping dust from the seat of her denims, picked up a lantern, and went into the tunnel to explore her mine.

At first everything was pitch-black; gradually, her eyes

adjusted to the darkness and she lit the lantern and began to move further into the tunnel. Her first impression was of the cold—a permeating, bone-chilling cold—as if she had slipped from summer to winter with one step. Then the absence of sound penetrated her senses; it was like a tangible thing. The walls glistened with mica and quartz, and great logs shored up the sides and ceiling of the tunnel. Ahead, beyond the edge of lantern light, she could see nothing but a vast velvet blackness. A trickle of sandy dirt sifted down in front of her from one of the ceiling supports. Her nostrils were filled with a characteristically musty odor of damp earth, mold, and old wood.

So this was her mine, she thought; seemingly dormant, torpid. But she knew that it would come alive under her hands and supply her with riches beyond belief, like a great cornucopia of wealth. She smiled to herself in the dark, thinking of the gleaming silver.

Suddenly her dreams and the echoing silence of the mine were shattered by a muffled shout just outside the entrance. Whirling around, she ran the few steps back to the circle of light, snatched up the rifle, and held it before her as she emerged from the tunnel.

She blinked her eyes in the unearthly brightness, buffeted by the heat and noise of the outside world.

"Erin."

She could not mistake that low, self-assured drawl. Of course, it had to be Matt.

"What do you want?" Her voice was wary, and she kept the Sharps rifle pointed at his midsection.

"Whoa, Erin! Don't shoot." He held up his hands, feigning fear, a mocking smile on his thin lips. "I won't claim-jump your precious mine, don't worry." He smiled charmingly at her. "Can I put my hands down now? See?" He showed his hands to her. "No guns or knives."

Lowering the rifle wearily, Erin rested the stock on the ground. "Why did you come up here? You'll get your city duds all dirty."

"Erin." His voice was intimate, soothing. "I only came up here to talk to you. That's all, just talk."

"What about? We've nothing to discuss." Her voice was cold and flat, belying the rapid beat of her heart.

"I just don't want to see you work yourself to death over

this—this crazy mine and then be disappointed. Erin, it'll break your heart, kid. I've seen it before, and so have you."

She narrowed her eyes. "What do you care, Matt Steele? Why should it matter to you if I choose to break my heart over it?"

"Erin, don't be ridiculous. Of course I care!"

"Liar!" she spit.

"I'm not lying, Erin, and you know it." His voice was insistent, alluring her with its promise of—what? Satisfaction, maleness, all those things she had hated and avoided. She shook off the spell.

"This mine has silver in it. I know that. Whether you believe me or not is up to you, and frankly, I don't give a tinker's damn."

"So fierce! A real, true, red-haired Irish lass defending her own! You sure make a pretty picture standing there with your back up, spitting fury." His tone was bantering now, and she could feel her anger draining away in spite of herself.

"Oh, Matt. Go away. Leave me alone. Haven't you done enough to me? What do you want?"

"I *am* going away. I'm leaving on the stage tomorrow. I have to be in Utah soon. But I wanted to say goodbye—properly—and try to persuade you to forget this no-good mine." His tone turned serious.

"The Silver Lady is *rich,* I tell you! I'll never let her go. Remember that, Matt Steele! I'm glad you're going. Now I've got work to do." Erin turned around, dismissing him, and began to approach the mine entrance. But Matt was at her side in two long strides and closed his hand over her arm.

"I won't apologize for the other night, Erin. I want you to know that. It's something I'll always remember . . ."

"Sure, Matt. Put another notch on your gun and stash it along with all your other *memories.*" She shook his hand off.

"Damn you, you little red-haired vixen! Can't I get through to you?" He spun her around easily and held her immobile in front of him for an endless moment. She saw the anger in his face, *real* anger. His blue eyes darkened, shooting cold fire at her, and she began to feel afraid. She had never seen Matt so furious before.

"Damn you!" he repeated hoarsely. Then he bent his head and buried it in the soft hollow of her throat, his lips brushing her skin.

"No, no, please," she begged, her fierce courage gone now. She tried to push him away, but her strength was no match for his.

His mouth found hers and he crushed her to him. She felt an overwhelming temptation to give in, to relax, to let him have his way; it would be so much easier than trying to fight him. Always fighting him. So tired . . . His hands stroked her arms and back, cupping her buttocks and hips to mold them to him, and Erin's vision seemed to blur and dim. She felt a part of herself go away, and seem to be watching herself and Matt, as two figures in the distance. The Erin figure could not seem to move, to resist as she knew she should, to fight away Matt's exploring hands. From far away she watched as Matt removed first her clothes, then his own, touching, touching all the while. And then the feeling those touches evoked brought her back into herself again and a wave of sensation, of wanting and longing so strong it made her faint, washed over her. She could feel that her breathing had changed; it was coming so fast. A hot ache spread from her core; it was separate from her, yet it took control of her senses, whirling her on wave after wave of desire. Her body began to move with his; he was in her at last. She pulled him closer, her breath panting now as her movements urged him to penetrate her deeper, more deeply still, until she was filled completely with the maleness of him.

Matt felt the change in her; surprised that she did not struggle against him, amazed when she joyfully and willingly gave herself to him, fully matching his passion. His mind registered all this fleetingly, but the idea was quickly lost in the cascade of sensation, in the feeling that they were truly one.

"Oh, God, Erin," he whispered against her throat. "This is so good . . . so good."

Then he withdrew from her slightly, teasing her throbbing hunger, until she began to moan with her craving for release. He plunged inside her again; their whirling sensations reached the dizzying heights of consummation and then exploded into the ethereal beyond.

The moments passed slowly, lazily, as they lay beneath the hot, embracing sun. He propped himself up on an elbow and regarded her. One hand was flung over her eyes to protect them from the bright sunlight, but he could see her wide, full-lipped mouth; amazingly, the corners were turned up in a secret, satisfied smile. A thin film of perspiration covered her face and breasts, and one knee was bent, showing the long, graceful line of her leg.

"Erin?" he said softly.

She removed her hand from her eyes, then raised a finger to his lips to silence him, still smiling that secret smile. Her finger moved to his cheek to trace the bloody line she had left there.

"I'm sorry," she whispered. "But you deserved it, after all. I should have done worse."

"Thank the Lord you didn't." He smiled tenderly at her. "You're something . . ." He bent his head and nuzzled her neck, loving the long line that flowed into her jaw. She slid an arm around his shoulder and played idly with the curling hairs that fringed his neck.

"And just think, I'm leaving tomorrow," he groaned.

"It's just as well, and you know it." Her voice was distant, caressing him lightly. "I'll never *be* this way again, Matt."

"You're crazy, Erin, you know that?" His finger traced her lips and he nibbled at her ear lobe. When he lifted his head again and looked into her eyes, now a deep blue from the sky's reflection, he could see that the smile had left her lips.

"You know, don't you, that sleeping with every woman you meet won't erase what your mother did," she said slowly.

"What the hell has my mother got to do with us?"

"There is no 'us,' Matt. Only you, and your ghosts from the past."

"Well, I'll be damned! A philosopher! Erin, try out your theories on someone else. I don't fit them. And what my mother did is none of your goddamn business!"

"I'm not so sure, Matthew Steele. Now shut up and come here." She pulled his face down to hers, reveling in his lithe, muscular body.

The long shafts of the afternoon sun striped their bodies as they lay together in the warm grass. Far below them, the streets of Aspen churned with life, unknowing, uncaring. Across the valley, on the crest of Red Mountain, a prospector casually noticed the feminine silhouette of Aspen Mountain.

"Now, there's a lady for ya," he muttered, continuing his solitary climb, unaware of the white glint of two naked bodies coming together again.

Chapter 18

Matt stared blankly through the dust-streaked window of the moving train. He was hot and uncomfortable even in his shirt sleeves, and he debated whether it was better to swelter with the window closed or choke in the dust with it open. He pulled Charles Adams' letter from the pocket of his leather jacket, opening its well-creased folds once more. It was addressed to him, in care of the stationmaster, Union Station, Denver City, and had been forwarded to him via Ogden, Utah.

So he was to be sent on another "mission" by the exacting Mr. Adams. He skimmed the contents of the letter again, his eyes coming to rest on the crucial part of the document:

> . . . *proceed directly to the B/W Ranch, Bitter Creek, Wyoming, and report to Mr. Martin Beechwood. He requires your assistance on our behalf to remove a stubborn squatter from the right of way on the railroad spur we anticipate building for Mr. Beechwood. This squatter's land is apparently perched right on the pathway the tracks must follow, and he will not move for love or money.*
>
> *Something must be done, Matthew, and I leave it to your discretion, ingenuity, and good sense to solve the problem so that the contract company can get started before the winter snows; you have shown great aptitude for this sort of thing in the past. Mr. Beechwood will fill*

you in on the details. As always, you have a free hand, and I look forward to hearing of the satisfactory solution to this problem.

The story was familiar, repeated again and again as the railroads spread their steel tentacles ever wider. Matt felt a slight distaste at what he had to do. His job as personal troubleshooter for Charles Francis Adams, the president of the Union Pacific Railroad, had not turned out to be quite the exciting undertaking he had imagined. It consisted mostly of long, tedious train rides and equally long, boring meetings with narrow-minded, selfish men. He had found in himself a surprising facility for going to the heart of the problem, whatever it was, and giving all parties concerned just enough of what they wanted so that a resolution could be accomplished. He had not been above using force, trickery, or, indeed, bribery from time to time, as needed. Anything so the railroad can go through, Matt mused. The stout, cigar-smoking men sitting in their plush board rooms on State Street, Boston, had the long-distance advantage of great money and absolute power.

He put the letter down and stared out the window again as the train, heading west, passed the last of the foothills of the Medicine Bow Mountains. Rawlins was coming up soon; he could get off and stretch his legs for a few minutes at least. The clear, hot blue of the sky reminded him suddenly of that afternoon with Erin at the Silver Lady Mine. The same deep blue of the sky had hung over them then, and Erin's eyes had reflected that color, but darker, stormier, more diverse. He remembered the half smile of satiation on her lips. She was an enigma, fascinating but unreachable. She was the first woman he had ever bedded who had not cried and nagged, begging him to stay with her, offering marriage, love, a home. She was also the only woman who had kept him interested long after she was out of sight. All his other women had merged into one, forming a compound image of smiling mouths, naked limbs, and heaving breasts. But Erin was different. She had sat at the table that night, perfectly calm, quiet, distant, but Matt had had the distinct feeling that she was laughing at him, even though she hadn't even met his eyes. Hell! He'd better forget her. That girl—or any other girl—was not for him. What would he want with a woman, anyway?

As he dozed in the stuffy car, images of Erin floated

through his mind in spite of his efforts to the contrary. He saw her slender back as she bent over the stove, her copper curls sliding over a shoulder, a slim bare leg with tiny blond hairs glistening in the sun . . . Damn! Why couldn't he get her out of his mind? She was just another female, and a young, inexperienced one at that.

The train finally arrived at Bitter Creek, a town not even big enough to have a post office. It consisted of the railroad depot, a water tower, and a combination saloon-hotel, its dusty street typical of every small Western town. But fifty miles to the north lay the B/W Ranch, a vast, sprawling spread that was an empire unto itself, with enough cattle to fill a hundred railroad cars. And Mr. Beechwood wanted a railroad line to his front door so that he could transport his cattle with fewer men and fewer losses, and because the Boston moguls agreed with him, some poor dirt farmer would have to go.

Matt hired a horse at the hotel, having to pay dearly, had a quick lunch of greasy potatoes and beefsteak in the dining room, then loaded his blanket roll and saddlebags onto the big roan. He checked his .45 and slapped it into his worn leather holster. After he had slipped his rifle, a Winchester .76, into its place on the saddle, he swung his leg over the high cantle and departed.

Tim McCarthy proved to be far more intelligent than Matt had expected of a farmer, and much more obdurate. He was a tall, lanky Scotsman, a slight burr still clinging to his words. His spread was well tended and productive; Matt could see that immediately. McCarthy had no reason to budge, and he knew quite well that Beechwood would be tied up in court for years if he tried anything illegal. The fact that McCarthy and his two young sons carried rifles at all times told Matt they were well aware that Beechwood was ready to try sheer force.

As he sat in the clean kitchen and finished his second cup of strong coffee, he tried once again to reason with the farmer.

"Look, Mr. McCarthy—"

"That's Tim."

"Okay, Tim. You know the railroads are big business. They're not going to turn aside for you or anyone else. Eventually, you have to let Beechwood get his right of way."

"The answer-r is nay, Matt. That strip would go through me best pasture land. I'll not be havin' it, and that's final."

"Let me talk to Beechwood again. He's willing to compensate you . . ."

"Matthew." The tall Scotsman leaned over the table and rested on his folded arms. "I dinna want compensation. I want me land, that I worked and slaved to git. If that's all the impor-r-tance the U.S. government puts to my deed, the hell with 'em!" He spit expertly, disparagingly, into the hearth.

Martin Beechwood was also obdurate, but much louder. His seamed red face turned almost purple as he pounded the gleaming dining-room table with a big fist.

"That old fool! He thinks he can stop progress! Listen, Steele, you've got to change his mind. We can't delay any more. I've contracted to supply five thousand head of beef to Chicago by next spring on your damn railroad!"

"Martin, dear, calm down. Mr. Steele is doing the best he can." The quiet voice came from Grace Beechwood, a lovely, gray-haired woman.

Beechwood ignored his wife and continued. "You get him out of the way, Steele. Use your gun! I'll give you as many men as you need. It's your job to get the railroad through—so do it! That damn Scotsman! What the hell does he want with that dry spread he's got?"

"I have the option of using force, Mr. Beechwood, but I also have the responsibility of getting the job done *in the best way for all concerned.*" His crystal-blue eyes bore coldly into the muddy ones of the older man. "I carry guns, and I've used them, but I will not be pushed into violent action on anyone's behalf unless I am convinced it is the only solution. Is that clear?"

Beechwood mumbled his reply. "Yeah, sure, Steele. Do whatever you have to. But, by God, in two weeks the construction crew will be here"—his voice began to rise again—"and they better be able to lay rails!"

Matt's face relaxed into the charming smile he employed to end conversations and disarm belligerent clients. "Don't worry, Beechwood, the Union Pacific will get here. Now, if you'll excuse me, I'll get to work."

Matt made good use of the B/W's string of cow ponies, choosing a new one each day on which to do his exploring. He carried long rolls of survey maps and plat sheets in his saddlebags, and checked them constantly against the terrain, marking the proposed right of way and ranch boundaries with red-flagged stakes. He enjoyed the long, solitary rides; the land stretched away, undulating, to distant foothills, and hefty red cattle grazed freely on the high grass. Antelope bounded out of nowhere, coyotes slunk away, and even a few eagles swooped low to inspect the intruder.

July faded into the burning days of August, and Matt rode back and forth between McCarthy's place and the B/W, neither threatening nor offering anything, merely talking casually, adding to his knowledge of the situation daily. One hot afternoon he crossed from McCarthy's land to Beechwood's and, spying a stand of shade-giving trees in a hollow, turned his horse in that direction. Much to his surprise, he found a cool, clear spring bubbling up in the center of the low area. Gratefully, he knelt down and drank the cold water, so much better than the warm, rusty liquid in his canteen.

At dinner that night, he answered Beechwood's questions patiently but offered little beyond his repeated promise to get the railroad there on time.

"Stop harassing the young man, Martin," Grace Beechwood chided gently. "He's doing the best he can, I'm sure. We've lived without the railroad for all these years, and we can live without it for a few more."

"You won't have to, Mrs. Beechwood," Matt said. "I'm working on an idea."

"An idea! Steele, you better come up with more than an idea," Beechwood insisted.

Matt sipped his after-dinner brandy. "Nice cold spring you've got down on the lower hundred. I had myself a welcome drink there today," he said, adroitly changing the subject.

"Oh, that one. Yeah, Indian Spring. It's nice, but too far from the main grazing land, so we don't use it much."

"Well, folks, I'm off to bed. If you don't mind, I think I'll mosey over to McCarthy's tomorrow and stay the night there. I have a few things I want to clear up." Matt turned to Grace. "Thanks for the delicious dinner, ma'am. Haven't eaten so well since . . . Aspen, I reckon."

McCarthy greeted Matt politely, if not with enthusiasm, and agreed to put him up for the night. His wife, Nancy, was a stern-looking, silent woman, but she prepared a succulent beef stew for supper, as if vying with the Beechwoods' elegant meals.

Between McCarthy, his two sons, and Matt, the big pot of stew disappeared quickly, along with the fragrant baked rolls glistening with fresh churned butter, homemade pickle relish, and raspberry pie.

The men pushed back their chairs as Nancy and her daughter, Rosemary, cleared the table. Tim took out a well-worn pipe and filled it, then commenced to puff steadily.

Matt began nonchalantly enough. "Did you ever think of just pullin' up and leavin', Tim? This must be a hard life."

McCarthy laughed, showing strong, yellowed teeth, then drew on his pipe again. "I canna say I haven't thought on it, many a time, but I'll never-r leave here, and I think ye're beginnin' to realize that, sonny." He looked far away, focusing beyond the cloud of smoke that wreathed his head. "Th' only time I seriously consider-r-ed it was, oh, about five years back. It was a drought year-r—dreadful dry, it was. The milk cows dried up and we barely got through, but we did it." He leveled his eyes under bushy gray brows at Matt and pointed the stem of his pipe at him. "And we'll be doin' it again, if need be."

"I'm sure you will, Tim McCarthy," Matt said quietly. "Do you mind if I take a turn outside? I need to walk off this meal." He patted his flat stomach. "That last piece of pie did me in."

"Oh, Rosemary baked the pie," one of the McCarthy boys chimed in. "We can only get her to put a hand to it when someone special comes to dinner," he added innocently.

"Hush, Donald!" Rosemary cried, flushing prettily. "Mr. Steele will think we live like poor folk here, with you sayin' things like that!"

"Mighty good pie, Rosemary," Matt said politely to the McCarthys' oldest offspring, eliciting another blush from her.

He excused himself, then went out into the hard-packed back yard. He wandered aimlessly to the barn, a weathered log structure half buried in the ground, in which the milk cows and a large draft horse stood placidly in their stalls. The barn smelled of horse sweat, manure, and oiled leather, a familiar smell from Matt's Pennsylvania childhood. It was reminiscent of summer visits to his uncle's farm on the Susquehanna, before his mother had left them. A bitter smile pulled at his mouth, then he heard a rustle of straw behind him and turned quickly.

"Rosemary! I didn't see you."

"Oh, Mr. Steele, I'm sorry. I have to milk Brandy, here. Didn't have time before dinner." She spoke softly and hesitatingly, as if she were afraid of him.

"Mind if I watch? I haven't seen anyone milk a cow in nigh on to twenty years."

"No, I don't mind." She sat on the three-legged stool and leaned her forehead into the cow's flank, her strong hands rhythmically drawing long spurts of milk from the udders.

"Mr. Steele . . . is it true there's a hotel in Denver City where they have a real orchestra you can dance to? I heard of it once." She looked up at him shyly.

"Yes, and there are several in Leadville, too. One has a real fountain of water in the lobby."

"God, I'd love to see that!"

He was surprised at the intensity in her voice. Poor kid, he thought, stuck out here and longing for the bright lights of the city.

"Rosemary," he said gently, "you aren't missing a thing. Those dressed-up ladies dancing to the music are not any happier than anyone else."

"Still, I sure would like to see it, just once."

He looked at her closely for the first time. She was a pretty girl, he supposed, small-boned, with big brown eyes and a band of freckles across her nose. But she had none of the strong dignity of her mother or the enduring stubbornness of her father.

Rosemary finished milking the cow and started carrying the heavy bucket back to the root cellar, but Matt took it from her hand and followed her. He could see she had a trim figure and a small waist, but she didn't measure up to Erin's more brilliant beauty. Erin! Why did her image superimpose itself upon every woman he encountered?

He put the bucket down, and as he straightened, he felt a soft hand on his arm.

"Take me with you . . . please." Rosemary's voice was filled with desperation; her eyes brimmed with tears.

"What do you mean? I can't do that . . ."

"I knew it!" she cried fiercely. "Look, you don't have to marry me—just please take me away from here!"

"Rosemary, you're much too nice a girl to think of things like that."

"I'm sick and tired of being a *nice* girl. I want to have some fun, see something besides this damn farm!"

"You will, someday."

"I want it *now*, Matthew Steele." She looked him straight in the eye. Her surface gentility fell away, making her oddly exciting to him.

"Rosemary . . ."

"No, don't talk, just kiss me." She sagged against him, offering him more than he could refuse. They sank down together onto the straw, and the silence around them was broken only by a few passionate, whispered words.

"Those work crews'll be here tomorrow," Beechwood growled, "and McCarthy's still sittin' on his butt down there."

Matt halted his pacing of the rancher's study. "I know, I know. But I think I have the answer. Here's a document giving McCarthy the water rights to your Indian Spring—"

"Hey, wait a minute, Steele. You crazy?"

"—in return for a railroad right of way through his property. Sign this, and I'll ride down to McCarthy's and get his signature."

"What in hell makes you think he'll sign this—this paper?" Beechwood flicked it with a thick nail. "Or that *I* will, for that matter?"

"I think you will, Beechwood," Matt replied quietly, a steely undercurrent in his voice. "And I'm quite sure McCarthy will, too."

"Why should he?"

"He needs water. It's simple. Find a man's weakness. Yours is the railroad spur, McCarthy's is water."

"It just might work." Beechwood looked at Matt with sudden, new respect. "It just might—I'll be damned!" He took the paper and signed it with a flourish, then turned to Matt again. "And if that damn sodbuster won't sign, I'll go down there and blast him off the face of the earth! You can tell him that!"

"I'll tell him, Beechwood, but it won't make a bit of difference. McCarthy's immune to your threats." Matt took the document, folded it carefully, and put it in his pocket.

"I'll be off, then, and you should see me sometime this evening with your right of way. Tomorrow I'll ride back to Bitter Creek and be out of your hair for good. Just make sure you register the deed with the county, Beechwood, so there won't be any trouble." He tipped his Stetson and left the room, his boot heels sounding loudly on the polished wood floor.

"I'll be damned," Beechwood muttered to himself. "Now, I wonder what in hell *his* weakness is."

Chapter 19

When all was told, Erin could not believe how much her happiness depended on Lew Steele. True, now she had all the money she could ever need, she had her house on elegant Bullion Row and had furnished it with pieces from as far away as Paris, but what she did not have was the doctor's guarantee that Lew Steele would live.

Just yesterday morning Dr. Barnes had said, "If it were up to me, Miss Conner, I'd let Lew Steele live forever, just to pacify you. But as I've told you a dozen times before, his lungs are full of coal dust." He had placed his hat on his head. "I'm afraid it's in God's hands now. I am truly sorry for you."

"Sorry for me!" Erin had shrieked. "Be sorry for yourself, Doctor. All your fine Boston training, and you can't even cure a cough!"

"Now, Miss Conner . . . Erin, we've been through all this. Thirty years in a Pennsylvania coal mine is responsible here, but certainly not my profession."

"Well, I'll take him to New York—Boston—London! With my money, I'll buy him a cure!"

"Erin," he had said sternly, "you can take Lew to China, and he'll still die there. Why not let him remain in Aspen, where he's loved, and quit all this foolishness? You're only hurting him."

"Does . . . does he know?"

"I think so. He's too proud to say, though."

Erin had seen Dr. Barnes to the door. Somehow everything in the vestibule had seemed soiled, the gleaming floor tiles and mahogany drop-leaf table pitifully unimportant compared with Lew, lying above in his room.

The doctor had called back from the gate. "The most humane thing you can do now, Erin, is to put a smile on your face and keep it there."

But Erin had not smiled as she quietly closed the door. She had gone into the drawing room and sat for a long time, staring blankly around with a heart that was wrenched in sadness. The rest of the day had crept slowly by, with Erin torn between sobs and silent but abject misery. She had even allowed the servants to watch over Lew, for the good doctor was correct, she would only upset him.

After a sleepless night, having lain awake with her torturous thoughts, she had vowed to sweep away the pain and try her best to cheer him. She owed him that, and a lot more besides.

Today saw a marked change in her. She placed a smile on her lips and decided to make the most of what time was left to Lew. After all, she was the strong one, the so-called Silver Lady of Aspen. Had it really been only a year since she had flipped that coin? Why did it seem like a lifetime ago?

Erin looked at her reflection in the vestibule mirror. In her chic cream silk blouse and blue taffeta skirt, with her hair fashionably styled, she was still youthful at twenty-one, yet somehow more mature. And in spite of her efforts to the contrary, she was repeatedly sought after. Perhaps this was a result of the new dresses, for men certainly did not seek her out for her sweet personality. Hardly that! She had a reputation for having an acutely honest tongue and was well known for her stubborn attitudes.

Picking up the silver tea service, Erin climbed the polished hardwood steps up one flight to Lew's room, with the large bay window overlooking Bullion Row.

"Good afternoon, Lew." She smiled gaily.

"Hello, Erin. What have you got there now? I swear, girl, you'll have me fat as that Abraham by the time I'm up and about!"

"Good! I'm planning exactly that." She poured Lew a steaming cup of tea and served him a huge helping of his favorite, her rum cake. Then she pulled a chair to the bedside. "I've been to check on the emporium—the account books are downstairs, and everything looks in fine order. John's a good manager. I think you should give him a raise."

"I'll think on it, Erin. And how goes the mine today?" He laughed lightly, but then had another coughing attack. She sat there helplessly, trying to appear calm, but her soul was being torn apart by despair.

When he had quieted, she continued the conversation as if nothing had happened to interrupt it. "No complaints. The strike seems bottomless. I'm thinking of starting a new tunnel. I have a feeling . . ."

"Then, by God, girl, if you have a feeling—dig the tunnel!"

Erin giggled. "Oh, Lew, it's all happened so fast—overnight. You know they call me the 'Silver Lady' around town, and one old geezer said I'm known in Leadville and Denver City, too!"

"Well," Lew said pensively, "there's times I think you ought to save a little instead of spending everything you get your hands on."

"I know . . . and I will, as soon as the house is finished. I have my carriage . . . I guess I have everything." She almost wanted to add, "Everything but time with the one person I cherish—you." She bit her lip and poured another cup of tea, fighting back tears.

"Any letter from Matt today?"

"No, I haven't been to the post office yet, and you know very well I'd rush straight up if there were, Lew Steele." She laughed and went about tidying up the bedcovers. "I've got to do some shopping and stop back at the emporium. Now, you nap, and I'll check in as soon as I get back." She rose and shooed the cat from his resting spot next to Lew.

"Nap! I'm sick of napping!" But Lew looked wan, gray-faced, and she knew he'd nod off as soon as she left.

It was July second, and already Erin could feel the afternoon heat as she closed the white picket-fence gate behind her. The first half of 1886 had seen a great influx of people to Aspen, and every day she noticed another house or store. Sometimes it even seemed as if entire streets had been cleared and staked in a matter of a few short days. But the worst eyesores were the huge, sprawling mines that sat almost in town. Still, there was a serene, lovely quality to some parts of Aspen that soothed her. And, of course, there was the Silver Lady, which made her life complete.

It didn't matter that some of the local folk considered her cold and remote. She was too busy to care about that, what with trips to the mine, watching over the store, and fussing over her new, elegant home.

Erin walked down Third Street to Main, turned into Mill, and headed toward the emporium. She returned the account books to John and briefly discussed a possible raise in his salary. Then she walked up Mill Street to the new lady's shop, called Lottie's Dresses and Things, to pick up her custom-made silk chemises. When she entered the shop, she cringed on seeing two ladies of the evening who were haggling prices with Lottie.

Erin picked up her neatly tied box and left quickly; although there were many *nymphes du pavé* in Aspen, and they seemed harmless enough, she could never bear to be around them. They reminded her of Madame Lucille's in Denver City.

A short stop at the bank, and she was on her way to the post office. The postmaster, Mr. Sweeny, greeted her. "Got a letter here for Lew—looks like it's from Matt—all the way from Wyoming."

She looked at him askance. "Thank you, Mr. Sweeny, I'll take it to Lew."

Somehow, no matter how long it had been, no matter how little she told herself she cared, Matt's letters to Lew always seemed to burn her fingers. His letters these days were precious few—one perhaps every four or five months. As Erin neared her home, she knew that soon she would have to write Matt and tell him about Lew. The idea of writing him didn't bother her. She had finally purged him from her mind, and that hadn't been easy. The hard part would be telling him about his father.

Besides, she thought tiredly, he's probably married by now. Matt was twenty-seven—or was it twenty-eight? She couldn't remember.

Erin unlocked the front door and tossed her hat carelessly onto the vestibule table. It was then, as she was about to put down the box and the letter, that she had a quick whisper of intuition.

Her mouth opened and she called lightly, "Perry?" Then,

more loudly, as she rushed toward the drawing room, "Perry—oh, God! You're here!"

And as she rounded the corner into the room, she could hear him say, "Haven't changed, have ya, Sis?" So he remembered her "gift!"

Erin's first glimpse of her brother, after nearly six years, was one of shock and disbelief. Perry was still tall, still fair-haired, but now he was also immensely overweight. His eyes protruded redly from his puffy face, clearly revealing the years of dissipation, whiskey, and rough living. Patched and faded, his clothes were nearly rags, and were dirty enough to surround him with a faint odor of staleness.

"God, Erin!" He took a step closer. "You're absolutely beautiful! You look like Ma!"

"Why, thank you, Perry." Erin turned away from him in confusion. "Would you . . . would you like a brandy?" She gave a short laugh. "I think I could use one."

She poured the amber liquid from the cut-glass decanter into two crystal glasses and seated herself across from him. She still could not believe that her brother had returned after so long an absence. Suddenly all the fear, loneliness, and bitterness she had felt when he had left her in Denver City washed back over her and filled her with remembered pain.

She managed to speak at last. "For a time, Perry, I thought you were dead. I really don't know what to say."

"I ain't dead, that's for certain!"

"Where did you learn to talk that way, Perry? Mother and Father would be furious if they could hear you."

"Yeah? Well, that's too bad, Sis. I've been here and there—been busy."

"Oh, I see." She narrowed her eyes. "Drinking, too, I'd say by the looks of you, Perry."

"Pretty smart, ain't ya, Sis? And damn rich, too."

Lord, but he sounded odd, she thought—jealous, she realized. "How did you find me? It's been a long time."

"That was easy. Ran into this here miner from Aspen . . . Fred something . . ."

"Zimmerman."

"Yeah. That was him. Kept tellin' everyone 'bout this pretty Irish girl, Erin."

"I know the rest, Perry."

They were silent for a time, each observing the other. Finally, Erin could no longer contain her resentment toward

168

him. "Perry," she began, "you abandoned me in Denver City, do you realize that?"

"Come on, now, Sis." He seemed truly taken aback. "I couldn't take ya with me, ya knew that."

"No, I never did think that. What you left me to was so horrible . . ."

"Yeah, I heard tell. And it ain't all true. I did go back to that place, maybe a year later." He thought a moment, then added, "And boy, they sure remembered you!"

"That'll do, Perry. I don't want to relive any of it." Erin felt near to tears, a sickness rising in her throat, but she fought for control. "If you'd come back sooner for me, maybe I wouldn't have had to kill! Can you understand how I feel now? Why seeing you here now is so . . . difficult for me? I've made a whole new life for myself, tried to forget . . ."

"You had to . . . *kill?"* he said slowly.

"You said they told you."

"Oh, yeah, guess I forgot about that. It's been a while," he lied easily. "And I suppose it wasn't your fault."

"Of course it wasn't! And all these years I've been afraid someone would come for me—find me and arrest me!" She could feel her heart beating heavily at the utterance of these words, which had not been said aloud for years.

"Calm down, Sis . . . Ahh, got another brandy for your long-lost kin?"

She took his glass and was thankful she could turn her back so that he couldn't see the expression of honest loathing on her face.

While she took her time pouring his brandy, Perry was thinking furiously. Erin had knocked out that man back in Denver, the girls all remembered that, but no one had mentioned his *dying.* And for certain they would have told *him,* Erin's brother. Yet she really believed she had killed the lout. For an instant Perry felt a twinge of hatred for the man who had raped his sister, but then it was gone. He couldn't afford to feel sorry for her, not now, with the law hot on his heels and him needing money. He steeled himself against any uncalled-for sympathy. After all, she had everything, and he had absolutely nothing.

"Thanks." He took the glass she handed him. "Look, Sis, I'm kinda hard up right now."

"I can see that, Perry." She looked at him stiffly, again feeling her nausea rise.

"What I mean is, I could use a few bucks . . . heard ya had more than ya could use." He emitted a forced chuckle.

Erin went to the front window. "Perry, you still owe me five dollars."

"Five dollars?"

"Yes, Perry." She whirled on him, her taffeta skirt rustling opulently. "The only money I had was sewn in my hem. You took it from me back on that horrible prairie . . . the day you said you were leaving me."

"Oh . . . that. Well, guess I ain't got it. And I'm not kiddin'—I need some money, bad."

"Then I suggest"—was that really her voice?—"that you get a job and earn it."

"On, no, Sis, I ain't got the time. 'Sides, it won't hurt ya to fork over a little."

"You're wrong, Brother. It would hurt. I think you should leave now."

"Just like that? Kinda stuck-up, ain't ya?" He was growing angrier by the minute. Well, she had what was coming, trying to turn her own brother out. "How would you like it, Sis, if I was to tell the Denver City police where they could find ya?" There, it was done.

Erin's eyes flashed an icy blue-green as tingles of fear prickled her spine, fighting for ascendancy over the white-hot rage she felt. "You . . . you wouldn't!"

"I ain't saying they'd hang ya—the guy probably had it comin'—but no doubt they'd throw ya in jail for a spell."

With her fists clenched tightly at her sides, she stood speechless before him. He was bluffing—he wouldn't turn his own sister in to the law! The authorities probably knew where she was, anyway, and had for years. Hadn't she thought that for a long time? Still, terror threatened to engulf her.

"Well? What's it gonna be?"

God! She needed more time to think! Her mind spun as she came to the realization that her own brother was blackmailing her. "I . . . I need a few days, Perry."

"Two. That's all I got. Two days, Erin. And," he added hastily, "I want ten thousand."

"Ten thousand dollars?"

"Yeah. Two days. See ya." Perry eased his huge frame out of her gold brocade chair and left without another word.

Two days! She had two days to decide what to do! Erin

paced the pale gold and green Oriental carpet in agony. Once again, for the thousandth time in her life, she wished she were a man. She would call Perry out and shoot him! It didn't matter that he was of the same blood—no, that's not true any more, she thought with sudden insight; he was no longer her brother.

Involuntarily, the tears she had suppressed came streaming down her cheeks and onto her cream-colored blouse. She didn't care if the two servants saw her; she knew only that she felt alone, lost in a dark world of despair.

"Erin?" Lew's voice floated weakly from the stairs. "Erin, is something wrong? Thought I heard voices . . ."

She quickly wiped her cheeks with her lace handkerchief. "Wait there, Lew . . . don't come down. I'll be right up."

Once she had him tucked back in his bed, she attempted to leave. There was no reason why Lew should know about her dire predicament.

"Erin, don't go. Not until you tell me what's going on. I've never seen you so upset."

She hesitated in the portal for an instant. But the tears began to flow uncontrollably again, and she flew to the only person she could trust.

Chapter 20

Of course, Erin came to realize, Lew was perfectly correct in his assumption that the police no longer cared about her whereabouts. Not only that, he had assured her, but they would probably have questioned her briefly at the time of the incident and then let her go. Erin and Lew had come to the joint conclusion that she should simply refuse to see Perry again, and if he persisted, she should call in the local sheriff and press charges.

The dawn of July fourth, Independence Day, broke bright and cloudless. It would be a magnificent day for a summer celebration. One hundred and ten years had passed since the signing of the Declaration of Independence, and only ten years since Colorado had proudly become a state, the Centennial State. Aspen itself celebrated its sixth year of existence this summer of 1886. Nonetheless, Erin did not feel up to joining the long-planned local festivities; she was concerned about Lew's health and praying, too, that Perry would again disappear from her life.

Around midday, when she could already hear the boisterous cheers from the town's core and the occasional echoes of harmless gunshots, she decided to trek up Aspen Mountain and check on the mine while the crew was on holiday. In the past, she and Lew had always taken part in the activity around Aspen on the Fourth, but Lew lay upstairs napping, coughing sporadically in his sleep, so there was little room in her heart for joy this day.

Erin changed into a tan, fitted riding skirt, a red plaid blouse, and high-buttoned boots. She twisted her curls carelessly into a knot at the nape of her neck, pulled on her pigskin gloves, then left the house in a rush, hoping to avoid seeing Perry. When he came and found her gone, perhaps he would just leave town.

Deciding to go on foot to pass the time, she was rounding the corner of Durant Street when she heard her name called from a distance. Erin's heart lurched and she quickened her pace. It must be Perry! If she didn't stop, perhaps he'd think she was someone else.

"Erin? Erin, hold up!" came the insistent masculine voice.

She was spun around by a pair of strong hands, and her mind whirled in renewed fear.

"Erin, are you running from me?"

Her eyes widened in shocked disbelief. The man wasn't Perry—he was Matt!

"Dear God! Matt? Is it really you?" In spite of her quick effort to show no emotion, she could not help but feel relief, and a timid smile played on her lips.

"Lord, woman, you acted as if the very devil pursued you!"

For a moment Erin could only stare into his face. He looked different—older. Around his deep blue eyes there were tiny sun lines crinkling the corners, and yet, amazingly, they served to heighten his complete masculinity, to give him a tantalizing air of virility. His clothes were expensive, although dusty from the ride, and he still wore the same Stetson, tilted in his devil-may-care fashion.

"I'm sorry, Matt . . . guess I was staring. But I certainly didn't expect to see you."

"Didn't you get my letter?"

"Letter? Oh, Lord! Yes, we did . . . I'm afraid I forgot to give it to Lew . . ."

Matt's smile faded for an instant, then returned with full force. "Well, never mind. Can I walk you home?" He started to take her arm, but she held back. "What's wrong? Don't want me to see that new house Dad's been bragging about in his letters? You know, you're all he writes about, Erin."

She could not help but smile genuinely now. "Of course I want you to see the house!"

"And, Erin"—his finger barely brushed her chin—"I like your outfit. No more pants?"

"Nope! And I'm probably the best-dressed woman in Aspen," she boasted, against her better judgment.

"I like it . . . the glamour becomes you."

Flattery! He was always so good at that when he wanted to be. Erin's eyes twinkled. Well, why not enjoy it? She was over succumbing to Matt Steele's charm.

"Come on, let's go to the famous house of our little Silver Lady."

Abruptly, Erin lost her beguiling smile. She had completely forgotten to tell Matt about his father's condition! Why had she delayed writing to him? But deep down she knew why; it was because she had refused to believe the truth about Lew for so long.

Matt saw the quick change in her. "What's wrong, Erin? Has it something to do with why you were running just now?"

"No, Matt." Why couldn't she just bury herself in his arms and cry out her constant worry about his father?

"Then what is it?"

"It's Lew." She took a deep breath, feeling an empty desolation sweep her. "He's very sick, Matt."

His eyes narrowed perceptively. "How sick?"

Silence hung in the air for a terrible moment.

"He's dying."

Erin saw so many emotions at play in Matt's face that she

173

could only stand there silently, her heart thudding. One moment he looked surprised, the next angry and frustrated, and finally his eyes took on a glassy, distant stare.

"How . . . how long does he have?" His tone was so low that she had to strain to hear him.

"Dr. Barnes said it could be a week or a month. He just doesn't know."

Suddenly Matt grabbed her arms with a violence he could not restrain. "Why in hell didn't you write?" he demanded.

"You're—you're hurting me!" she cried.

"I should break your damn arms, Erin!"

For the second time in her life, she was afraid of him. "I . . . I didn't know for sure until a few days ago . . . and, Matt, I didn't know how to tell you!" she concluded in a rush.

As quickly as he had grabbed her, he released his bruising hold. "God, Erin, I'm sorry . . . I was just so . . ."

"I know. I felt that way, too. Go to him, Matt." Tears sprang to her eyes.

"Are you coming?"

"No, not right now. I'll be along later." Erin gave him directions to her Bullion Row house and watched sadly as he strode down the street and disappeared around the corner.

She climbed the steep approach to the Silver Lady and went about checking the work on the new shaft, but her mind was not on her business; nor was she thinking about Lew or even her brother. She was fixed on Matt's surprise return and felt a need to gather her wits together.

As the afternoon shadows lengthened across the valley floor and she began the long hike back to town, Erin recalled how casually Matt had addressed her, like old friends. But certainly that was all they were now. She had no regrets about their shared passion—and that was all it had been, a physical joining, nothing more. She was lucky he hadn't left her with a child! Well, she wouldn't risk *that* again!

She dusted her boots and skirt with her hands and walked back across town. The usual frivolity was in high gear this Fourth—the volunteer firemen's tug-of-war, the wagons and carriages cleverly decorated for the parade, the loud boom of gunfire from the wild street drinkers. Perhaps she would persuade Matt to walk downtown later and try to cheer him up. In time, he, too, must come to accept Lew's illness.

Rounding the corner of Third Street, Erin was surprised to see Matt sitting on the steps of her house as if he awaited her, a grim look on his face. Yet just seeing him there caused her heart to leap unexpectedly in her chest. Again she told herself she had reacted only to his extraordinary good looks, and for no other reason.

"Hello, Matt. Is everything all right?"

"No, Erin, it's not." He rose and stood with his hands on his hips, towering above her from his position on the first step.

"Lew—it's Lew!" she cried in sudden dismay, her fear surfacing again.

"No, he's fine for now."

"Then what?"

"Your brother. That's what. Why didn't you tell me right away?"

She could not believe her ears—but of course, Lew had told him. Yet why was Matt so furious? What possible business was it of his? "Perry? I don't understand . . . This is absurd, Matt!"

"Absurd? That your own brother turns up after six years and tries to blackmail you?"

"Matt! Calm down . . . *please.*"

"I *won't* calm down, dammit!" His eyes turned a darker shade of blue. "He's the very reason you were raped, and forced to attack that bastard in the first place!"

"Matt, I know all that, and I detest Perry for it. But this is my business and," she added, "I'll handle it!"

"Like hell you will!"

"Stop swearing, Matt. You . . . you frighten me. What's come over you?"

He adjusted his belt, checking his gun unconsciously, and swept down past her toward the gate.

"Where are you going, Matt?"

"Let's just say I'm going to do something that should have been done years ago!" And in spite of her pleas to him, he quickly vanished from sight.

Erin's mind raced. The image of his familiar motion with the gun flew into her head, and she knew she had to find him immediately. Perry was half crazy, true, but Matt was behaving insanely.

As Erin reached for the gate latch, she began to sway slightly and groped blindly for support. The gate, the dusty street before her eyes, were quickly replaced in her diffused vision by a man's broad, lightly furred chest, the outline of his buckskin shirt, and the silver nugget—*her silver nugget*—suspended in front of him.

When her normal vision returned, she was damp and perspiring from the intensity of her sight. Each time the same vision recurred, she felt it drawing nearer; most importantly, the faceless man was growing more special to her. She did not know why, but she felt that *he* was the one—the man whom she knew so well, and yet not at all.

The sounds of celebration reached her ears again. She took a deep breath, then threw open the gate and raced down the street. She had to find Matt!

Erin searched the crowds frantically, asking anyone who might know Matt if he had seen him. Dear God, where on earth was he? In his wildly furious state he would do anything. At last she found herself standing before the swinging doors of the Red Dog Saloon. As soon as she had pushed her way inside, she was certain she could see Matt. At least that looked like his hat, she thought. But the man's back was turned.

Before she could make her way through the throng, everyone began to crowd out the doors in a frantic race to leave the saloon. Erin tried desperately to shove her way further inside, but the tide of bodies was far too strong, and soon she was out on the street again, futilely crying, "Let me through!"

And then it happened: first one, then another sharp, crashing report of gunfire. Erin grew dizzy and faint with horror, almost collapsing in the dusty road.

"Oh, God! Matt!" she shrieked. "Please, God . . . don't let it be him!"

She sank down onto the road, helpless and shocked, unable to enter the saloon in her agony of trepidation, unable to face the fact that it was Matt she feared for, his name that she had cried aloud.

A short moment later, voices flowed in and out of her consciousness.

"That big guy sure had it coming!"

"Did ya see that lightning draw of Steele's?"

"Guy never had a chance—but he damn well asked for it!"

Finally, as terror coursed through her veins, Erin became aware of a hand on her shoulder and the faint but distinct odor of gunpowder. She looked up through wet eyes to see the blurred image of a face, a familiar Stetson . . . She jumped to her feet and clung to Matt's tall form while her pulse raced. She could feel his gentle urging as he began to lead her away from the onlookers. The cheers of the crowd echoed nightmarishly in her brain, cheers for what he had done.

She stopped quickly. "Matt . . . is he . . . is he dead?" The words were wrenched from her lips. She felt as if this couldn't be happening to her. Any moment now, she'd wake up from this ordeal and everything would be fine . . .

"I tried to reason with him, get him to leave Aspen . . . but he drew on me, Erin." Matt paused briefly. "He's dead."

She drew back weakly, in horror. "You went there! With a gun on! To—kill him! You're—you're a murderer!"

"It wasn't like that, dammit." He took her hands. "I know my business, Erin."

She fought to snatch her hands away. "Your business? And *what*, really, is *your business?*"

"Never mind."

"I think you finally betrayed yourself, Matt Steele. I'm beginning to see much more now—it clears up a lot of questions! A surveyor? You were never a—"

"Dammit! Calm down!"

"No, I won't," she shrieked. "You're a hired killer! I always knew by the way you wore that gun!"

Matt twisted her hands behind her back, crushing her against his hard chest. "I am *not* a hired killer, Erin. But my work is *my* business, and I'll thank you—"

Her foot came up and caught her sharply on the shin. Instantly, Erin was racing down the street, disappearing into the masses of people who were drinking, dancing, or watching the fireworks bursting over Aspen Mountain.

She had almost reached her home when she felt a strong arm tackle her so forcefully that she fell to the ground, Matt on top of her.

"No!" she cried breathlessly, her brain spinning confusedly.

"Hold still—we've gotta talk." He clamped his hand over her mouth and pinned her securely under his unyielding weight. "Now, lie still and listen . . . I don't want to hurt you. Erin, I know what you're thinking—that you asked me to stay out of your business and I didn't." He could see sparks of fury in her eyes. "But don't you see? When my father told me about Perry, I was so damn mad and worried about you, I just couldn't let you handle it alone. At least give me credit for that." Slowly he took the pressure away from her mouth. "You can cry or tell me you'll never speak to me again, it won't matter. I'd do the same to any man who threatened you."

Her heart bounded involuntarily. In spite of her horror over Perry, even her wild notions that Matt was a hired gun, she could not prevent her response to his admission that he would always protect her. Surely, in all his experience, he had never told another woman that!

He removed his hand completely from her mouth.

"I . . . Matt, I don't quite know what to say . . . or think . . ."

"Then do neither!" His lips came down over hers in a fierce, longing kiss, and the fact that he had just killed her brother made absolutely no difference to Erin. This was Matt, his mouth searching hers with a kind of desperation, the same urgent need as her own; his hands freeing her hair and crushing it with his fingers; his lean, muscular body pressing her into the cool earth. Blessed forgetfulness . . . God! how she yearned for it!

The former nightmare turned into a dream, and he was leading her inside the house and up the stairs. She could hear Lew's low snore as they passed his room, then Matt threw open her own door, paying no attention to the racket he was making.

Erin came to, shaking off the trance. "No, Matt, we can't do this. It's wrong!" And at his quick, disparaging laugh, she grasped at straws. "I'll not risk having a child!"

He pushed her roughly down onto her blue satin spread. "That's your problem, Erin. I like children." His features remained impassive.

Her mouth flew open to protest his crudeness, his blatant assumption that she would allow him to bed her in her own house. He cared neither if she got pregnant nor that her brother's blood was still on his hands.

Before she could utter a scathing remark, he said, "Take your clothes off," and began to undress himself.

"Get out, Matt! I'll scream!" She breathed heavily, trying to dispel the oppression she felt.

Immediately Matt was on top of her, his hand moving urgently over the thin fabric of her shirt. "Scream if you want, Erin." His mouth pressed against her bosom. "My dad's known about us for a long time."

Her eyes widened in disbelief. "What!"

"He guessed." Matt raised his head to catch Erin's look of surprise and shock. "So, you see you've no way out . . ."

No, Erin had no choice at all. Nor did she care when he took her fully and with demanding passion; nor later, when he took his time, teasing her flesh until she cried out for release.

And afterward, when he flung an arm possessively over her naked hip, it didn't matter either. In the morning she would once more rid herself of his spell. She had done it before and she would do it again. It would be easy this time . . . and now, more than ever, she had good reason to despise him. He was nothing more than a murderer, therefore a man for whom she could feel nothing.

Chapter 21

Erin stood outside the door of Lew's room, unconsciously wringing her hands. She could hear the doctor's voice speaking quietly inside but could not make out the words; Lew's tortured breathing and weak fits of coughing reached her ears, causing her to cover her face with her shaking hands. There was nothing she could do but wait—and Lew was dying! All her money could not save him, the mainstay and focus of her life. Her mother's and father's images had dimmed to faint, beloved memories, but Lew had sheltered and fed her, had raised her through the difficult years of her youth, and for no other reason than because he was kind and generous and loving. What would she do without him? She would be alone again, totally alone. A familiar ache settled over her, even though it had been six years since she had felt that kind of emptiness.

Dr. Barnes emerged from the room, quietly closing the door behind him. "He wants to see his son," he said.

"Of course." Erin nodded, trying to control the trembling of her lips. "I'll fetch him . . . Doctor, how is he?"

The physician looked at Erin, seeing beyond the beautiful young woman who stood before him, for her expression was like that of anyone who faces the loss of a loved one. Rich, poor, they all had the same look of misery and supplication in their eyes. He had seen it so many times before. He shook his head gently and said nothing.

Erin, near tears, descended the stairs to where Matt was waiting in the drawing room. For once, he was not wearing his mocking smile. The other night—but she would not think of that now.

"Matt." She saw his face turn white, harden; he expected the worst. "He wants to talk to you. I'll wait here. Please tell me if there's any . . . change."

He nodded and began to climb the stairs, passing the doctor on his way down. They greeted each other, then Matt started forward again, but the older man detained him.

"Don't stay too long. He's exhausted. But his mind is clear, so there's no use trying to deceive him . . . Your father is a fine man."

Matt looked into the physician's eyes. He saw the truth there; he had no need to ask how his father was. He nodded brusquely and continued.

It was close and dim in Lew's room; the heavy velvet draperies were partly drawn, but a breeze pushed at them through the half-open window.

Lew was propped up on several pillows to facilitate his breathing. He looked pale and shrunken, but his face lit up in a smile when he saw Matt.

"Come here, Son. We have to talk."

Matt sank into the chair by Lew's bed. "Dad, how do you feel? If you're in pain, I'll come back another time . . . tomorrow."

Lew smiled sadly. "There may be no tomorrow for me, Son. No, don't say anything. I know what I've got—saw enough old codgers die of it back in Pennsylvania. To tell the truth, I feel surprisingly well, peaceful . . ."

"Dad . . ."

"I know. It's hard for you, and worse for Erin. That's what I wanted to talk to you about . . . Erin." He stopped to cough, then caught his breath again. "She thinks she's tough, that kid, and now she's rich—well, she thinks nothing can hurt her. But there'll always be someone like that damn brother of hers . . . or worse, much worse."

"What can I do, Dad? She won't listen to me."

"Yes, so I've noticed . . . and I think I know why, too. You used to be her idol." He leveled his gaze on Matt and had the obverse satisfaction of seeing his son's eyes shift away. "I won't ask . . . I may be sick, but I'm not deaf to what has gone on again since you got back. Matt, she's young and helpless, so vulnerable . . . I'm terribly worried about her . . . she's been my responsibility. And now . . . there's no one else." He coughed again, and when he had finished, Matt held a tumbler of water to his lips.

"Thanks, boy." He fixed his eyes on Matt and spoke very clearly and slowly, as if to give his son no opportunity to mistake his words. "And that's why I want you to marry her."

"What?" The word burst from Matt's lips.

"You must promise me that you will marry her and care for her, always. Then I can go to my grave peacefully."

Matt was silent for a time, his face drained of all color, his eyes glittering like blue ice in the dim room. "Dad, you know I'd do it, if only for you, but she won't have me. Have you approached her?"

"No, and I don't intend to. That's *your* job, Son. She'll have you, all right."

"What on God's earth makes you think so?"

"Son, I just know it. Call it a 'vision,' you know, like those she has."

"You crazy old goat!" Matt grinned affectionately at his father.

Lew's face became more gray and drawn. "Matthew, you *will* promise me, swear to me, that you will marry Erin Conner. You owe her that much." He coughed again, racking his frame and gasping for breath. "Swear it!"

"Dad, I promise. I'll do everything in my power . . ." He took his father's hand and was shocked at its cold frailty; Lew Steele had been such a robust man.

"Good . . . good." Lew's eyes closed and the animation drained from his face. Then his eyes flew open again. "Matt?"

"Yes, Dad, I'm here."

"Matthew, see if you can find it in your heart to forgive your mother. I have come to forgive her . . . perhaps it was better . . ." His voice faded and his hand felt limp in Matt's strong grasp.

"I'll . . . I'll try, Dad."

". . . need a rest now, Son."

"Okay, Dad. Sleep well." Matt released his hand and left the room quietly, surprised to find tears prickling his eyes. "Damn!" he muttered, roughly wiping his shirt sleeve across his eyes. "Damn!"

He was met at the bottom of the stairs by Erin, white-faced and obviously holding herself tightly in control.

"How is he?"

"Not good, kid. He's so weak."

Her eyes filled with tears and she dabbed at them ineffectually with a lace-edged handkerchief. "What will I do? What will I do? He's all I have!"

It was on the tip of his tongue to tell her what Lew thought she should do, but now was not the time.

"Take it easy, Erin. Get some rest." He steered her toward the stairs, wanting to be alone, away from her eyes that reminded him of his promise to Lew.

He went to the sideboard and poured a glass of brandy from the stoppered decanter, then changed his mind and took the decanter with him, setting it down on the embossed leather table to one side of the sofa. He sat there sipping the liquid, then tipped the thin-stemmed glass up, emptied it, and poured himself another.

"Here's to a miracle, Dad," he said bitterly to the empty air. He raised the glass, then drank the burning brandy in one gulp.

Hours later, he was jolted awake, confused. Something had awakened him, but the darkness was silent now. He rubbed the back of his neck, stiff from his uncomfortable position on the sofa, then lit the lamp next to him and rubbed his eyes; they felt dry and scratchy. The cut-glass decanter was three-quarters empty.

Then he heard a noise, a strangled coughing. He saw a light go on in the upstairs hall and heard footsteps. Matt's heart contracted with dread and he rushed up the stairs, taking them two at a time. He strode quickly down the hall, passing Erin's door; it was open. Lew's door was open, too, and the dreadful sounds of a person choking came from within, freezing his blood. He went into the room and saw Erin, her red-gold curls in disarray, her scanty nightgown barely concealed by a hastily donned dressing gown, bending over Lew, trying to raise him up against the pillows.

"Here, let me," Matt said quietly.

Erin stood back, pallid and trembling, while Matt rearranged his father's position. But still the terrible, tearing cough continued, and Lew seemed barely conscious. She wondered fleetingly why Matt was still dressed and why his clothes were wrinkled, but her mind could not pursue these concerns, she was so filled with fear.

They could do nothing for the next few hours but sit by Lew's side while he slowly coughed his life away. Erin realized abruptly that she was holding Matt's hand tightly but she could not remember taking it. She looked down at their entwined fingers, then up at his face, ashen in the lamplight.

"It's all right, kid. Hold on if it helps," he said gently.

"Oh, God, Matt. It's awful . . ."

"Yes . . . I know."

As the fragile fingers of early light spread over Independence Pass to touch the top of Aspen Mountain, Lew took a deep, rattling breath. They waited, as they had waited all night for each breath of his, to hear him exhale. But there was only a heavy silence.

Erin gave a strangled sob and rose from her chair to shake his shoulder. "Lew, Lew!" He did not respond and she shook him harder, frantically crying his name over and over.

"It's no use, Erin. He's gone." Matt's low voice brought her back to reality, and she stopped suddenly, staring down at the gray, quiet face. Yes, he was gone; she could see that the spirit of Lew, her beloved friend and protector, had departed the still figure on the bed. She turned and buried her head in Matt's chest, sobbing out her grief. He slipped his arms around her, trying to protect her from misery and loneliness, but he knew that it was only temporary.

And for the second time in Erin Conner's young life, a void engulfed her. It had been the same with the death of her parents, and as she stood in the comforting arms of Lew's son, she again knew deep, spiritual pain.

There were many degrees of pain, she knew, but this was the darkest and loneliest of all. It was as if she had been whirling around in a frightful maelstrom, a black funnel of fear and confusion, and now, as her swollen eyes fell on Lew's still form, she knew that she had sunk to the very depth of misery. Oh, God, how she would miss him; God, how she would miss him . . .

The room lightened as the sun's rays reached into the valley; they lit upon the two figures locked in close embrace and then rested on the peaceful features of Lew Steele.

The afternoon of the funeral began to turn gray and windy shortly after midday. Erin kept glancing nervously out the window of her bedroom, toward the west where great, black, billowing clouds were amassing.

I knew we should have had it in the morning, she told herself as she drew on her long, black kid gloves. It *never* rains in the morning. Oh, blast it all! She felt tears begin to well up in her eyes again and she bit her lip, staring into her floor-length mirror. Her face was as pallid and gray-splotched as a daytime moon. Her elegant black voile dress flattered her, but she was in no mood to care. She wanted only to look respectable, for there would be many of Lew's friends at his funeral; he had been a well-loved man in Aspen, his kind heart recognized by many. She perched the ridiculous little black bonnet on her curls, stuck in the long pins, and pulled the veil down. At least it hid her reddened eyes and pale cheeks.

Matt would be arriving soon. He had been very kind lately, and subdued from grief himself. He had not pressed her in any way, but had tried to comfort her during her many stormy crying fits. Strange, she thought, that he had moved out so suddenly on the very morning Lew had died. She had protested, but he had insisted that he move into the rooms above the store, sharing them with John, the manager.

"There's no need, Matt. I've got lots of room here," she had said.

"I know, kid. But it doesn't look good. With Lew gone, there's no—chaperone." Matt had seemed almost embarrassed.

"For God's sake, Matt, I've never given two hoots what anyone thinks, nor have you. What's come over you?"

"Maybe you should begin to care, Erin. With Lew gone, you shouldn't leave yourself wide open to gossip."

"They'll have nothing to gossip about, Matthew Steele."

But he had moved anyway, and she had seen him only

when he had chosen to come and visit her empty, echoing, beautiful house. He seemed unlike himself now, oddly reticent, thoughtful. The mockery and the brilliant smile were gone, but his new soberness was just as attractive to her.

She heard the front door open and Matt's voice greet her servant politely. Her eyes again filled with moisture; it was time. She pushed the veil up over the hat, and giving Abraham a pat, went down to meet him.

It did indeed rain at the cemetery, a quick mountain shower that pelted down onto the dry dust in separate balls of moisture. Matt had had the foresight to bring along an umbrella—he always remembered things like that—and they stood huddled under it while the minister intoned the words of the service, then went on to speak eloquently of Lew as one of Aspen's first citizens. Erin was happy to see so many people at Ute Cemetery; Lew would have been as touched as she was.

Erin felt dried up and empty; she could not cry now, although her eyes burned. Later, she thought, later, when I have the leisure to feel his loss; later I shall cry. Her heart thumped heavily with every spadeful of dirt that fell on the pinewood coffin. At last the painful ordeal was over, and she and Matt returned to the house, both remaining silent in the elegant black carriage, both wrapped in their own dark thoughts.

"Matt . . . come in and have some coffee with me. The servants are gone for the afternoon and I can make it myself. We can . . . talk." She did not really understand what had prompted her to ask him in. Loneliness? A reaching out for another presence? Fear of her lovely, empty house?

He did not answer but followed her up the walk and into the tiled vestibule. She stood in front of the small mirror and took off the black hat that perched on her curls. Her slim arms reached up to withdraw the pins, pulling the fabric of her dress taut over her breasts, accentuating her tall leanness. Matt could not keep his eyes off her.

He walked up behind her and put his hands on her waist; he could feel her involuntary stiffening. He looked into the mirror and saw her white face, eyes huge and staring, while her hands were frozen in their attitude of removing the hat. He held her eyes in the mirror. "You're beautiful," he whispered, not wanting to disturb the tableau.

"Don't . . . please don't," she breathed. "Lew's hardly

cold in the ground and you're already thinking of . . . like an animal." Her words fell tiredly, weakly, into the air.

He turned her around slowly until she faced him. "You make me feel a little like an animal," he said quietly. He bent his head and kissed her on the lips, searchingly and thoroughly. He could feel her body relax as she returned his kiss, molding to his frame.

They broke apart, and she put a black-gloved hand to her lips. "I didn't mean to do that," she said, watching him intently.

"Neither did I," Matt answered simply.

But Erin knew that her words were not altogether true; perhaps she hadn't intended to let Matt kiss her, to respond to him, yet she desperately needed him to do exactly that. She wanted him to hold her, comfort her, help her put aside her grief for a moment.

She turned her eyes up to meet his and realized that her pulse was beating far too rapidly. "Let's have that coffee before you get any more ideas." She laughed shakily as she walked into the green and gold drawing room.

The sun had come out again and the sky was innocent and blue, daring anyone to believe it had rained only an hour before.

Erin disappeared into the kitchen, emerging a short time later with a silver coffee service. The pungent odor of the hot brew filled the room as she poured. They sipped in silence until Matt put his cup down.

"Erin."

She looked up, startled by the purposefulness of his tone.

"Lew made me promise something before he died. It concerns you." He stopped, unsure about how to continue.

"I figured he would . . . He wants you to watch over me, see that I'm all right. That's it, isn't it?"

"Not quite," Matt said slowly, keeping his gaze fixed on his cup. He glanced up then and met her smoke-colored eyes. "He made me promise to marry you." As soon as the words were out, he knew he'd done it poorly. He could see the shock and pain that crossed her face.

"He *made* you—what?"

"What I meant to say is, I promised Lew that I would marry you."

"Oh, yes, *that* makes it much better! The fool! How could he possibly . . . ? Oh, it's like him, I suppose." She had risen and was angrily pacing up and down. "And what did *you* say to that?"

"I told him I didn't think you'd listen to me."

"And I won't! You egotistical bastard!" She stopped in front of him, her hands on her hips, spots of red staining her cheeks. "If you were the last man on earth, I wouldn't marry you. I don't need *you,* no matter *what* Lew thought." Her voice was low and full of fury, and she felt the blood rushing to her head.

"Well, I tried. That's twice I've offered you marriage, Erin, and you've turned me down twice. I've done my duty, and I don't think even Lew could have expected more." His tone was light, but the darkness of his eyes betrayed his anger.

"Your duty!" she spit, then strode to a window. She kept her back turned to him and stared unseeingly out at the sunlit street, trying to regain control of her emotions. The branch of a tree scraped gratingly against the window in the mild breeze, jangling her taut nerves.

Erin did not know which feeling was stronger, her pain or her anger; each battled for ascendancy in her heart. Lew she could understand and forgive—he only wanted someone to take care of her—but Matt . . . Matt . . . that despicable, arrogant bounder! *His duty!* Her mind screamed the words soundlessly. Perhaps if he'd asked her himself, without any prompting from Lew . . . but that was not to be. Now that she'd given her body to him willingly, he thought he owned her—lock, stock, and barrel!

She felt her fury rising in a hot flush up the back of her neck, and she clenched her hands at her sides, whirling around to face him as he sat, relaxed and nonchalant, on her—yes, *her*—sofa.

"You can just get out of my house." Her voice had been low, but now it climbed rapidly. "Get out and stay out! I never want to see you again!"

Matt rose from the sofa, his face cold and menacing. "Oh, yes, your precious *house!* You've got your house, Erin, but not much more. Who do you think you are, throwing your money around like a rich tart? Do you think all that money makes you special?" His tone turned scathing. "Don't try to put on airs. You're still just a little orphan girl whom we picked up in the streets—a used one at that!" He heard her sharp intake of breath. "I'll be glad to leave. I have nothing to keep me in Aspen any longer." He picked up his Stetson and started for the door, leaving her standing in the middle of the room, the black dress making her face appear much too waxen under the copper curls. He turned back to her at the last minute with a sardonic "Goodbye, Erin. I hope you enjoy your wealth." Then he was gone, the front door gaping open to permit a band of sunlight to spill in over the colored tiles of the vestibule.

Erin remained frozen in the middle of the room. When she was certain he had really gone, she walked stiffly, slowly, to the front door and closed it gently, leaning her forehead against the cool, smooth wood. Was it possible that only a few minutes ago she'd been serving coffee to that bastard in her own drawing room? Watching him from under the veil of her lashes and devouring what she saw? What was worse, her lips were still burning from his recent kiss, from the sensuous feel of his mouth covering hers. What an absolute idiot she was!

For a brief whisper of a moment, her heart lurched in her chest. She could have had him then, could have known the secret, fulfilling bliss of his body consuming hers night after blessed night. But at what price? How much was she willing to pay in the way of pride to know that joy when, in the morning, in all her mornings, she'd have to face the degrading, humiliating fact that Matthew Steele had married her out of duty?

No, her mind screamed. She'd done exactly the right thing by tossing his revolting offer in his face and not giving in for a moment. The price for having him, for the privilege of looking into those hypnotic eyes, was far and again too high.

At last Erin turned around and rested her back against the door, the door through which he'd just stormed for the last time. And then her tears came, racking her frame with their ceaseless intensity. She sank slowly to the floor in a circle of black skirts, the sound of her rending sobs filling the empty hallway.

PART III

Chapter 22

Although it would have been simpler to have taken the stage to Leadville and then the train to Denver City, Erin chose to travel by carriage on the barely existent road to Glenwood Springs, by stage to Georgetown, and finally, by train to Denver City. How she traveled made little difference to her; she was not on any particular time schedule. The Silver Lady had a competent crew and did not require her presence, and the same was true for her house.

She spent two days in Glenwood Springs and even visited its famous mineral springs, which had been called Yampah by the Indians. It was hard for her to believe that this bustling town was only forty miles from Aspen, yet the condition of the road, to which she could easily attest, was treacherous at best. No doubt her carriage was ruined, or would be by the time the hired driver returned it to Aspen.

Several hours before her coach was due to depart for Georgetown, Erin had her luggage carted to the depot. She checked her attire one last time in the wardrobe mirror. Her pale yellow linen traveling suit looked chic, a jabot of white lace frothed at her throat, and her straw hat covered with bright silk flowers tilted rakishly on her stylish pompadour. She slid on a pair of light-colored kid gloves and looped her reticule over a wrist, then left the hotel.

She spent her remaining time strolling the downtown streets of Glenwood Springs and stopped to purchase several bottles of Yampah water, purported to be beneficial for ailments such as rheumatism, colds and coughs, giddiness, aching muscles, and—of all things—stunted growth. Erin giggled merrily as she left the apothecary while continuing to be fascinated by the bottles' labels.

"Pardon me, ma'am." The gentleman tipped his wide-brimmed hat as Erin nearly bumped into him.

"Oh, no—it wasn't your fault, sir. I was merely reading when I should have been watching my step." She smiled up into the slightly dissipated yet handsome face, noting the man's luxurious handlebar mustache.

"Haven't seen you around before, Miss . . ."

"No, you haven't. I live in Aspen, up the Roaring Fork Valley about forty miles."

"Yes, I know." He coughed suddenly. "Excuse me, Miss . . ."

"Erin Conner, sir." His persistent cough caused her to blanch momentarily; it reminded her so much of Lew.

"Damn cough," he muttered. "I certainly hope, Miss Conner, that you remain in Glenwood for a spell." Then he smiled at her. "The name's Holiday, Miss Conner . . . Doc Holiday."

"The Doc Holiday?" Her shock was undisguised; she even looked down to see the bulge of his famed derringer under his coat.

"Yes, ma'am—came here to cure this wretched cough. Doesn't seem to help, though."

And then the notorious man made Erin an offer that she would remember all her life: he invited her to dinner at the new Hotel Glenwood.

Of course she had to refuse; not only was she due on the stage in a few minutes, but whatever reputation she had would certainly be ruined.

"Thank you again, Mr. Holiday, but I must be going now." She turned and left, but not before she saw an odd twinkle in his eye as he tipped his hat again.

Erin was so utterly entranced by her accidental meeting with Doc Holiday that she barely noticed the sights along the stagecoach ride. Her eyes fixed unseeingly on the thundering Colorado River and the splendor of the immense granite walls of Glenwood Canyon—a spectacular combination of raging water, towering rock masses, and brilliant September sky. The day was already printed indelibly in her memory.

The coach rattled and pulled and tunneled its way up through the mountains, crossed the Continental Divide to the eastern slopes, and headed for Georgetown, where Erin caught the train. She had to admit that traveling by train was far more practical, not to mention more comfortable, and she thoroughly enjoyed this last part of her trip.

At the Union Station in Denver City, Erin hired a carriage to take her to her hotel, the Windsor, on 18th and Larimer. She had engaged an elegant suite there for an unlimited stay.

Her days were spent in the shops and boutiques, where she indulged herself lavishly in the purchase of gowns, hats, shoes, two furs, and a supply of the latest Parisian cosmetics. Even though she knew that she would probably never use a third of these items, she could think of nothing else to do with her time. Spending money seemed the perfect antidote to all sensible thought.

Evenings were the loneliest time, however. After spending hours preparing for dinner, she still sat and ate alone in the handsome Windsor dining room. She knew that many male heads were turned in her direction, but this meant nothing to her. At first she had attempted to return the men's polite greetings, but after a few meals she had grown bored with the trite banter. Now she kept her eyes coolly averted when addressed.

Only once did she attempt to make friends, and that day she joined a group of wealthy miners from Leadville to see a play at Elitch Gardens. Afterward, their company became tiresome, so she retired to her hotel room with a newly purchased pulp magazine, donned a lacy, yellow silk night-gown from New York, and stretched out on her wide bed. The dresser mirror sat a few feet from the foot of the bed, and she could not help but stare at her reflection. Since Lew's death, she had somehow changed. But how?

As she carefully looked at herself in the mirror, she suddenly saw where the change was most apparent. It was in her face. Her fingers traced the lines of her nose and mouth and chin. She had not noticed it before, but in the past year she had actually become a woman. And—she blushed at her immodesty—a rather beautiful woman at that!

Without wishing it to happen, Erin remembered the time Matt had said she was beautiful. She clenched her teeth but could not tear her gaze away from her reflection. Wanting to recall, yet fighting against the memory, she envisioned his hands and mouth on her body, teasing, arousing, tracing its hollows and curves.

A soft sheen of perspiration broke out over her flesh as the image refused to disappear. She loathed herself all the more, knowing that the very thought of Matt could weaken her limbs and cause her stomach to flutter. Damn! Undoubtedly, at this very moment, he was wooing some young innocent into his arms, his lips exploring the firm round curves of her breasts, her slim legs wrapped tightly around him . . .

"No!" Erin cried aloud. "No! No! No! Leave me alone, Matt Steele! Leave me alone!"

She threw herself off the bed and paced the room in agony. Damn! There were hundreds of men equally as attractive as he, equally as sensual, and she had been cheating herself by wasting her precious youth comparing all other men with a conceited killer. An egomaniac who was an expert in the art of carnal pleasure.

Suddenly, as she fought against his ever-present ghost, a notion flew into her head. What she, Erin Conner, needed was a man to wash away her painful memories. A man equal to Matt in some ways, but infinitely more kind and soft-spoken. This, she realized, would erase him from her mind once and for all. Her habit of avoiding men would have to stop; that had been her childish protection from a cruel incident that had happened long ago. Now she knew what a man could do for her, the pleasure he could give her. All she had to do was to find someone, and, if necessary, use him—marry him, perhaps, but bend him to *her* will.

It was still early in the evening, and abruptly, Erin felt like joining the throb of city life. She dressed in a rush, tidied her hair, and casually tossed one of her new furs, a red fox, over her shoulders.

The cool night air struck her flushed face as she walked out onto 18th Street, where she hired a carriage and instructed the driver simply to drive around. She sat back, a warm woolen blanket covering her legs, and studied the people on the Denver streets. There were dozens of men and women strolling along the rough sidewalks, occasionally disappearing into a saloon or a doorway of an open shop. Why hadn't she noticed the crowds before? There were others like herself, many who faced life unmarried and alone. And she was the lucky one, the one with youth and money—a great deal of money. She was, after all, the Silver Lady of Aspen—wealthy, beautiful, and strong. She had survived the death of her parents, Lew's death, her brother's death—and, most of all, she had survived Matt Steele. Survived him and won the battle!

The driver took Erin east of her hotel to the Capital Hill area, where she had heard there were more millionaires per square foot than anywhere else in the world. Many homes were still under construction, most of them looking very much like her own elegant house in Aspen. After a short drive around the new streets, she grew bored, and on a sudden impulse asked the coachman to return to Larimer Street and head north slowly. Her heart began to throb wildly; she would purge all the old ghosts this night. She had already dealt with Matthew Steele; now she would face the primal horror in her memory.

It occurred to her that Madame Lucille's house might not be there any more, but as the horse plodded north on the rutted street, she saw it—at least it was the same building, for she recognized the ugly stone turrets.

"Stop the carriage."

When Erin climbed down, the driver looked aghast. "Miss! Do you have any idea . . . ?"

"It's all right. Wait for me here."

She slowly approached the front door—it looked exactly the same. Timidly, almost turning to run away, she lifted the brass door knocker and rapped lightly. The small, familiar wooden panel slid cautiously aside.

"Go away—you're at the wrong address," a feminine voice instructed.

"No, wait, please," Erin said quickly. "I—I would like to see Madame Lucille—please!"

"Wait there, then."

Endless minutes later, the door opened soundlessly and Erin forced her cold feet to move up the last step, into the garishly decorated entryway of Madame Lucille's. She was then led past the formal greeting room, where she could hear the whispers and lusty laughter of men and women. The young girl who showed her to Lucille's private office was dressed outrageously in a black and white French maid's uniform that elicited in Erin the desire both to giggle and to sigh in disgust.

The girl tapped lightly on Madame's door.

"Entrez! Entrez!" came the shockingly familiar voice.

Erin was ushered in hastily; the door closed quietly behind

her. There sat Madame Lucille, the same black-haired presence whom she remembered so vividly, but so much older and wrinkled that Erin gasped audibly.

"What is it that you want? I am *très occupée*."

So! Lucille did not recognize her—but, of course, it had been six years. "You don't remember me." Erin's voice remained steady and impassive, yet she wondered what she could have been thinking of to come back here.

"I should remember? There have been many *jeunes filles . . .*"

"My name is Erin Conner . . . it was six years ago, when I was only fifteen."

"Ah, *oui!* I do remember! *Oui*, the girl with the copper hair who attacked the customer!"

"Yes," Erin said slowly, "that was me."

"Well, what is it that you want?" Lucille's voice turned suspicious.

"What I would really like to do would be to tear out your dyed black hair, madame." Was that really her voice? So casual? So cool?

"What! How dare you!" The woman's French accent suddenly disappeared.

"I only came to tell you that. I'll go now—I can see this is pointless." Erin turned to leave; then, dissatisfied, she turned back. "I'm going to put my mind to it, Lucille, and, I assure you, I'll find a way to hurt you—like the sick way you hurt me!"

These words, however, did not give Erin the pleasure she longed for, and even before she was out the office door she knew that her threat was idle. Her ghost was gone, there was no need for vengeance any more, she felt only emptiness inside. Oh, well, she mused, let Lucille stew for a while—forever—I really don't care.

As she was turning the knob on the front door, a hand touched her shoulder.

"Erin? Is it really you?"

Erin spun around in surprise, almost defensively. The woman's face was hauntingly familiar.

"It's Hattie, Erin. Don't you—"

"Yes! Oh, yes, I *do* remember! Hattie . . ." It seemed natural to her when Hattie embraced her warmly.

"Quick," Hattie said, "let's go outside. Madame wouldn't like it if she saw us talking."

When they were out on the front steps, the night air chilling them, Erin took stock of Hattie's appearance. She looked older, too, and thinner; her face was painted miserably. Yet she was still an attractive woman under all the cosmetics.

"You must tell me quickly what became of you that night," Hattie urged. "You remember, the night you hit Ben Mortimer on the head. We laughed about that for days."

"Laughed! How could you?"

"What do you mean? He deserved it," Hattie said. "The old reprobate liked young kids too much."

"But did he deserve . . . to die?"

"Die? All the fat pig got was a bump on the head and some singed hair."

Erin could not believe her ears—*she hadn't killed him after all!* And all these years she had tortured herself . . . A great weight lifted from her as the knowledge slowly seeped into her consciousness.

"Oh, my God, Hattie, I thought I killed him! You can't imagine what a relief it is! I've even been blackmailed over it! If only I'd known!"

"Well, you know it now, so don't worry yourself another minute. I'm sure he's forgotten. He still drops in occasionally to see if Madame has any more young ones."

Erin's mind turned to Perry's blackmail attempt. Oh, dear God, it had all been for nothing! He needn't have died. Why had he deceived her? He must have known that Mortimer was alive, and through his greed and dishonesty Perry had brought on his own death.

Erin shook off these thoughts and focused on the present, on the old friend who stood before her now in a fit of excitement to hear all that Erin could tell her about the past years.

Erin took a deep breath and hurriedly related everything she could remember, the important things. She omitted telling Hattie about Matt, mentioning him only once, casually.

"Your coat, it's so lovely and expensive, too," Hattie said, touching the fur carefully.

"Yes, it is. I'm wealthy now, Hattie. The mine I told you about has brought me so much."

"I'm happy for you, Erin. After what Madame did to you, well, you deserve it!" She looked downcast for a moment. "You know, Erin, sometimes I wish I had the guts to run away like you did. Madame's gotten so cruel through the years, and she's terribly ill, too. Why, some of the things she does now would make your experience seem like a Sunday school picnic!"

"Hattie, why do you stay?"

"Oh, that . . . well, it won't be for much longer. Madame says I'm too old now, and good only to tend the servants and do the books."

An idea came to Erin, something that would both help Hattie and hurt Lucille. "Come with me. Tonight. I have a place for you in my home, Hattie. But," she added to save the woman embarrassment, "you'll have to earn your keep as my companion and housekeeper."

"Oh, Erin, I don't think I could just . . ."

"Yes, you can! You owe *her* nothing! You've made thousands of dollars for Lucille, and she's given you nothing but cheap clothes, a little food, and a lot of misery."

"Well . . ." Hattie's eyes brightened.

"Say yes—oh, please, Hattie. I need you!" She truly meant it.

"Well . . . could you come for me later, maybe tomorrow?" Hattie took Erin's hand in her own trembling one.

"Any time. I'll come any time you say," Erin assured her.

At three P.M. on September 28, 1886, Erin hired a carriage and drove along Larimer Street to pick up Hattie. She had the immense satisfaction of seeing Madame Lucille standing in the middle of the road, arms flailing and tears of rage rolling down her painted, wrinkled cheeks. In the light of day, Erin could appreciate that the woman was truly ill, perhaps even dying; her face beneath the makeup was lifeless.

Hattie Nelson, in a very short time, became Erin's loyal companion, friend, and substitute sister. And she gloried in her new, respectable position.

Erin, on her part, found herself confiding things to Hattie that she had never dared voice even silently. One evening, while they were eating a delicious dinner at the Windsor Hotel, Erin told her all about Matt; she also discussed their affair and her frequent visions of the man dressed in buckskin.

"And that's why I'm certain Matt Steele was only an interlude in my life," Erin said, between bites of Colorado tenderloin.

"Yes, Erin. But do you still love him?"

Erin almost choked. *"Love* him? You must be mad, Hattie! Only a crazy woman would love a man like that!"

If Hattie was skeptical about Erin's flat denial, she kept silent on the subject. It was clear that Erin had convinced herself that she loathed him.

"Hattie, I've been thinking. I'm getting bored in Denver City. Let's go home—to Aspen."

"I was wondering when we would. I'm dying to see your house and begin my duties. I only hope I can really earn my keep—I won't be taking your charity!" She gave a short, nervous laugh. "There's only one thing that worries me, though, and I won't have you laughing at me. I've heard tell of the '79 Indian uprising. It scares me, all those filthy savages . . ."

"Don't be ridiculous, Hattie." Erin smiled knowingly. "It's true there was an uprising of the White River Utes. But the government moved the whole tribe off the western slopes to the Utah territory back in '81. There's not a redskin to be seen in the valley these days." Then she remembered something. "There is old Gray Hawk, but he's at least a hundred and is drunk most of the time.

"To get back to the subject. We're definitely leaving soon. And as for your job, Hattie, I've told you time and time again that the work is endless there. Your just being around will allow me to tend to business at the mine and at Lew's store. Besides, my housekeeper is getting married in November, so I'd have to replace her, anyway. Now, eat your meal and stop worrying."

"Erin, will it be hard returning to Aspen now that Lew Steele is gone?"

Erin thought a moment, then realized that Hattie was forcing her to face an unpleasant fact. "Yes, it will be hard, but I'll manage. I always do, you know."

And now she had a plan—to find a man of strength, yet with weaknesses of her choosing, to fill the empty place in her life.

Still chatting, the two women rose and walked out of the dining room into the hotel lobby. Erin was relaxed and cheerful; for the first time she had another woman, a friend, in whom to confide. She stopped at the kiosk to buy one of the latest Paris fashion magazines, and as she was paying the lady behind the mahogany counter, she heard a booming voice that caused her to glance in its direction.

A huge man was standing at the lobby desk, gesticulating and arguing with the clerk. There was something very crude about the man in spite of his expensive clothes and ivory-headed cane. He turned in Erin's direction, his face suffused with anger; their eyes met and locked.

Suddenly she felt all the blood drain from her face and a cold wave of fear wash over her. She could have been fifteen again and back in that dreadful red room. The man was Ben Mortimer. She would never forget that face, that shining, bald head, that huge girth.

With unutterable horror, Erin saw slow recognition dawn on his repulsive features. Ponderously, he began to walk toward her. She could not move; she looked wildly around for help, but Hattie had gone upstairs and the few strangers in the lobby were occupied with their own interests.

"Oh, yes, miss, I remember you!" The wheezing tones of the fat man made her jump in fear; her skin crawled with disgust. She tried to move away, but it was too late. A meaty hand encased her arm and led her forcibly toward an alcove behind a potted fern. "And you remember me, too, I can tell . . ." Mortimer chuckled, an obscene sound deep in his throat.

He pushed her down onto a leather settee, then sat next to her, squeezing her against the wall and still holding her arm.

"Oh, yes, I remember you." The little piglike eyes turned hard and cold. "You made a fool of me. And left me scarred to boot. Let me tell you, I got every penny back from Lucille, but I never got anything back from you, you little twit!" He gripped her arm harder and she bit her lip in pain. "I've been waiting many years for you, little miss redhead. And I never forget a face." His bulk was very close to her, giving off a mixture of cigar and whiskey fumes. "It was Erin, wasn't it? A little Irish girl . . . *Bitch!*" he hissed at her, causing her to shrink back into the cushions.

"I've had years to think of what I'd like to do to you—and just fancy my luck bumping into you here!" He sat back and smiled at her wickedly.

Erin gathered her strength, tensing her muscles and hoping that Mortimer wouldn't notice. Suddenly she sprang to her feet and swung her reticule at him with all her might. The bag caught him square in the face and he let out a bellow of rage.

A few people turned their heads and saw a white-faced young lady almost running across the marble lobby floor, to disappear up the stairs in a swirl of skirts.

Erin reached her room and had to knock on the door for Hattie to open it because her hands shook so badly she could not use her key.

"Lock it!" she cried harshly when she was inside.

"What's the matter, Erin?" Hattie gasped. "You look like you've seen a ghost!"

"I have. Ben Mortimer—in the lobby!" Erin shuddered. "He tried to—oh, I don't know what! Something awful. I hit him in the face with my reticule and ran away."

Hattie sat down next to her and put an arm around her shoulders. "He can't hurt you, honey. He's just a big fat, nasty man, not a ghost. Look, we'll leave early in the morning and ask the desk clerk to call us a trap at the back entrance. Mortimer will never find us. He doesn't know where you live."

Erin gave a great, shuddering sigh. "I guess so, Hattie. I don't know what I expected him to do in the middle of a hotel lobby." She laughed weakly. "But I can never forget what he did to me. He's so—repulsive!"

"Erin, I know. My stepfather made me feel the same way before I ran away from home. I know exactly how you feel."

"Oh, Hattie, I'm so sorry. I didn't mean to bring that up."

"Never mind. Let's get some sleep. We're leaving early, remember?"

Erin checked the lock on the door again, then pushed a heavy chair up against it. Once undressed and in bed, she thought she'd never be able to sleep, but eventually she drifted off.

Sometime in the middle of the night she awoke with a start, her heart pounding. The sound that had awakened her was the loud rattling of her doorknob. It went on and on, until she thought she would scream. Then she heard the thick door panels creak, as if a heavy weight were pressing against them.

She lay in the darkness, terrified, her fists clenched whitely on the satin comforter. Surely someone would hear this noise!

Then, abruptly, everything was quiet, and after a few

moments Erin drew a shaky breath. But she lay awake the rest of the long night, bathed in a cold sweat of fear as she waited for the dreadful rattling and creaking to begin once more.

Chapter 23

"We haven't all day," Erin called to Hattie from the vestibule. "And don't forget your coat!"

Undoubtedly Hattie was still fussing with the draperies in Erin's bedroom—that woman never wearied of cleaning and tidying up, Erin knew. How in heaven's name did she expect to wash and dry draperies in January?

"Hurry up! The bank closes in an hour—we'll never make it."

Hattie finally emerged from the upstairs hallway, tugging her coat on. "I'm so sorry, Erin. They just wouldn't hang out properly!"

As the two women walked carefully through the snow, they chatted about the new owner of the bank, Andrew Cartwright, lately of St. Louis. Erin was not certain she liked the idea of a new bank president; Mr. Jeffery had been just fine, in her opinion, and had handled her account very satisfactorily. But along came this Easterner who bought the bank outright, and Mr. Jeffery's house as well, which was down the street from Erin's. She would meet this Mr. Cartwright and judge him shrewdly, and if she didn't like his ideas, she would transfer her account to the new bank across Mill Street.

The slight wind was biting today; but after all, this was January. The minuscule, powdery snowflakes whirled up from the streets and sparkled like diamonds in the air. Erin loved days like this, when the cold put a glow in her cheeks and the sun arched its way brightly over Aspen Mountain. To her, it was like living in a fairyland, unreal and splendid.

She and Hattie joined the flow of shoppers dressed warmly in woolen coats, capes, and high leather boots, and proceeded up Mill Street to the bank.

Tucking the stray locks of copper curls under her fox hat, Erin caught her reflection in the window. Through the gold lettering on the pane she saw that she looked proper indeed. The elegant fur coat and hat lent an air of maturity and wealth to her bearing, an air that she liked and which gave her confidence.

The women entered the stifling warmth of the bank lobby—a small area that had only one teller's window—and Erin spotted the new owner in his glassed-in office, engaged in conversation with a familiar-looking miner.

For a brief moment she thought simply to interrupt their talk; she was miffed without really knowing why. Then she settled herself, not too comfortably, on the wooden lobby bench and sent Hattie off to do a few errands.

After a few minutes her eyes wandered to the figure of Andrew Cartwright, whom she could assess quite clearly through the glass. He was evidently tall, judging by the length of his torso, and also lean. His graying hair and dignified features told Erin that he was close to fifty years old. His clothes were finely tailored for a perfect fit, the dark blue broadcloth frock coat displaying the broadness of his shoulders. Cartwright looked exceedingly healthy for a man of his age. But Erin would not judge him on looks alone—no indeed!

It took another fifteen minutes before the miner, along with Cartwright, emerged from the office. After the men shook hands and parted, Erin rose and approached the banker, a look of impatience crossing her features.

"Excuse me, sir. My name is Erin Conner and I—"

"But of course! Miss Conner . . ." He placed a hand on her fur-clad arm and ushered her directly into his office. "I'm Andrew Cartwright, Miss Conner, and I must apologize for allowing you to wait so long. If I had known the lovely lady sitting out there was you . . . well, promise me that next time you'll just come straight in." A warm smile gathered around his mouth.

For a moment Erin was silent. Already, against her better judgment, she liked this man. He reminded her of Lew, with the same note of sincerity in his voice. "Thank you, Mr. Cartwright, but I shouldn't like to interrupt . . ."

"No indeed, of course you wouldn't. You know, Miss Conner, as I was going over your account, I had a marvelous idea that should benefit both yourself and my bank." He went on to suggest diversifying her holdings to bring in more interest, on which she would pay points to the bank. Although Erin did not understand his exact meaning, he seemed to know his business—in fact, far better than the previous owner, she thought.

"Well, Mr. Cartwright, I'm not very good at this sort of thing. I've always kept a straight savings account here . . ."

"I realize that, which is exactly why I should like to handle this tedious business for you. If, of course, you would like to check my credentials—" His lips turned downward for an instant. "No, I insist that you *do* check. That way there'll be no doubt in your mind that I have only the best of intentions." Andrew Cartwright proceeded to tell Erin that he had previously owned a well-known St. Louis bank, and after the death of his wife a year ago, had decided to sell out and start anew in the West.

As she listened to him talk so easily about his past, she grew to like him more. He seemed so open and forthright. He was not an arrogant man, nor was he weak, yet she had the feeling he possessed an inner strength that displayed itself naturally through his manner.

Erin rose to leave. "Mr. Cartwright, if you're not otherwise engaged, I should like to have you to dinner tonight. Perhaps you could explain more fully your plans for my investments."

He smiled openly and broadly. "I have only an empty, twelve-room house awaiting me. I'd love to visit with you, Miss Conner. And dinner would be delightful. I'm a dreadful cook myself."

Erin shook his hand. "Seven, then?"

"Seven it is."

Hattie could not help but comment on the length of time it took Erin to dress and the inordinate fuss she made over the dinner menu. Nonetheless, by a few minutes before seven, it was obvious that the ado had been well worthwhile. Erin emerged from her bedroom looking devastatingly elegant in a midnight-blue velvet gown that sported a bustle, was cut low in the bodice, and was decorated with swirling rows of a lighter blue ruched lace and satin ribbon. Her creamy flesh was quite deliciously displayed. She had tied up her hair in matching blue ribbons; the style was casual, but only Erin knew how long it had taken to achieve just that effect. She had even dabbed perfume between her breasts, behind her ears, and on her wrists.

"Erin Conner," Hattie gasped as Erin descended the stairs, "you plan on seducing the man?"

Erin swept past her into the drawing room. "You're just jealous, Hattie! I'm planning no such thing. This past winter I've had lots of callers, and I always dress well."

"Not *this* well," Hattie observed.

Erin went to the sideboard and poured a small glass of sherry. "I'm entitled to enjoy an attractive man's company, aren't I? Besides, he's new here—he needs to meet people."

Hattie went over the legs of the tables and chairs with a feather duster. "Yes, of course he does, Erin. And I know it's none of my business, but I think it's high time you started to take men seriously. For the past few months you've played with their affections and never allowed yourself to have any real feelings."

"Oh, Hattie, you're a dreadful philosopher. Of course I have real feelings. It's just that no one has interested me." Erin walked over to the sofa and sat down with her crystal glass. Hattie shrugged her shoulders and disappeared into the kitchen.

Real feelings! Erin thought. Hattie doesn't know *everything* about what I've suffered. Every inch of my way up the ladder to get where I am has been painful.

The image of Matt crept into her mind, but with no resultant ache. She saw him on the day of Lew's funeral, when she had had to face the reality that he would marry her, not because he wanted to, but because he had a duty to fulfill. How very self-righteous of him! And now Hattie thought she was cold and reserved, unable to let herself feel. Well, with Matt Steele purged forever from her, it was time to feel again. And if she got hurt in the process, so be it; she would survive.

The doorbell rang. Erin flew out of her seat and checked herself in the vestibule mirror before admitting her guest.

"Good evening, Mr. Cartwright. Won't you come in?"

"Please, my given name is Andrew. I'd feel much more comfortable if you would call me that."

She took his hat and coat, gently laying them aside. "Well, Andrew, then you must call me Erin."

They laughed easily while she led him into the drawing

room and poured another sherry. For a time they chatted about Ireland, St. Louis, and then Aspen. Erin became an animated storyteller, amazing the banker with her vast knowledge of every facet of Aspen's brief history.

During dinner she could sense his interest in her—not in her money or her humorous stories, but in *her*. His eyes betrayed him when they kept coming to rest on her low-cut bodice. And, of course, hadn't she planned just that? Did it matter if he was old enough to be her father? He was a very attractive man who flattered her outrageously with his quiet appreciation.

At the evening's end, well past midnight, Andrew asked Erin to join him for lunch the next day, confiding to her that he had not enjoyed a woman's company so much since the death of his wife.

As the weeks of February came and went, the luncheons, the dinners, the evening carriage rides, all fused into one in Erin's mind. She felt she was wanted and needed, securely cherished by a good man. Andrew brought her candy and perfume, even small baubles of jewelry, each time they met. She always scolded him but loved the gifts, nevertheless. Every facet of her life seemed perfect; he brought her happiness along with a handsome interest rate on her money. Most importantly, he never pressed her sexually. Only once had the subject arisen, and Erin had managed to put him at bay with a casual word. She was not certain that she had done the right thing, but when she was ready to accept him that way, it would be easy enough to let him know.

Early in March a snowstorm occurred, the kind that carried heavy, wet flakes and cloaked the town with four-foot drifts. The aspen branches sagged to the earth with their white burden; everything wore the pristine beauty of nature's wonderland.

As the snow continued to fall thickly from a dark sky, Andrew decided this evening would be perfect for a sleigh ride.

He came for Erin at eight. She waited for him by her gate, and when he hopped down from the horse-driven sleigh, she caught him playfully in the chest with a snowball. Their moments together were always like this, lighthearted and joyous. Erin brought youth and clarity to Andrew's lonely life, and he gifted her with caring and respect.

The horse, frisky in the moist night air, pulled the sleigh

steadily along the drift-covered road to Independence Pass. Erin and Andrew were covered with snow, but they laughed and sang and listened to the bells jingling to the horse's gait. They were mindless of the damp cold, unaware of the smooth white fields around them.

It was then that Andrew asked her to marry him. ". . . you don't have to answer right away. Take some time to decide—it's a big step for you."

Had she heard him correctly? Erin's heart fluttered in her chest as her smoky eyes met his warm brown ones. Yes, oh, yes, she had understood his words perfectly! His broad smile convinced her of that.

To love, cherish, honor, and obey! For a lifetime! Andrew wanted her to be his, and yes, she wanted him, too. A hot, tingling sensation spread from her core as she realized the impact of his proposal. It was really too wonderful to be true, but at last she had met a man who suited her needs perfectly and who wanted her as much as she did him.

For a brief, fleeting instant, while she snuggled warmly against Andrew, a dark cloud scudded across her mind. What of Matthew Steele and her past relationship with him? Would she find that same secret, fulfilling thrill with Andrew? No, of course not. She felt no base, animal attraction to this man seated next to her. And that kind of passion hurt too much to live through again. With Andrew she would find a different passion, one abundant with happiness and a peaceful warmth.

Erin blinked the snowflakes from her lashes and looked deeply into Andrew's hopeful eyes. He had said that marriage was a big step, and indeed he was correct. But she didn't care. "Yes, Andrew, I'll marry you."

"What—do you mean that?"

She answered him by throwing her fur-covered arms around his neck and pressing her cold lips to his. It was not a passionate kiss, but one filled with love and adoration. I do love him, in a very special way, she told herself.

"Oh, my! Oh, Erin!" Hattie cried, apparently not knowing just how to react.

"It will be a June wedding. Hattie! I'm so very, very happy!" Erin whirled around the vestibule and shook snow all over the polished tiles. "Can you believe it? *Mrs.* Andrew Cartwright . . . Erin Cartwright . . . Mrs. Erin Conner Cartwright!"

Hattie picked up Erin's hastily discarded fur. "Oh, my. Oh, my," was all she could say.

"What's wrong? You think I'm making a mistake, don't you? Now, don't fib, I can see it in your eyes."

"No . . . well . . . what about that certain person who's bound to come back someday—even if it's only to check on his store?"

Erin's eyes flashed. "I absolutely forbid you to mention *him* and ruin my happiness! Is that clear!" And then, less harshly, "It's been months and months. I'm over him completely. And if you don't believe me, then you're a fool."

"I believe you, Erin. Honestly, I do. But you once told me about a man you often saw in your visions, remember? What about him?"

Erin did not answer for a moment. Then she said, "That vision isn't important now. It must have meant something else, something I've forgotten that's happened already." She picked up Abraham and nuzzled him to her cheek. "Besides," she added gaily, "I can always buy Andrew a buckskin shirt and make him wear my silver nugget!"

Hattie turned down the oil lamp and led the way upstairs. "That's ridiculous, Erin, and you know it!"

"Oh, no, it's not." Erin walked into her bedroom and sat Abraham gently down on the bed. "If that's the way *I* want it, that's the way it will be. Now, good night, Hattie."

As Erin increased the flame of her bedside oil lamp, the room was cast in semi-shadow and the walls glowed with strange, light and dark shapes. Why did Hattie have to mention that silly vision of the faceless man in the buckskin shirt? Erin wondered irritably. She stared at the odd, flickering shadows and vividly recalled the imaginary figure. Suddenly she felt her nerves jangle and grow raw.

"Oh, damn it all, anyway," she whispered. "I'll have what I want in spite of my silly visions. *I will!*"

Chapter 24

Erin had hoped that Andrew would stop by or at least send her a note, but she knew he was entertaining a distant cousin of his wife's and probably could do neither. She sat in her drawing room, surrounded by luxury, bored and oddly tense. Hattie had gone to bed early, complaining of her "damn spring cold," and only Abraham, growing fatter and lazier by the day, was left to keep her company.

It had rained all afternoon, despite the morning sun's attempts to break through the thick gray clouds, but Erin was used to April in the Rockies after all these years.

Leaning back in an overstuffed brocade chair, she absently stroked Abraham's tawny fur while setting her mind to the plans for her June wedding. She was still undecided whether to have a large affair or a small one. True, there were all of Andrew's family from St. Louis, even his grown children . . . A sudden qualm seized her. His children were her age! They would resent her, she knew, and laugh behind their hands at their father in his dotage, taking a wife less than half his age. Erin's brows drew together and her mouth hardened. Let them! she thought. Andrew and I love each other and we'll be happy together. That's all that matters.

Dusk had darkened the room, and Erin thought to rise and turn up the lamps, but the twilight of the day held her enthralled. She felt suddenly giddy and a little strange, as if one of her visions were about to come upon her; sometimes she had such a feeling before an image appeared to her, but often it passed without further incident, as it seemed to be doing now.

The rain continued its steady, monotonous patter, the street lamps appearing as blurry bright circles through the bay window, the trees showing only a sprinkling of new growth.

Erin finally got up and struck a match, then lit the oil lamps. She rang for the kitchen maid before remembering this was her evening off. Sighing, she left the parlor and went down the hall to the sparkling kitchen, where she made herself some hot chocolate from the special Swiss cocoa she had ordered. Then she carried her cup and saucer back to the drawing room and seated herself. She sipped at the sweet, hot liquid—she adored chocolate—and could not help thinking of the many evenings she and Lew had partaken of a cup together. Lord, she still missed him terribly. So many times she had told herself, Lew would like that—I must tell him, or Lew should see this, he'd appreciate it. Then she would remember that he could no longer share a joke or a cozy evening with her.

Sometimes a small, nagging question formed in her mind: was she looking for Lew in Andrew Cartwright? But when she considered her relationship with Andrew, she persuaded herself that this could not be; she was charmed, thrilled, caressed, by Andrew's presence, and not in a fatherly way at all. He was everything she could want in a husband; in a word, he was perfect.

A sudden whim caused Erin to open a drawer in the corner secretary and withdraw the gleaming silver chain with the irregular, molten silver lump suspended from it. She swung the necklace back and forth, watching it catch the lamplight. She would always treasure this first chunk of silver from the mine; it mesmerized her and had a significance she could not quite explain. It was the beginning of her mine, the talisman of her success, but it was also the shining object she had seen in her visions so many times. Well, she thought, she would just have to give it to Andrew—as a wedding present. That was it, a wedding present! He would wear it, and the faceless man in her visions would have Andrew's kindly features. *She* would spin the threads of her *own* destiny.

A sudden, boisterous gust of wind rattled at the windows, obscuring for a moment the sound of a knock at her front door. When the sound was repeated, she spun around in anticipation. It must be Andrew! He had come after all—how wonderful! She walked quickly out of the room, dropping the necklace in the card tray on the drop-leaf table in the vestibule, and pulled open the door, a welcoming smile on her face.

A tall, shadowed figure stood on the threshold, the light rain glistening on the broad-brimmed hat that sat jauntily on the back of the man's head. Oh, Lord, no. It couldn't be . . . But of course it was! Her mind registered shock and an unthinking, irrational fear as if from a child's nightmare.

"Evenin', Erin, Can I come in? It's a bit wet out here." That familiar low drawl . . .

She backed away as he entered, until she stood in the archway that led to the stairs, unreasonably afraid to allow him to come too near. "How dare you . . . how dare you come back here . . . after what you said . . ." Her voice was a hoarse whisper, forced from a constricted throat. Her heartbeats were like drums in her ears.

"Erin, I did want to apologize—some of the things I said were . . . uncalled-for. Let bygones be bygones," Matt said quietly.

"Oh, I see," was all her tight throat would allow.

"I came back to check on the store and, well, because I found that I missed the valley."

"You're dripping water all over the floor." Had that inane comment came from her lips? Her voice sounded so strange, so far away.

"Guess I am," he said, smiling, and began to remove his long, rain-drenched coat.

Erin stood frozen, watching him as if he were a cobra about to attack her. She saw, as if in slow motion, the long coat fall away to reveal what he wore underneath: a fringed, beaded buckskin shirt, open to the waist between thongs that laced it together. Erin gasped and blanched, her hand going to her throat and her eyes searching frantically for the missing piece of the puzzle.

He noticed her horrified gaze. "Sorry. I didn't have time to change my shirt. Been workin' in some rough country lately."

She continued to stare, unable to speak, and Matt narrowed his eyes at her. "You okay?"

She nodded slowly, as if in a trance. He shrugged his broad shoulders. "Mind if I have a drink?"

She nodded again, still feeling as if she were under a serpent's glare. He walked toward her, passing the drop-leaf table and spying the gleaming ornament in the card tray.

"What's this? An interesting piece . . . unusual." He picked up the chain and dangled it in front of him. The swinging nugget threw off dull sparks in the light from the hallway.

Erin's heart leaped, beating at her ribs as if it wanted to flee from her body. The vision! There it was—all the missing pieces joined together! The lightly furred male chest in the buckskin shirt, the gleaming pendant dangling before it! But something was terribly wrong; the face should be Andrew's—warm, comfortable, beloved. Instead, to her horror, it was that of the handsome, brilliant-eyed Matthew Steele!

Erin gave a low moan and sagged against the arched doorframe, closing her eyes tightly. Abruptly, she felt strong hands around her shoulder, leading her to a chair, lowering her into its soft embrace. Still she could not bear to open her eyes, but kept them shut while a horrible, sick fear gripped her.

Finally, after endless minutes, she opened her eyes and faced him.

"You feel all right? You look . . . strange." Matt appeared concerned.

"I'm to be married in two months." Her reply made no sense, but it was all she could think of to say. "I'm marrying Andrew Cartwright . . . he's asked me to marry him and I said yes." She intoned the words as if they were a prayer that, repeated often enough, would come true.

"What?"

Erin stood up, straightening her back with effort. "I am to marry—"

Matt cut across her words. "I heard that. Mighty sudden, isn't it?"

"Whatever it is, Matt . . . it's none of your business!" She found her strength returning.

"I think it *is* my business, Erin." His eyes narrowed as he faced her across the drawing room.

Her shock had passed; she forced the image of Matt and the silver nugget from her mind and felt her fury rising. How dare he walk in here out of the night, out of nowhere, and complicate her life again? He had no right!

"Get out of here, Matt! I told you that last time, and I meant it! Get out of here and go to your own kind of hell! I won't go with you! Get out!" Without waiting for his reaction, Erin whirled, the white ostrich feathers on the neck and hem of her red satin dressing gown fluttering wildly about her, and fled toward the stairs and the safety of her bedroom.

Once inside, with the door locked securely behind her, she flung herself on the bed and buried her head in the pillows.

Why did he have to turn up like the proverbial bad penny? she fumed. And every time he did, *she* ended up feeling miserable. Now, just when everything was perfect, he had to come back and step into the blank outlines of her vision, as if he belonged there, coloring the picture, filling in the details. She should have known something would happen to spoil her happiness. And, of course, he would be the one to do it!

Well, she vowed, this time he wouldn't succeed. She would marry Andrew, and Matthew Steele could go to hell. He wouldn't hold any further power over her, she wouldn't allow it—despite her vision, despite his infernal good looks, despite the fact that she could still conjure up the hard, lithe feel of his body. She would do exactly as she pleased, and what she wanted to do was to marry Andrew.

Nevertheless, no matter how hard or how many times she cried her anger, her anguish, into the pillows, she could not rid herself of a sick feeling about the future. Somewhere, in the deep recesses of her subconscious, Erin knew that her plans were falling to ruin around her. Yet, through sheer determination and willpower, she managed to convince herself that she alone could forge her destiny and that nothing could stop her.

Matt stood in the middle of the drawing room, still staring at the stairs up which Erin's flamelike figure had fled a moment ago.

"Christ!" he muttered. What the hell had caused such a violent reaction from her? Naturally, he'd assumed she would still be angry at him. That Irish temper did not cool easily. And their last meeting had been . . . well, rather unpleasant, to say the least. But she had acted so strangely tonight, staring, white-faced, too shocked by his return. She should have expected him to come back eventually, after all.

He turned slowly and retraced his steps to the front door. What had she said? That she was getting married to someone named Andrew Cartwright. He felt an odd, sinking sensation in the pit of his stomach. Cartwright was probably some greedy, down-at-the-heels miner, looking to get his hands on her money. But Matt could not picture Erin wanting to marry anyone like that; she was too proud, too strong—and too damn smart!

Why should he care? he asked himself. She's grown, she can do what she wants with her life. But a faint despondency settled over him as he grabbed his coat and left her house, closing the door carefully. Somehow he felt she wasn't doing the right thing, that she wouldn't be happy with this . . . whoever the man was. Matt wondered why he should feel that way, or be at all interested in whom she married. They'd had a few pleasurable interludes—nothing more. He'd never cared whether any other female he'd bedded was going to be married. In fact, that usually gave him a great sense of relief. So let Erin Conner marry—what was it to him?

He walked through the drizzle toward Steele's Emporium and pounded on the door, jingling the bell. When his rapping was not answered immediately, he grew impatient and pounded again. Then he saw a light appear in the interior. John, the manager, strode through the dim aisles carrying a lantern, then peered narrow-eyed through the glass window.

"Oh, it's you!" he cried, relieved, when he finally unbolted the door.

"Can I stay here the night, John?"

"Sure, Mr. Steele, but Miss Erin's house is more comfortable . . ."

"Not to me, John. I'd rather stay here."

Matt had a hard time falling asleep that night. Images of Erin in bed with a faceless man, her new husband, were superimposed by flashes of a sad, dispossessed band of Indians. The small remnants of a tribe had to be moved, again, because they were living on one of the railroad's land grants, and the Union Pacific, in poor financial straits, had sold the land to an Eastern speculator. The dispirited group had fatalistically shouldered its belongings and climbed aboard a railroad car to be resettled elsewhere. That had been Matt's last "mission," and he felt soiled, disgusted with himself for being connected with such a huge, impersonal conglomerate. He was tired of kicking around the small folk, the poverty-stricken, the defenseless, to make room for the steel rails that writhed further and further into the country's innards. It was time to call an end to it; the job was wearing him down. Let some other idealistic young fool do it. He was completely disillusioned.

He finally slept, only to dream of Erin staring at him, terrified, screaming "No! No!" over and over again. Yet he had no idea why she was screaming at him, and although he tried to reach her, a thick fog obscured his path. Then she reappeared, smiling and happy. But another man went to meet her, gathering her into his arms and kissing her. Then the fog swirled in again, blanking out the scene, and Matt was powerless to reach them . . .

Chapter 25

It had been over a week since Matt's nightmarish visit, Erin realized, and she was quite in control of herself. No more weeping, no more depression. And she was still going to marry Andrew. A smile lit her face as she thought of her betrothed; she was dressing to meet him for lunch at a new restaurant that was reputed to equal any in New York or even Paris. No one can stand between us now, she told herself, now that I've seen the face of the man in my vision and know the worst. I cannot be *forced* into marriage with *him!*

She smiled gaily and put on the jacket of her new suit, which had a mauve, draped taffeta skirt and a short, matching cape trimmed with rows of swirling black braid. Her swooping straw hat with ostrich plumes was topped by a mauve velvet bow. She tilted the hat at just the right angle in the mirror, noticing that her eyes looked almost purple today, reflecting the color of her costume.

"Hattie! I'm going now! Be back in a couple of hours," she called down the hall.

She had her man drive the trap so that he could return home with it; hopefully, Andrew would have the time to drive her back himself.

As she jounced along the rutted, muddy streets, she suddenly felt dizzy, as if the blood had drained from her head.

The back of her driver's head expanded, his black cap becoming a spreading black cloud, and a picture appeared in the center of the deep miasma: a stagecoach falling over a rocky cliff, pushed by a blinding torrent of snow. Then the vision focused in close, revealing the wrecked coach buried under masses of snow, frozen limbs groping out of the stark whiteness. One of them was—oh, God forbid, it couldn't be true—one of them was Andrew's! Then the picture disintegrated and Erin was staring at the driver's black cap again, her heart in her throat, her hands clenched in her lap. She could feel a sick, cold sweat break out on her brow, and for a moment she sat perfectly still, her mind working furiously. Andrew was in terrible danger! She knew he was planning to take the stage to Leadville tomorrow on business; she also knew now, with a dread certainty, that he could not go.

Curtly she told the driver to hurry, and the horse increased its pace, clip-clopping through the mud. By the time they reached the bank, Erin had worked herself up into a near-hysterical state. She jumped down from the trap, disdaining the driver's attempt to help, gathered up her skirt, and ran inside, unaware of the customers' raised brows. She pushed open the door of Andrew's glass-enclosed office and, panting, leaned over his mahogany desk.

"Erin! What's wrong?" he cried.

"Andrew! Listen to me! I've just seen something—a terrible accident—and you were in it!" She stopped to catch her breath, then looked deeply into his eyes. "Andrew, you must not, under any circumstances, take that stage tomorrow!"

"Erin, dear, sit down and calm yourself." He rose and pulled up a chair, then pressed her into it. "Now, tell me, what's this all about?"

"I have these visions sometimes," she said fiercely, "and I just had one on the way over here. It was a terrible accident—on Independence Pass, I think. And you were there . . . Oh, Andrew, you mustn't go!" She pulled at his hand, trying to make him understand why her heart was gripped with fear.

Andrew's voice was calm, smooth. "Erin, dear. I can see you feel very strongly about this, but one cannot go through life following 'visions,' you know." He stroked her hand, finding it cold and damp. "You're really frightened. Now, what can I do to make you feel better, my love?"

"Don't go tomorrow, Andrew!"

"Tell you what. I've some business to keep me here, so I'll take the stage the next day. Will that suit you?" He smiled at her, still holding her hand.

"I . . . I don't know. Maybe." Erin's brows met in a frown, then her face cleared. "I know! *I'll* go with you! The vision had nothing about me in it, so if I'm there, nothing too bad can happen. Oh, Andrew, say yes! We'll have such fun in Leadville, and I promise I won't bother you during business hours."

"All right, I can see there's no other way to pacify you. We'll both take the stage the day after tomorrow. I do hope people won't gossip, Erin. It's really not proper for an unchaperoned girl to go off—"

"Andrew, don't be silly. We'll have separate hotel rooms—it'll be proper enough. And in Leadville no one gives a hoot, anyway."

He laughed, throwing back his gray, leonine head. "Erin, I'm glad the business world can continue now, with your approval. It cannot stop, you know, even for the premonitions of the most beautiful, charming, and delightful creature west of St. Louis."

She suddenly felt embarrassed. She was making a terrible fuss, barging into his office like this, demanding that he change his plans. She began to fear that he would think her a meddling, flighty female, a drawback as the wife of a respectable banker. Of course he was right—life could not stop because Erin Conner had visions.

"I'm sorry I made such a scene, Andrew." She looked at him shyly. "It's just that I was so worried about you. I couldn't bear to think that you . . ." Her voice faded.

"I know, my love. We'll just forget the whole thing. Now, let's go to lunch. I have a little surprise for you."

The "little surprise" turned out to be a chilled bottle of the restaurant's best French champagne and a small, velvet-lined jewelry box.

Erin opened the box, her heart beating with excitement, and gasped in delight. "Oh, Andrew, it's lovely—so beautiful, so different!" She leaned over and kissed him on the cheek, not caring who in the crowded dining room noticed. "Thank you. Now we're *truly* engaged." She slipped the ring on her finger and held out her hand to admire the sparkling diamond, surrounded by clusters of smoky opals.

"It reminded me of your eyes, Erin. I could not resist it."

"Andrew, I don't know what to say . . . I'm so happy . . ."

The morning of the trip to Leadville, Erin was in a frantic rush to finish the last-minute packing; even with Hattie's help, everything had been topsy-turvy.

"Are you sure you don't want me to come, too?" Hattie asked once again.

"No, really." Erin smiled mischievously as she buckled the last strap on her trunk. "This is to be, well, a sort of honeymoon—only before the wedding!"

They both chuckled, and Hattie finally gave in, saying, "I hope you know what you're doing, Erin."

"Of course I do. Don't I always?" She laughed, then glanced out the window. "Oh, there he is! Help me with the bags. His man will get the trunk."

"Lord, you'd think you were goin' for a year!" Hattie exclaimed, shaking her head.

Besides Erin and Andrew, there were four other passengers in the coach: two businessmen, a reverend, and an elderly spinster lady.

The coach bounced along the rough road toward Independence Pass, retracing the path Erin had been on many times before. The day was warm and overcast, but snow still sat heavily in the high country. Erin paid little mind to the scenery; her attention was fixed on Andrew. Having him to herself for such an extended period of time was a luxury, and she could talk with him to her heart's content.

After crossing the bridges, the stage began the steep ascent through the giant boulders. Erin was listening to Andrew plan their first trip after they were married, when suddenly she heard a far-off, echoing thunder.

"Heavens, it's going to rain again, Andrew. I do hope the road doesn't get washed out—"

Her words were cut off as the thunder grew louder and the coach gave an abrupt sideways lurch. The passengers were thrown in a heap against the door. Through the confusion Erin heard the driver's loud curses and the horses snorting and whinnying in fear, but her overwhelming reaction was one of bewilderment. Then oddly, terrifyingly, the stage seemed to be floating off the road; she could see snow coming in through the windows, pressing against the doors, as if a huge white ocean were engulfing them in its embrace. My God, she thought, an avalanche! The white death!

Erin felt the heavy coach being swept along uncontrollably, and then the doors collapsed. She was pushed tightly against the hard wood, the snow covering everyone inside, sweeping them away from her, pressing around her. In an agony of icy terror, she saw Andrew's face disappear beneath the whiteness and she tried to scream. But the waves of snow bore down on her chest unmercifully and left her gasping for breath. Then came a dizzying, sickening spin . . . darkness . . . murky oblivion.

Matt casually dropped by Erin's house to see if she had calmed down enough to talk; there were some details about the store he wanted to discuss with her. Actually—and he even acknowledged it to himself—this was merely an excuse to see her, and to ask more about the man she was going to marry. Matt had heard from the townsfolk that Cartwright was a good enough fellow—rich, attractive, well mannered—but at least twice Erin's age. What the hell did she want with an old man? Matt wondered in puzzled frustration.

Hattie informed him that Erin had left for Leadville with Cartwright that very morning. "She had one of her visions," Hattie said as she served Matt a cup of coffee in the drawing room, "and insisted that if she went along, nothing would happen to him." Hattie shook her head in mock dismay. "That girl."

"I know what you mean, Hattie. I've had to deal with her stubborn streak for many years. When Erin gets a notion . . ." He laughed.

A knock sounded at the front door and Hattie disappeared to answer it. Matt took this opportunity to study the room for the first time; before, he had been too busy looking at Erin or fighting with her. He thought the parlor was elegant, yet warm and inviting. The colors provided just the right background for Erin's burnished hair and smoky eyes.

Matt's appraisal was cut short by the reappearance of Hattie, followed closely by Sheriff Johnson.

"Mr. Steele," Hattie began, her throat working convulsively until she could continue. "Erin's had . . . an accident. An avalanche . . ." She put her face in her hands and moaned. "They don't know if she's dead or alive!"

"What in hell—!" The words exploded from Matt as he turned to the sheriff.

"It's true, Steele," Johnson said. "The stage to Leadville was caught in one of those spring slides—must have been that rain the other day. The driver was thrown clear—pretty banged up, but he managed to get down to a ranch and ride into town. He was real shaky. Said all he saw was the stage rolling over and disappearing under the snow—horses and all, by damn!"

"My God," Matt whispered, suddenly picturing Erin—beautiful, vibrant Erin—buried under a mountain of white death. "No!" The word escaped unnoticed from his lips while his mind went blank, frozen with horror. Silent moments passed before he could shake off the paralyzing fear and once again become a controlled, detached machine.

"Are you doing anything to rescue them?" he asked the sheriff.

"Doubt if there's much left to rescue, but we're gettin' together volunteers to go on up there and dig out the bodies," Johnson replied flatly.

"I'll meet you there," Matt said, tight-lipped, then turned on his heel and strode purposefully out to the stable.

After saddling up one of Erin's horses, he spurred the mount unmercifully along the tortuous miles, his senses numbed. Eventually, he reached the site of the accident. Men were already gathered there, digging desultorily. Two men were bent over a woman's body, and Matt felt his heart constrict in horror until he saw the face and knew it wasn't Erin's.

He quickly organized the volunteers into a line to probe the hard-packed snow with anything they could find; most had had the presence of mind to bring along a shovel or a pick. More men arrived and joined the group. After several minutes one man shouted, "I've struck something hard—must be a corner of the coach!"

Matt began to dig frantically with his hands, almost clawing away at the snow. He could not admit to himself that Erin was dead. Damn it, no! he swore mutely. She's not dead! He uncovered a limb, cold and stiff, a man's leg in gray pinstriped trousers. He dug further, using a shovel now, and at last succeeded in reaching the inner body of the coach.

"Take it easy, for Pete's sake. There ain't no one left alive in there."

Matt glanced quickly up at the man who had spoken and turned back to his work. He *knew* Erin was in there alive; he had to find her!

The man muttered under his breath at the withering look Matt had given him and spit a brown stream onto the tracked-up snow, hefting his shovel once again. "Damn fool," he said to no one in particular.

Several other workers came to Matt's assistance, but he hardly noticed them, so consumed was he by his single-minded purpose.

Exhausting hours later, their hands blistered, their shirts dark-splotched with sweat, they had found a total of four distorted bodies—but not Erin's. Daylight was beginning to fade into evening. A brilliant red sunset bloomed in the west, on the cloud banks; then it, too, began to fade. The men brought out lanterns, and jugs of hot coffee and sandwiches were sent up by their womenfolk.

A few men sat down to rest and have something to eat, occasionally gulping mouthfuls of whiskey from flasks and bottles. They watched Matt continue his furious assault on the snow and shook their heads in amazement.

"Sure as this snow's cold, there's no one alive in there."

"He's gone daft—won't quit."

"Killin' hisself, the fool."

But Matt heard none of this; nor did he slacken his pace or look up as lantern light took the place of sunlight.

Finally, he felt something soft under his shovel and threw it aside to dig with his bare hands. The snow gave way to a small air pocket in the corner of the coach, and it was there that he found Erin's body, crumpled in a pitiful heap against the smashed wood.

He couldn't extricate her immediately because her legs were still held fast by the snow and the wrecked stagecoach, but he managed to remove the white stuff from her face and shoulders.

Someone held a lantern above his head, and he saw that she had the look of frozen death: pinched, cold, and a little blue around the mouth. But, unbelievably, her skin felt warm to his touch, and her breath showed in tiny puffs of white in the chilly evening air.

"Christ," Matt sighed fervently, suddenly aware of his exhaustion and the soreness of his torn hands.

The other men soon had Erin out and placed her on a

rough woolen blanket, muttering their amazement at the miracle of her still being alive.

Matt bent over her, chafing her hands. "Erin? Erin, can you hear me?"

Moments passed before her eyes fluttered open, focusing blearily on Matt's face. Her voice, when she spoke, was weak. "Where am I . . . ? Matt . . . is that . . . you? What . . . happened? Oh . . . I'm so cold . . ." Her eyes closed wearily, then opened again, shining silver in the light of the lantern. "Andrew?"

"We haven't found him yet, Erin. They're still searching," he said gently, unable to ignore the pain in her eyes.

She turned her head away and murmured, "I knew it . . . I told him . . ." Then she looked back at Matt. "I suppose it's a miracle I'm alive—some miracle! Oh, God, I've lost everything again. I can't bear it!"

"Yes, you can, Erin. You can bear anything you have to. You'll see." He brushed her wet, matted curls away from her forehead. "Come on, kid, I'll take you home." He lifted her from the blanket and carried her to his horse.

"Hold me, Matt. Please hold me. I'm so cold, so cold . . ." Her voice was faint, and full of a sadness that he could hardly bear to hear. He set his horse slowly down the road toward Aspen, cradling Erin sideways across the saddle. She clung to his neck and whispered a wrenching plea, almost as if she were delirious: "Hold me, Matt, hold me."

Chapter 26

It was a full three days after Matt had brought Erin home before she swam up out of a gray murkiness to hear Dr. Barnes talking to Hattie.

"I reckon she'll be all right now, Miss Nelson. Her fever's

gone down. Keep up the hot compresses and steam, and try to get a little nourishment into her."

"Oh, I will, Doctor. I'm so glad to hear she's improving! . . ."

"Tough girl," he remarked admiringly, shaking his head as he went out the door.

"Hattie." Erin's voice surprised herself; it was as faint as a shadow.

Hattie jumped as if stung and ran to the bedside. "Erin! You're awake! Thank the Lord!"

"I'm all right, Hattie. Have they found Andrew?"

"All right, my foot! You've had a fever and been delirious for three days and—"

"Three days! You mean I've been lying here like this for three days?" Erin tried to rise, but fell weakly back on her pillows.

"Yes, honey. And poor Mr. Steele has been here every night, askin' for you."

"Matt? Here?"

"Yes, and furthermore, the man's almost killed himself looking for poor Mr. Cartwright up there, all day, every day." Hattie caught herself. "Oh, I'm sorry. You couldn't know, but they haven't found him yet."

"Matt? Looking for Andrew?" Erin's mind whirled in confusion.

"Yes, Erin, and I'll tell you something from my long years of experience with men. That man *cares* for you." She wiped Erin's damp forehead with a cool cloth.

"I don't know . . . But if he's been searching for Andrew . . . Oh, it all seems so hopeless!"

"There, there. You'll feel better when you've eaten something. You'll mend quick now. Oh, Erin, it's like you were returned from the other side of the grave! What would I have done without you?" Hattie leaned down and gave Erin a quick kiss on her cheek. "Mr. Steele has been askin' to see you. Should I send him up when he comes again?"

"I guess so, Hattie. I do owe him my thanks, after all . . ."

"Yes, you do, Erin. My God, he saved your life."

"I know, Hattie, but I wonder if it would've been better if he hadn't . . ."

"Stop that! You've no right to say such a thing!"

"They had no right to die and leave me all alone!" Erin cried weakly.

"You're not all alone, just remember that. Now, try to rest. I'm going to cook you up a good broth, like the doctor said."

When Hattie reached the bottom of the stairs, she was not surprised to find Matt waiting there, hat in hand.

"She woke up, finally, and Dr. Barnes thinks she's on the mend. But she's still weak." Hattie put a hand on his arm. "Go up and see her, if you want, Mr. Steele. It'll make you feel better."

Climbing the familiar stairs, Matt gritted his teeth, knowing that he alone had to break the sad news to her. He entered her bedroom and bent over her still form, whispering her name. At last he saw her eyes open.

"Matt." It was said so simply, yet so full of feeling. "Thank you."

"Erin, I must tell you straight out. We found Cartwright's body this morning. He's at the mortuary now, and they're waiting for instructions. I didn't know what to tell them . . ."

"I'll see to it, Matt. He would have wanted me to, I know. I'll get Hattie to take a note over tomorrow. I'm so tired now . . ." Erin spoke with control, yet inside, she again felt the black hand of doom seize her heart.

"Of course you're tired. You've been terribly ill, and at first we were afraid of frostbite. Lucky it wasn't any colder out there." He took her hand in his. "Take it easy, kid. That was a close one."

She smiled sadly, thinking to herself that she always survived somehow, but that being a survivor wasn't necessarily a blessing. Poor Andrew . . . but Matt didn't want to hear her grieve over a lost love. That wouldn't be fair to him. He'd already been through enough these past days.

"Remember when I nearly froze my hands trying to hang up the wash?" she asked him. "I think that hurt worse, to tell the truth."

"I remember. You always were a fool kid, biting off more than you could chew." He grinned at her, his blue eyes crinkling. "Rest, now, and get better, Erin."

She lifted a finger and traced the cleft in his stubbled chin. "You look awfully tired yourself, Matt."

"Yeah, sure, kid."

The next two days passed fitfully for Erin. Matt did not come to see her again, but Hattie was there constantly, trying to get her to eat, brushing her hair, regaling her with anecdotes of the household. Erin began to feel better physically and left her bed from time to time, to sit in the blue velvet chair by the window. There she would stare for hours at the expanse of Aspen Mountain, but the view did not alleviate her apathetic state of mind. Something had been obliterated in her—a spark, a vitality. She had no real desire to proceed with her life. Matt had told her that she was strong enough to bear whatever she had to, but to be strong, to be a survivor, was burdensome. It meant she had to go on alone, picking up the broken pieces and trying to mend them. And this time it was Andrew who had suffered and died. She had a terrible conviction that he had died because of her, because of her sin of pride in trying to defy her vision. Anyone who stood between her and her destiny was bound to be destroyed; she should have known that.

She leaned her elbow on the windowsill and rested her forehead against her fist, a fresh spill of hot tears coursing down her cheeks. Hadn't she shed enough tears for Andrew? How could there be any left after so much sobbing? And because her future seemed bleak, she felt afraid to start a relationship with another man, for surely he would be taken away from her, too. The only man who kept coming back again and again was Matthew Steele; *he* was the one who had fleshed out the man in her visions, the man she had built up in her mind as someone significant in her life. What a fool she had been, thinking she was in control of everything, happy, secure!

Erin had taken care of the funeral arrangements for Andrew, sending word through Hattie. The date was set for the day after tomorrow. Erin was determined to attend the funeral, despite Hattie's concern for her health. It was the least she could do. She had decided that if his family protested his burial in Aspen, she would fight it, for she knew that Andrew Cartwright had loved his adopted city and would want to rest forever in the earth that was a part of it.

Erin spent the next two nights lying awake in bed, reliving her time with Andrew, wondering if she could have done better, could have saved him somehow. She also thought of Matthew Steele. He had saved her life, as Lew had once done—how ironic—and what had Lew said then? Something about being responsible for a person forever after you'd saved his life. She knew that Matt had worked frantically to find her, long after a sane person would have given up. Why? Why had fate chosen *him* to do it? Why couldn't Andrew have been the one to rescue her? Then they could have lived happily ever after, as if they belonged in a fairy tale . . .

On the day of Andrew's funeral—a bright, warm spring day—Erin donned the same black voile dress she had worn to Lew's funeral. Now the garment hung loosely on her, for she had grown thinner, almost gaunt, and it emphasized the dark circles under her eyes.

She and Hattie rode to Ute Cemetery behind the carriage bearing the pinewood casket. A small group of people stood around the freshly dug grave. As Erin approached the mourners, a figure detached itself from them and greeted her.

"Erin, I'm terribly sorry. I just wanted to tell you that."

She felt so drained of emotion, so empty and cold inside, that Matt's low drawl had no effect on her now.

"Thank you, Matt. I appreciate your sympathy."

"Can I do anything, Erin? Anything at all?" He took her elbow as if they were good friends, as if he belonged at her side, and guided her close to the minister, who was beginning the eulogy.

Erin had not answered Matt, but he accepted her silence with grace. Throughout the service he stood by her side, and in her grief and loneliness, she was comforted to have someone she knew from the past standing next to her. This was proof that not everyone from long ago was dead. She tried to remember that Matthew Steele was the one man she should avoid at all costs, but grief had dulled the intensity of her ambivalent feelings toward him.

She sneaked a quick look at his profile through her black veil. Matt was still as handsome as ever. Today he wore an elegantly cut black broadcloth suit, not a buckskin shirt. Was he really the man in her visions, or had that been merely a coincidence? He kept reappearing in her life in spite of her wishes—even, she thought suddenly, in spite of his own. Could it be possible that they shared the same destiny? How unfair, how terribly unfair.

For the first time since Erin had arrived at the cemetery, she began to weep uncontrollably. She did not try to stifle her sobs, but let them come forth freely, from the depths of her soul. She could not have said whom she cried for—herself or Andrew Cartwright—but two words kept whirling relentlessly through her head: *how unfair, how unfair, how unfair . . .*

The minister's voice carried above the sound of her weeping. "The Lord is my shepherd, I shall not want . . ."

Chapter 27

Erin's hand trembled so violently that Matt came over to the sideboard and took the decanter from her.

"Would you like a brandy, too, Matt?"

"If it's not too much trouble, I'd prefer black coffee." He looked at her closely, doubting that she was capable of even such a small task. "Listen, if you don't mind, I'll just go to the kitchen and fix it myself."

"Oh, no, I'll have the cook—"

"Erin, don't you remember? You said you gave the servants the afternoon off."

"Oh . . . I suppose I did at that." She sighed deeply, suppressing the urge to weep again. "Well, then, let's go to the kitchen . . . I feel like keeping busy."

Matt followed her down the hall into the cooking area; he remembered her in that black dress at Lew's funeral. Somehow she seemed older now, yet it wasn't quite a year since his father had died. He watched her reach for the coffee canister on the shelf, catching the way her breasts curved so softly when she moved.

"Here, Erin, I'll do that." Their hands brushed for an instant while he measured the coffee beans.

She sat down at the small wooden cook's table near the rear window. She seemed to forget his presence as she stared unseeingly through the pane and sipped from her brandy glass.

"Would you like to talk? It might help."

"I don't know . . . I really don't feel . . . anything." Erin finished her drink. "You could get me another brandy."

"Are you sure? I mean, it's bound to make you feel worse in the long run."

227

But she had turned her attention to the window again. Matt shrugged his shoulders and left the kitchen with her empty glass.

When he returned, his cup of coffee was ready for him.

"Matt, you've been awfully kind, considering . . ." Erin smiled at him timidly.

"Look, kid, I didn't know the man, but I'm sure if you loved him, he was a good sort."

"I didn't love him." Now, why had she said that? It wasn't true at all. Matt's intense blue gaze seemed to bore into her. "I'm so confused right now. Of course I loved him, but . . . but not like . . ."

"I know what you mean, Erin."

"No, you don't—you don't understand."

Matt smiled noncommittally. "You're tryng to tell me that you never slept with him."

Good Lord! Were there no limits to his arrogance? She bit her lower lip and said sharply, "Matt, there are some things that are none of your business. Is that quite clear?"

He laughed. "Yes, Erin, quite. But nevertheless, it's true, isn't it?"

"I've never liked that about you, the way you constantly need to have your male pride reaffirmed. But, if it will make you feel any better, no, I didn't sleep with Andrew. Mind you, if I'd wanted to I would have."

He was silent for a time while he sat gazing at her, liking what he saw. "I guess you're right about that. It was important for me to know that about you. It makes what I have to say easier."

She took a long swallow of brandy. What was he up to now? "Matt, don't mince words with me. I'm just too tired, too drained."

"Erin, there's no better way than just to come out and say it—my offer of a year ago still stands."

Her eyes widened in surprise. "Marriage?"

"Yep. Lew was right. You know it and so do I. You can't go through life alone—and take that indignant look off your face. I sure don't want to argue."

"Neither do I. The answer is still no, Matt. I'll pick my own husband." Erin hoped he could not see how her hand trembled. "Get me another brandy, please. I think I'm going to need it."

This time Matt did not argue, but left her alone once again

to refill the glass. She could not believe he would still offer her marriage. What was in it for him? Was he so full of himself that he couldn't take a simple "no" for an answer? Or . . . did he care for her? She dismissed that idea quickly. There had to be a reason, but it eluded her completely. Well, she mused as she watched his tall frame approach her, she would find out this time.

"Matt, why do you want to marry me?" she asked bluntly.

He sat back down, his face an unreadable mask. "Good question. It's partly for Lew, true enough, but it's also because I really think you need to be taken care of." He saw her brow arch, but he continued. "And I also feel a certain duty for the times I . . . I let my desires, ah, run free, shall we say?"

Erin was embarrassed, but it wouldn't do to show him. "That's ridiculous—what I mean is, that's no reason at all to get married." Then she quickly added, "Besides, you'd probably have to marry half the girls in the West if that were the case." What had she stooped to now? She drained her glass again.

Matt's lips spread in a wide grin. "Does that bother you, Erin?"

"Certainly not!"

"Then marry me. You've nothing to lose."

Would he never quit! Yet in the back of her mind flashed the undeniable fact that *he* was the man in the buckskin shirt! What could she do?

"Look, Erin, I know this is a bad time, what with Cartwright gone—"

"It's a bad time, all right, Matthew Steele!" Her eyes blazed with anger. "Do you realize that *I'm* the reason he died? It was *my* fault!"

"Lord, I knew you'd drunk too much!" His warm hand covered her trembling one.

"You don't see, do you? It's that crazy vision—any man I tried to marry would die! I just know it."

Matt dropped her hand and rose, a look of irritation gathering on his features. "A vision! I really think you've lost your mind."

"I don't care what you think." Erin rose, too, then blurted out everything that the vision contained. "So all along it *was* you! But for once I'm going to fight it! I'll change my destiny somehow—"

"Like hell you will!" He grabbed her arm and pulled her to him. "If—and I say *if*—you really *can* see things, then why don't you just stop fighting and say yes?"

"Because—because we'd be miserable! I don't love you! I don't even *like* you most of the time!"

Matt let out a string of oaths and drew her closer, nearly crushing the breath from her. "And *I* am starting to dislike you, too, my dear. But we always have this . . ." His mouth came down on hers, forcing her lips apart in a painful kiss. Abruptly, he tore his mouth away. "You don't hate *that,* do you? Do you? Dammit!"

She fought against his overpowering strength while also fighting against her brimming tears.

"Answer me!"

"You—you just love to shame me, don't you? To see me lose control!"

"You bet I do. You think you're so damn strong, but you're not—not when it comes to—"

"Stop it!" she sobbed bitterly. "Stop it . . . *please!*"

"No." He backed her up against the wall. "That's one thing you can't hide from me—your response."

"All right! I admit it! And I hate myself for being so weak!" She turned her head to one side, unable to face his penetrating stare.

"Have there been others?" His tone was dangerous.

"You're a bastard! I hate you!"

"Answer me!"

"No! No!" she shrieked. "Only you—and that other son of a bitch in Denver!"

Matt had not expected such a lashing. He quickly snatched his hands away and strode across the room. When he faced her again, his expression was almost sheepish. "Look . . . I didn't come here to fight, or to hurt you. I don't even really care if you've slept with every man in Aspen . . ." He grinned slowly. "We do seem to hurt each other, don't we?"

She slumped weakly against the wall. The funeral, the exhaustion, the brandy, were taking their toll—and Matt had pushed her beyond her limits. She tried desperately to regain her composure.

"All I want," she said with great effort, "is to live in peace . . . to have my mine, my house. Why must you always torment me?"

"Damn your house and damn your mine! You don't need

all this." He made a sweeping gesture with his hand. "You need a *man,* Erin!"

Her head was swimming, aching abominably. She pressed her fingers to her temples. "I don't love you . . . I loved Andrew . . . the nugget . . . the buckskin shirt . . . I'm so terribly confused."

Matt was at her side in one long step. He picked her up in his arms and carried her down the hall to the stairs. "I warned you about the brandy, and you've been sick," he muttered roughly.

"You'd make me give up my silver mine . . . I wouldn't be myself . . ."

Once upstairs in her room, he placed her on the blue silk spread and began to undo the tiny buttons at her throat. "You can keep the damn mine, you can do whatever the hell you want, I don't care. But just never deny me your bed. That's the one thing I'll not give in on." His lips grazed the soft flesh of her bosom and he murmured, "God, Erin, you're so lovely."

Matt quickly shed his clothes, his eyes never leaving the intoxicating sight of her creamy, rose-tipped breasts, her coppery hair spread luxuriously over the blue coverlet. He reached down and eased Erin carefully out of her dress and chemise, revealing her legs as he pulled off each stocking. And when he was done, and Erin lay staring mutely up into his face, he stood there for several minutes just regarding her perfectly formed body.

Erin felt his gaze fall hotly on her flesh; a gnawing ache spread through her stomach. Wasn't this the moment she had so often dreamed of and fought against, that of Matt standing over her with a look of longing in his eyes?

"Marry me, Erin. At least we'll always have this."

He was right! Oh, God, it was bitter, ironic! But he was right . . . what else could she do? He said she could keep the mine, do anything she wanted. There was no choice left . . .

"Yes," Erin whispered, "I'll always loathe you, Matthew Steele, but yes . . . yes." She repeated the word again and again as he sat on the edge of the bed and expertly stroked her smooth flesh from her ankles to her shoulders until she moaned aloud with desire. Still his hands explored her every hollow and curve, eliciting further cries to escape her lips. She was desperate to feel him inside her.

Yet Matt took his time; she was his now to explore, to

arouse, to enjoy. He traced the path of his fingers with his mouth, shocking Erin with the intensity of her own passion. She stiffened momentarily when his lips and tongue caressed her inner thighs, then a stabbing shaft of pleasure overcame her reason. Involuntarily, she screamed aloud from the sweet, blessed ache that threatened to consume her until she had been completely fulfilled.

With each flick of his tongue, each far-reaching thrust, Erin's body whirled and spiraled. Again and again she reached a peak, each one shocking her with its newness. When at last Matt entered her, she climbed aloft with him to the summit of ecstacy, moaning, "Yes, oh, yes . . ."

It was well past noon the next day when Hattie's knock awakened Erin. "Just a minute," she mumbled, stretching languorously. Suddenly her hand touched Matt's shoulder blade. "Oh! I'll—I'll be down shortly."

He rolled onto his stomach and propped himself up on his elbows. "Good morning, Erin. Did you sleep well?"

That incredibly low drawl of his! "You know darn well I didn't—you kept me awake all night! And probably the servants, too!"

"We're to be married, aren't we? They'll just have to get used to the noise!" He chuckled deeply.

"Oh, Matt, you're infuriating! But that does mean we'll live here, doesn't it?"

He thought a moment. "I guess we'll have to, for a time. I can't really take you to some of the places where I go on business."

Erin sat up and covered her breasts with the bed sheet, which caused Matt to quirk a dark brow. "Matt, about your business . . . I think I have a right to know—well, if it involves using your guns." There, it was said, and she did have a right, after all.

"Sometimes . . . only as a very last resort." He pushed himself up to a sitting position. "I've never drawn first, if that's what you're asking."

Why did he sound so embittered? Erin wanted to ask him more, but she feared he would retaliate by bringing up the subject of her mine. For some reason, the fact that she had more wealth than he seemed to grate on him. She best let the subject of his "business" alone for now.

Matt tugged on his pant legs and pulled in his flat abdomen

to do up the buttons. Erin noticed how perfectly his muscles flexed as he dressed.

"When should we tie the knot, Erin?" he asked.

"Oh," she said blankly. "I hadn't really thought about it. When do you want to?"

"Soon. I have an appointment in Denver in a few weeks." He buttoned up his white shirt.

"Just set the date, Matt. We'll have it here, with just a few friends."

"Oh, no, Erin." His voice was edged with anger. "We'll marry in the church."

"But, Matt! This is my home. I want to be wed right here!"

"Look, kid, I've given in to all your whims for some time now. You can keep the mine, the house, even wear the same wedding dress you planned for Cartwright—I really don't care. But I'll have my way on a few things." He stuck his hat on, letting it tilt back recklessly. "I thought I made it plain last night what I want from you."

Erin gasped. "What did you say?"

"I meant, before you fly off into a rage, that there are a few husbandly rights I want when I'm around. One of them is to find you here, in Aspen. The other is to pick the place of our wedding. All right?"

Erin thought for a minute. There was no point in arguing now; she would get her way in the end. Matt wouldn't be that adamant about it. Furthermore, he was openly allowing her total freedom—at least when he was away, which was often. And then there was this feeling of fate between them, that the vision would indeed come true. But for how long! Nothing in it had ever told her that she had to love and obey him. In a peculiar way, marriage to Matt would set her free—free to do what she pleased!

She drew a deep breath. "In the church. That's fine, Matt."

"Good." Leaning over her, he brushed his lips against the nape of her neck, then lower for an instant. "By the way," he whispered, "I enjoy the way you loathe me." And with that he was out the door, closing it quietly behind him.

Erin took a long, hot bath after Matt had left, and let all her conflicting emotions surface, testing them one by one. Yet the main focus of her attention was the fact that her life had changed remarkably in a relatively short time. She missed Andrew's company dearly, but, like her immediate family and Lew, he was gone. For a brief, fleeting moment she was almost sorry she had not allowed him to bed her. Then she could have thrown that little truth in Matt's shocked face yesterday afternoon.

But as Erin relaxed in the tub, she recalled the feel of Matt's hands on her naked, tingling flesh. He had been right about one thing, she thought with grim amusement. They would always have that glorious, deep longing for each other, would always need each other for fulfillment.

Chapter 28

Amber fingers of predusk crept across the western ridge of Smuggler Mountain, faintly streaking the Oriental carpet in the drawing room. Matt had been gone all afternoon, and as Erin sat watching the dust motes in the pale light, she began to wonder if he planned on dining with her or eating with John at the emporium. And where did he intend to sleep that night? Certainly not at her house again! There were some proprieties they had to observe. She rose and started to pace the floor, annoyed that she didn't know what Matt planned to do or when he would appear on her threshold.

Hattie entered the drawing room. "Should I have Cook hold dinner?" she asked.

"Of course not! Why do you ask such a question? You never have before."

"Well . . . I just thought you might want to wait for Mr. Steele, that's all. You needn't bite my head off."

Erin narrowed her eyes. "Hattie, this is still *my* house. You behave as if Matthew Steele had something to say about *my* affairs!"

"That's unfair, Erin. I only thought, since you told me you are to be married that you might want to dine later."

"That's another thing, this business of the marriage—I

don't know how I let myself be talked into it, I truly don't. It must have been the brandy . . . and Andrew's funeral upset me terribly."

"Why in heaven's name did you say yes if you weren't sure?" Hattie appeared dumbfounded.

"I . . . I really don't know why." Erin sat back down on the settee, a look of confusion clouding her brow. "All I know is that Matt has an odd power of persuasion—it's as if he doesn't hear, or understand, the word 'no.'"

Hattie would have loved to pry more out of Erin, but a knock at the front door distracted her and she went out to answer it.

A few moments later Erin heard Matt's easy laughter echoing from the vestibule, then a lilting chuckle from Hattie. How deftly he charmed the ladies! She could picture the enchanted smile on Hattie's face while Matt chatted with her as if they were old friends. Hattie should know better than to allow a flirt like Matt to affect her so foolishly.

"Hello, Erin. Sorry I was gone so long, but I ran into a couple of old friends. Then there was the license to see about." Matt poured himself a brandy as if he owned the house. Only as an afterthought did he say, "Mind if I help myself?"

"Not at all." Erin's tone was edged with annoyance, and she felt a tight knot in her stomach.

"I talked to the minister today. He seemed to think—"

She rose nervously and interrupted him. "I don't care what he thought! The very least you could've done was to consult me before going!"

"Would you like me to go out and come back in again, or are you looking for a fight?"

He was right, of course; she was spoiling for an argument. "Hattie," she called, "have dinner served," and without another word, she proceeded toward the dining room. If he's hungry, he'll follow, she thought to herself.

As she seated herself at the long mahogany dining table, Matt appeared in the portal. But instead of sitting down to the meal or chastising her, he just stood there quietly and stared at her.

Erin was unnerved to see a closely guarded mask of indifference cloak his face. It was as if they were total strangers viewing each other for the first time. Erin, however, refused to speak first; she quickly ladled soup into her bowl and began to eat, displaying the most casual facade she could put forth.

If Matt Steele thought he was going to barge in and out of her life at any given time and then proceed to act as if he owned her, he certainly had a surprise in store! She fumed. The wedding had not yet taken place, and at this point, she wondered if it ever would. Why had she said yes? To have a few shared moments in her bedroom? Impossible! She couldn't be that weak!

Silence hung in the air like an October mist blanketing the valley. At last, when Erin's nerves were raw, Matt spoke.

"I think we'd best come to an understanding."

"I agree," said Erin, laying aside her spoon.

"I've always thought of you as capable—brave even, considering all you've been through. But there are a few things that have to change."

She remained silent but felt somewhat more relaxed when he finally sat down and spread his napkin across his lap; at least he was speaking to her now.

"You're entirely too independent, which is fine up to a point, but in the long run it's bound to cause you trouble." He saw her look of bewilderment. "Listen, your independence caused that scene in Denver City way back—"

"That's not true!" she snapped.

"Oh, yes, it is. Any other young girl would have stayed with the wagon train that gave her shelter; you tried to take care of yourself. The result being . . ."

"No, Matt, You're wrong. The *man* who brought me into Denver City was too . . . difficult, and he wouldn't take me along," she cried painfully. "He sold me into that house!"

"Maybe, I don't know. Just seems to me there were other ways, other jobs. And then that business of killing Mortimer instead of leaving it to the police—"

"Oh, Matt, didn't I tell you? He lived! I found that out when I went back to Madame Lucille's."

"When *what?* Damn it all, Erin, explain that!" Matt slammed his spoon on the table and jumped to his feet.

"But you knew, of course you did . . . Hattie is from Madame Lucille's. I went there to—well, just to return to the place. Never mind. You wouldn't understand."

"Christ! Are you telling me you actually went back to that

whorehouse? And alone, no doubt! Are you insane?"
He strode over to her, his fists clenched whitely at his
sides.

"It was after Lew died, and I had a lot of things to clear up.
At least I found out I wasn't a murderer . . . and I found
Hattie, too." She could see that Matt's temper was strained to
the breaking point. Oh, why did he have to be so—so
possessive?

"And that damn mine! That's the biggest farce of all! A
mine is man's work!"

"A farce!" Her hand indicated the rich furnishings of the
dining room. "You call all this a farce? I assure you, it's quite
real!"

He turned abruptly and went to stand at the window near
the mahogany breakfront. After a time, he said, "You just
don't understand, do you? You've had to fend for yourself a
long time." He glanced back at her. "Maybe marriage will
settle you down, help you ease into a proper role."

"My life is proper enough right now, thank you all the
same. Why should I want to change it?" Erin pushed herself
away from the table. "I've been thinking. Maybe a marriage
between us would be a mistake."

"Back to that again? Well, forget it—the wedding is on. I
started to tell you that the minister thinks we should keep it
private, under the circumstances of Cartwright's recent
death."

"I refuse to be drawn into an argument, Matt. And it seems
that last night you promised some things you've no intention
of carrying out." He began to say something, but Erin held
up a hand. "No, wait. Let me finish. You said I could keep the
house and the Silver Lady and that you'd give me no trouble.
Now all you can talk about is how things are going to change.
I take it that means you'll start dictating to me the minute
the wedding is over!" She headed toward the drawing
room.

He followed her inside. "You're certainly taking no
chances, are you? Gonna make me swear on a stack of Bibles
that I'll say nothing to interfere in your life? Come on, be
reasonable, Erin."

She seated herself on the settee. "I think I am. I've got a lot
of things that are special to me—I know you don't understand
that—but I've worked hard to get where I am. I'm . . .

grateful you're concerned about my welfare, but I don't want to change my lifestyle. It's important to me, Matt."

"All right, all right. I'll stick by what I said. You can do whatever pleases you with this damn house—the mine, too. Just remember, I meant what I said about your being here when I want you. I'll not change my position on that."

Erin thought he sounded too obliging, that he was giving in too easily, not like the Matt who always got his own way. Perhaps he really didn't care what she did, which would suit her just fine. On the other hand, it was unlike him to possess something he did not control completely.

The hour was growing late, the dinner spoiled as far as she was concerned. Yet as physically tired as she was, Erin could not help but wonder about so many things. She walked over to the bay window and gazed out at the darkness beyond. "Matt, why are you really marrying me?" she asked. "I'd like a straight answer."

He came up behind her, his hands resting on her slim waist. "Look, Erin, I told you before. For one thing, I promised Dad, but mostly, I guess a man ought to take a wife at some point. I've never afforded myself the luxury of falling in love so why shouldn't I marry someone I desire physically?"

"You have a way with words, Matt," Erin replied bitterly, wishing he wouldn't stand so close.

"You know what I mean."

"Yes, although I'm not sure I care for your attitude. Just allow me my freedom, that's all I ask." Marry him, she surmised, and the vision will at last come to pass; there was no fighting it any more. Accept the reality of her strange fate and pray that her marriage would usher in a broader kind of freedom than was afforded a single woman.

She turned around to face him. "I guess, in a way, we need each other . . . we need the respectability that a marriage can give us."

"And we always have this." His lips brushed her neck. "What I said a moment ago, about wanting you . . . I like what we have." It was inevitable that his mouth would cover hers, slowly at first, then with a growing urgency that left her clinging to his tall frame.

Even while her mind rebelled against her desire for him, her lips parted involuntarily and she began to return his kisses. There was no doubt where Matthew Steele would sleep tonight.

At one o'clock the following afternoon, when the sun beat warmly on the dusty Aspen streets, Erin and Hattie were stopped in their tracks while entering the post office.

Several yards away, two grizzly old miners had come to drunken blows over a claims dispute, each struggling ineffectually to pull a gun on the other.

Erin backed up against the doorframe of the post office, her hand covering her mouth in shock. As her gaze was transfixed by the two men, her vision became hazy; she swayed dizzily, fighting desperately against the oncoming sight.

Hattie tugged on her arm. "Oh, God, this is dreadful— we've got to get out of here!"

Hattie's voice reached Erin as if from a great distance, but she was unable to move.

And then what had been two fighting men became a single entity, a well-remembered figure from Erin's past. It was her uncle Edward; tall, proud, and despicable, his thin lips pulled back in a slow grin, his mouth moving as if to speak.

For a moment Erin could not understand him, but soon his voice sharpened and his words echoed in her mind. "Thought you were high and mighty, didn't you? Now look at you . . . you had it coming." He repeated these odd words, and then his image was superimposed by a wave of fragmented limbs, until Erin once again saw the miners before her, surrounded by others engaged in the act of separating them.

"Are you okay, Erin? Oh, my gosh!" came Hattie's welcome voice.

Erin wiped the perspiration from her brow and breathed deeply. "I . . . I'm fine, now. I'm sorry . . ."

Sheriff Johnson approached the two women. "Understand you witnessed the whole thing, Miss Erin."

"Well, yes . . . actually, not really. We only heard a few harsh words, and then, before anyone could intervene, they both tried to draw on each other."

"No one drew first?"

"It all happened so fast, Sheriff. I'm afraid I'm not much help, am I?" In truth, she was not. Her head was swimming with the memory of her vision, and she was barely able to answer the few simple questions Sheriff Johnson put to her. She heard Hattie reply for her; still she could not shake off the dreadful sinking feeling left by the sight of her uncle. What had he meant by the words "you had it coming"?

Suddenly Erin found herself hurrying down the streets in a frantic attempt to get home. She had to check on the Silver Lady as fast as possible. Or perhaps something had happened to her house—a fire? She was certain that through the image of her uncle she had received a message of impending disaster. It might even refer to Matt, but somehow she sensed not.

At the house—which appeared safe and secure—Erin changed into denim pants and a blue plaid shirt, hastily tossing her print chambray dress on the bed. Her carefully arranged hair fell loosely around her shoulders, but she didn't care how she looked. She cared only about reaching the Silver Lady to reassure herself that all was well. In her mind's eye she envisioned a cave-in, perhaps an explosion, the timber supports blazing unimpededly. She grabbed her jacket and flew down the stairs into the vestibule, tearing open the front door.

The next thing Erin knew, she was lying in a heap on her front steps and gasping for breath. She had collided with Matt and the air had been knocked out of her.

"You'll be all right in a minute, Erin," he assured her. "I can't leave you alone for a minute, can I?" he added teasingly.

She could not speak, but through her blurred vision she saw the minister, Reverend Arnold, standing next to Matt. What on earth was *he* doing here? she wondered. What was Matt up to now?

When her breath returned, so did her panic over the mine. "Oh—I've got to go—the mine—something's wrong up there!" She jumped to her feet and began to race toward the street.

Matt grabbed her by the back of her belt and forced her to halt. "Wait a minute—what are you talking about?"

"Let me go! I . . . I had a vision—something's terribly wrong!"

Surprisingly, he appeared concerned, as if he had finally come to believe in Erin's gift. "Are you sure?"

"Well, no . . . it wasn't clear this time. But something's wrong, something I can't see exactly. Please—come with me!"

Matt led her through the gate to the middle of the street,

from where they could view the face of Aspen Mountain through the foliage. "Look, you can practically see the Silver Lady entrance from here. There's nothing wrong at all."

Erin stood frozen, her eyes searching the area; she could see the pale green stand of aspens that fronted the entrance to her mine. Everything seemed peaceful, undisturbed. She let out a deep sigh. Matt was right; she knew it, felt it. Yet the nagging feeling of impending trouble would not leave her; she was positive that some form of disaster lurked in the shadows, but she did not know where or when it would strike.

"Erin, I've got to leave soon," Matt said as they walked back across the pebbly street. "I've been thinking that we haven't time for a big wedding, or even a small one."

"What?" The breath catching in her throat, she stopped and looked up into his face, then over to Reverend Arnold, who was still standing at her front door.

"Listen," Matt said gently, "I was pretty selfish to demand a church wedding. We'll do it your way—right here, right now." A charming smile upturned his lips.

"But I—I need more time! I haven't a dress—"

"Hurry up and change. We'll wait."

Her mind whirled. They would be married today—*immediately*. She would be Mrs. Matthew Steele. It was really going to happen; no more secret encounters in bed to bring a hot blush to her cheeks. They would be legally wed. Her heart threatened to burst with a strange unfamiliar sensation of excitement.

While Erin stood motionless, seemingly unable to cope with the suddenness of Matt's plans, Hattie appeared around the corner.

"Oh, there you are! I couldn't imagine where you'd run off to!" she said breathlessly.

Before Erin could reply, Matt took Hattie by the arm. "Erin and I are getting married today—right now, in fact. See if you can help her dress—it doesn't have to be fancy."

It took a full two hours for Erin to ready herself. But when she slowly descended the stairs, Matt's growing impatience fled instantly. She wore a gown of pale beige silk, the low neckline and fitted sleeves trimmed in off-white Belgium lace, the skirt section full and without a bustle. Her skin was peachy, glowing from her bath, and her hair was coiled atop her head in loose ringlets that shone like spun gold. She wore tiny diamond earrings and a single strand of emeralds and diamonds around her neck. Only Erin and Hattie knew that the gown was a simple, hastily altered lounging robe.

When Erin reached the bottom step, Matt stepped forward to take her trembling hand. He leaned over, his lips brushing her hair. "Shouldn't have bothered to dress so beautifully, kid. Now all I can think about is undressing you!"

She could feel a warm blush spread from her chest up to her cheeks, a hot surge in her stomach. "Don't . . . you embarrass me . . . they'll hear!" she whispered.

Arm in arm, the couple walked into the drawing room, where Hattie and the servants stood in a line to witness the ceremony. Reverend Arnold waited patiently near the south window. Matt looked devilishly handsome; he wore a white silk shirt, open at the throat, under a casual brown suede jacket. His thick dark hair gleamed wickedly where the late-afternoon sunlight struck it.

Erin barely heard a word that Reverend Arnold spoke; she could feel Matt's intent gaze on her face and on the firm flesh swelling above the deep cut of her gown. She tried to fix her smoky eyes on the minister's lips, to answer his questions without stumbling over her words, but it was as if she were part of a dream and unable to function properly. Ironically, Matt was completely at ease as he replied to Reverend Arnold's simple questions.

To Erin the seconds dragged by endlessly, and when the final, binding question was put to her, all she could hear was Abraham's "meow" from the couch behind them. The minister had to repeat himself. "Do you take this man to be your lawfully wedded husband?"

"Yes . . . I do." I *think* I do, her mind cried silently.

An eternity later, Matt bent his head and kissed her soundly, but all she could feel was the reassuring grasp of his hand. Then he broke the embrace and spoke a few quiet words to Reverend Arnold, who nodded his head, smiled, and took his leave.

The servants and Hattie congratulated them warmly, then also departed. Erin, feeling rather awkward, was left alone with her new husband.

"It wasn't exactly a wedding befitting the famed Silver Lady of Aspen, but I'm kinda glad now," Matt sighed. "Don't think I could have stood all the to-do." He walked over to the sideboard.

"Well, I guess I'm glad, too. It's funny, but I'm so nervous now that I couldn't possibly have gone through weeks of preparation." Erin laughed weakly, the blood still pounding in her head.

"How about a brandy, Mrs. Steele?" He grinned widely at Erin's flush. "I thought the chandelier was going to fall, the way you were shaking!"

"I'll take that drink, Matt." She seated herself on the settee and placed a hand on Abraham's long fur. "Mrs. Steele," she murmured. "I guess I really am Mrs. Steele now. How odd. Do you feel different, too, Matt?"

He chuckled deeply, a rakish look on his face. "Of course. Why, already I'm henpecked!" Approaching Erin, he lightly traced a finger over the firm flesh rising above the gown's bodice. She felt like scolding him, but then remembered they were married and that he was entitled to this sort of freedom.

He stood for a time behind her, his brandy in one hand, the other playing casually with her hair, slowly freeing the loose curls until they draped over the back of the settee.

"What on earth are you doing, Matt?"

"Simply enjoying your company. I may never get over how much you've changed from that young kid I first met." He came around the settee to face her. "No, don't move. You look absolutely beautiful just like that."

She remained nervously fixed under his close scrutiny. She could feel the soft rise and fall of her breasts straining against the beige silk, her hair spreading in wild disarray over the green velvet sofa, Matt's eyes seeming to strip her of the delicate gown. She felt breathless, weak, desirable.

Setting his glass on a table, Matt leaned forward and kissed her cheek as if she were a fragile porcelain doll. Erin was both bewildered and excited by this new approach to lovemaking. Each time he touched her, it was a shockingly new sensation; her skin tingled in anticipation of his next artful move.

"Tired?" he whispered.

"It's early yet . . . we haven't eaten, or anything . . ."

Matt took her by the hand and helped her to her feet. "I told you it was a mistake to wear that dress around me. As soon as we're upstairs I'm going to take great delight in removing it." His low, coaxing drawl was irresistible.

She followed him up the stairs in a half trance. It was all right this time, she was married to him, Matthew Steele was her husband. She didn't have to like his overbearing arrogance, but she had every right to savor the pleasure he could bring her.

When they were in her bedroom, Matt ushered Abraham, who followed her everywhere, gently out and locked the door behind him. He went to the blue velvet wing chair by the window and sat down casually, leaving Erin standing mutely in the stream of golden-pink light coming through the glass.

Matt seemed oddly pensive, his eyes trained on her and yet somehow looking through her. At last he said, "Undress, Erin. And do it slowly."

"Matt!" She was upset that he considered her a private play toy, to stand meekly under his heated gaze and unclothe herself.

"It can't hurt—do it for me." The smooth tone of his voice was compelling, leaving her with butterflies in her stomach and willing to do his bidding.

As her fingers fumbled with the silk sash tied at her waist, Erin once again begrudged Matt the hold he had over her; while she desperately wanted him to take her, she would be equally glad when he went away on business.

The sash fell aside, splitting her lacy beige gown down the center and leaving her chemise exposed. She kept her eyes averted from Matt's and slid her arms out of the fitted sleeves, letting the creamy silk folds drop to the floor. The chemise was next; she felt a hot, pounding blush suffuse her body when that, too, was slowly cast aside. Then came the lacy petticoat, which she undid and let fall, and finally the ruffled pantaloons. Her slender form was now completely naked beneath his intense blue stare.

He observed the rapid rise and fall of her breasts and saw their firm tips grow taut, aroused. "Come here," he said hoarsely.

She walked slowly, hypnotically, over to the chair. Gently, he urged her onto his lap and began to stroke her sensitive flesh, exploring her, exciting her. His lips caressed the rose peaks of her breasts, then moved lower, to the delicate curve of her hip.

Erin felt her hands grab Matt's thick hair, involuntarily urging him to continue. Even before his mouth found her inner flesh, she had reached a fever pitch of desire, her breath coming in quick, gasping snatches. Arching herself up against his tender arousal, she experienced unbearable pangs of delight that soared and ebbed, then soared again, until she was consumed within them.

Later, when Matt carried her to the bed and undressed himself, Erin could not believe that she still longed for him. Time and time again, during the short twilight and the long night, they knew the bliss of a shared sensuality, falling into a brief slumber of exhaustion only to awaken and begin anew.

That Matt barely spoke to her mattered not to Erin; the feel of his powerful body next to hers was enough. That they would undoubtedly argue in the morning, and she would dislike him thoroughly did not matter, either. She had these moments now; she wanted his body as urgently as he wanted hers. Words would only spoil their time together.

Chapter 29

The delicious odor of Hattie's cooking tickled Erin's nose as she approached the kitchen. This was to be a wonderful day, away from the ever-looming presence of the tall mountains surrounding Aspen. She needed a few hours to herself—with her new husband, of course. But the last few weeks had provoked in her a long string of confused emotions, and it would be wonderful to have a change of pace, even for a short time.

A smile upturned the corners of her mouth as she entered the kitchen and saw Hattie, bent over the table, stuffing a few items into a leather pouch.

But Erin's smile faded as Hattie glanced up at her for a moment with a mixed look of shock and admiration.

"So you're really going to wear that—that thing!" Hattie exclaimed indignantly.

"Why not?" Erin demanded. "It's comfortable and practical. I can ride astride. Do you think I give two hoots what the old biddies will say? Why, this venerable old town is becoming much too respectable for me!"

She looked down at her suede riding skirt, split in the middle so that she could ride comfortably, but giving the appearance of an ordinary ankle-length skirt when she stood straight. She'd had it tailored especially for her by a local seamstress who had made disapproving faces while Erin had explained what she wanted.

"Leave it to Matt to insist on a trip to where only a horse can go," she said for Hattie's sake, but in all honesty, the ride they were to take to Snowmass Valley excited her. She hadn't ridden like this in a long time, and she anticipated the feel of the June wind on her face, the horse flesh under her, the green mountains around her.

Matt hadn't given a reason for wanting to travel the twelve miles to the base of Snowmass Mountain; in fact, he'd been somewhat mysterious about the outing. When Erin had asked him that morning, he had merely smiled, kissed one pink-tipped breast, and told her it was a place where he had often hunted in the past.

Hattie packed them a lunch that would suffice for an army, under the guise that they might be snowbound for a few days. Erin had to laugh. "Think we'll make it on this skimpy meal?" she asked facetiously, eyeing the fried chicken, potato salad, rolls, and chocolate cake. There was even a bottle of wine and a jug of Yampah water, just in case.

"I know you're making fun of me, but it's better to be prepared," Hattie said with a sulk.

"I know. I'm sorry." Erin gave her a quick kiss on the cheek. "Don't be angry at me. It's such a beautiful day; Hattie, you should get out yourself."

"Well, as a matter of fact, since you'll be gone all day, I accepted an invitation from Mr. Lloyd Rumplemeyer. We're going riding, too." Hattie looked distinctly uncomfortable, both from Erin's raised brow and because she had never ridden a horse before.

"Who is this Mr. Rumplemeyer, Hattie?" Erin tried to keep her laughter under control. "Is he a new beau of yours?"

"Goodness, no, Erin. He's just a . . . friend. He thinks I'm a nice, respectable housekeeper and he likes my—my company."

"And so he should, Hattie," Erin said, suddenly serious, "and he'll never know any differently."

She carried the heavy saddlebags out to the stable, where Matt was saddling their mounts. He burst out laughing when he saw her struggling under the weight of the two leather pouches.

"Are you sure the horses can carry those? Maybe we need a pack mule just for lunch."

"Now, Matt, don't hurt Hattie's feelings. She likes to take care of me."

The ride west out of town took only a few minutes; then they followed the road along the Roaring Fork River, through sage-covered hills, a few aspen groves, and stands of tall cottonwoods closer to the water. The sky was a dazzling, resplendent blue—Colorado blue, Erin called it. One small puffy cloud peeked from behind Mount Sopris, far to the west, until it was lost to sight around the shoulder of Buttermilk Mountain. They finally turned into Snowmass Valley, and the path—evidently a game trail—became narrower and rocky, winding its way along steep bluffs. At last they rounded the cliffs to stand at the entrance of a huge, bowl-shaped valley surrounded by mountains that grew taller in the distance. It was a breathtaking sight: the brilliant green of the grass, the darker patches of trees on the smooth hillsides, the majestic peaks in the background, some still capped with snow.

"It's beautiful, Matt! What's that strange peak with the diagonal stripe on its face? I've never seen anything quite like it."

"That's Mount Daly. Unusual, isn't it?" He leaned on his horse and pointed out landmarks to her. "The next big peak to the east is Capital, and the one closest to us is Snowmass. Impressive." He turned to her, his face grave. "Someday this land's going to be valuable. I don't mean for mining, I mean as ranch land and farmland. This valley needs beef. It's foolish to keep shipping in food from Leadville or Denver City at today's high prices. We could grow it all right here."

His voice took on a reverent tone. "Erin, I want to buy land here, lots of land. It's cheap, to be had for the asking. I've always pictured my ranch here, ever since I hunted in this valley that first winter. My job with the railroad is getting stale. You weren't too far wrong when you asked me about my work. It's not exactly my idea of a lifelong profession."

He slid down from his horse and helped her to dismount, then took her hand and gestured at the wide expanse of emerald valley. His blue eyes were intense as he described his dream to her. "Picture this valley covered with red cattle, and a ranch house over there." He pointed to a flat area protected by the hills. "Erin, I want to quit my job and settle down here—be a rancher. What do you say?"

Erin's mind whirled in confusion. Matt a gentleman rancher? She almost wanted to laugh. Erin Conner a ranch wife, sitting at home in the evening by the wood stove, knitting? Ridiculous! She looked at him but did not see the intensity of feeling on his face; if she had, she might have held her tongue.

"Matt Steele, I can't believe I'm standing here listening to you say these things. You want me to give up my house? My life in Aspen? To help you run a ranch? You must be daft! I thought we'd agreed to live separate lives when you were gone—I with my interests and you with yours. What would a ranch do to that idea? Good Lord, Matt, you can't expect me to agree with you!"

He stood very still for a moment, a muscle ticking in his cheek, thin white lines radiating out from his compressed lips. "No," he said slowly. "No, I guess I shouldn't have expected you to see things my way. You rarely do." His tone became sarcastic. "That damn house of yours. I'm sick to death of hearing about that pile of wood and brick. You really think it's so damn important . . . And the mine, the great Silver Lady! Erin, one of these days you're going to learn that the things you value so highly are merely objects—they can't bring you happiness, or even security. Why, there're people we both know who've been rich one day and broke the next! Who do you think you are to escape their fate?"

"The Silver Lady will never let me down, I know it," she replied stubbornly.

"One of your visions?"

"No. It's just a feeling I have." But she felt a prick of fear, nevertheless.

"A feeling. Good. Then I hope your feeling feeds you and polishes your fancy floors when the Silver Lady goes broke!"

"That won't happen, Matt!" she insisted.

"Eventually it will. Then, my dear, you'll have no one to turn to but me, your loving husband." He laughed, a short, harsh sound. "If you're smart you'll buy some land with your silver money, Erin. In the long run, it's the only thing that lasts."

"You'd like it if I went broke, wouldn't you? To see me poor and dependent, like the other ignorant, rundown ranch wives. Well, I'll never turn to you for help, never! I'll keep my mine and my house, and you can live up here on your precious ranch all by yourself!" She turned and ran back to her horse, yanked his head up from the rich grass, and mounted, not waiting for Matt, only knowing that her stomach was in knots from their argument.

Her temper must have communicated itself to her horse, for he snorted, laid back his ears, and began to rear, sinking on his haunches. Abruptly, she felt the reins snatched from her, and then Matt's strong hands pulled her down from the saddle.

"I'm not through talking to you, Erin." His low, drawling tone belied the anger that sparked in his ice-blue eyes. "You're a fool, a damn stubborn fool. Can't you see that this silver boom won't last forever? That it's a flash in the pan? You're acting like a child, putting all your eggs in one basket." His tone turned gentler and he held her by the shoulders, looking into her eyes. "You're my wife now, and that means something to me even if it doesn't to you. I don't want to see you get hurt."

"If you don't want to see me get hurt, then kindly take your hands off me and leave me alone!"

He dropped his hands and stood back, regarding her in a detached sort of way, almost with amusement. He watched her turn away, catch the trailing reins of her horse, mount, and start down the valley. The stiff, angry line of her shoulders was visible to him as she rode off, and he shook his head in bewilderment.

She was soft, yielding, passionate in bed; they reveled in each other's bodies at night. But during the day her temper still flared at him, and he, in turn, still tried to dominate her fiery spirit. They were obviously not going to get along very well; perhaps this marriage idea had not been so smart after all.

A little too late to think of that, Matt mused wryly. But the fact that he was married would be very welcome in his dealings with the women he met on his travels. They'd have no hold over him now. Actually, his married state might prove to be a very convenient reality.

He caught his own horse and swung a leg over the cantle, pressing his heels to the gelding's flanks to catch up with Erin. Both of them rode silently back to Aspen, neither one admitting thirst, hunger, or fatigue. It was dusk by the time they reached the stable.

Matt heard a muffled groan as Erin dismounted, and he smiled to himself. The stubborn brat! She wasn't used to riding these days and would be as stiff and sore as an Eastern dude. Well, it served her right, he thought as he carried the saddlebags into the kitchen and lit the oil lamp.

Erin followed him slowly. She sank down into one of the kitchen chairs but winced as her sore backside touched hard wood. She squirmed on the seat, unable to find a comfortable spot.

"Hattie's not home yet," she murmured. She looked up at Matt, suddenly shy, her eyes almost silver in the lamplight. "I'm starving, so if we eat all this food now, Hattie will never know we didn't have it for lunch."

"Sure, kid," he laughed. "We wouldn't want Hattie to know we'd had a lovers' quarrel and didn't eat all her goodies."

"Oh, Matt!" she cried, exasperated. But she dove into the nearest bag and pulled out a package of fried chicken, which she began to consume with great gusto. They even opened the bottle of wine and sampled some Yampah water.

Later, sitting back contentedly, they viewed the ruins of Hattie's lunch lying on the table: chicken bones, an empty bottle of wine, smears of chocolate frosting. Erin licked the cake crumbs from her fingers.

"Umm, that was good. Whatever would I do without Hattie? She's really far better than Cook herself." She sighed, satisfied, then looked at her husband. "Matt, I'm sorry I ruined your surprise for me . . . up there. I've been trying to understand your side of things. But it wouldn't work. I'm not cut out to be a ranch wife, not after I've scraped my way up from nothing to get where I am. I think it's better if we live more . . . apart. It's too difficult otherwise."

"Sure, Erin. You're probably right. We'd never get along anyway. We're both entitled to our freedom."

Erin thought she detected a note of resignation in his tone, quite unlike his usual forceful manner with her. She changed the subject abruptly.

"And another thing, Matt. There's something that's been mulling about in my mind for a very long time . . . I want to go back to Ireland."

"You want to go where?" His casual tone suddenly turned hard.

"I want to go back to Killarney and show everyone that the Conners, or what's left of them, have become rich and successful. I want to throw it in their faces. And especially in my uncle's, after what he did to us."

"Erin, I can understand your feelings, but you're married to me now, like it or not, and you've made promises to me . . ."

"Don't worry, Matt. I know what I promised—to be here whenever you returned and to be available in bed. I know." She heard the bitterness in her voice. "I won't go back on my word—I respect a contract. I'll go to Ireland when you leave on your next job, and I'll be back before you."

"I absolutely forbid it, Erin," he growled.

"You can't forbid me to go, Matt."

"I'll be damned if I'll see my wife gallivanting around the world by herself!"

"You won't have to see it, you'll be gone; and besides"—her eyes narrowed—"I'm not stupid enough to ask what *you* do all those months you're on a *surveying* job. You've no right to question *my* behavior."

Matt tried to control his temper. "I am your husband, Erin, and the only person in the world who has any interest in looking after you. Therefore, I'm telling you you're not going."

"Don't worry, husband dear, I'll be perfectly safe. Hattie will accompany me. Why, I can take the train all the way to New York, and those new steamships—"

"Erin, don't be coy. I just told you you're not going—and that's that!"

"Yes, Matthew," Erin said sweetly, her eyes downcast. It was better not to fight him; he was stronger and would always win. She would agree with everything he said and then do precisely what she wanted. He'd be gone in a few days and then she could make her plans. He couldn't stop her.

As Erin undressed for bed that night, she wondered how the years ahead, with Matt Steele for a husband, could be endured. Perhaps marriage had been a terrible mistake on both their parts. At the time it had seemed so inevitable—fated, actually—but now . . . She drifted off to sleep, feeling trapped by her marriage and hating Matt for making her feel that way.

She was awakened shortly by his hands stroking her body. Immediately she entered a state of languid desire. Matt did not engage in foreplay tonight, but took her fiercely, with a desperate urgency.

When she awoke in the morning, all of his belongings were gone. He hadn't even left her a note. The only reminder that he had ever occupied her room was the black broadcloth suit hanging lifelessly in the wardrobe.

She pulled a loose, jade-colored dressing gown around her and went to the window overlooking the stable and the carriage house. Yes, his horse was gone, too. For a brief moment she had thought he might still be below. An inexplicable pang seized her heart and was quickly replaced by a dull emptiness. I'm glad he's gone, she told herself. I'm glad I told him about my plans to go to Ireland. She had done exactly the right thing. She had stood up for her rights and held him to his marriage promise, and she would abide by hers, too. She would be here when he wanted her . . . This thought left her slightly shaky, and she sank into a chair, her hands clasped tightly in the folds of her dressing gown.

The unbidden image of Matt sitting at the kitchen table, his eyes crinkled in amusement, rose to her mind. Oh, he was handsome, so devastatingly virile! Hadn't she always thought that? Suddenly she felt queasy, and the image of him flew around in her head, torturing her. It was possible that he had even gone away forever. She didn't want to dwell on this idea.

"Well, damn him anyway," she whispered. "I'm going to Ireland. I've got my own plans, my own life to live. And I'm far better off without that conceited lout!"

Erin stood up and moved toward her wardrobe, anxious to rid her mind of these disturbing thoughts of Matt. "Now, what to pack?" she said to the empty room. "I suppose these dresses are fine for Aspen, but I'll need lots of new things. Perhaps I'll shop in New York for a few days . . ."

And before Erin had dressed for breakfast that morning her head had cleared and was full of the exciting prospect of a shopping spree in New York. She was determined that absolutely nothing would ruin her trip, not even a husband who had forbidden her to go in the first place.

PART IV

Chapter 30

The shining, closed coach Erin had hired rolled to a stop in front of a thatched-roof cottage in Killarney. The driver sat straight-backed and kept his eyes fixed ahead while she and Hattie stepped down from the elegant interior into an atmosphere of obvious poverty, overladen with foul street odors.

Her dainty boots immediately mud-splattered, Erin took a few hesitant steps forward on the familiar yet somehow foreign path leading up to the crumbled stone wall surrounding the cottage. She saw a tattered white curtain in the front window part slightly for a moment and then fall back into place.

"Erin, let's go," Hattie said, behind her. "You're only torturing yourself, and we've a long trip today."

"I suppose you're right." Erin turned back to the coach. A few thin children stood around it and giggled nervously when she smiled at them. A long time ago she had been one of them herself, dressed in poor clothes, looking like an urchin. But that time seemed like yesterday, and she could feel the burden of those years weighing heavily on her shoulders. How could she have forgotten the misery, the pathetic faces?

She stole a backward glance at her former home and her eyes filled with unbidden tears; yes, it might have been just yesterday that her own mother had stood by the stone wall and called her in for dinner. Dinner! There had been little food in those days. And her mother—how quickly that life of poverty had aged her.

Erin and Hattie reentered the coach, and Erin instructed the driver to continue their journey. She did not look back as the vehicle lurched forward, scattering the children, and rounded the narrow corner. Soon they had left the impoverished Killarney district.

"I'm sorry, Hattie, but I just had to stop and see the place again. We've come a long way, and I thought, since we were so close, that I should do it."

"I understand, Erin, I really do—but maybe we shouldn't have come to Ireland at all." She reached over and touched Erin's clasped hands. "You seem so . . . unhappy, and maybe we should just turn around and go home."

"Go home? After all these weeks of traveling—oh, no! Not until I've seen Norwood Manor again and cleared away a few cobwebs!"

Erin sat back and stared pensively out the coach window, not really seeing the lush Kerry countryside. Unconsciously, she straightened the rich gray linen of her traveling skirt and buttoned-up jacket. After removing the pins from her gray plumed hat, she took it off and placed it next to her on the seat cushion, then reached down with her handkerchief to rub the mud from her laced boots until they shone again. It was still a distance to Norwood, and she wanted to appear rested and stylish when she confronted her uncle. Edward would certainly be surprised, she mused, for she hadn't written to him of her intended visit—after all, he had long ago told her father never to step foot in Norwood again.

The coach jounced on past the tiny rural cottages and rolling, stone-fenced hills. Hattie dozed, and Erin wondered again what had prompted her to insist on coming back to Ireland. When the notion had first entered her mind, she had never stopped to think about it. Now that she was actually here, what did she hope to accomplish?

The road narrowed perceptibly, telling Erin that they had traveled more than half the fifteen miles from Killarney to Norwood Manor. Familiar cottages and neighboring estates could be seen from her coach window, and her heart began to beat more rapidly with each passing mile. She felt the nervous thrill of a child who had gotten away with a naughty deed.

At last Hattie stirred. "Aren't we there yet?" she mumbled.

"A few more miles, Hattie. You look done in, and I guess it's all my fault for dragging you on this venture." Erin tried to smile, but her nerves were raw.

"Dragged me all over—I'd say that's a fair assumption. St.

Louis, Chicago, New York, across an ocean!" Hattie shifted her stiff bones miserably on the seat. "I wish we'd stayed home! I'm not a young chicken any more, you know."

"I do know—haven't you told me that a thousand times these past weeks?" Erin snapped, irritated. "We came first class the entire way, so I'd say you have little to complain about. Why, just think of all the new places you've seen!"

"If it's an argument you want, Erin, it's one you'll get. I'd happily have stayed right in Aspen—I happen to like it there! And those idiot women you left in charge of the house—"

"That's enough!" Erin commanded. "When I've finished what I came here for, we'll go home. Does that suit you, Hattie Nelson?"

"Yes—the sooner the better, too!" She leaned forward with narrowed eyes. "And what did we honestly come here for?"

Erin bit her lower lip. "Honestly?" She thought for a moment. "I came to throw my wealth in dear Uncle Edward's face. And mostly, to make him pay for my parents' death. That's why I returned, and when I'm satisfied, we'll leave."

"God, Erin, what's come over you? Sometimes I think you're mad! Don't you care at all for others—for instance, people like your husband? Doesn't it matter that he'll find out what you're up to?"

"I couldn't care less. And if you want my opinion, our so-called marriage is a farce—has been since the beginning." The carriage rounded the gates that led into the mile-long drive to Norwood Manor. "When I look back now, I realize why he wanted to marry me. It wasn't for Lew and it wasn't because he felt responsible for me. It was simply because I had turned him down, and Matt couldn't swallow that! Oh, no, not him! Do you think I don't know how many little chits have had their eyes on him?"

Hattie raised a brow. "Lots, I'd say. You sure question a lot, don't you? Can't you just accept that he married *you*, and not some giggling female who caught his fancy for a night?"

"You're an old romantic, Hattie. Now, hush up, please, and let me gather my wits. We're nearly there."

The hired coach came to a swift halt in front of the stone-faced Georgian house that she had not seen for almost twelve years. Norwood Manor, where she and Perry had been born and raised; where her grandfather had given them a secure home; where they had found happiness for a time.

She stepped down from the carriage and paid the driver handsomely, instructing him to unload their luggage and place it by the front steps.

"Erin, don't you think we should have him wait?" Hattie asked somewhat fearfully. "At least until we're sure we can stay."

"Absolutely not. This is my ancestral home—we're definitely staying." Yet as she stuffed her banknotes back into her beaded purse, she could not help but notice that her hands trembled and her knees felt weak.

The coach turned in a semicircle and made its way down the long drive. Erin watched until it was gone from sight. Now she knew there was no turning back, at least not today.

She gazed around her and suddenly realized there was no one about—no gardener, no saddle boy—and that no one had come to the door. She shook the travel wrinkles from her skirt, smoothed the fitted lines of the smartly cut jacket, then checked the pins in her plumed hat. She straightened her back and walked up the four stone steps, but before she had lifted her hand to knock, the carved double doors were opened by an old man who looked familiar to her. His mouth gaped wide in utter shock, and then slow recognition spread over his countenance.

"Clarence? Is that really you?" came Erin's unsteady voice.

"Miss . . . why, it's Miss Erin, come home to us!" The elderly butler put out his shaky, brown-splotched hands for her to grasp.

Erin could hardly believe that twelve years had aged the faithful servant so drastically. He was bent and seamed; his uniform, which had once held the wide breadth of his shoulders, was now loose and sagging, and his skin hung flaccidly around his face and neck. Yet this was indeed Clarence, warm and dignified, genuinely glad to see her. She felt an edge of confidence return.

"Clarence, I'm certainly happy to see you still at Norwood. Is Uncle Edward about?" Erin crossed the threshold, and the sight that met her eyes staggered her. The entrance hall, once grand and elegant, was now in sad disrepair. Pale rectangles of empty space stood out on the walls where the portraits of the Conner ancestors had once hung. Erin's grandmother's pianoforte was gone from its accustomed place. Dust covered every piece of furniture.

"Clarence! This room . . . what's happened?"

The smile on the butler's lips remained; it was as if he hadn't heard her at all. "Sure an' all, for a moment, Miss Erin, I thought 'twas Miss Claire, your mother . . ."

Of course people in Kerry would think that now. Abruptly, the notion that Edward would also think so occurred to her. Edward, who, like her father, had desired Claire, but had turned bitter toward her when she had married Patrick instead.

Erin shook her head, dispelling the thought. "Where is my uncle? Take me to him, please, Clarence."

"He's in the study . . . A bit chilly today, isn't it?" the butler remarked as he led the way. Indeed, she felt a raw dampness in the house. There were no fires lit, she noticed, and everywhere she looked she saw unpolished furniture, fallen pieces of plaster, dull silver and glass. What in heaven's name had gone amiss at Norwood? And why had Clarence avoided her earlier question?

The elderly servant opened the door to the library, from which the distasteful odor of mildew and stale smoke assailed her nostrils. In the far corner of the large room a gray-haired man sat slumped in a cracked red leather chair, a faded plaid shawl draped around his bony shoulders. His eyes squinted narrowly at Erin across the expanse of threadbare carpet separating them.

No! Erin screamed silently. This couldn't be Uncle Edward—tall, imperious, arrogantly dignified. It simply couldn't be!

"Squire Edward," Clarence announced, "Miss Conner, sir."

"What?" the man whispered. "Who'd y' say? Come closer, girl." When Erin walked near enough for him to make out her features, she thought she had never seen so ashen a face. Edward pushed himself up out of the chair, his face growing red and tense. "Claire? By God, sure an' it can't be you!"

"No," Erin replied in a cool voice that did not sound like her own. "It's not Claire, Uncle. It's Erin, her daughter."

"Erin? But I don't understand . . ." He slumped weakly back into his seat.

"Your Claire, my dear uncle, is dead." Erin approached him slowly, purposefully, wondering to herself why she couldn't have waited for a more opportune moment to tell him. As it was now, he merely put his head in his hands and said nothing. Shouldn't he have been more upset, more shocked?

After a long moment, Edward Conner looked up at his niece. "So . . . one of you has come back . . . Well, now you can just leave."

"Leave? Don't be silly, Uncle. I have no intentions of leaving." She walked over to a smudged, rain-streaked window. "Perhaps my father was too weak to stand up to you, but I'm not. This is my home as much as it is yours, and I'll be *damned* if I'll leave."

"How dare y' speak to me—me, yer own uncle—that way! Why, y' little peasant! Yer no better than that mother of yers!"

Erin spun on her heel, eyes flashing a deep green color, lips pulled back in a mock grin. "You despicable old pig! My mother was twice the woman you could handle and you know it! As for being a peasant—yes, I'm of lowborn stock, Uncle Edward"—she spit his name—"but I'm also half Conner, your brother's daughter, too. You cast us out once, but you'll not do it again!"

Edward rose to his former height, seeming, to Erin, to be making an enormous effort to intimidate her; she held her ground and faced him squarely, feeling every muscle in her body grow taut.

"I suppose yer not alone, girl. Where's the rest of yer kin? Waiting outside, no doubt, to sack me home?"

"Hardly." She drew a deep breath. "They're all dead . . . Mother, Father, and Perry, too. They're dead because you tossed us out into a world of poverty, a world where your brother could not provide for his family." Erin made a sweeping gesture with her arm. "And by the appearance of Norwood Manor, I'd say you are already being punished for your sins, my dear uncle!"

He nearly fell back into his leather chair. "They're both dead? Patrick, me own brother?"

"That's right. Dead and buried halfway across the world, with not even a gravestone to grace their memory." The words were wrenched from her.

"Dear Lord," he mumbled hoarsely. "It wasn't any doing of mine . . . not me fault . . . I couldna known . . ."

"Don't you *dare* try to shirk the responsibility!" Erin shrieked. "Fool yourself now if you want to, old man, but before I leave Norwood, you'll accept the blame!" Erin went to the library door. "Yes, I promise you'll suffer yet!" She looked long and hard at him before departing; he appeared aged now, even pathetic. Yet in an odd way, he still possessed an aura of cruelty; it was evident around his eyes, she realized, the way they emerged from under his hooded lids and seemed to sear a hole through her.

A distasteful shiver ran down her spine as she closed the door behind her. Certainly she had nothing to fear from him now, and she would think of a sound way to belittle him before all the people of Kerry.

She found Hattie seated comfortably in the morning room, sipping tea. Clarence stood close by, awaiting the guests' wishes.

"Clarence, tell me, is your wife, Maude, still cooking in the kitchen?" Erin asked.

"Yes, miss, and our son, Kevin, is still with Squire Edward. Doin' odds and ends, he is."

Erin smiled and seated herself. "Please have Maude join us here for a moment, Clarence. I'd like to speak to you both."

The elderly butler did as Erin bade and returned shortly with his wife of forty years. Erin greeted her warmly, remembering the sweet taste of Maude's cinnamon buns and apple dumplings. Maude, like her husband, was old and stooped, and was also happy to see Erin, whom she obviously remembered with affection.

The couple stood by the dim windows and awaited Erin's words.

"Are you the only servants here now?" she inquired.

"Yes, miss," Clarence answered.

"Have you been paid anything recently?"

They looked at each other closely. "No, miss," Maude said slowly.

"Then I must assume my uncle is out of funds . . . I'll see that your wages are paid, though."

"Oh, no, miss, we wouldn't be hearin' of it!" Maude looked imploring at Clarence.

"I'm in charge here for a time—at least where your wages are concerned." Erin rose and paced the tiled floor. "How long has my uncle been short of money?" She waited for a reply, any hint of his financial status, but could see she would receive no information from the servants. At last she said,

"You're both very loyal. I'm sure my uncle doesn't deserve such fine people as you." She dismissed them kindly. "You may go now."

After the servants went back to their duties, Erin told Hattie of her meeting with her uncle. Hattie was shocked by Erin's strong words of loathing for the man and said as much, but Erin was adamant about her intentions.

Finally, when the afternoon shadows had lengthened on the tiled floor, Clarence returned and showed them to their rooms on the second floor of the east wing, where Patrick Conner had resided when his father was still alive.

Erin remembered the suite of rooms given her as if it were yesterday. The bedroom had belonged to her parents. Clarence apologized for the poor condition of the green room but did nothing to remedy it. Erin realized his limitations. She herself would hire several girls from Killarney; perhaps Kevin could be sent to town tomorrow to fetch some women.

She ran a slim hand across the bureau and shuddered at the thick dust, then built a fire in the hearth and sat near its warmth, wondering how she could have forgotten the dreadful September dampness in Kerry. After a time, she closed her eyes and dozed, only to awaken with her arms folded about her waist, shivering uncontrollably.

She rose, pulled a moth-eaten blanket around her shoulders, and dragged the wing chair even closer to the fire. During the time before dinner she allowed herself to concentrate on her impulsive urge to confront the only living member of her family—the man who she felt was at the very root of all her former misery. In the instant she had thrown the news of her parents' death at him, she had expected to feel an enormous sense of satisfaction, yet what she had felt was lacking in intensity. Perhaps I'm just exhausted from the long trip, she told herself, and *tomorrow* I'll be rested and able to think more clearly about how I'll make him suffer.

Suddenly an image of Aspen Mountain appeared in her mind's eye: the early-autumn leaves golden now in the sunlight; the rows of wood-framed houses and white picket fences; the stores and shops bustling with customers whose pockets were lined with riches. And then, came an image of Matthew Steele: his dark hair glistening; his crystal-blue eyes reflecting the Colorado sky; his thin, sensual lips split in a smile that could melt a woman's heart.

"Oh, damn!" Erin swore aloud. Why did his face always crop up in her mind, dogging her when she had so many more important things to think about?

She rose and unfastened the leather buckles on her wardrobe trunk; she would wear her red velvet gown for dinner and have Hattie pile her hair in ringlets atop her head. Jewels, too, she decided, would adorn her ears and throat—let Uncle Edward see her then!

As if her mother's voice reached across the years, Erin's head rang with her words. "I hold no grudges against your uncle, dear," she had revealed so long ago. "He acted out of a pained heart, and is not such a bad man."

As the words faded, Erin knew that what she wanted to do to him was motivated by pure selfishness. She was not avenging her parents from their grave; she was, instead, avenging the poor orphan girl she had been back in Denver City. All these years, in the dark recesses of her mind, she had blamed her uncle for every wrong she had suffered.

Erin began to pull off her traveling suit and dress for dinner. Confusion beset her as the sun cast its dying shadows on the bedroom walls. But she would not let herself be swallowed up in this emotion. She would continue with her plans, see the whole scheme through to its final conclusion, and whether she would be satisfied or not remained an unknown factor. She had gone through a great deal to be here. She had even left her marriage in the dust, and she'd be damned if she'd give up now!

She felt the flow of power course through her veins, comforting her, nurturing her.

Chapter 31

Erin swished down the once-elegant staircase the next morning as if she were sallying forth to do battle once again. Her uncle's uncertain manner toward her the previous evening, as well as his obvious infirmities, served to dull the edge of her victorious return. Nevertheless, she was aware that she wished her as far away as possible—in hell, most likely. The thought made her smile tightly as she entered the musty dining room.

The gaunt man rose from his place at the long table, causing the plaid shawl to slip from his bowed shoulders, and held out a firm hand to her.

"I've been thinking, girl. Let's be calling it a truce for now. I don't wish for us to quarrel any more—I haven't the energy for it." His voice was calm, but his rheumy eyes slid away from her, suddenly suspicious.

It would seem that Edward had renewed his energies after a night's rest; he was certainly more like the man Erin recalled so well.

"All right, Uncle. You treat me with respect and I'll *try* to do the same." She seated herself in the one place that was set with silver—tarnished she noticed—and waited for her breakfast to arrive.

Clarence appeared with a bowl of some sort of gruel, which she tasted and pushed away, grimacing. "Haven't you any fresh eggs, or at least toast?" she asked, remembering the sumptuous breakfasts of her distant childhood.

Edward's hooded eyes blinked once, then stared at her. "We've not much money for fancy breakfasts these days, Erin. Things have changed. The peasants can barely pay their rents, the potatoes are plagued by the devil himself, and the

266

English squeeze every penny out of us." He smiled thinly, showing his uncared-for teeth. "Not like the old days that you remember."

She sipped the cup of tea Clarence had poured for her; it was strong and delicious. "I had precious few years here to remember, Uncle. As I'm sure you recall, you chased us out when Grandfather died, and I was only ten then."

"Can we not let the past go? I've made mistakes, so have we all. I never meant for your family to come to harm. It was your father's decision to leave Ireland, and look where it got him." His voice took on a whining tone, and the nervous trembling of his hands was more pronounced.

Erin sipped her tea in silence. This morning her uncle aroused none of the fear or loathing she had expected; in truth, he was no longer the same cruel, powerful villain she had pictured in her memory for so many years. He was only a sad, pitiful, aging man. She almost resented his weakness, for it blunted the edge of her desire to better him.

"I have a business proposition for you, Erin," he began hesitantly, then paused. She knew he was referring to her money, since he had shown a great interest in her display of wealth last night. She only wondered how long it would take him to choke out his request.

"It would only be temporary, naturally, but these last few years have seen so many setbacks, and my health has failed . . ." The serpentlike eyes stopped shifting and rested on her own; she could read nothing in them but the reflection of light from the dining-room windows. "I need a loan." The words were wrenched from him, as if he were in pain.

"Ah, I wondered when you'd get to the point, Uncle. A loan, you say? And with what collateral do you propose to guarantee that loan?"

"Collateral?" He seemed genuinely puzzled.

"Yes, collateral. Do you think I'd loan you money without it? Gracious, my banker would skin me alive!"

"The title to the manor, then. Yes, you can hold the title, just until I pay you back . . ." He smiled weakly at her.

"If I know you, it's been mortgaged to the hilt, hasn't it?" The fading smile on his face answered her question. "And land isn't worth tuppence around here these days, with half the population of County Kerry living in America now. Isn't that true, Uncle?"

Erin tapped her fingers impatiently on the table, but

Edward seemed to be without energy, like an old machine that had run down. His only movement was to pull his shawl tighter around his shoulders.

"I have an idea, though, that would make it possible for me to loan you some money." She tilted her head and saw a spark of animation return to his pale face. "You make me and any children I may have heirs to Norwood Manor," she continued, "and I'll lend you whatever you need to bail you out. In addition, you may live here as long as you wish. Now, I think that's quite a fair deal all the way around, don't you?"

The wasted features of Edward Conner twisted, and Erin realized that he was grinning with the bitter humor she remembered from her childhood dreams.

"So, little niece, you've come back to revenge yourself on me, haven't you? To reclaim the inheritance I rightfully took from your father—that's it, isn't it? Oh, Erin, you've grown hard, and very sharp indeed. And you've won, too. I've no defense against you. You're young and strong and rich, while I . . . I am merely a sick old man, without even children to protect me from you. Ah, yes"—his face fell into old lines of misery and uselessness—"I should have married . . . once, when I had the chance . . . but no one suited me, no one." He regarded her with a wicked gleam in his eyes. "You've won, girl. Does it make you happy? Does it fulfill all your fantasies?"

Erin's eyes narrowed. "I want your will changed, now, Uncle, before you slip away from this world and leave the land to the Crown."

"Don't be daft, girl. I can't change it now. My barrister is in Killarney, and he's undoubtedly busy. I'll have to make an appointment. Tomorrow, perhaps . . ."

"No, today—now! Send for him. He'll get paid for his trouble."

"It's daft you are . . . but all right, I'll send Kevin for him. I can't promise he'll drop everything and come."

"You just make sure that he does, or you'll not see a penny of my money, not a penny."

She stood over Edward as he laboriously wrote a note to his barrister, one Gregory Claymore, and rang for Kevin, who turned out to be off on an errand. When Kevin was finally located, Edward carefully gave him explicit directions where to deliver the note. Erin's impatience threatened to overwhelm her while she watched Kevin slowly saddle the old draft horse and amble off toward town.

She bit her lips in vexation; things seemed to move in slow motion here, as if they were all still mired in the Middle Ages. It was then that Erin realized she was American through and through; she could almost see herself as an Irishman would— brash, impatient, rich, strong, and direct, like the brazen new country she came from. How strange, she mused in amazement, and I thought I was returning home! This is not my home any longer—I'm an American now!

With this in mind, she climbed the stairs and found Hattie trying to dust her musty rooms.

"Don't bother, Hattie. I'll ask Maude to do this work for today."

"Maude? That's a joke! She's so old she can hardly move around the kitchen. It's only habit that keeps her going at all. Why, she'd never be able to get up the stairs!" Hattie's voice was full of her annoyance with the inefficiency of the manor. Hattie was American, too, Erin realized.

"Well, never mind. I've decided to hire some women to do it anyway. Come with me, Hattie. I want to go down to the duck pond. You know, Perry almost drowned in it when he was eight, and Father was so mad."

Outside on the overgrown lawn, Erin described how the grounds had looked when she was young: emerald-green, smooth, perfectly manicured, with formal rose gardens. The women walked down the greensward to the duck pond, but when they reached its bank, Erin's face fell. The water was reed-choked and muddy, almost filled to the brim with debris; there were no ducks to be seen.

"I can't believe it, Hattie. It's awful now."

"That's what ails these rich old places. They need too much money and too many in help to keep 'em goin'," Hattie remarked.

"Well, I'll put it all to rights, for it's to be mine now!" Then Erin told Hattie of her understanding with Edward Conner.

"Well, I'll be!" Hattie exclaimed, eyeing Erin appraisingly, her head cocked to one side. "And what do you think Mr. Steele will say about it—remember him, your husband?"

"This has absolutely *nothing* to do with him, Hattie. This is *my* business. And why should he care, anyway, what I do? He told me I could conduct my own business, didn't he?" Erin was quite put out.

"Sure, Erin, he did say that, but I still wonder . . ." She also wondered if Erin had conveniently forgotten to mention her marriage to anyone here.

As they wandered about the grounds of Norwood Manor, they saw nothing but ruined elegance: sagging stables, unkempt lawns, dying shrubs, neglected old buildings.

Then they noticed a lone horseman galloping up the drive, to halt before the carved double doors. After tossing the reins onto the wrought-iron hitching post, he stalked up the stone steps and let himself into the house.

"Now, I wonder who that is," Hattie said. "Doesn't appear to be the sort who would visit Uncle Edward, does he?"

"I think I know who he is. If I'm not mistaken, Hattie, he's the Honorable Gregory Claymore, barrister." Erin had a triumphant smile on her face, and she began to stride purposefully toward the manor. "I may have some important business to transact with that gentleman, Hattie."

"What's this all about, Conner?" Gregory Claymore demanded as he advanced into the study. "Vital business that cannot wait? What the devil is going on here?"

"Calm yourself, Gregory. I had to get you out here. It's my last chance. Now, listen well, while she's still out . . ." Edward Conner rapidly explained to his barrister the gist of his arrangement with his niece. He saw the man's expression of increasing amazement give way to one of grudging admiration.

"The little chit!" Claymore cried. "Of all the nerve! Sure and she's got you in a tight corner, Edward."

"Yes, I'll have to do it, but for God's sake, Gregory, put her off if you can." Conner's hooded eyes glinted, and he pulled his shawl closer around him.

"Yes, well, it should be interesting meeting this young— ah—woman."

"She's no woman, she's a witch, a redheaded haunt from my past," Conner quavered, and Claymore realized how much strain the sick man was laboring under.

Just then the barrister's attention was drawn from Edward's face by the sound of a woman's tinkling laughter bursting through the doorway.

"I'm no witch, Uncle, but ordinary flesh and blood, like you!" Erin came forward with long, graceful strides, her hand extended. "So you are Mr. Claymore, I presume. And you've come to attend to the wishes of your client, Squire Conner, is that not correct?"

Claymore saw the smile on the young woman's face, but her eyes belied her expression, measuring him. He immediately sensed that she was intelligent and determined, but Edward Conner had not mentioned his niece's glowing beauty: the red-gold curls springing around her face; the wide, sensual mouth; the eyes like blue-gray jewels; the statuesque carriage. Claymore realized that he had not answered her question and shook off his state of fascination.

"Yes, Miss Conner, your uncle has been explaining to me the changes he desires in his will." He bent over her outstretched hand and kissed it lightly, then straightened and met her eyes again. This time they almost seemed to be laughing at him.

"Certainly, Mr. Claymore, just so. I would like to see this particular piece of business cleared up directly, if you don't mind, as I wish to enjoy my visit to Norwood Manor without having to concern myself with trivialities. I'm sure you understand." Her long, dark lashes veiled her eyes, so that Claymore could not tell how serious she was. What a woman! he thought. The mind of a shrewd businessman and the face and body of a courtesan! He could not help but compare her with his own poor Sophie, a pale, plump woman who stayed abed most days, nursing the vapors. Claymore had never seen a female so alive, so vital. Her presence filled him with an unbelievable shyness, and he found that he had little to say.

"Oh, go on, Gregory, get it over with," Edward Conner shrilled thinly. "There are quills and paper on the desk."

While the barrister drew up the document, consulting occasionally with Edward as to the wording of the will, Erin had an opportunity to study Gregory Claymore. He was tall, dark-eyed, and dark-haired, with sideburns that were turning a distinguished gray, and an aristocratic Norman nose. He must be about forty, she thought, but his broad shoulders and slim waist under the frock coat showed that he was in excellent condition.

Then it was done, the document blotted carefully and signed with wavering script: "Edward Conner, Norwood Manor, County Kerry." Claymore held the will out to Erin and she read it carefully, from beginning to end. It struck her suddenly, when she saw the name "Erin Conner," that she had neglected to tell her uncle of her marriage. Her legal name was now Erin Conner Steele, but she pushed that thought out of her mind as irrelevant. If Matthew tried in any way to take Norwood from her, or protested her ownership, she would . . . yes, she'd divorce him. She could do it if she had to.

She felt a fierce pride in her ability to revenge herself and her father, but once again the surge of victory over her uncle did not come as she had expected. He had given in too easily. She handed the paper back to Claymore, frowning slightly.

"Will that be all, Edward?" the barrister asked, and Conner muttered a reply.

Erin walked over to one of the many-paned windows and looked out at the formerly elegant lawn that sloped gracefully toward a stand of trees. This land would soon be hers, and her children, if she had any, would inherit it as well. The shadows had grown lengthy, and the low stone walls that lined the drive stretched dimly away. A fine mist had begun to fall, blurring the scene slightly.

She swirled around and spoke quickly, the words emerging before she even knew what she meant to say. "Mr. Claymore, you will, of course, stay to dinner. It's late, and it's raining besides. We couldn't possibly turn you away without offering you our hospitality, could we, Uncle?" But she hardly paused long enough to let him answer. "After all, we owe you our thanks for concluding our business so speedily."

Gregory Claymore thought quickly. Sophie expected him home, but she would probably be in bed with a migraine. She had had one coming on that morning, and all because they had not been invited on to the Governor's Hunt Ball. The children would dine in the nursery anyway, and there was no one else to consider. He could always say he had been detained by Conner, which was close enough to the truth.

"Why, thank you, Miss Conner. I do believe that would suit me very well." He could hardly believe he had said this, but he *would* enjoy staying, if only to study the copper-haired Irish-American beauty further.

Erin served him a glass of rather thin sherry, all that was to be had, and excused herself to see about dinner and her evening attire. A faint scent of perfume remained in the room after she had gone, overshadowing the odor of mildew.

"See what I mean, Gregory? She's not quite human, is she?"

Claymore turned to see Edward grinning knowingly. "I'm not sure . . ." was all Gregory could reply as he sipped the sherry. "I'm not at all sure."

At dinner, Erin appeared somewhat subdued. Her blue silk dress made her unusual eyes seem to match it. When Claymore looked into the depths of her eyes, trying to pin down their color, he found that their shades shifted, like water in sunlight.

Edward was sullen and withdrawn during the meal. Erin was also quiet, much more reserved than she had been that afternoon. Luckily, thought Claymore, Hattie Nelson, introduced to him as Erin's companion, carried the conversation quite charmingly, asking him many questions about his life, and about Ireland in general. He was strangely reluctant to speak of his family, although Hattie asked him pointedly whether he was married, then how many children he had.

The food was quite plain and not very plentiful, but Claymore's appetite did not trouble him; he found himself staring at Erin often, fascinated. Her hair was pinned up in soft waves, but a bunch of ringlets fell over one shoulder—like molten copper, he mused.

After dinner they retired to the study and seated themselves before the marble fireplace. The library and the dining room were the only habitable rooms on the ground floor. A lull fell over the conversation as they stared into the crackling embers, and Erin rose to draw back the drapes from one of the windows.

"I believe it's stopped raining, Mr. Claymore. That will make your trip back to Killarney much more pleasant, I'm sure." She returned to the group around the fire. "It's never like this in Aspen; it's always either hot and dry, cold and dry, or storming—no in-between drizzling, as it is here . . . I'd forgotten."

She stared into the fire for a few moments, then spoke again. "I've decided to have a party here, a great party. A ball, in fact." She saw Edward begin to protest and cut him off. "*I'll* put it on, Uncle, no need for you to lift a finger. I would like to see all our old neighbors and friends, my parents' friends." She turned to Claymore, catching him unaware and seeing a hot flush cover his neck as her eyes met his. "And of course, Mr. Claymore, you are invited . . . and your wife, too." She smiled charmingly then, her American accent even more pronounced. "It will be an evening to remember, I promise you."

Chapter 32

The first carriages to arrive at the party rolled to a stop in front of Norwood Manor.

Erin sighed deeply; she was near to exhaustion from her frantic efforts these past weeks to restore the estate to something of its former grandeur.

Smoothing the lines of her silvery gray silk gown, she checked her appearance in the full-length wardrobe mirror. The skirt flowed with yards of the shimmering fabric, and the tight-fitting, low-cut bodice displayed her breasts in an almost indecent fashion. Diamond clasps sparkled on her shoulder straps; her arms were naked save for the elbow-length, white kid gloves. Hattie had piled a portion of Erin's hair atop her head and arranged the rest in long curls that cascaded down her back. And tonight, Erin had daringly applied a light touch of rouge to her cheeks.

She recalled the other day when Gregory Claymore had ridden to Norwood, ostensibly on business, but actually to see her. He had wanted to steal a few hours away from his wife, whose condition, he had confessed in a moment of unabashed candor, was a drain on his nerves and at times most tiresome. It would be amusing to flirt with Gregory, she thought slyly, and right under the noses of the Kerry gentry!

While Erin looped a black, lacy fan over her wrist, her mind focused inexplicably on Aspen—and, of course, on Matt. "Damn," she muttered. "Why must he always pop up to ruin my pleasure? I'll flirt if I like—why not?"

Nevertheless, she knew that flirting with Gregory was as far as she would go, for the idea of an affair with him was distasteful to her. She had no desire to have him touch her; it was only her detestable husband who managed to arouse her senses.

At last she felt ready to descend the polished steps and greet the first arrivals. She knew she looked elegant in her silver gown—the Silver Lady incarnate—and she felt confident of her ability to charm even the most stiff-necked of guests. Indeed, she was positive there would be those who would raise a brow at her display of "new" wealth.

The hired orchestra from Killarney was already playing quietly in the fern-bedecked, glassed-in solarium when Erin led the first waltz with Squire Mulligan, an old friend of her father's. She briefly noticed her uncle and was grateful to see that he wasn't wearing his moth-eaten shawl. He was obviously enjoying himself, for he was chatting with the same banker who only a few weeks before had been clamoring for money.

Erin spent the first hour dancing with a myriad of finely dressed gentry and reacquainting herself with old neighbors and friends. She even took a few minutes to assist Sophie, Gregory's wife, upstairs to lie down when the pallid-faced woman nearly swooned on entering Norwood. It seemed that one of the Claymore horses had shied at a rabbit during the ride to the manor. Erin's smile was polite, but inwardly she pitied Gregory his wife.

All in all, the party was proceeding very smoothly. Certainly everyone who had been invited was there, for precious few balls were given in Killarney these days, and a chance to shrug off one's worries was most welcome. Erin knew this and was pleased to have been able to spend a small fortune for their enjoyment. After all, what was money to her?

She danced a few waltzes with a twenty-six-year-old bachelor, Thomas Baird, who bowed like a butler at the end of his dances and confessed to being smitten with Erin for life. She laughed archly and allowed him to fetch her another glass of champagne. While Thomas was gone, she searched the colorfully dressed throng for a glimpse of Gregory, finally spotting him engaged in conversation with her uncle. She decided to slip away from Thomas as soon as possible.

In the end, it was Gregory who saved Erin from another waltz with Baird by tapping the young man on the shoulder and taking his place.

"And how is Sophie?" asked Erin, looking up at Gregory from beneath the fringe of her lashes, an impudent smile tilting her lips.

Gregory Claymore regarded the beautiful girl in his arms, her slim, lithe body fitting deliciously to his own. Her dress shimmered in the light of the chandeliers; she was a silver goddess, a vision of all that was out of his reach. He felt an involuntary hardening in his groin. What was happening to him? he wondered, aghast. Was he bewitched completely? But he managed to answer Erin's question calmly, hiding the fever that burned inside him. "Sophie? It's fine she'll be. She always does this, then makes her grand entrance later. I no longer worry over her as I once did."

He tightened his hold on Erin's waist as they swept around the floor, and was oblivious to the stares and whispers. He was aware only of the glistening opalescence of her eyes, her creamy shoulders, the sweet smell of her hair. It was exquisite agony to hold her while they danced, and a small death to let her go when the music ended.

On her part, Erin was aware of Gregory Claymore's infatuation but she refused to be concerned about it. He was much older than she, but Andrew had also been older; and, like Andrew, Gregory was attractive and debonair. He treated her with respect and dignity, and he would probably die before compromising her good name.

And so Erin spent the majority of her time in the company of a forty-year-old married man. That she was thoroughly enjoying herself was all that mattered. Even when Hattie commented waspishly on her behavior, saying she now knew why Erin was keeping her marriage a secret, Erin brushed her aside and continued to flirt openly with the barrister. He was safe; other young swain at the gala might not be so easily held at bay, and besides, in her eyes they were immature.

Only once during the festivities did she have a low moment, and afterward she would swear to herself that her overindulgence in the champagne had brought it on. Months had passed since she had been visited by one of her visions, and she had begun to hope they were gone for good.

She was talking with Gregory and a woman named Mrs. Lowery, and glanced over at her uncle. Immediately her vision blurred and a younger Edward stood before her, tall and threatening, shaking an admonishing finger at her, his mouth moving soundlessly. She gasped, so real was the image, and Gregory immediately helped her to a seat, where she fought to regain her composure of a moment before.

"What is it, Erin? Is something amiss?" Gregory's anxious voice broke through the fog of her confusion.

"No, I'm all right . . . I just drank too much, I guess." She tried to smile and looked up into his dark eyes. "Really, Gregory, I'll be fine in a second." Erin smiled. "I'm not very hungry. Why don't we take a stroll into the solarium? It's so close in here."

The couple made their surreptitious exit from the dining area and sought out a more comfortable, fern-shrouded corner near the musicians. She decided it wouldn't hurt to have just one more glass of champagne, and was soon feeling lighthearted and giddy again.

Gregory was leaning close to her bared shoulders, whispering compliments, when his wife appeared in the doorway, her fingers pressed to her temples and swaying slightly. If Sophie thought something was amiss, she said nothing, so great was her concern about her health that Gregory's actions were beyond her comprehension. But Erin felt oddly miffed when he was compelled to attend to his complaining wife for the remainder of the night, and she found herself growing bored with the dancing and with explaining her situation in America to the curious.

Shortly before three A.M. the last guest retired to his chamber, the others who lived nearby having already returned home. Erin was escorted upstairs in a state of near exhaustion by Hattie, who remained while Erin undressed, apparently to give her a good scolding.

"You've a lot of gall, flirting all night with that older man!"

Erin stretched out on her bed, still wearing her thin chemise and petticoat. "Oh, be quiet, Hattie. I felt like having a good time, that's all."

"What about Matt? Don't you care what may happen to your marriage?" Hattie sat down on the feather bed. "Let's go home, Erin. It's almost Thanksgiving in America, and we can't stay here forever."

"Thanksgiving . . ." Erin recalled her first Thanksgiving, that first winter in Aspen, her frozen hands and the comforting embrace of Matt's voice and strong arms around her.

She rolled over onto her side. "I've given it a lot of thought and I—I'm not certain about my marriage to Matt . . . I'm considering a divorce, Hattie."

"A what!"

"You heard me. And don't scold!" Erin reached over and patted her arm. "I've told you before how we were accidentally thrown together—about the time he—he took me. Well, that's all we've ever had in common, except for Lew, of course, and I think I've always disliked Matt. Even hated him."

"You don't *hate* him! You can't, Erin—you're fooling yourself."

"No . . . I've thought that for a while now. I had a schoolgirl crush on him when I was younger, but when he came back after being away for four years, I realized he was merely a conceited oaf. Don't you think I know what he does when I'm not around?"

"You're wrong, I'm sure of it," Hattie said dismally.

"He's always got women chasing after him, and frankly, he's only nice to me when my clothes are off! Well, I'm sick of that. I like the way Gregory treats me, and I feel wanted when I'm around him. At least he likes me for my good business sense and—"

"Erin! You can't be *that* ignorant! This Claymore fellow's after the same thing any man wants from a woman!"

"No!" Erin cried in exasperation. "You're absolutely wrong! He's . . . he's not like that!" The evening, the long weeks of preparation for the ball, finally took their toll, and she began to weep softly.

Hattie left the room, angry with herself for having argued with Erin. Erin, who had been so good to her, had given her everything. But for all her strong pretenses, Erin was foolish and confused where men were concerned. Hattie knew that her womanly sensibilities had been mortally wounded by the experience with Ben Mortimer, and then later by Matt himself, when he had taken Erin forcefully instead of gently wooing her.

Hattie retired late that November night with a worried heart and a troubled mind. Erin would undoubtedly continue to see Claymore and would spend the winter in Ireland. If indeed they ever did return to America, Erin would *have* to get a divorce—she was right about that! What man on earth would sit meekly home while his wife gallivanted around Europe?

It could not really be called dawn yet in Kerry, for the rolling hills and stone-fenced meadows were still cloaked in blackness, and only the faintest hint of gray could be seen to the east, only the slightest glow of what would become a rainy morning.

Erin woke with a start, her hand going instinctively to her pain-filled temples. Damn! She had known better than to drink all that champagne! Now her mouth felt cottony and she was extremely thirsty.

She rolled out of her soft bed and planted her feet firmly on the cold floor. She had to have something to quench the thirst—water, cider, anything. She moved slowly to the carved wardrobe, pulled out a green velvet dressing gown, and slid her feet into her slippers, her head throbbing unmercifully.

She made her way through the dark halls and down the stairs to the back of the manor, where the kitchen was located. A few minutes of searching produced a cool keg of cider. From its tap she poured the liquid into a mug and drank until she was satisfied. Through the rear window she could see the first streaks of light illuminating the sky. On a sudden impulse, she opened the kitchen door and breathed the fresh, moist air. Then she stepped outside, closing the door softly behind her, and strolled across the lush meadows toward the pond.

The chill morning air seemed to creep into her very bones, and she shivered in her velvet dressing gown as she approached the bank. But in spite of the dampness, she felt refreshed, and her headache was beginning to diminish. She seated herself on a smooth rock and looked up at the dawn breaking over the misted green hills, her mind wandering back over the hard years to when she and Perry had played pirates around this same pond. Erin wondered if the sudden death of their parents had caused Perry to become bitter. But it was pointless to speculate about that now; he was dead— quite dead, she remembered—gunned down by her own dear husband.

Erin shook her head and shivered, rubbing her arms vigorously against the cold. She had to stop blaming Matt for

Perry's death; it would have happened eventually anyway. And why did she always seem to forget that Perry had drawn his gun first? Hadn't at least a dozen people told her that?

"Erin?"

She jumped off the rock and gasped aloud, her hand going to her mouth. Then she realized it was only Gregory standing behind her.

"I'm frightfully sorry. I never meant to startle you." He put a gentle hand on her shoulder to calm her obvious shock.

"What . . . what are you doing up at this hour?" she whispered.

"Sophie hasn't slept yet and has kept me awake. I was sittin' by the window when I saw a lovely spirit wanderin' about the grounds." He laughed lightly. "Sure an' you looked unreal out here. A wood nymph, perhaps, in your flowing green gown."

A weak, drizzling rain began to mist the air, and Erin blinked up at Gregory. "We should return . . . Sophie might be looking out that same window and might misunderstand."

"In that event, perhaps we should be givin' her something to fret over!" He drew Erin into his arms even as she tried to pull away.

"Don't . . . I can't allow you to do this . . . please."

But as if he had not heard her plea, Gregory brought his mouth down on hers, demanding a response she could neither feel nor give. She struggled against his embrace, only compelling him to press his lips on hers more urgently and to bend her backward within his strong arms. The front of her gown fell away and his hand quickly sought her warm flesh.

She began to fight in earnest against his unwanted advances when she felt his hand hungrily kneading her bosom. Her mind revolted in panic; he would surely fall upon her in the grass and have his way, and she would be abused as before.

But when his other hand sought to force her lower body against his hard loins, she was able to free an arm and bring her hand up to slap his face smartly.

The stinging blow made Gregory come to his senses, and he released her abruptly, causing her to stagger backward.

"I'm . . . I'm so sorry. I don't know what came over me . . . Forgive me, Erin."

For a long moment she did not speak. Then she said breathlessly, "I won't forgive you. I'm not the type of woman you seem to think I am!" She rushed past him and fled toward the manor.

But Gregory was not to be put off so easily. He followed her into the kitchen and began to apologize again. "Erin, I don't think of you as *that* sort of woman at all. It's just that you're so—so irresistible!"

She was still trembling from his physical assault. Here she had thought he was very much like her Andrew! How wrongly she had judged Gregory Claymore.

"Go away, Mr. Claymore. I've nothing to say to you." She walked toward the hall leading into the dining room. Suddenly his firm but gentle touch stopped her.

"Please, if you'll just speak to me—anything, Erin! Sure an' I've been a cad an' all, attacking you like an animal . . . It's just that my life seems so dull. My wife, you see, is quite unable to . . . to comfort me and—"

"Stop it, Gregory! Don't blame your behavior on your wife. It certainly wasn't *her* fault that you kissed me!"

"I know . . . I know." He released his hold on her arm. "I only meant that married life can be difficult. Sometimes a man allows his eye to rove . . ."

"You needn't bother to tell me that. I already know about husbands with roving eyes!"

"What?"

"That's right, Mr. Claymore. I have one of my own who flaunts his good looks at every passing female!"

Gregory was momentarily overcome; never had he imagined Erin to be married—she was far too independent, too self-contained, to be wed. A sudden pang of jealousy shot through him, but when he had recovered from his initial shock at her confession, he remembered the deed drawn up between Erin and her uncle.

"Erin!" he gasped. "Don't you realize this nullifies the deed between you and—"

"Oh, no, it doesn't!" Erin took a deep breath. "You see . . . I was married . . . but I'm, ah, divorced now and have taken my former name . . ."

"Erin, what's come over you? You aren't bein' serious, lass. Why, a divorce is unheard of—just not possible, I'm sure." Gregory had almost called her a liar but had held his tongue. Perhaps she had really managed to obtain a divorce; after all, Americans were known to be headstrong, if not downright crude. Yet he remained puzzled. There was certainly no way to determine the truth from across an ocean without going to great lengths to check the validity of her story.

"Will you let me pass? I don't wish to stand here arguing with you."

Gregory softened his tone. "Erin, I know you detest me right now, but if you'll just give me another chance to be your friend, I swear I'll not touch you again. Please?"

"I don't know, Mr. Claymore . . . Gregory. How can I trust you after what happened at the pond?"

"You can! Oh, Erin, please do!"

"Well, I'll think about it. I don't wish to make any enemies here, naturally. I'll let you know," she concluded smoothly.

He let her pass, leaning back against the wall in an all-consuming effort to calm himself. This was the first woman he had desired—nay, lusted for, he admitted—since his marriage to Sophie nearly twenty years ago, and he would have to restrain his pent-up urges and give Erin Conner time to grow accustomed to him.

As Erin tried to get back to sleep that morning, she thought that nothing had gone as she had planned. Her desperate need to return to Ireland and avenge her family had turned out to be less than satisfying, a disappointment at best. And this situation with Gregory was more than she had bargained for. All she had meant to do was to carry on a small flirtation with him, and that had backfired on her. Well, she mused, all men could be handled if a woman but used her wits; certainly Gregory was no different. And since she considered spending the winter in Killarney, she decided to give him a second chance. Surely he would not dare touch her again.

Before falling into a restless slumber, she also decided to wash her hands completely of physical relationships. From now on, she would enjoy the company of men and even use them when necessary, but there would be no more touching, or kissing, or worse . . .

Then she recalled how foolish she had been to tell Gregory about her marriage. Now she would have to maintain the lie about her divorce. Yes, she rationalized as she drifted off, she would indeed see Gregory Claymore; that way she could keep him too enamored of her to think about looking into her past history. When she returned to Aspen, she would remedy the fact of her marriage. Immediately. The one thing she could not risk was to lose Norwood Manor simply because a document read "Erin Conner" and not "Erin Conner Steele."

Chapter 33

Matt Steele stared through the window of General Palmer's suite. Already a few yellow leaves were swirling down Larimer Street, and winter would be close behind. He forced his attention back to the general's words.

"We're offering you this job, Steele, because of your past history of success with this sort of thing. It was a stroke of luck for us that you quit working for the Union Pacific—although we're not above stealing a valuable employee, if necessary." The general laughed flatly.

Matt eyed the older man appraisingly; he was an aristocratic Easterner with a reputation in the upper echelons of the great railroads as a hard but fair taskmaster. Matt waited silently for the general to proceed with his proposal.

William Jackson Palmer leaned closer to Matt and stubbed out his cigar in the ashtray. "Steele, this is strictly confidential. It can go no further than this room, but I expect you're to be trusted. Otherwise, you wouldn't have lasted as long as you have." The general observed the young man seated across from him in an easy chair. The suntanned face was impassive; the bright blue eyes coldly level; the thin, sculpted lips under tight control; the long, lean body gracefully relaxed. A cool, cool customer, Palmer thought, but the one to get the job done.

"We're about to begin building a line from Georgetown, through Glenwood Springs, and down the Roaring Fork Valley to Aspen." Palmer saw Matt tilt his eyebrows slightly at this but give no other sign that the words meant anything to him. "We have received information that the Colorado Midland is planning something similar—a line from Leadville to the Frying Pan River and then on into Aspen." He leaned forward and tapped his fingers on the low table that stood between them. "It is *imperative* that the Rio Grande Railroad reach Aspen first. We cannot let the Colorado Midland win this race—for a race it will be, make no mistake about that—or else I'm afraid the standard gauge will take over in the Rockies. And I won't allow that. I've put too much work into the 'little giant' for that to come to pass." He sat back in his chair, pulled another cigar from his waistcoat pocket, and began cutting the tip off with a tiny diamond-studded knife, his eyes never leaving Matt's.

"What exactly do you want me to accomplish for you, General Palmer? I've retired from the railroad business, as I told you. My last job became a bit too . . . distasteful, shall we say? I have no wish to get involved again."

"I know, Steele, but this would be a one-shot affair and you'd be in charge of the operation, so the use of . . . physical persuasion would be entirely up to you. And we'd pay you fifty thousand dollars at the successful completion of the contract, free and clear, no strings attached."

Matt watched Palmer wet the fine cigar tobacco with his lips and savor its rich taste. "It's tempting, General, but I have to know just what's expected of me."

"Very simple, Steele. It would be your responsibility to get the Rio Grande into Aspen before the Colorado Midland by whatever means you can, short of going too far outside the law."

Matt gave a brief laugh. "Simple, you say? General Palmer, you have a bizarre idea of what's simple." He paused, thinking of the ramifications of the railroad man's offer. "I could use the money, all right. I've bought some land in Snowmass Valley and I'd like to stock it, build a house there. How long would the job take, General? You must have made some projections."

"Not more than a year, Steele. We have to get there before the winter of '88." Palmer rose and went to the oak sideboard, poured two brandies, and set one down in front of Matt. "I have all the reports right here, some roughed-in routes and so on. We need more right of ways, especially along the Roaring Fork, and I thought you'd be especially useful there, since it's your home ground. This has to be kept pretty quiet until rail construction actually starts."

"Well, General," drawled Matt, "it seems you are very sure of my answer."

Palmer's bushy gray brows quirked slightly and a smile curved his lips. "Steele, this is a job that will excite your imagination and give you a great deal of satisfaction when it's done. I hope I don't underestimate your professional pride by offering you this opportunity."

"No, you don't." Matt smiled in return. "You know I'm hooked. All right, I'll do it. The Rio Grande will get to Aspen first, General. But this is my last job. Don't expect me to come running again. After this, I'm gonna settle down."

"Steele, I don't give a damn whether you sit in a rocking chair in front of the fire for the rest of your days—just get my railroad to Aspen before the Midland!"

Matt left the suite and walked slowly down the stairs to the long, dim bar of the Hotel Denver; he needed a stiff drink before he went back to his room, and Samantha. He envisioned her waiting patiently there, most likely in bed with very little on, thumbing through a ladies' magazine. He could see her dark, thick hair and could almost feel her warm skin under his hands. Cheerful, undemanding Samantha, one of the few women he'd bothered with for more than a night. Maybe it was because she was so different from Erin. Erin! The very thought of her could make his blood rise. The bitch! The lying, cheating, bitch!

He ordered a whiskey at the bar and sipped it slowly, trying to control the unreasoning fury that formed in his breast every time he thought about his last return to Aspen—home, he had thought. Ha! He had come back after a brief but nasty job, ready to settle down and even live in Erin's house until she was ready to move with him to the land he had bought. He had realized it would take time to convince her, to build her a house she would love in Snowmass Valley; he had been determined to be patient with her. But only Erin's maidservant had answered his summons, explaining that Mrs. Steele had left for Ireland a short while before. The woman had had no idea when Erin would be back, but her orders were to make Mr. Steele most comfortable if he should return.

Matt felt the strong whiskey burn its way down his throat and tried to tear his thoughts away from that day, but the impotent rage returned, fueling his imagination. Erin had broken their agreement, deliberately, and had left without informing him. And for what? To revenge herself in some insane way upon her uncle, whom Matt remembered her speaking of with bitter contempt. Damn her! What the hell was a wife for but to be home when her husband wanted her! And, he admitted to himself, he still wanted her—missed her, even. Matt Steele, womanizer, was caught in a trap of his own making. He hated himself for feeling that way, yet he longed to have her near him, to stroke her smooth skin . . .

He ground his teeth and took another swallow of whiskey. Women! They were all trouble—he should have known better than to hitch himself up to one. And now she had left him, just like his mother had done! Well, he'd have an explanation from her when she returned, and he knew she would, because her house and her mine were still there; she'd leave her husband, but she'd *never* leave the Silver Lady and that fine house of hers!

Matt finally cooled down enough to climb the stairs to his room. Samantha would be there, he thought. She wasn't the type to go anywhere on her own; she needed a man. That was the trouble with Erin. *She* didn't need him enough, she was too damn independent. He stopped outside his door, deliberately pushing all thoughts of Erin from his mind.

Samantha was sitting on the bed in her corset and petticoats, her hair spreading lushly over the pillows behind her. The vivid darkness of her hair and eyes struck him again; her beauty was that of a Rubens painting—generous, unsubtle, and ripe. She was amusing, pleasant company, a willing mistress. She loved big cities and had so far refused to travel with him, which was fine with Matt. He liked her to be waiting for him in Denver City whenever he put in an appearance. He had meant to write her a note, ending their relationship, but had neglected to do so when he had found Erin gone. And when the tempting letter had arrived from General Palmer, he had had a perfect excuse to go to Denver City and take up with Samantha again.

"Was your meeting interesting?" Samantha asked, putting aside her fashion magazine.

"Yes, sweet, very. But you wouldn't want to hear about it . . . Let's see, what were we going to do tonight?" He sat down on the bed next to her and stroked the plump white flesh of her arm.

"Oh, Matt, you know you promised to take me to the Tabor Grand Opera House tonight! I simply can't miss the play they're giving there!" Her full lips pouted exquisitely.

Matt leaned forward, kissing a swell of her voluptuous breast. "Ummm! You smell good, Sam." He ran a hand through her loose, flowing hair, then began to undo the laces of her corset.

"Don't, Matt! I have to get dressed!"

"We have plenty of time, sweet. Just give me a little kiss." He tilted her chin up and kissed her thoroughly, deeply. She wrapped her arms around his neck, arching her body to meet his. He drew back, seeing the open adoration in her eyes. That's the way a woman should look at you, he thought, not with cold contempt or green-eyed fury. "That's better, Sam," he said, kissing her again, then buried his head between her ample breasts.

He had a lot of hard work ahead of him, Matt mused as he sat in the stagecoach bouncing over the rough road past Independence. Palmer had briefed him thoroughly and given him a stack of surveys and land-elevation diagrams, as well as a detailed report on the Colorado Midland's plans. He had immediately seen that he would have to secure a right of way on the north bank of the Roaring Fork, thereby avoiding crossing two deep canyons where Maroon Creek and Castle Creek emptied into the Roaring Fork on the south side. If he could do that, the job would be half done.

The coach was approaching the spot where Erin had been buried alive in the avalanche; Matt could never pass it without feeling the same dreadful gnawing he had felt then. In spite of his angry resentment of her, he had never wished her dead. Merely brought down a peg or two so that she would depend on him, show him she needed him.

The jolting trip finished at last, Matt made his way from the stage depot to Erin's house. It was in excellent condition; her servants obviously obeyed her orders. He wondered whether she was still in Ireland. Had she triumphed over her uncle? Was she satisfied now? Matt shook his head as if to clear it and poured himself a glass of brandy.

He settled down on the settee and waited for his dinner to be prepared, knowing it would be done to perfection. This idea drove him to slam his glass onto a table and pace the floor angrily. This was Erin's house, these were Erin's servants; the whole smothering blanket of her authority suffocated him. He wanted to flee to the apartment over his store, but John had married and there was no room for him now. Maybe he would just go to a hotel. But he knew he would stay, because it was easy and because Erin owed him that much. He had work to do, and her servants might as well take care of the details of his existence.

Several days later, the housekeeper announced that Mrs. Steele's banker, Jeff Wilcox, had come to see him. Matt was annoyed. He was studying the reports Palmer had given him, and he hated to be interrupted.

"Mr. Steele," the banker said as he entered the library, "I don't like troubling you with your wife's finances, as she told me never to bother you with them, but since she's out of the country . . ."

"I understand, Mr. Wilcox. What's the problem?"

"Well, her account has been greatly depleted by several large drafts that she's drawn on a bank in Killarney, and to tell the truth, the silver from her mine is reaching a lower grade and isn't bringing in as much as it once did. And with the costs of her house here, the servants' wages, and so on—"

"I see . . . I'll write her immediately, Mr. Wilcox, and tell her. Meanwhile, if there is a shortage in her account, I'll cover it—is that understood?"

"Yes, of course, Mr. Steele. We'll advise you if that's necessary. I just thought you ought to know . . . It's very odd, her insisting on keeping her finances separate from yours. Usually the husband takes care of such things."

"Yes, I know, Mr. Wilcox," Matt said dryly, steering the man to the door, "but *those* husbands aren't married to Erin." He closed the door behind the banker, and a smile began to curve the corners of his mouth. So! Erin was getting a bit too high and mighty. Well, he had warned her that the mine wouldn't last forever, but she had been furious at his word of caution. She was bound to find out sooner or later that her sense of security was just as low-grade as the silver in her mine. Poor Erin, she'd need him yet; he'd just have to be patient.

He sat down at Erin's mahogany desk and went to work again, turning his mind to the task at hand: tomorrow he'd have to ride out to meet with several ranchers who owned land on the river. He'd have to be sharp, but not too overbearing in his efforts to convince them of the benefits a railroad would bring. It was delicate work, like tinkering with the insides of a machine; everything depended on the wheels meshing precisely, in perfect balance and harmony.

Chapter 34

Erin opened the envelope with trembling hands; how could a mere letter from Matt upset her so? She read it quickly, then once more, more slowly, searching for his true meaning. But the words were there in boldly written script; nothing further was to be found between the lines. The letter gave no hint of what he might be feeling about her absence, or about anything else for that matter. Strangely, it almost disappointed her.

She finally put the letter down and turned to Hattie. "He says there are some business problems and I should return to Aspen to settle them. No hint of what they are. I wonder if something's seriously wrong. Well, whatever it is, it'll wait a few weeks. Mr. Wilcox can handle it. I don't want to miss the Winter Cotillion." She saw Hattie's sour expression and pouted. "Now, Hattie, don't look like that. I'm in no rush to get back home. I'm having fun in Killarney, the social whirl I missed when I was a girl. I've been accepted into society here—it's my rightful place, you know."

"Erin, what on earth are you doing here? You've showed off your wealth enough to impress the entire county. You've flirted with every male between six and sixty for miles around, gone to every party and soiree. You're married and your life is in Aspen, and you know it! I thought you were a brave girl, but now I'm beginning to think you're really a coward, putting off facing your own husband."

"That's not true! I just like it here! Why should I go back to Aspen and fight with Matt? I'm tired of it!" Erin paced the room, a frown creasing her forehead.

"You're a coward, Erin. Admit it," Hattie said quietly. "You're afraid of what Matt will say to you."

"Oh, Hattie, be quiet! Why do you talk like that?"

"Because someone damn well has to . . . and because I'm homesick. I want to go home where I belong. Here they all look on me as some sort of maiden aunt. It makes me nervous, afraid I'll say something wrong and blast their top hats off!" Hattie glanced down at her hands, an embarrassed smile on her lips. "And there's something else, too. I'd kinda like to see Lloyd again . . . that is, if he's still around and single."

"Lloyd?" Erin was puzzled.

"Yes, you remember. Lloyd Rumplemeyer. I went out with him a few times. He's a nice man."

"Oh, Hattie, I'm so sorry. I forgot you might not want to traipse all around the place with me. I've been selfish. Look, I promise we'll leave right after the cotillion, all right?"

"At last!" Hattie sighed.

"Yes, I suppose it's time . . ." Erin sat down in a chair and rested her head on her hand, a sudden chill falling over her at the thought of facing Matt again . . . Matt, with his cool sapphire eyes, his frightening powers over her. How would he react? His letter sounded as if he didn't care, but maybe he had deliberately tried to be casual.

"We'll have to make some plans, then, Hattie—book passage, pack, say goodbye. Uncle Edward will be quite happy to see us go, I'm sure." Erin giggled. "We've upset his routine enough as it is. The old reprobate! He got what he wanted, and so did I."

"Well, I'm sure he got what he wanted, but are you sure you did?" Hattie asked.

"Of course I am! I'll own Norwood Manor when he's gone, and so will my children."

"Humph! Not likely you'll have any, if you don't get together with that husband of yours."

"Hattie, that's crude! I don't want that conceited boor's children, anyway!"

"I may be crude, Erin, but that's how I see it—lowdown and true. And if you don't want *his* children, who *do* you expect to father them?"

290

"You're not fair, Hattie."

"The hell I'm not. You're just too stubborn to face the truth."

Erin turned away, upset by Hattie's sharp words. She *was* being unfair, Erin thought. I've been trapped into a bad marriage and she seems to think I should make the best of it, but why should I? He doesn't love me, and besides, he's got plenty of women all over the West to dally with. If only he'd told me he felt something or wanted my companionship, if not my love, I could almost be content to settle down with him. But no, he treats me like a child, with no respect for my feelings. Well, maybe he's used to treating women that way, but I can't accept it.

Erin sat down at her uncle's desk in the study and wrote a short note to Gregory Claymore, saying that she planned to return to America in a few weeks and was advising him in case there was any business he had to discuss with her. It would look better stated that way if anyone else in his office saw the note; no need to compromise him. He would probably want to see her again to protest his everlasting affection and loyalty. Well, let him do so; she owed him that much. He had been a good friend, an interesting companion, an intelligent and sometimes cynical interpreter of Ireland and its customs. Also, he had respected her wishes and treated her with distant but ardent gallantry. She would probably miss him. Indeed, she thought wryly, Matt could take a few lessons in manners from Gregory.

When Matt heard a door open and close, he swore under his breath. Another disturbance—undoubtedly one of the servants using her key to return early from an afternoon off.

He rose from his chair in the study and heard a female voice coming from the vestibule. There was something familiar about it. It sounded like . . . but it couldn't be! Had Erin returned home at last?

Matt walked to the study door and opened it, leaned his shoulder against the wood frame. He looked very casual in his faded denims and green and black plaid shirt unbuttoned at the neck. His hair was unruly, as if he had been unconsciously raking a hand through it while he worked.

Toting her reticule, at first Erin did not notice him standing like a statue at the far end of the hall. "Hello," she called. "Isn't anyone here?" Then her eyes came to rest on Matt's immobile form. "Oh!" she gasped. "Oh, Matt—I—why, you've grown a beard!"

He finally moved, placing a hand on the neatly trimmed dark growth. "Is that all you can say? Come, now, my dear wife, surely you can think of a better greeting after these many months."

Erin narrowed her gaze at him and then put her reticule on the hall table. "My trunks, and Hattie's, are outside. If you wouldn't mind bringing them in . . . there seem to be no servants about."

"Certainly. Make yourself at home, and I'll be back shortly." He strode past her nonchalantly, stopping only when he had reached the door. "Have a sherry, Erin. I'll see you alone in the drawing room."

How like Matt, to demand that she await him at his leisure! She shrugged at Hattie, who quickly disappeared upstairs, then walked into the familiar drawing room, which somehow seemed smaller to her now.

She poured herself a little sherry and began to breathe deeply to keep her exasperation under control. He hadn't changed a bit, she mused. He still had the same old air of coolness and arrogance that she detested. Well, Matthew Steele was in for a shock. This time it would be *she* who played all the aces, it would be *her* turn to run the show, and soon he would be gone—out of her house and out of her life!

She was calm and smiling to herself when Matt returned from carrying the trunks upstairs. For a fleeting moment she felt a weakness in her limbs when their eyes met, but it was quickly gone. Hadn't his devilishly handsome features always affected her like that? And with his dark beard he looked downright satanic.

"Erin," he began, "I think we better just sit down and have a good, long talk." He walked past her and picked up a glass at the sideboard. "Take off that damn silly hat—I'll think I'm talking to a bird!" He poured himself a stiff drink.

Erin bit her lower lip and began to remove the pins from her expensive headpiece, then tossed the hat on a chair. What did a gun fighter know about fashion anyway? she grumbled silently. She also removed her gray fitted jacket and placed it next to the hat. Her hair, when undone, sprang loosely down over her tailored white blouse, and she relaxed into the overstuffed chair near the south window.

Matt glanced at her appraisingly, then walked over to the

mantelpiece and rested his elbow on the cool marble. "Did you enjoy Ireland, my dear?"

"Yes." She sipped at her drink. "I had loads of fun."

"Spent a lot of money, too, didn't you?"

Erin raised an eyebrow; he was going beyond his rights where her business was concerned, yet she remained silent, seeing that familiar flare of his nostrils when he was angry and the way he stood motionless, like a cat before it pounces.

"Answer me, Erin."

"What was the question?" She crossed her legs, looking down casually at her button-up boots as if they might need a buffing.

"Let me put it this way. How much money do you think you went through on this Irish adventure of yours?"

"I haven't the faintest notion, nor do I see what business it is of yours. We had an agreement, if I remember correctly."

"Damn you, Erin!" He crossed the distance between them in long, furious strides. "It *is* my business! You've always failed to see that—except with Lew; when he advised you, you'd listen. Hell! I'm your husband!" Matt took her chin roughly in his hand, forcing her head back, so that she was compelled to look at him.

"You're angry because I went to Ireland!" she cried. "But *you* left *me* without a word! Not even a note!"

To say that he had written later seemed pointless, and besides, it was time he told her about the house and to whom it really belonged. And to think he had considered putting her name back on the deed without letting her know what had happened!

He withdrew his hand from her chin as if he had been burned. "Erin, like it or not, you're going to have to accept some unpleasant things, and Lew's not here to console you any more. You're going to have to turn to me for once, kid, and live with it!"

What in heaven's name was he talking about? she wondered. Turn to him for what?

"Your mine—that damn Silver Lady—when flat broke!"

Erin felt her heart clutch, then cold fury took over as she realized what he had just told her. She leaped to her feet and shrieked, "You're lying! Of course you are! You've always been jealous of the Silver Lady—and besides—Wilcox would have written me."

"For Christ's sake, Erin, calm down. Why would I lie about

something as important as that? Get hold of yourself." He tried to take her hand, but she swatted him away. "Erin, everything's all right, believe me. I bought the house and you're out of debt and—"

"What!" Tears of disbelief streamed down her cheeks. "You? *You* own *this* house?" She flew at Matt with closed fists, pummeling his chest.

"Stop it, Erin! You'll hurt yourself!"

His cool assumption that she would hurt herself only enraged her more. She attempted to rake his face with her nails, but he grabbed her arms and pinned them behind her back, causing her to emit a loud string of street oaths.

Gritting his teeth with self-reproach, he pressed her to his chest. "Damn it, Erin . . . are you all right?"

"Let me go," she whispered. He led her back to the window chair and she slid into it gratefully.

"I'm sorry about the mine, Erin . . . but we've money enough now. Let me worry about it from here on out." He stood over her, a muscle working under his newly grown beard. Abruptly, he turned on his heel and went to the cigar box on the mantel, then came back to her. "Erin, here's the deed to the house. I bought it for back taxes. It's free and clear now, and I'll sign it over to you . . . just stop shaking like that, please!"

She turned her wet, smoky eyes up to him, his words pounding in her ears. "You'll—you'll sign *my* house over to *me?*"

"Something like that, yeah. But you've gotta promise to let me take care of the finances from now on." He reached down to fondle a stray golden curl. "It's high time I wore the pants in this family, kid. You may have thrown yours out a long time ago, but you've never let yourself be a woman."

"You own the house now . . . and you'll sign it over to me if I submit to your will . . . Is that correct?"

"I didn't mean it that way, Erin, and you damn well know it!" To try to save further argument, he dropped the neatly folded document into her lap. "It's yours, Erin. Always has been."

She picked up the deed and opened it, quickly scanning its contents to reassure herself that his name was really on it. Naturally, it was. Matt was a lot of despicable things, but he had never lied to her. So the house, *her* house, was his—and the mine was gone, too. She was left with absolutely no source of income save the generosity of her husband. Her uncle's warnings in the vision had come true! she suddenly realized. Oh, how he would gloat if he knew!

A tear slid down her cheek and she wiped it away roughly with her fingers. "Thank you for the gesture of the deed, but I'm afraid I cannot accept it."

"You can't what?"

"I won't take charity. I've worked hard for everything I've ever got, and I can't accept it."

Matt spoke in a deep, uncharacteristically soft tone. "Erin, I am your husband. *I'm* the provider here, not you. Can't you get that through your thick head?"

"Matt, everything I've ever had or loved has been taken away from me. I guess the house and the mine are the same. But somehow I've managed—managed on my own—and that's important to me."

"Then, for God's sake, I'll keep the damn house and you can live here! Get a job, pay me rent—whatever it takes to satisfy you!" He could feel his anger rising again. There was no other female on earth as hardheaded as Erin. Lord, he was doing everything in his power to pacify her. What did she want from him?

"Matt, maybe this is for the best. There was something I wanted to talk to you about, and maybe now it will be easier." She watched him walk to the sideboard and pour himself another drink. She suddenly felt drained, empty, unable to cope with this latest blow of misfortune. But what she had planned to tell him still stood, doubly so now, since if the marriage were to continue, she would be completely beholden to him. Yes, now more than ever she had to end this travesty between them.

He turned to face her. "Let's call it a day. I'm done in, and I'm sure you are, too. Maybe we should have some supper—I don't feel like talking any more right now."

"I want you to divorce me. If you don't, I'm leaving anyway." The words were out. Erin sat in an agony of nervousness, waiting for some reaction from him. But Matt simply stood there unmoving, a strange tilt to his lips, and she couldn't tell if he were elated or furious. A feeling of depression slowly enveloped her as she faced him across the room. Wasn't a divorce what she wanted? To be done with this man, with all men, for good? Of course it was, she sighed inwardly.

Matt spoke at last, measuring his words carefully. "So now that you're financially ruined, you want a divorce."

"That's not why. I've been thinking about it ever since we were first married, if you must know the truth."

"I see," came his steely reply. "And I suppose it's because you can't stand men, even your own husband—whom I might add, you've known since you were fifteen."

Erin was silent under the weight of his words. He was right; she had no use for men in her life.

"Aside from my father, and Lew, and Andrew, you're absolutely right, Matt. Men are . . . well, they want only one thing from me."

"Erin, it's perfectly natural for a man to want a woman that way! You're a beautiful girl, and many will want—"

"To rape me?" she cried suddenly.

"No, of course not." But his tone belied his words, for hadn't he desired her enough to force her into submission?

She looked tiredly over at him, knowing that she was correct, at least about that. "What about the divorce, Matt? You haven't answered me."

"There won't be any divorce, Erin. Forget about it."

"Why not?" she demanded, rising quickly to her feet. "You could remarry, do anything you want. You'd be free again!"

It would be a hopeless impasse, he knew, for he would never give her a divorce, and it appeared she would fight him tooth and nail if he didn't relent.

Erin bent down and picked up the deed, which had fallen from her lap. "I'll be gone in the morning. I believe this is yours." She tossed the document onto a table near him and went to the drawing-room door. "I'll fight you in court, Matt, if I have to. I'll get that divorce somehow."

Upstairs in her room, she threw herself on her familiar blue spread, and let her emotions flow freely. As his wife, she was entitled to absolutely nothing in her own name, but if she were a Conner again, at least Norwood Manor would be hers someday.

After a long fit of sobbing, in anger and frustration, Erin felt drained. She lay on her side, staring blankly toward the window. The single thought that floated dismally through her mind was that everything she had ever cherished was gone from her now. Matt would never divorce her, and Norwood would drift away from her grasp. She had been too busy for friends, and even Hattie would have to seek a new life, for Erin could not ask her to remain.

She was about to let her eyes close, to slip into the blessed forgetfulness of sleep, when her gaze fixed on an object under the blue velvet wing chair. After a short while, curiosity bested her exhaustion, and she rose and went to retrieve the black object under the chair.

Long moments later, her mind racing in puzzlement, she faced the fact that what she held in her hand was damning proof of Matt's infidelity. She walked to the door, dangling the black silk stocking on one finger. But she did not have to go far to seek out Matt, for he was, at that instant, standing there indecisively with his hand on her doorknob.

At first their eyes met in confusion, and then he glanced down at the stocking she held. Neither spoke for a time, and finally he ushered her back into the bedroom, a grim look darkening his features.

Erin's eyes flashed in barely suppressed fury and she whirled around to face him squarely. "How *dare* you bring another woman into *my* bedroom!" She threw the stocking into his face.

Matt grabbed her by the shoulders and shook her until she was dizzy. "Listen, you bitch, if you'd been here where you belonged, I wouldn't have looked elsewhere for a woman!" He pushed her onto the bed. "And furthermore, she stayed in Lew's old room. I've never been able to stand the sight of this one when it's empty. About the stocking—I haven't any idea how it got here."

"I hate you, Matt! Get out of here before I find a gun and—kill you!" She rolled over and reached for the china water pitcher next to her bed. But Matt was faster than she and grabbed it away from her.

"Like to kill me, would you?" He jerked Erin to her feet and held her against him, almost knocking the breath from her. "You're not jealous, are you, Erin?" He didn't allow her to reply; instead, his mouth covered hers in a harsh, brutal kiss.

As abruptly as he had kissed her, he broke away and pushed her toward the door. "I'm going to show you something, Erin, something I hope will bring you to your senses."

"I'm—I'm not going anywhere with you—you adulterer!"

"Oh, yes, you are. You're going for a ride with me, to a place I want you to see before you leave."

Within moments, Matt had dragged her down the stairs and outside to the stable. While her hand clutched her chest as if she couldn't breathe, Matt saddled his chestnut, then swung her up on the saddle, mounting behind her. He was oblivious to the chill of the late-March afternoon.

"Please . . ." she managed to whisper.

"Please, nothing!" He took the horse through the back gate and then west toward the Roaring Fork River, ignoring her weak pleas.

Erin's mind was racing. Seldom had she seen Matt this angry, this forceful toward her. Why now? She could feel his arm crushing her ribs and molding her into his lean stomach, and each time she turned her head to complain, he tightened his hold until she thought she would faint from the pain.

The sun had dipped below the western peaks, and orange shadows enveloped the gullies and ravines. Erin began to shiver in her thin blouse and she sagged against his shoulder; she was too weak to fight him.

As if Matt sensed her surrender, he loosened his grip around her waist, feeling the soft breasts against his forearm, acutely aware of her hips resting between his lean thighs. As he guided the horse southward into Snowmass Valley, he almost wished he had let her pack her things and disappear. What did he expect to prove by bringing her to the ranch site? To show her that he had actually been foolish enough to plan for the future? That he was ready to settle down with her?

Darkness had nearly fallen over the valley when Matt finally stopped and dismounted, waking Erin roughly from her daze and lifting her down beside him. In the fading light he could see how ashen she looked, the way her body shivered in the chill evening air. She hardly resembled the Silver Lady of Aspen now, with her blouse askew and her light hair tangled and matted. Her perfect, creamy skin was smudged from the tear paths on her cheeks. She looked almost like the fifteen-year-old he and Lew had found on the city streets of Denver.

Matt grabbed the tender flesh of her upper arm. "Come on, there's still enough light to see." He led her to a wide knoll that overlooked the valley and from where she could make out the majestic outlines of Capital and Daly peaks against the sparsely starred sky.

"You see those stakes?" He pointed to four heavy wooden stakes driven into the ground the shape of a huge rectangle. "Those are the corners of the ranch house. We're standing in the front room, near the fireplace."

Matt pushed her forward, causing her to stumble dazedly over the rocks. Then, he spun her around and held her by the shoulders. "And this spot is the bedroom—it was to be ours, Erin."

"Matt, please, take me back. You're scaring me, and I'm freezing out here," she muttered between chattering teeth.

"I'm frightening you? Come, now, Erin, I've never scared you before."

"And you've never been so cruel before . . . Matt, I'm covered with bruises and I'm really cold . . . Please."

"There's a way to get warm, only I doubt you'd be interested." His tone was lazy, dangerous, and she felt the blood drain from her head.

"No! I—I won't!" And then she burst out, unable to hold back the words, "Why not bring your mistress out here!"

He forced her down onto the rough, cold earth. "Goddamn it, you're the one who's here now!"

"You bastard!" She tried to roll away, but he held her firmly to the spot.

"I'll never let you take me! I'll kill you, Matt!"

"And how do you plan on stopping me?" He tore open the front of her blouse and then forced her skirt up while she struggled frantically against his overpowering strength.

Even how as his hands stroked her flesh and her pleas reached his consciousness, he could not stop; she would submit in the end, he knew. It was as if her curves and soft skin were indelibly etched in his memory as he played slowly on her senses. No, he would not force her, he would wait, arousing her with his caresses, until she surrendered and held him to her, moaning aloud his name.

After a time, Erin could no longer fight against his strength and will, and lay weakly under his searching hands. And when she gave in to her exhaustion, it was inevitable that his expert touch would awaken her involuntary response and bring her body aflame. But while she clung to him and he drove himself deep within her, she never stopped crying "No"; she never aligned her spirit with the joys of her flesh.

And later, after Matt had built a fire and was holding her close, watching the early streaks of dawn light his valley, he knew she had still not surrendered completely. She would leave again, this time for good, as soon as they were back in Aspen. There wasn't a thing he could do to stop her—there never was and there never would be. He would build his ranch and go on without her. He had done all he could to uphold his promise to his father, but the arrangement had not worked out. However, there would be no divorce. If he couldn't have her, no man would. And perhaps in time she'd realize what he could give her and where she rightfully belonged. For that he would wait as long as he had to.

PART V

Chapter 35

Erin would never forget that train ride across the western landscape of the United States. Even when she had arrived in San Francisco on schedule, and with ample funds to make a new start, she had still felt as if she had lived through a nightmare. The hot, dusty journey to California had underscored the reality of her separation from Matt in a way that the trip to Ireland had not.

It had been a typically dreary spring day in Aspen when Matt had driven her and Hattie, and Abraham in his traveling case, to the stage depot. Erin had argued bitterly with Matt over his insistence that she accept a bank draft to secure her future, but in the end she had taken the loan, promising to repay him as soon as possible. He had not been pleased at the idea of her repaying him, but that had been the only basis on which she would accept his money.

Once she and Hattie had reached Leadville by stagecoach, it had taken what seemed like endless days to cross the severe, ocher-hued miles between the boom town and San Francisco—days filled with haunting memories for Erin and sharp words from Hattie, who had not wanted to be dragged away from Aspen again. But Erin had shut out her friend's voice and stared fixedly at the jagged mountains in the Utah territory and at the brush-dotted deserts of Nevada. Often she had had misgivings about her decision to go to San Francisco. It was just that returning to Ireland, or traveling to New York or any place eastward, had seemed like the wrong thing to do. "A new start must be made in a new setting," she had flatly explained to Hattie.

Yet leaving Aspen had not truly unsettled Erin, nor was it the uncomfortable train ride; what had disturbed her was the shocking discovery that her monthly visit was overdue. The fear that she was pregnant had tormented both her waking and her sleeping hours. And by the time she had purchased a small but adequate building on Market Street, she had known she was indeed carrying a child.

Even now, while she laboriously climbed the steps to her apartment above the boutique, she could still not believe that she would give birth in less than a month. And what had revived her memories of her departure from Aspen was the thick envelope in her hand, postmarked from Aspen on December 2, 1888, and addressed to her, in care of general delivery, in Matt's handwriting.

She opened the door and called, "It's only me, Hattie," while hanging her heavy coat on the door peg and giving Abraham a loving pat.

"Miserable day," Hattie replied, rounding the kitchen corner. "Never even got this foggy in Ireland."

"Yes, but it'll clear up soon. You'll see." Erin eased herself onto the couch in the small parlor.

"What have you got there?"

She glanced at the letter still in her hand. "Just a letter from Aspen."

"Just a letter! It's from Matthew, isn't it?"

"So what if it is, Hattie? I'll read it later."

"You'll do no such thing!" Hattie stood over her with arms akimbo. "Look, Erin, I'll leave you alone now . . . there're some new hats downstairs that need pricing and sorting. When I get back, I'll want to know what he said."

Erin laughed weakly. Hattie would never stop hoping, never stop pestering her about Matt. But by now Erin had grown used to her constant prattling and scolding; she regarded it with affection.

When Hattie had gone below, Erin suddenly remembered that her old friend was going to leave her, for Hattie had received a letter from Mr. Rumplemeyer only last week. She had insisted on remaining until the summer, when the baby would not need such constant care and when Erin could find a suitable replacement for her. As if Hattie believed anyone could replace her! Erin smiled. She was glad she had convinced Hattie to return to Aspen, possibly to marry this man who professed to love her.

Erin dismissed her thoughts about Hattie and turned the letter over in her hand. She knew she was behaving as if she were terrified to open it, afraid to read Matt's words.

Undoubtedly, he had written only to acknowledge receipt of the money she had sent him last month. He was probably amazed that she had been able to repay him so soon.

Erin slipped her fingernail through the seal and shifted her weight heavily on the couch. The baby moved constantly now, reminding her of how near her time was and of how uncertain she felt about carrying a child whose father was Matt Steele.

Unfolding the many-paged letter, she was surprised to see another, smaller envelope fall onto her rounded lap. It was from Ireland, and bore Gregory's precise script on its face. She decided to read Gregory's letter first and save Matt's for last. Briefly, she wondered if Matt had read the letter from Ireland before forwarding it to her, but it appeared untouched.

"Dearest Erin," it began. "I write to inform you of the recent death of your uncle. Mercifully, he closed his eyes in sleep one night and slipped into the other world without pain or knowledge. Naturally, Norwood is yours now, and I am given to understand that Edward confided to an old friend that he was quite pleased to leave the manor in the expert care of his niece. I thought you might want to know this, Erin, and I hope it may comfort you."

Her uncle had actually been pleased to leave Norwood to her! What an odd turn of events. Yes indeed, the knowledge that Edward had come to see her as a worthy heir did comfort her.

Gregory's note went on to say: "I have taken it upon myself to install an excellent young family at Norwood. The Owens recently lost their own estate, north of Killarney, through no fault of their own. I shall personally see to the affairs of Norwood, and, if possible, rents will be paid into your account.

"Also, I would advise you to have a will drawn up immediately and to forward the instructions to me."

Erin paused in her reading. A will! Her baby would be heir to Norwood Manor—but was that true? After all, she had been foolish enough to put her maiden name in Edward's will, and legally, she wasn't entitled to the estate. If she could somehow persuade Matt to have the date changed on their marriage papers, or to deed the property to her now, since he would inherit it, Edward's will would then be legal. Perhaps if Matt were told about the baby, he would be willing to do this, knowing that his child would someday inherit Norwood. She would have to think hard about it. But oh, how very foolish she had been to get herself into this situation in the first place.

She went back to Gregory's letter:

"I am quite content these days. Sophie has borne me a son only last week, and her spirits seem to be improving with the birth of this child.

"Should you ever need anything, please know that you can depend on me."

So, she thought, Gregory would attend to all her affairs in Ireland. She was grateful, for certainly that would make things easier for her. Now, if only Matt could be brought around to her point of view. Perhaps she should write to him and explain the situation, but that would mean telling him about the baby, and she wasn't ready to do that just yet.

Erin rose and went into the kitchen to prepare a cup of hot chocolate. It was a miserable Sunday in San Francisco, she noticed as she glanced out the window. Even if she had kept the shop open, there would have been few customers out in the damp fog rolling in from the Bay. But Christmas was coming soon, and Erin knew that she and Hattie would spend long hours below in the boutique, fitting elegant dresses to fussy women or making selections for indecisive men. Nevertheless, the profits were excellent, and the young Chinese seamstress she had hired was not only tireless but also expert in her custom designs.

Turning away from the dismal scene outside, Erin carried her cup back to the couch and sat down with a deep sigh. Her legs often cramped these days and her back ached terribly. How would she ever make it through the Christmas season? she wondered.

She picked up the sheets of Matt's letter and her hands began to tremble. Coolly, she reminded herself that Matt was part of her past, the part that was buried. He no longer mattered to her—only in terms of Norwood. The shop, the baby—they were what counted. However, she could not stop the surge of giddiness coursing through her as her eyes fell on the words "Dear Erin" at the top of the first page.

"I have received the draft drawn on your San Francisco account," the letter stated, "and am happy that you seem to have done so well. The interest, not to mention the balance of the money, was not necessary. You know I never wanted to be repaid. I have deposited the sum into your old account in Aspen, and should you ever need to draw on it, it's there for your personal use. No arguments, please?"

Damn him! she thought futilely. Now it was as if she had accepted the money for good. He simply wouldn't relent!

"It was quite typical of you to avoid telling me where you are living," his letter continued, "or, for that matter, the location of your business. I suggest that at some future date you send me your address, as there might be further letters from Ireland, or documents concerning the Aspen house that need your attention. By the way, the house remains empty and is now in your name. If you want, I can rent it out; at least that way someone could look after your expensive furnishings."

Oh, how like Matt to make it almost impossible for her to avoid writing him! She would let *him* take care of any papers or rentals; she was finished with the house anyway.

Abraham jumped up on the couch and attempted to settle himself in her lap. She laughed and stroked his graying muzzle. "Well, Abraham," she said, "in a short while there'll be room for you again."

Erin discarded the first page of Matt's letter and was surprised to see a well-drawn map on the second. "The Rio Grande Railroad is now in Aspen," he wrote. "Thought you might want to see the route from Glenwood Springs. Also, I'm done working for the railroad—retired, you might say, from all that backstabbing and deceit. For me, it's the life of a rancher now."

She studied the map. The route was obviously an engineering feat of some magnitude, and to think that Matt had laid the difficult groundwork for the Rio Grande to beat out the Colorado Midland. I'll bet he was paid a dear sum for that job, she surmised. No wonder he was able to retire into ranching! Of course, Matt Steele always got what he went after.

She turned the page, only to find a hasty sketch of Snowmass Valley and his new ranch house. Why had he bothered to inform her so thoroughly of his situation? Had he actually thought she would care *what* he did?

The fourth page offered newsy items: how Aspen had prospered with the arrival of the railroad; how the streets had changed; how new buildings were sprouting all over, how silver fortunes were lost and found overnight. Erin was amazed to discover that Matt took such an interest in the town. He had never really done so before. Somehow, this information both pleased and saddened her. She dismissed her musings and proceeded to read the last page.

"I hope, whatever your situation in the city, that you are happy now. I've often thought that your leaving was for the best. We couldn't have made a marriage based on your running affairs—I can see that now. I trust you have given up the notion of divorce, since I haven't heard otherwise. I'm truly sorry if my firm position on the subject causes you any problems with your suitors, but I've no intentions of remarrying, so a divorce is permanently out of the question."

Erin gritted her teeth in abject frustration. How dare he assume that she would meekly take on lovers without the hope of a decent marriage! *Damn him!* she cried inwardly. He was condemning her to a life of loneliness and he knew it! He had written a honeyed-sweet letter for that sole purpose!

That Erin had already resigned herself to a life without a man mattered nothing to her now. Matt was pulling the strings of her existence from afar and throwing that fact in her face. He had managed everything very well. First he had put the money she had repaid him into her Aspen bank account, and then he had changed the deed of the Bullion Row house. Worst of all had been his open mention of her "suitors" and the hint that she could never remarry. Why had he gone to such obvious lengths to ensnarl her in his life? His supreme arrogance was more apparent to her now than it ever had been, for his actions had to stem from the simple fact that she was the one woman in his vast experience who would not submit meekly to his will.

Erin gasped suddenly as it occurred to her that if Matt ever found out about the baby, he'd surely take it from her. Involuntarily, she touched the life-filled swell of her stomach. He could never find out about the child. Never! Or, like everything else in her life, she would lose that, too.

Abruptly, her mind was racked by a picture of Matt holding the infant in his powerful arms, carrying it away from her, disappearing into the dense San Francisco fog. Moments later she broke out into a fearful sweat and her mind cleared, but she could not tell if she had had one of her visions or if she had merely contrived the image because of her panic.

Rising to her feet, Erin moved sluggishly to the apartment door. She would talk to Hattie, busy herself below in the shop—do anything to dispel the churning emotions that threatened to consume her.

It took a full week for Erin to calm down, a week of hard work interspersed with constant reassurances from Hattie that everything would turn out for the best. But even the myriad Christmas shoppers who purchased one feminine item of apparel after another could not fully relieve Erin of the feeling that someday Matt would reenter her life. Often, she would curse herself aloud for not moving to a place where he'd never find her or hear about her. She knew she had gained a reputation for providing women with elegant clothing and the latest undergarments from Paris, and that her boutique was a frequent topic of conversation in the finer hotels and salons. She had become known as the beautiful Irish widow of Market Street, a rumor she did not deny. The gentlemen who stopped by to purchase a hat or a pair of gloves for their wives or mistresses did not let Erin's obvious pregnancy stem the flow of their words of flattery for her. That she was a charming "widow" was enough to keep them entranced. After the baby was born, they would probably become bolder with their suggestions, but Erin was confident that she could hold them at bay while relieving their pockets of the weight of banknotes.

Eventually, as the year 1888 drew to a close, her anger and misgivings over Matt diminished, until she no longer worried about him at all. Time was an excellent healer; hadn't she learned that simple lesson so often before?

Chapter 36

The baby's tiny mouth sucked and pulled at Erin's breast. She loved the feel of nursing him, the hungry urgency of his tugging at her. His dark head was so like his father's, she mused, but even the thought of Matt could not dampen her pleasure at holding the warm roundness of her child. Her lips curved in a sudden smile and she told herself, He is worth everything. He is worth my losing the house, the money, even the Silver Lady. He is worth my living in a strange city, having to work hard for our keep. She bent over to kiss his soft, dark hair. He continued nursing, but his blue eyes closed and his tugging at her breast grew fitful. Patrick Llewelyn Steele, she thought. Such a big name for such a little baby.

She had decided not to let Matt know he had a son. If that was being cruel to him, she didn't care; he deserved it. Her heart contracted at the recurring thought of what would happen if he ever found out. Would he try to take the baby away? Her arms tightened possessively around Patrick. Maybe Matt wouldn't care at all; maybe he would be as unconcerned about his child as he was about her.

Erin thought back to her first weeks in San Francisco, when she had felt so homesick that she had been tempted to sell the shop and return to Aspen. But her pride and her subsequent success had kept her from acting on that feeling—as well as her desperate need to stand on her own and not live on handouts from her husband. She had persevered, and all was going well now; thank God, Hattie was with her. What would she have done without her dear friend? But there were times that she ached with desolation and with something else, too—a need to have a man lying next to her in bed, to hold and comfort her. And no matter how hard she tried to ignore it, her mind's eye conjured up a picture of only one man in her bed—Matthew Steele. She could envision only his face, his slow, mocking smile, his penetrating blue eyes, his long, lean body.

She kept thinking of the sketch he had drawn of his ranch at Snowmass. He was obviously proud of his spread, but she focused only on the fact that he had forced himself upon her there, and that the baby had been conceived there. Matt would be overjoyed to know that his son had been conceived on the very spot where his house now stood; Erin thought he would consider it poetic justice. It would be a long time, if ever, before he'd be able to throw *that* in her face! she fumed inwardly.

Then her thoughts would soften, with the contentment of motherhood coloring her imagination, and she saw her son romping in the green valley with his father, or riding on a pony, or visiting Ute Cemetery, where his paternal grandfather was buried. But this could never be. Matt didn't want her and she didn't want him; she would never give him the satisfaction of knowing about his child.

Patrick was asleep, his lips still puckered and making sucking motions at the empty air. Erin rose carefully and laid him down in his cradle. He didn't move; his face was angelic in repose. She covered him and left the room on tiptoe. She would relieve Hattie in the shop and take care of the customers for the rest of the afternoon while Hattie puttered around the apartment and cooked their dinner.

Erin sat on a high stool behind the counter, trying to catch up on her accounts ledger in between customers. It was a pleasant day in early April, without the usual damp fog, and many people were riding around in carriages or picnicking, not shopping. The shop was, therefore, quiet and peaceful. The bell over the door tinkled faintly, and Erin glanced up from her book work. No one was there, the door had not opened, so why had the bell rung? How strange. Then the edges of her vision became blurry, and her eyes focused only on a tunnel-like opening through the gray mist. She could see the door of her shop opening and a man in a dark frock coat and brilliant white shirt sauntering in, a silk hat pushed casually to the back of his dark head. He smiled and held out his hand, saying something to her, then the image faded. Erin squeezed her eyes shut, trembling violently. It had been Matt in her vision, Matt walking into her shop! But he was a thousand miles away; he had no idea what she was doing or where she lived, beyond the fact that she was in San Francisco. He could never find her!

But the sight unsettled her; her strange imaginings so often came true. She could no longer concentrate on the columns of figures in front of her, so she walked around the shop, tidying shelves, arranging the new hats more attractively, her heart pounding in her chest. It was only her too-sensitive imagination, nothing more, she convinced herself.

While she was fidgeting with a high, lacy collar on a Parisian day frock, the doorbell tinkled again, and Erin jumped as if she had touched a live current. She looked around in fear, but this time the door was opening normally, admitting a dark-haired, pretty woman in a burgundy, bustled dress. Erin smiled politely, relieved to see a flesh-and-blood customer. She quickly assessed the woman's style, as was her habit; that way she could dispense with time-consuming preliminaries and offer the best possible service. This was her job now, and she did it well. She hardly glanced at the man who had followed the woman into the boutique; when men accompanied ladies here, their purpose was only to pay the bill, and usually they remained in the background.

"Good afternoon, may I—" But Erin's words froze on her lips as she looked more directly at the tall, dark-coated man who now stood just inside the door. Her face turned white and she felt an immediate rush of dizziness; she closed her eyes and groped blindly behind her for the counter. Everything receded farther and farther away, until her ears were ringing with the echo of her rapid heartbeat.

"I'm sorry, Erin. I didn't mean to shock you so." A strong hand steadied her arm and the familiar low drawl penetrated her hearing.

She opened her eyes at last, to see Matt's blue eyes staring into her own, a slightly worried frown on his face. She licked her dry lips and tried to speak. "How . . . how did you . . ." Nothing more could escape her closed throat.

"First of all, maybe you better sit down. You look a bit peaked." He led her to a blue satin Louis Quinze chair. "Is there something to drink here, a glass of water?" he asked solicitously.

"Yes," Erin whispered. "There . . ." She gestured to a curtained alcove.

He strode behind it, found a pitcher of water and a glass, and reappeared. "Drink some of this," he said, forcing the cold liquid into her mouth.

She swallowed convulsively, then pushed his hand away. "I'm all right now. It was just . . . a surprise to see you here." She could feel her self-control returning, the dreadful weakness passing. "How did you know . . . ?"

"San Francisco's not all that big. I just asked at my hotel. Seems everyone has heard of the beautiful young *widow* who opened an elegant shop on Market Street."

She could not miss his emphasis on the word "widow," and looked down at her hands, feeling undone. "It was easier that way, Matt, that's all." Then, abruptly, she remembered the young woman who had come in ahead of Matt and who was now standing, ill at ease, in a corner of the boutique. A sudden anger flared within Erin. "Your . . . friend is waiting, Matt. How cruel and thoughtless you are." Her eyes blazed like green stones.

"Samantha, come here. I'd like to introduce you to Erin Conner Steele, my wife." Not even a hint of embarrassment colored his manner; he was as cool as a man introducing two business acquaintances.

"Matt, if you don't mind . . . I'd rather go. I'm sure your *wife* has no great desire to meet me, nor I her." Samantha's face was flushed; her dark eyes had grown brilliant with unshed tears. She turned to the door, trying to muster her dignity.

Matt leaned down over Erin. She could feel his warm breath on her, the faint smell of cigar smoke. "I'll be back in a minute, Erin. Let me see to her—I'll send her on ahead to the hotel. But I'll be back to talk to you."

He walked quickly out after Samantha, leaving Erin sitting mutely in the chair, but seething inwardly. How dare he bring his mistress in here! she fumed. And what is he doing in San Francisco? Did he come to lavish his money on Samantha? A tart? Erin's head spun dangerously, and she tried to regain her composure.

Then Matt was inside the shop again. "There, I've sent her off, slightly mollified."

Erin looked up, then rose and walked away from him.

His voice reached her from across the room, low and intimate. "You're looking well, Erin."

She whirled around to face him. "How *dare* you—"

He cut her off sharply. "I dare any damn thing I please. You're my wife."

She laughed bitterly. "So you keep reminding me! What are you doing here? I won't flatter myself to think you've come looking for me!"

"No." The low drawl, the mocking smile, were so familiar. "I had some business here, which I could have done by mail, but I felt like a holiday. Nice city you've got here."

"I'm glad you're enjoying it, Matt. Now get the hell out of my shop!" Her eyes narrowed, flashing green lights.

"Not yet, my dear." His tone was suddenly harsh as he stepped closer, taking hold of both her arms and looking into her face for a long, silent moment. She was still beautiful, vibrant, but there was a new maturity about her, a subdued quality. Suddenly he had a great urge to crush her in his arms, to taste her lips, to caress her flesh, until the anger and bitterness on her face fled, as he knew they would. But afterward, as always, she would turn away from his demands, from his passion, from his need to dominate her willful stubbornness. His eyes moved over her body then, and he noticed that her figure looked fuller, more rounded, and that her breasts were more prominent.

"What do you want, Matt?" Erin's voice was cold and flat. "What do you really want from me?" She stared at him, remaining unmoving, tense, in his grasp.

"Nothing, Erin," he said lightly, releasing her. "I don't want a damn thing from you." He gazed around him for the first time, taking in the elegant decor, the rich and feminine ambience of the boutique.

"Nice little shop you've got yourself here."

"It's adequate. We're not starving. If you've come to push your help on me, it's not wanted."

"No, you never wanted any money from me, Erin, or anything else, either." His tone was dry, amused. "And how is Hattie?"

"Hattie's fine."

"Erin, listen to me." He cupped her chin in his hand. "Our marriage hasn't worked out, but we don't have to be enemies. It would be so much simpler to be . . . well, if not friends, then at least reasonable adults. Stop being so afraid of losing your independence. You didn't have to go to such drastic lengths to get away from me. I gave you your freedom when, by law, I could have forced you to live with me."

"Do you have to keep reminding me?" she hissed angrily. "Do you think I like having to lie, to say I'm a widow? You've put me in an intolerable position, and I hate it! I resent that you can go anywhere, do anything you want, while I have to keep up a front. Why won't you give me a divorce? That's what I really want."

"Lew wouldn't have liked the idea." Matt's tone was mild.

"Lew? What do you know about Lew's likes and dislikes? What does he have to do with us?"

"He was my father, Erin, and I love and respect his memory and his last wishes, which is more than you seem to be doin'."

"Don't change the subject, Matt Steele," Erin flared.

"I'm not, believe me." He paused. "This is no place to talk. Next thing you know, we'll have your customers listening to our marital problems. I want to talk to you some more. I'll be tied up for a day or two, but how about coming to my hotel room on Wednesday? I'm at the Grande—we can talk in privacy there."

"No!" Erin retorted quickly. If he insisted on speaking with her, she'd rather have him here, with Hattie around—but she couldn't invite him upstairs, he'd see the baby. "Not your room. I'll meet you in the lobby."

"What's the matter, Erin, don't you trust me?" The mocking smile returned, causing her to sigh with exasperation. The same old Matt! "All right, Erin, in the lobby—at seven o'clock. Maybe we can have dinner together, talk about old times . . ."

"And what are you going to do with your lady friend? Will she join us?" Erin asked sarcastically.

"Hell, no. Sam's used to keepin' her own company. She's patient."

"Why do you want to see me, Matt? We've nothing to discuss, except that I want a divorce and you won't give me one." She wouldn't dream of discussing the child, *his* son, who lay sleeping peacefully upstairs. My God, she thought suddenly, what if Patrick wakes up and cries? Matt might hear him. Dear Lord, she prayed silently, please don't let him wake up now.

"Well, that's a start. I'm sure we'll think of something."

"All right, seven on Wednesday." She had to get Matt out of here quickly.

"If you're not there, Erin, I'll come looking for you. I'm not used to being stood up."

"Fine, fine. I promise I'll be there."

Matt noticed her faint agitation and wondered about it. Was she expecting another man? A spark of jealousy flickered in him. She was so beautiful; surely other men had noticed her. A woman all alone was fair game. His blue eyes went hard and opaque, and he spun around to leave, then turned back to look at her again. She stood very still, her teeth worrying her bottom lip, her glorious hair piled stylishly on top of her head. His grave regard seemed to make her more nervous.

"See you the day after tomorrow, then, kid," he said, and rambled nonchalantly out the door.

The bell tinkled as he left, jangling her nerves. As soon as she was certain he had gone, she ran to the door and locked it, putting up the "Closed" sign with shaking hands. Then she turned to the stairs, her heart pounding. *Why* had he come back into her life? She had just been growing accustomed to the peacefulness and serenity of her life, and *he* reappeared, like a recurring nightmare. Would she never be rid of him? Would she never be free of his powerful charm, of the strength of his maleness? Would she never be free of *her* response to him? Why did she suffer such a debilitating disease, such a profound weakness, when she was near him? He was not worth her anguish or her response. He kept after her merely because she had rejected him, had hurt his precious pride. She would see him once more, if just to convince him that a divorce was the only solution to their relationship.

Chapter 37

Tonight, Erin thought dismally, she was to meet Matthew, and if she didn't he'd come to the shop. She couldn't risk that; if he found out about the baby, Lord knew *what* he would do!

While she busied herself in the boutique, her mind raced with the possible words of persuasion she could use to sway Matt to give her the divorce. She had lain awake most of the last two nights worrying herself sick over the problem, and now she had only a few hours left in which to come up with something. As she began to devise a workable plan in her mind, the door opened, and the woman named Samantha entered.

Just what I need, Erin thought to herself in disgust. Now I have to stand here and mince words with a trollop whom I don't dare throw out for fear of angering Matt!

"Good afternoon, Mrs. Steele," came the woman's overly polite greeting.

Erin conveniently forgot Samantha's name. "Look, miss, if you've come here to shop, that's fine. But if you want to talk, which I suspect you do, let's get it over with."

"Just like Matt always said—you're a woman of business, aren't you?" Samantha seated herself stiffly in the chair. "Well, I just wanted you to know I'm on your side."

"My side?" Erin's eyes widened in hesitant surprise.

"Yes, Mrs. Steele. You see, over the long months that Matt and I have known each other, I've come to think of him as mine—mine alone. And I'm all for a divorce."

Erin eyed the woman carefully. Samantha was not as dull-witted as she appeared. Nevertheless, Erin could not help but dislike her, and wondered how Matt could possibly appreciate her overblown demeanor.

She straightened a beige, plumed hat on a mannequin's head. "If that's all you have to say, then please leave. I assure you, I have every intention of divorcing my husband, and I don't need your help."

"Oh, but you might, my dear," Samantha remarked lightly. "Perhaps if we both work together, then—"

"I told you, I can do it on my own!" Erin snapped. "After all, I know Matt much better than you do!"

Samantha narrowed her eyes. "Maybe you really don't want to be rid of him . . . or why else won't you accept my help?"

"Please leave now. I think our little talk is over."

Samantha smiled, but her politeness did not reach her eyes, which glared their jealousy at Erin. She walked to the door, her hand lingering on the knob, and was about to speak when she was pushed backward by a customer who had entered the shop.

Samantha gasped, and then coughed to cover her rudeness; the man who had just come in was perhaps the most repulsive-looking individual she had ever seen. He was immense, both in height and in girth, and his head was completely bald. But it was his small, piercing eyes that almost caused her to stagger when he looked directly at her. She froze for an instant before she wrenched her stare away and noticed that Erin was also taken aback by the man's appearance.

And then she heard Erin's indrawn breath, sounding as if she were utterly shocked. For a moment Samantha thought that Erin was overreacting to the distasteful sight of this customer.

"Mortimer . . . Ben Mortimer . . . oh, my God—no!" Erin whispered.

"Well, well, the little Irish virgin! I'll be damned! I'll just be damned if this isn't my lucky day—and to think I only came in here on a whim!"

Samantha was stunned; it was obvious that Erin knew this crude man, knew him and was terrified. And what had this Mortimer person meant when he called her an Irish virgin? How disgusting! But Samantha was not so confused as to be unaware that Matt might be interested in this tidbit—that the man seemed to have known Erin intimately at one time. Had he taken her virginity?

Mortimer strode heavily over to Erin, and Samantha strained to hear his mumbled words.

"Remember Denver City? When you hit me? I sure haven't forgotten . . ." He grabbed the soft flesh of Erin's arm and shook her roughly for a moment before releasing her.

Erin appeared to be speechless, her face ashen and her eyes wide with terror. Samantha could not hear what the man continued to say to Erin, but whatever it was caused Matt's wife to tremble and back away from him. Then Mortimer seemed to sense Samantha's presence again, and he moved toward the front door, amazing her by the way he nearly filled the tiny shop.

Finally Erin spoke. "Get out of here, Mortimer—get out of here before I call the police!"

"Oh, I'll leave, all right. But make no mistake, you owe me, owe me real good for this scar on my head and that little scene way back when. You'll pay, and soon."

Samantha watched in bewilderment as he made his awkward exit, slamming the door behind him, so that the glass rattled severely.

"My God . . . oh, my God," Erin cried, sagging into the chair, fingers of terror creeping up her spine.

"Are you . . . all right?"

Erin could not reply for several moments. At last she muttered, "Yes, I'm fine now."

"Listen, if you like, I'll stay . . . Maybe you want to talk about it." Briefly, Samantha had felt sorry for Matt's wife, seeing the look of stark horror on her face. But when Erin seemed under control again, she saw an opportunity to find out more about what she had just witnessed.

But Erin halted her plans. "No, it's nothing I want to think about, much less discuss. I'm sorry . . . thank you for the offer. And I'll do anything I can to obtain that divorce."

"Well, all right, Mrs. Steele. I'll leave you now, if you really feel you don't want to talk about that grotesque man."

"No, I don't. I was just shaken for a moment. It's over now . . . So much has happened today . . ." Erin spoke as if to herself.

When Samantha had gone, she went upstairs to check on the baby and to calm her nerves. While she rocked little Patrick, the full weight of the last few days fell heavily upon her. First Matt appeared, toting his woman on his arm, and now another face, a dreaded one, popped up out of her past.

Hattie locked up the shop at six and came back upstairs. Erin had decided not to tell her about Mortimer; Hattie worried too much about everything as it was. Besides, Erin had more urgent things on her mind.

"I've got to hurry or I'll miss the meeting with Matt," she said. "Will you be all right here alone with the baby? He's fed now, and I won't be long."

"Don't be silly. The baby and I will be just fine, but I don't like your going out alone at night."

Erin thought briefly to herself that Hattie was quite right, but for a different reason.

"Maybe you should postpone this meeting. The more I think about your being out on the dark streets . . ." Hattie grimaced.

"If I do that, Matt will come here—he'll find out about the baby. I've got to go." Erin rose from the rocker and handed the sleepy infant to Hattie.

"Did you hire a carriage to take you to the hotel?"

"Well . . . no, I was going to walk. It's only a few blocks."

"I'll go with you."

"No, you won't, you'll stay right here with the baby. I'll stick close to the street lamps and ask Matt to walk me back." Erin ended the debate firmly.

The hour was growing late, and she barely had time to change her dress, fix her hair, and check her appearance in the mirror. And to make matters worse, she had not yet fully planned what she would say to Matt. Well, she would still come up with something . . .

The damp evening air chilled Erin right through her full-length fur as she hurried north along Market Street toward the Grande. Even if she were a few minutes late, she was certain Matt would wait.

Only another two blocks, Erin thought, and she would see Matt, perhaps for the last time. Her mind was suddenly filled with the idea: if he would grant her a divorce, then most likely this would be their final meeting. She was vaguely aware of the sound of a lone carriage behind her, the horse's hooves ringing hollowly on the cobblestones. She also heard the carriage slow its pace, but she was in too much of a rush to look around.

"We meet again so soon!"

The man's voice threw a stab of terror into her heart, and she felt herself spun roughly around and thrown off balance. Her sole reaction was to open her mouth to scream; surely there was help nearby. But before she could emit a sound, everything before her went black, and she did not know that her huge foe lifted her unconscious body like a feather and shoved her into his carriage.

Much later, when Erin's eyes flew open in confusion, the first sensation she had was a nauseating, choking feeling in her mouth. She tried to gasp for air and discovered that her mouth was stuffed with some sort of cloth. Then she realized that her arms were bound above her head, but that her feet, at least, were free. And then, to her absolute horror, Erin saw that she was stark naked.

Everything flooded back to her: the intended meeting with Matt, the hurried walk down Market Street, the fog, those hands spinning her around . . .

"'Bout time ya woke up—I didn't hit ya that hard!"

Ben Mortimer! Of course!

Erin tried to scream, but the effort only served to gag her and to elicit a hoarse chortle from her tormentor. And from where she lay tied helplessly to a bed, she could see his small, beady eyes riveted on her shrinking flesh. The look on his face vividly brought to mind that dreadful red velvet room at Madame Lucille's.

She began to sob, a series of muffled moans.

"Cry all ya like, bitch . . . won't help ya now."

Chapter 38

Matt pulled out his pocket watch once more and looked at the time. Eight-thirty. Erin was an hour and a half late. The lying little *bitch!* he fumed. She was probably out with some admirer, dining in a candlelit restaurant, while he paced the lobby of the Grande Hotel like a fool. She had never meant to meet him—why had he ever believed her? He should have known better.

He strode angrily across the polished marble floor and entered the dark, hushed men's bar, all heavy oak and smoke-shrouded. He ordered a double whiskey and slammed a silver dollar down on the counter. Taking great gulps of his drink, he felt the warm glow in his stomach, but his fury persisted. There was no woman in the world who could irritate him like Erin, who could get beneath his skin and dig her claws in. Maybe, he mused, it was because she had known him for so long, or maybe she simply liked to aggravate him. He finished off the rest of his whiskey. There was nothing for him to do except to go back upstairs, but he knew he wouldn't be very good company for Samantha. Still, she was used to his moods; for that he was grateful.

He let himself into their room with his key. Samantha sat propped up in bed, wearing only a red negligee, a box of bonbons on her lap and the usual magazine in her hands. Her eyes met his, limpid and surprised, over the top of the periodical.

"Matt! I thought you were seeing that—your wife. Has she gone already?"

"Damn bitch never showed up! And I've been waiting like an idiot for an hour and a half!" He threw his hat and gloves on a chair, then began to pace.

Samantha felt an immediate glow of joy—Matt would spend the evening with her, then. But this feeling faded rapidly as it occurred to her that perhaps Erin had changed her mind about the divorce.

"That's funny, Matt," Samantha said, popping another chocolate in her mouth.

"What's funny?" he asked absently.

"Well, just a few hours ago she said she was planning on seeing you . . ."

Matt whirled around and fixed her with his intense blue gaze. "What the hell are you talking about?"

Samantha stopped chewing. She hadn't planned on ever telling Matt that she had taken it upon herself to visit Erin, for she knew that would drive him wild. As it was, his reaction to her words left her breathless; she had never seen him so angry.

"I . . . I'm sorry, Matt," she said in a small voice.

"I . . . saw her this afternoon. She was getting ready to come over here . . ."

"Then what happened to her?" He looked genuinely puzzled. "Look, I don't know in hell you were doing there or what you two females said to each other. That's *your* business. But *my* business does concern her—so where is she?"

Samantha was frightened. Matt's cool control had always bothered her but now he appeared menacing as he held her wrist in a tight clasp.

"I don't know, Matt—honestly I don't!" Then she tried to satisfy him. "But there was this strange man who came in while I was there. He seemed to know her, and they had an argument. I almost felt sorry for her, the man was so . . . awful. Maybe . . ."

"Maybe what?" His voice was harsh, almost unrecognizable.

"Oh, I don't know. Matt, you're hurting me!"

He let go of her abruptly and attempted to calm himself. It wouldn't do him any good to upset Samantha. "Just tell me everything you can remember about him, Sam."

She took a deep breath before answering him. "He was *huge,* crude and ugly, but he looked rich. And he was bald. He got purple in the face and muttered something to her. It sounded threatening, but I couldn't hear the exact words." She gave a delicate shiver. "I hope nobody ever talks to me like that."

"What was his name? Where was he from? Do you know any more about him, anything at all?"

Samantha put a finger to her lips and thought for a moment. "His name . . . She said it like she was shocked or scared. It was something like . . . Montgomery, and his first name was Ben, because I remember thinking, 'Ha! Big Ben.'"

"Ben . . . Mortimer. Was that it, Sam?" His voice was so quiet, so somber, that Samantha was frightened all over again.

"Yes," she whispered. "Ben Mortimer."

Matt's face was very taut, his blue eyes glinting like splintered glass. A muscle ticked in his jaw. "Ben Mortimer," he murmured. "Jesus Christ!" He grabbed his hat and turned to leave.

"Where are you going?" Samantha cried.

323

"I'm not sure. Don't wait up for me." The door closed behind him with a determined click.

Matt rushed down the stairs, through the lobby, and out into the dark, fog-hazed street. His first stop would be Erin's shop, since it wasn't far from the hotel. Had the man really been Mortimer? If so, what was he doing here? Matt's brain spun. Poor Erin, he thought. He knew, had known for years, how terrified she was of Mortimer, even though her ghastly experience with him had occurred so long ago.

Everything was black inside the boutique. Matt knocked on the door loudly, but there was no answer. He stepped back into the street and glanced up at the lace-shrouded bay window on the second floor, then gathered a few stones from the gutter and threw them at the glass. Soon Hattie's pale face appeared. She held up a hand, motioning Matt to wait, then disappeared. He cursed impatiently as the cold mist settled on his face and shoulders.

The door opened, the bell tinkled, and Hattie stood there with a lamp. "Matt! What are you doing here? Where's Erin?"

"That's what I came to find out," he answered tightly.

"Come in—I'm sorry." She put down the lamp and locked the door behind him. "Isn't she with you?"

"No. She never showed up, and I take it she's not here."

"What on earth . . .?"

"Hattie, never mind how I know this, but I think Ben Mortimer was here this afternoon, threatening her."

"Ben Mortimer!" Hattie's eyes were huge. "Oh, poor Erin!"

"Yes, exactly."

"I was upstairs most of the afternoon. I didn't hear a thing . . . but, come to think of it, she seemed very rattled before she left." Hattie looked at him searchingly. "Do you think something's happened?"

"Could be, Hattie."

"Oh, dear God, what can we do?"

"Don't worry, I'll find Mortimer, if it's him. I'll find him if I have to search every inch of the city."

"I knew him—I can tell you what he looks like."

"Hattie, can we go upstairs? I'd like a drink, and you can tell me all you know."

At that moment, Hattie knew she had to decide whether to

keep Erin's secret or to help Matt find her. She had no choice. He *was* the child's father, after all, as she had so often reminded Erin. She sighed, knowing Erin would hate her forever if this was a false alarm. "Come on up, Matt."

Once they were in the apartment, she poured him a stiff drink and one for herself, tossing it down with gusto. "That's better. Now, what do we do? Go to the police?"

"Hell, no. They won't be much help. They'd wait a week before they'd believe she was gone! Does she have any friends—any men friends, for instance—with whom she could be?"

"Absolutely not. She's never gone for very long. She has to—" Hattie stopped, flustered.

Matt's eyes narrowed. "She has to what, Hattie?"

As if on cue, the sound of a whimper was heard in the adjoining room, whose door stood ajar. The whimper became a thin wail, then grew to a lusty bellow.

"Oh, dear," Hattie said mildly. "Oh, my."

"What the hell!" The words exploded from Matt's lips.

"He's hungry," Hattie explained weakly.

"Who's hungry?"

"Come and see—you may as well."

He followed her into the next room. It was dark inside, but Hattie walked unerringly to the cradle and picked Patrick up.

"You better light the lamp—he won't be sleeping for a while. He's hungry."

Matt's hands fumbled at the simple task. Then the wick flared, the shadows receded, and Matt saw Hattie standing a few feet away from him, a baby in her arms. This is crazy, he thought. What is Hattie doing with a baby?

"Meet Patrick Llewelyn Steele," Hattie said solemnly, holding the blanket-swathed bundle out to him. The walls reverberated with the red-faced infant's wails.

"Who?" Matt asked blankly.

"Patrick Llewelyn Steele," Hattie repeated. "Your son."

"My *what?"*

"This is your son, Matthew."

"Hattie, this is no time to joke!"

"Matthew Steele, you simpleton, this child is most certainly *not* a joke!"

"But . . . she never . . . never said a word . . . I never heard anything." He was stunned, his face a mask of confusion. "Oh, my God, she never . . ." He grabbed Hattie's arm. "You're not just saying this to hurt me—or her?"

"You numbskull! That's a damn insult!" She turned and began to croon to the baby, rocking him gently. "You're hungry, I know, and your mother isn't here to feed you. Now, what are we going to do?"

Matt went out into the parlor and poured himself another drink. He felt numb, his mind devoid of everything but what he had just seen and heard. He had a son! Erin had borne him a child and had never let him know about it—even when he had seen her the other day in her shop! Why in heaven's name had she chosen to keep his son from him? What kind of perverse pride had driven her to do such a thing?

Hattie appeared with the baby; he had quieted down and was blinking in the light. Matt looked at him more closely, noticing the dark hair and bright blue eyes so like his own, the mouth and chin so like Erin's. Yes, this was his child; and when he thought back to when Erin might have conceived—it had to have been that time at Snowmass—he no longer questioned the reasons for her silence.

Then it hit him: the mother of his child was missing, and the child was hungry, crying for her. Erin would never leave her baby hungry. Someone—Ben Mortimer—was preventing her from coming home. Matt had to find him quickly and get Erin out of his clutches . . . if she was all right. If she wasn't . . . He refused to acknowledge that possibility.

"Hattie," he said briskly, "I have a lot to do. I'm going to check the hotels, boarding houses, restaurants. From what I understand, this Mortimer is an easy man to spot. Now, tell me everything you know about him—every detail."

"Well, it's about time you came out of your fuddle and decided to do something!" She proceeded to describe Mortimer, and to relate what she remembered of his habits from Denver City. "He's a big drinker and eater, very fussy about his food. Try the places with good dining rooms first. And he likes to get barbered every day and have a manicure." Hattie shuddered. "He's a wicked, disgusting beast!"

Matt felt a familiar calm ease into him, one that transformed him into a cold, analytical machine, capable of efficient, implacable operation. He put all emotion, all gentle thoughts, from him for now; he had been trained to function in this manner until the task at hand was completed. The technique had always worked before, and it would again.

It was very late now, Matt realized. Had it really been a full twenty-four hours since Erin's disappearance? He was only now beginning to feel the first twinges of fatigue from his relentless search for Mortimer's whereabouts, but he had to keep going. Erin's very life might depend on his ability to maintain an alert mind and body.

Already he had been to a number of hotels and restaurants in San Francisco; several employees had recalled the man described to them but had been unable to give Matt any pertinent information. As Hattie had suggested, he had stopped by the barbershops and haberdasheries but had found no new leads there either; the only remaining hope was the boardinghouses and more permanent lodgings. Eventually, he knew from past experience, something would break in his favor.

In a boardinghouse belonging to a widow named Mrs. MacIntosh, the fifth such establishment Matt had entered in the past hour and a half, his luck was with him. The widow at first shook her head in response to Ben Mortimer's description, but then became reflective.

"Seems there was a man like that . . . a huge horse of a man in here only last week. But I was full up, so I—" Mrs. MacIntosh hesitated a moment. "Listen, you offering a reward or anything?"

"Why not?" Matt pulled a roll of bills from his pocket and peeled off two of them, but did not give her the money right away.

"Well, like I was saying, I had no rooms, so I sent him down to Jenkins's Lodgings. Pretty sure he got a room there, too, 'cause old Jenkins don't keep a real tidy place like I do."

Matt thanked the woman, handed her the money, and left.

Jenkins's Lodgings turned out to be only a few doors down the street. When Matt entered the small lobby area, he knew this was the right place, the way a jungle cat knows where to ferret out its prey.

He approached the thin, shifty-eyed man lounging behind the front desk. "Do you have a Ben—Benjamin Mortimer registered here?" he asked flatly, his face impassive.

The clerk narrowed his eyes and pursed his lips. "My dear

sir, I am not allowed to give out any information about our honored guests."

"Oh, no?" Matt's expression became dangerous. "Perhaps you need a little persuasion." He reached over the counter and took a firm hold of the man's lapel. "I'll ask you just one more time—do you have a man named Mortimer in these lodgings?"

The clerk's face paled considerably. "Why . . . I think there's a man by that name . . ."

Matt gritted his teeth. "What room?"

"Ah—ah—number twenty, I—ah—believe."

Matt turned on his heel and sped up the flight of stairs. Room 20 was located at the end of the second-floor hallway, in a dark, out-of-the-way corner. He stood for a moment outside the thin wooden door, his heart pounding. He would have to be very careful now; Mortimer was a man whose strength might equal his size.

Tuning his senses to a sharp, perfect pitch, Matt put his foot to the door and gauged the force needed to break it in. Erin's life might well depend on his surprise entrance and quick assessment of the situation. He backed up a few feet, lunged forward, and kicked one leg straight out with all his strength. The door crashed inward, splintering off its hinges. Matt crouched inside the entryway, scanning the dimness beyond for a sign of possible retaliation, but could detect no movement.

Slowly he unfolded himself to an upright position. Then he noticed that a shaft of lamplight from the hallway fell on the room's bed, and to his horror he saw Erin lying naked on it, her wrists tied to the bedposts. The sight of her in such an undignified, degrading condition, with purple bruises and wicked-looking welts lacing her flesh, wrenched Matt to the depths of his soul.

It took every ounce of courage for him to light the lamp on the table and walk to the bedside. She has to be dead, he told himself; she couldn't have lived through this . . . this diabolical brutality. He put a finger to her throat and, mercifully, felt the faint but steady pulse beat. Releasing his breath slowly, Matt undid the gag around her mouth and set her wrists free, his hands trembling violently. For an instant his eyes froze on her bruised breasts, the full bosom of a nursing mother, he suddenly realized. A vile, bitter taste rose in his throat, and he fought back the urge to vomit the hatred for Mortimer that engulfed him. Then he reached out and drew the bed sheet up over Erin to cover her abused body.

Matt stood looking down at her for a few moments before seating himself on the edge of the bed and cradling her head in his lap, his eyes filling with hot tears. "Oh, God . . . Erin . . . wake up." He saw her lips move spasmodically and feared she would slip away from him for good. *Wake up, Erin, wake up!* he pleaded silently.

Calming himself as best he could, he began to speak to her slowly, softly, urging her back to reality. "I'm here, Erin . . . It's Matt . . . you're gonna be fine . . ."

A low, agonized moan escaped her lips.

"That's it, kid . . . wake up . . . It's me, Matt."

"Matt?" she whispered faintly, her tongue licking her dry lips.

"That's right . . . It's Matt . . . Open your eyes, there's nothing to fear now."

Her mouth formed his name; she felt a strong hand stroking her hair, her forehead, and she opened her eyes slowly. "Oh . . . Matt . . . you came for me."

"That's a damn crazy thing to say, kid!" He laughed tightly in relief, carefully sweeping her up into his powerful arms and clasping her to his chest. "Of course I came for you." He felt her stiffen slightly then, but not from pain. He knew it was from his touch, a man's touch. "Erin, don't be afraid, I won't hurt you. You'll never be hurt any more. I swear it."

She grew limp again, as if she couldn't fight the comfort and security of his embrace. "Oh, please, Matt, get me out of here," she wept. "Take me home."

He was about to lift Erin from the bed when he heard a heavy footfall coming down the hallway. He released her quickly and put a finger to her lips. "Hush, don't make a sound."

Erin's eyes widened in fear; her heart threatened to burst as the footsteps neared and then halted abruptly.

From the dim hall a voice bellowed, "What in hell is this?" And then Ben Mortimer's huge form filled the portal, his small eyes taking in the scene before him. "Who're you? What's going on—"

"You filthy son of a bitch!" Matt roared.

Erin curled up in a corner of the bed, one hand clutching

the sheet, the other grasping the bedpost. She began to shake in fear, not for herself, but for what Mortimer might do to Matt.

Mortimer stepped over the fallen door and came face to face with Matt.

Even though Matt was well over six feet, the other man loomed over him. Mortimer's mouth was twisted into a sick grin that said he was fully confident of his tremendous advantage of height and bulk.

But Matt was ready to meet the challenge. A muscle worked in his tight jaw, and his blue eyes narrowed at his opponent. "I'm going to kill you, you pig, and slowly." Matt's voice was barely audible, but filled the heavy silence in the small room.

Mortimer laughed. "Look I don't want to hurt you . . . Why not just share her?" His face still wore that ugly grin.

Matt kept his fury under control and did not rise to the bait.

"No? Well, then, why not use that pistol bulging under your coat?" Again the grotesque man let out a laugh.

"I might," Matt said dangerously, "but I'd rather kill you with my bare hands."

Erin heard this in mute disbelief. Matt couldn't possibly win against Mortimer—not at all! Oh, God, she prayed, don't let him try! Please . . .

As if it happened in slow motion, she saw Mortimer bring up his fist and swing at Matt, yet her husband easily ducked the punch and stepped aside with a catlike movement.

"Quicker than I thought," Mortimer said, looking more serious. "Underestimated ya, maybe." His hand went to his pocket and emerged with a razor-sharp hunter's knife.

"Use your gun, Matt!" Erin screamed. But Matt's lips were pulled back in a snarl, and he stood like a statue, waiting for his foe's next move.

Before Erin could tell who had moved first, Mortimer's quick side-slash had caught Matt in the ribs. Blood welled up through his white shirt and waistcoat, and she was certain he couldn't fight now.

Yet Matt did; he provoked Mortimer time and time again with every insult he could fling at him, as if he had planned to goad him into an uncontrollable rage. He ignored his wound, too, as if by allowing Mortimer to win the first round, he could catch him off guard.

Mortimer flung himself around the room, knocking over

330

the few pieces of furniture in a white-hot fury to get at Matt, who still ducked the man's attacks while continuing to provoke with insults. Suddenly Mortimer stumbled and fell heavily over the chair. Matt was on him like a panther, his foot grinding Mortimer's knife hand into the floor.

Erin found herself staring at them in silent fascination. The sound of Mortimer's cries mingling with the crackling of the bones in his hand should have disgusted her; instead, she was thrilled in a strange, primeval sort of way that would have shocked her if she had considered its implications.

"Jesus! You've broken my hand—crushed it!" Mortimer groaned.

Matt made no effort to back off; he leaned over the sprawling figure and placed his left forearm tightly up against Mortimer's fleshy neck, causing him to arch his back above the chair beneath him.

"Dammit! You win!" Mortimer choked. Still Matt continued to press deeper, his eyes narrowed in hate.

Suddenly Erin knew that Matt was furious enough to crush the breath from Mortimer's body. Was this what Matt was really like? she wondered. Was this how he had performed for the railroad? "No, Matt, don't!" she cried in terror.

For a split second he turned to her, his eyes dark, unfathomable pools, then directed his attention to Mortimer again. The fallen man mumbled unintelligibly, flailing his legs in the air, seeing the same deadly look in Matt's eyes that Erin had seen a moment before.

"You better make peace with your Maker . . . but I doubt it'll help." Matt's words fell on him like icy pellets.

"No!" Mortimer gagged. "No! You wouldn't kill an unarmed man!"

As his blood dripped onto Mortimer's chest, Matt slowly increased his strangle hold against the fat man's throat. Whatever words of pleading Mortimer uttered were lost when he sputtered and choked, fighting and twisting uselessly against the strength of Matt's arm.

Matt issued a final decree. "Go to hell, Mortimer."

The indescribable sound of flesh straining against bone permeated the room, and then all was silent for a few unearthly moments. Matt slowly came to his feet, perspiring, his face white from exhaustion. He drew a deep breath and steadied himself.

"Erin . . . we've got to go now . . . back to your place."

With an effort, he moved to the bedside and lifted her into his arms. "Don't look at me like that, Erin. Of all the people in the world, you should know he deserved it. I'm just sorry you had to watch."

She swallowed with difficulty. "You didn't . . . have to . . . for me."

"I'd kill anyone who hurt you."

Yes . . . of course he would. She knew that, and in his own way he was telling her something she couldn't yet fathom. But in spite of her revulsion over what had just taken place, she put her arms around his neck and rested her head on his chest.

Suddenly she remembered his wound. "Oh, Matt, you're hurt! You can't carry me. I'll try to walk," she offered, while knowing she could not.

He pressed her tightly to him, wrapped in the bed sheet, and made his way out of the room and down the dim hallway. Neither Erin nor Matt took notice of the few lodgers gathered in a frightened huddle in the corridor. Once they were outside in the cool night air, Erin again begged him to let her walk.

In answer, he whispered against her hair, "I'll find a carriage—it'll be all right. But when we get to your shop, you may have to carry me. Think you can?"

She could not believe he had laughed, that crazy, devil-may-care laugh of his. She snuggled up closer to him, feeling the warm, sticky blood on his clothes, his inner strength seeping into her like a forging, a molding together, of their spirits.

"You know what?" Her voice was a murmur. "If it had been you in my place, with someone like Mortimer . . . I would have killed him, too."

Matt looked down into her eyes, but they were closed now. Was Erin making a commitment? he wondered. Finally? Or was she just saying thanks in her own way?

An empty carriage came into view along the deserted street. Matt hailed it, ignoring the surprised look on the old driver's face, placed Erin carefully inside, seated himself next to her, and fell back against the cushion with a muffled oath.

Chapter 39

Erin was barely conscious when Matt carried her up to the door of the shop. As for himself, his right side throbbed painfully every time he moved, and he had lost a lot of blood. He set Erin on her feet at the door, but she sagged against him and he had to support her with one arm; with the other he rattled the doorknob loudly and then knocked.

A light came on instantly, and Hattie ran to admit them.

"Thank God!" Matt muttered as the door opened. He almost fell against Hattie; Erin stumbled along with him.

"Lord! Oh, Lord!" Hattie cried. "I've been so worried! Are you both all right? You don't *look* all right!"

Matt laughed weakly, pressing a hand to his wounded side. "I *think* we'll both live, but I'm not too sure at this point. You better get us upstairs, then call a doctor. See to Erin first—she's had a bad time."

"I knew it! I knew it! I *told* her not to wander around alone! Was it . . . ?"

"Yeah, it was Mortimer." Matt drew back his lips in a wolfish grin. "But he won't be bothering Erin any more."

"I don't think I want to know about it, Matt." Hattie transferred Erin's arm to her own shoulder and half carried her friend up the narrow stairs.

Matt followed behind, holding his arm tightly against his side. He took the steps one at a time, gasping with the effort, until he finally emerged into the lighted sitting room and collapsed on the sofa.

Hattie was busy with Erin in her bedroom; he could hear her soft voice and Erin's weak replies. At least he had gotten her home. Someone else could take care of her now. He felt dizzy and nauseated, and he closed his eyes wearily.

Moments later he felt gentle hands stripping off his coat and shirt, probing the deep wound. He mumbled, "Good ol' Hattie, you're a cool one' in an emergency, you know that?" Then he grunted with pain and opened his eyes to see Erin kneeling next to him, a basin of water on the floor and a cloth in her hand. Her hair was still wild and tangled, her face still bruised, but she wore a fresh dressing gown and appeared calm.

"You need a doctor, Matt. I've sent Hattie for one."

"Erin, what are you doing? Get back in bed . . . you've been hurt. I'll wait . . . let the doctor take care of it . . ." His voice faded to a weak mumble.

"Matthew Steele, you're in no condition to tell me what to do. You've lost a lot of blood and I'm afraid to wait." Then her voice softened and she put a hand on his arm. "I knew, somehow, that you'd find me. I had to believe it—I had to, to survive."

"You were always gettin' into trouble, Erin . . . always, damn fool kid . . ."

Erin felt hot tears prick her eyes and spill onto her hands as she tried to arrange clean toweling against his wound.

Matt asked trying to smile, "Erin . . . how's my son?"

She busied herself with the bandage, ashamed to meet his gaze. "He's fine. Hattie fixed a bottle and fed him. I'll have to wake him up soon to feed him myself."

"Erin," Matt said faintly, "you should have told me . . . it's hard to forgive you for that. No matter what you felt for me, or didn't feel . . ."

"Will you be quiet? I'm trying to stop the bleeding, damn it!" Tears still fell on her hands.

Matt touched her cheek. "Don't cry, Erin."

"Oh, stop it!" She wiped at her eyes with the back of her hand and drew a great, wavering breath. "There, that's all I can do for now. I wish Hattie would hurry!"

"You won't get rid of me that easily, Erin."

They heard footsteps on the stairs then. Hattie appeared first, followed by a small, thin man dressed in black and carrying a black case.

"Dr. Stein," Hattie introduced him.

Erin nodded. "Please see to—to my husband quickly. He's lost so much blood."

"This is quite irregular, young lady. Miss—ah—Nelson

tells me it's a knife wound. Is he a criminal?" The doctor frowned and pushed his spectacles up on the bridge of his nose.

"No, he was protecting me . . ." Erin said. "I just haven't had time to notify the police. Please help him!"

Dr. Stein let his spectacles slip lower again and gazed down through them at her, seeming to note the hastily thrown-on dressing gown, the wild hair, the pallid, bruised face. "Looks like you need some doctoring, too, young lady."

"Never mind me. For God's sake, take care of him! I'm all right!" Erin's voice was desperate now.

"All right, all right. Don't upset yourself."

He examined Matt's wound efficiently, murmuring to himself over it. Erin felt her deep sense of worry begin to ebb slightly, but she had to oversee everything the doctor did.

"Is it serious, Doctor? How bad is it?" she asked, hovering over him.

"It's a deep wound, but nothing vital was damaged. He'll be right as rain again soon—strong young fella."

"Thank God!"

"He'll need a lot of rest and care for the next few days. I'll give you instructions. But first we must move him to a more comfortable spot. Where's the bedroom?"

Erin blushed, realizing that the doctor naturally assumed they slept in the same bed. "In there." She motioned to her own room.

The three of them carried Matt inside. He groaned with pain, and his face was pinched and gray. At last he was lying in Erin's bed, stitched up and neatly bandaged. He seemed to have drifted into a delirious state, mumbling at times but making no sense.

Erin let herself be examined then, feeling every inch of her body ache unbearably. Dr. Stein expressed concern over her condition and gave her a sharp look through his spectacles, but asked no questions.

"You'll be plenty sore for a few days, Mrs. Steele, but no permanent harm was done. I'll leave you some laudanum for your husband." Then he shook a finger at her. "But I will have to report this . . . accident first thing in the morning, I warn you."

"Of course, Doctor. And I will also," Erin replied haughtily. "And thank you so very much for your help." She ushered him out with all the dignity she could muster, then let Hattie take him downstairs and attend to the fee while she collapsed on the sofa in the parlor.

Dr. Stein said to Hattie, "I'll stop by tomorrow to see how my patients are." Then his voice faded and the bell tinkled faintly as the door closed.

"Well," Hattie remarked as she reappeared in the sitting room, "this has been quite a night! You wanna tell me what happened?"

So Erin lived through the horror once again, until the shuddering sobs took over and she cried out her pain and torment on Hattie's thin shoulder.

Hattie offered only one very succinct statement. "You've got your man back now, Erin, and if you're smart you'll damn well keep him!"

Erin made no reply. Exhaustion finally took over and she fell asleep, with Hattie's hand gently stroking her hair.

A stripe of sunlight fell across Erin's eyes and woke her. She sat up, noticed she was on the sofa, and tried to remember what she was doing there. She looked around slowly and felt a great surge of relief that she was in her own apartment, for now she recalled bits and pieces of the horrible events of the last two days.

"Matt," she whispered, and rose quickly. But her body was still very stiff and sore, and she groaned aloud. She made her way slowly to her bedroom, holding on to the wall for support. Matt was asleep, his face as white as the sheets. He looked so young and vulnerable lying there, like a sick child. She reached out and touched his forehead; it felt cool, slightly damp from perspiration.

Then Erin heard the first morning wail from Patrick, closed the bedroom door quietly, and went back to the parlor to lift the baby from his cradle. She kissed his dark head and crushed his warm body to her. For a while she had thought she'd never see him again, that Matt would have to raise him, that he'd never know his mother at all. She should have known—she *had* known—that Matt would be there to save her. He always had been before. It would be so easy to let him take over for us, she mused, to let him rule my life, take care of me. But part of her mind rebelled against this thought; she couldn't let go like that; allow herself to be taken over completely, as Matt would do. Something held her back from wanting to reveal her weaknesses, her doubts, her needs. He would see them and twist them to his own desires.

Erin carried Patrick into her room, sat down in the upholstered chintz chair in the corner, and held him to her breast.

A short time later Matt woke up gradually, at first feeling an enormous sense of peace and security. Then he remembered Mortimer, and even before his eyes had opened, his hand went to his right side: a thick piece of gauze was bandaged over his still-tender wound. If I lie still, he thought, I'll feel fine, but I wonder what will happen when I try to move? He opened his eyes and looked up at the ceiling, then around the room—a very feminine room—done in blue and white flowered chintz with many ruffles.

His eyes settled on Erin sitting in the chair; at first he thought she was asleep because her head was bent forward, so that only the top of it showed, but then he realized that she was nursing the baby, *his son*. He remained silent, enjoying the sight of her nursing the child with such absorption. Somehow it seemed so reassuring, so right. And in that moment Matt admitted to himself that he loved Erin, that he had loved her for a long time, and that it had taken a near tragedy to expose the truth to him. He wondered if she was ready to accept him now, but decided he would feel her out carefully and not push too hard. If he gave her time, and the freedom to choose for herself, then maybe . . .

Erin's coppery head rose and her eyes met his, then widened in surprise. "Matt, you're awake," she almost whispered. "How's your side?"

"Don't rightly know yet. I've been afraid to move . . . and besides, I liked watching you feed him." He smiled at her.

Her face flushed. "He's almost done. I just wanted to keep an eye on you. You were sleeping so deeply . . ."

Matt frowned. "And how are you feeling? *You* weren't in such good shape, as I remember."

"I'm okay—sore, that's all." Her smoky eyes held more than a hint of embarrassment, and she bit her lower lip. "Matt . . ."

"Don't say it, kid. As far as I'm concerned, the whole episode is forgotten."

Erin sighed with relief, closed her dressing gown, and carried the baby to the bed. Matt clenched his teeth and pushed himself up into a sitting position.

"Oh, Matt, be careful. You'll start bleeding again."

He laughed. "Not with this great wad of bandage on me! Tell me, what happened after we got here last night? It's all sort of hazy."

"A nice doctor came and fixed you up . . . but, Matt, he said he'd have to report it to the police this morning."

"Don't worry. We'll send Hattie down there with a note, that's all. They can come up here and ask me anything they want." Matt fixed stern blue eyes on her. "And I'll keep you out of it, kid." Then he slapped a hand to his head and winced from the movement. "Damn, I hate to bring this up, Erin, but Sam—Samantha—is still sitting in that hotel room waiting for me. She'll be hysterical by now. I've got to let her know—"

"Don't worry. I'm not going to quarrel about her. We'll just have to send Hattie with a note to her, too, saying you'll see her later . . . or something," Erin finished lamely. She sat on the edge of the bed carefully. "Would you like to hold your son, Matt?" she asked, suddenly shy.

"Hold him? Sure it's okay?"

"Of course it is. He's as strong as a bull, Matt, and just as stubborn as you are!" She handed the baby to him. Patrick looked blearily at the strange visage bent over him, then, screwed up his face to cry.

"Here, Erin, better take him back. I'm afraid I'll drop him, or worse." Matt grinned somewhat foolishly.

"Want some breakfast? I'm starved." She suddenly realized that she had not eaten in over two days.

"Sure. A little." He put out his hand to stop her from rising. "Look, maybe you'd better stay put and take it easy. You've had a rough time."

"I'm all right, Matt, really. It'll do me good to keep busy."

He tugged at her arm, drawing her closer, then leaned across the baby and kissed her gently on the mouth, surprising her. "That's for taking such good care of me, Mrs. Steele."

"But—but I haven't done anything yet!"

"You will, Erin, you will." His eyes twinkled with laughter as she made a hasty retreat.

Hattie was sent off to the police with Matt's long, laboriously written note, which explained the circumstances of Mortimer's demise and where Matt could be reached for questioning. He had also given Hattie a note to deliver to

Samantha at the Grande Hotel. This letter, although brief, had been difficult to write. Matt had apologized for his absence, saying vaguely that his wife had needed his help and that he had been hurt, but not seriously, and was remaining in his wife's apartment for the time being. He had folded a couple of large bills into the envelope for Samantha's trip back to Denver City, expressed his hope that she would remember him without rancor, and told her that if she ever needed his help, she knew where to reach him.

Matt could picture Samantha after she received his letter; she would probably pout and cry and then buy herself a box of chocolates. He knew she was very fond of him, perhaps more than fond, but she had never really expected him to marry her. She would go back to her frilly flat, entertain her old friends, and maybe make a few new acquaintances to bury her sorrow. He felt a sincere affection for her. If she hadn't seen Mortimer in the shop . . . he didn't like to think about it.

When he had handed the envelope to Hattie, meeting her sharp eyes calmly, he had felt a new era beginning for him. He would be a different man now, capable of great tact and forbearance. Erin would see that he had changed, that he would accept her as she was and would cherish her. Lew had been right after all, Matt thought suddenly. His father had known the truth all along.

After Hattie had left, Matt fell back on the pillows, exhausted, and slipped into a half doze, dreaming that Erin confessed her love for him and promised to return to Aspen with him; but when he reached out to hold her, she was gone.

Erin would always remember that the days that followed were a serene interlude. Matt grew steadily stronger, even getting out of bed on the third day. Dr. Stein returned a few more times, checked Matt's wound, then admitted he could do no more for his patient. Hattie spent most of the working hours in the shop, tactfully leaving Matt and Erin alone. It was an idyllic respite for the married couple, suspended as it was from the outside world and from reality.

Erin often thought that she would dearly love being married to Matt and living with him if he were like this all the time, but she was convinced their present existence was make-believe and would last only until he had recovered. Then he would try to force her to submit to him again. But she gloried in every moment nevertheless, trying to tuck away each memory so that she could call it forth later, at her leisure, and examine it: Matt sitting on the sofa, bouncing Patrick on his knee and smiling; Matt at the dinner table smiling across from her; Matt opening his shirt for her as she changed the dressing, gently smiling at her. This new Matt, relaxed and happy, becoming more easy in his role as a father, confused her. He could never remain this way, she knew; he was really a selfish, conceited man, insistent on having his own way. But in spite of herself, Erin felt her heart soften toward him; she tried to please him in small ways, just to see his face light up with a smile. In the many years she had known him, he had rarely smiled with delight; usually, it had been a diabolical, mocking grin.

Matt, true to his promise to himself, never touched her, except to kiss her gently on the lips or to hold her hand. None of the old powerful, sexual innuendoes existed in the new Matt. Sometimes she caught him with a slight tilt to his lips as he watched her make a meal or take care of the baby. And then Erin would be amazed to find herself wanting him, but afraid to let him know it. So she would hold back, forcing herself to be satisfied with his chaste kisses while she burned restlessly inside.

Chapter 40

Early one morning in May the idyll ended.

Hattie had gone downstairs to open the shop while Erin and Matt finished breakfast. Patrick was perched on his father's knee while Matt tried to feed him some oatmeal. Erin and he both laughed when the baby grimaced and spit out the cereal. Erin wiped Patrick's face with a cloth, then put him down on a blanket with his favorite rattle.

"This is terrible, Matt. I'm such a malingerer, making

Hattie spend so much time running the shop. I'm perfectly capable now—it's been weeks! I have to start working again; there's last month's books to do, and more material to be ordered. Hattie can't do it all." She pushed her chair from the table and sighed as she looked around the kitchen, at the baby playing, at Matt sitting across from her, contentedly finishing a cup of coffee. "But this is so nice, so easy . . . It'll be hard to become a successful businesswoman again."

Matt's voice, when he spoke, was quietly pensive, and his gaze was grave. "Erin, as far as I'm concerned, you never have to set foot in that shop again. I have a home waiting for you on my ranch, which I built for myself, but it's a darn sight too big—it needs a family to fill it." He leaned across the table and took hold of her suddenly limp hand. "Erin . . . please."

Her thoughts whirled disconnectedly. Through the confusion one clear fact emerged and would not dissolve: the parting of the ways. She had known this would happen eventually; there was no longer any reason for Matt to stay now that his wound had healed. He didn't live in San Francisco, and he would want to go home, of course. But Erin was not ready to relinquish her newfound happiness. It was quite unlike her to put something off, especially something this important, but she simply could not make a decision now. Matt had been so different of late, so giving. She had even managed to tell him about Norwood, and, amazingly, he had smiled, saying he understood and would do everything to ensure that the estate remained hers. And now she was unable to return his kindness.

"Matt, please, give me some time to think . . . I just . . . don't . . . know."

He let go of her hand and gave it a pat. Careful, he thought, go slow—she's as nervous as a green filly. "Sure, kid, take your time. I'll be around a few more days. Kinda like it here. Can we get some more of that crab for dinner?" Change the subject, that's it. Don't show your disappointment. She needs time.

Matt did not say another word, but a pall fell over Erin, and she could not recapture her recent mood of gaiety. She tried desperately to search her heart, to decide what to do. It was very tempting to think of going with him and not working any more. Her child would grow up with his father; there would be so many advantages. But all these reasons paled before her fear. Yes, she admitted to herself, she was deathly afraid of returning to their old relationship—the quarrels, the bitterness, the physical force. She was not really sure how she felt about Matt, and she was equally confused as to his feelings for her. He seemed to like her, to enjoy her company, to appreciate her, but was this only because of the baby, because she was the child's mother? Was there something else in his feelings for her? Sometimes she thought—but no, he had never loved her, and he never would. She was convenient right now, that was all. He had asked her to go back to Aspen with him, but he had never said he *needed* her, or *loved* her. These were the words she craved.

Erin had moved back into her bedroom and Matt slept on the sofa; he had insisted on this. He never approached her in any way but with open friendship. She alternated between feeling grateful to him and puzzled; didn't he want her any more? Had she become undesirable to him since Mortimer? Often, as she tossed and turned in her bed at night, knowing Matt lay in the next room, she had been tempted to go to him, to stretch out along the strong, warm length of him, to feel the curling ends of hair on the back of his neck, to stroke the sinews of his arms. But she had never done so, because she still resented the power he held over her.

The next few days drifted by, bittersweet. Erin and Matt were polite to each other, but the warmth had gone out of their being together. She had no answer for him, not that he prodded her for one, but she felt his eyes on her often.

One night Erin was particularly restless and finally fell asleep a few hours before dawn. But her sleep was broken by a nightmare; she dreamed she was tied to Mortimer's bed again and that his bloated face was leering down at her, his huge fingers reaching out to pinch, to squeeze, to degrade. She tried to scream, but her mouth was filled with a foul-tasting cloth, and the hands were coming closer—

"Erin, shhh! You were having a bad dream!"

She started violently, then felt a reassuring hand on her shoulder and heard a low voice whispering calming words.

"Erin, easy, now. Nobody's here but me. Take it easy, kid." The bed creaked as Matt sat on the edge; then the lamp flared, dispelling the dark shadow. "Lord, kid, I could hear you in the other room! It must have been a grandmother of a dream!" Matt's hair was tousled from sleep and his chest was bare, but his smile was as welcome as anything she had ever seen.

"Oh, Matt! It was Mortimer, coming after me . . . and I was tied to the bed—" She trembled with remembered horror.

He took her in his arms, stroking her hair tenderly. "Hey, now. He's gone. He'll never hurt you again."

She let Matt hold her. It felt good to lean on him, to have his strong arms around her. His presence chased all the ghosts away, and her heartbeat gradually became normal once more.

"Are you okay now?" He held her at arm's length, searching her face.

"Yes . . . better."

"Then I guess we should both try to get back to sleep." He started to rise, but Erin grasped his hand, almost involuntarily.

"Don't go—please! I don't want to be alone!" The words were out before she could stop them.

Matt looked at her for a long moment. Was she actually ready to accept him, he wondered, or was she only frightened because of the dream? He slipped under the bedcovers and took her in his arms. She was still trembling; he didn't know whether it was from the nightmare or from his nearness. She buried her head in his neck and he could smell the sweet scent of her hair. It had been a long time since he had held her like this, a very long time. He could feel her heavy breasts pressing into his side, her long, slim legs touching his own. He kissed her hair tenderly and she lifted her head, her mouth eager for his. Their lips met and locked in a passionate kiss.

Suddenly he drew back and gazed at her. "Are you sure?"

"Yes," she whispered fiercely, moving against him. "Yes."

He was gentle, remembering what she had been through, and she gave herself to him eagerly, wantonly, as if to prove something to herself, absorbing him in her stormy abandonment until her convulsive movements ceased and he was completely drained.

They lay entwined together, the only sound in the room that of their heavy breathing. Matt finally raised himself on one elbow and kissed her lips.

"It's been too long, kid," he said softly.

Erin turned her head away so that he could not see her expression, but he heard her muffled words: "I know."

"Will you come home with me now, Erin?" he asked quietly, turning her to face him.

She felt empty, desolate. "I can't," she whispered. Two tears traced paths down her cheeks. "I just can't."

Matt's patience cracked. "Why in hell not?" he demanded harshly.

"I . . . I don't even know . . . It's just . . . I feel so strongly that we'd ruin it."

"Erin, at this point we don't have anything to ruin, not any more. We can start all over, at the beginning."

"No," she murmured. "It wouldn't work. I'd rather have *this* to remember than the agony we used to know. I couldn't bear that."

"And can you bear it better to live alone for the rest of your life, to raise my son alone, never to live in Aspen again? Is *that* better?"

"No, no! I don't know!" she cried. "I just can't go with you—I know that much!"

Matt swore softly, almost to himself. He sat up in bed, the lamplight flickering on the play of his bare muscles. "Look, Erin, I've delayed going home, but I have a ranch to run, and I can't stay here any longer—much as I've enjoyed my *holiday*," he added ironically. "I've given you more than enough time to decide. I'll be on the train leaving the day after tomorrow. Just thought you should know."

"Oh, God." Erin's voice was full of her anguish.

Matt felt his own heart wrench at the thought of leaving her, and his son, but he had to put a stop to her procrastination, and force her to decide. After tonight, he was pretty sure Erin would give in and come with him.

He blew out the lamp. "Let's try to get some sleep. Think about it in the morning. Things always look better in the morning."

Matt's bags were packed, his train ticket lying on the table in plain view. Erin felt tears near the surface as she dressed to accompany him to the station. He had told her that he would get a carriage and go alone—he had told her this several times—but it was as if she wanted to punish herself by being with him to the bitter end. Hattie would stay at home with Patrick.

Erin wore a dark gray velvet suit, a color to match her somber mood, with a tucked, tailored white blouse. She put on a huge hat whose sweeping, cloud-colored plumes shadowed her pale face, and pinned it into place. After donning her gloves, she drew a deep breath and went into the sitting room, where Matt waited.

He looked so handsome, she thought, seeing him as if for the first time; tall and straight in his elegantly cut beige frock coat, his dark hair waving luxuriously, his brilliant blue eyes as compelling as ever, if a little sad. She longed to throw herself at him and beg him to stay, or to take her with him, but it was too late to do that now. In an hour he would be gone from her life forever, for what man would be foolish enough to return to a woman who had spurned him so thoroughly? Apart from her own misery, she experienced the additional feeling of guilt for keeping Matt from his son through her decision. She wondered, for the hundredth time, if she was doing the right thing, but a clear answer still eluded her. If it wasn't the right thing, she told herself, it was the only thing she *could* do.

"Are you ready?" Matt asked.

"Yes." Her voice was very low.

Hattie stood nearby, holding Patrick. Matt turned to her and the baby cooed, holding out his arms to the now-familiar face of his father. Matt embraced the child and gave him a kiss on the cheek.

"Goodbye, Hattie," he said gravely, taking her hand, "and thanks for everything. I mean it."

Hattie did not reply, but she squeezed his hand, and her eyes were bright with unshed tears.

Erin and Matt walked down the narrow stairs and out of the boutique. It was a warm, sunny day in San Francisco, and the streets were crowded with people promenading in all their finery past the elegant shops and restaurants.

Matt hailed a coach, loaded his bags on the top rack, and helped Erin to climb inside. The trip to the station seemed to last forever, and yet to take no time at all. Erin stared straight ahead, unseeing, quiet. Matt sat against the back of the seat, deep in his own thoughts.

Finally he broke the expectant silence. "You can leave me

at the station and go back in the carriage—no use prolonging this any further."

Erin looked at her gloved hands, pulling at a stray thread. "No, Matt, I'll go with you."

"What for?" he asked bluntly.

"I don't know. I guess I want to."

"It's your life, kid, do what you want."

Within a few more minutes they had reached their destination. The walk down the long, echoing platform to Matt's train was exquisite torture for Erin, knowing that each step brought her closer to a loneliness without end. Passengers and friends embraced around them, and small children ran in circles, chased by frantic mothers. Puffs of steam hissed from the front of the train; the conductor glanced at his large gold watch and began to intone: "All aboard, ladies and g'men, all aboard!"

"Guess this is it, kid," Matt said, bending to kiss Erin on the cheek. "Take good care of my boy. I'll expect him to spend summers with me when he's old enough." He looked at her, his head cocked to one side, the old mocking grin on his thin lips. "And take care of yourself, Erin. I mean that. Don't get in any more trouble—I won't be around to pull you out of it."

He picked up his bags and swung himself up lithely onto the metal steps, disappearing into the dark interior of the train without a backward glance.

"Goodbye, Matt," Erin whispered. She stood as if in a trance while the train, a smoggy leviathan, chugged slowly past her and out of the station into the sunlight. Long minutes later, she was still staring at the distant point beyond which the train had vanished.

Chapter 41

A deep void chilled Erin's heart; her mind was blank. Matt was gone. Never again would she hear his exasperating low drawl calling her "kid," or feel his warm hand on her skin. He had never said he loved her, nor, she had to admit, had she declared herself. But it struck her abruptly, and so simply: she *did* love him. Why else would she now feel as if her body and mind had been wrenched in half?

All these years she had fought him so desperately, but the desperation was of her own making, not of his, she suddenly realized. He had begged her—as much as Matt could beg—to come back with him. He had forgiven her every cruelty toward him, every stubborn tantrum, every nasty word. Her mind was filled with a pure, uncomplicated lucidity. He wanted her and she had rejected him, for no other reason than that of her overweening pride. And she loved him! How incredibly foolish she had been!

Erin's lips curved in a smile as she turned around and walked back quickly to the gate and then toward the ticket window. It occurred to her that she must appear ridiculous, smiling like a madonna while she waited in line.

"Two tickets to Aspen, Colorado," she said firmly to the clerk, digging in her reticule for some money. "First class, a compartment, please, and there will be an infant along. The next train, please."

When she walked out of the station clutching the tiny pieces of cardboard, she felt as light as air, as if she could fly. The smile would not leave her lips even while she stood on the street and hailed a coach.

"Western Union, please," she told the driver. He nodded, clucking to the spavined nag.

San Francisco had never looked so beautiful, Erin thought. The buildings, climbing laboriously up the steep hillsides, sparkled in the sun, and the Bay—cobalt blue—gave off glints where the sun touched the crests of the waves. Everyone looked well dressed, happy, and wonderful to Erin—even the beggars and the ragged sailors.

She sent a brief wire to Matt at the house in Aspen, praying the message would reach him before he went out to his ranch, or that one of the servants would find him before he left town. It was the best she could do. The wire stated only when she would be arriving, nothing more. Words could not begin to describe her feelings; Matt would understand. If he did not choose to meet her in Aspen, she would find him, throw herself at his feet, if necessary, and make him understand.

Erin was still smiling when she pushed open the door of her shop on Market Street. She looked around as if she had never seen the interior before. She belonged with her husband and child, not in a shop full of frivolous, expensive things for rich women. Everything seemed so simple to her now.

"Erin, how can you look so happy when you've sent your husband home alone?" Hattie asked reproachfully.

"I know, and it was a foolish, crazy thing to do!"

"What?" Hattie was dumbfounded at Erin's lightheartedness.

"Yes, it was, so we're all going home on the next train!"

"We are?"

"Yes. I've bought the tickets, and all we need to do is pack—"

"Erin, excuse me, but what in hell are you going to do with this shop, and the apartment, and all the stock?"

"Oh . . . close everything up. The bank can sell it all for me—they'll be glad to," Erin replied nonchalantly, pulling off her gloves and smoothing her hair back. "Now I must get busy." She approached the stairs, holding up the hem of her skirt daintily.

"Well, I'll be a drunken sailor!" Hattie exclaimed, staring up the stairs after her. "I'll be damned!"

It was dawn when the train started its descent into Roaring Fork Valley from Glenwood Springs. Erin sat near the window, straining to see out. The Rio Grande had laid these tracks only six months ago, Matt had told her, and she couldn't help but recall her carriage trip to Glenwood Springs

348

almost three years before. The road had been barely passable then—rough, rock-strewn, and dusty. Now the train rode along the shiny rails, and with every turn of the iron wheels she was coming closer to home—to Matt. Her heart lurched at the thought. Would he be there to meet her? Maybe he had missed her wire; maybe he wouldn't meet her even if he had received it. She drew a breath and calmly decided that it didn't matter; she would find him and convince him that she loved him.

Hattie sat across from Erin, also pressed to the window. Abraham slept in his traveling case at her feet; Patrick was asleep in his cradle. The morning sun slowly sent its pale golden rays toward them, along the valley floor.

Erin had noticed that the trees were thick and green in the town of Glenwood Springs; it had looked like full summer there. The wild rose bushes that had lined the tracks were already budding, and the sagebrush was silvery green. But as the train continued up the valley, it was as if Erin were traveling backward in time. The trees became covered with an immature green that gave way to the feathery gauze of new buds as the train climbed and descended. From summer they retreated to late spring, then to early spring: a pregnant waiting time of year in the mountain valley. Snow still clung to the peaks, extending long white arms in places.

Erin drank in the familiar sights of the valley: the river flashing by below them; the rolling red hills near Glenwood Springs; the cone of Mount Sopris, dazzling white in the early sun; the craggier vistas as they neared Aspen; the winding curves where the valley narrowed; the slanting, sage-covered slopes. The sun rose higher; it would be one of those glorious late-May days, the kind that promised the advent of summer.

Erin smoothed her traveling suit. She wanted to look her best, in case Matt was there, but it was difficult in the confines of their compartment. She had risen very early, in the dark, her heart pounding with excitement the moment she had opened her eyes. She had put on one of her favorite outfits, a tailored linen suit in a warm shade of burnt sienna that accentuated her coppery hair and made her eyes appear deep gray. A jabot of white lace showed at the neck of the jacket, which was trimmed with intricate swirls of brown velvet braid. She had tried to put her hair up, but had found that chore almost impossible, her hands had shaken so in her excitement. Well, it will just have to do, she told herself, trying to secure one stubborn curl that had already tumbled down her neck.

She felt a hot flush rise involuntarily to her cheeks, and her heart began to thump nervously again. What if she had made a serious mistake in coming back? If Matt didn't want her, what would she do? He might even have Samantha, or some other woman, living with him! The dire possibilities crowded her brain, fevering her imagination. What if he laughed in her face? Where would she go? She had burned all her bridges behind her, she had nowhere to run to this time. Erin played with the strings of her reticule and watched the scenery float by, trying to clear her mind of doubts. If Matt wasn't at the station, she had to remain calm. He might very well not have received the wire by going directly to his ranch, or he might have something else to do today, something important. Oh, dear Lord, she groaned silently, if he isn't there . . .

The train stopped at Aspen Junction, where the Frying Pan River emptied into the Roaring Fork. The new station was bustling, even this early, and several freight cars full of silver ore stood in the train yard, ready for the long haul over the pass to Leadville. Halfway home, thought Erin, and she had to clench her jaw to keep her teeth from chattering.

Hattie put a hand on Erin's knee and smiled reassuringly at her, but said nothing. As the train started up again, lurching forward, Patrick awoke and began his first cry of hunger. Erin was glad to have something else to think about besides her own fears. Nursing her son always relaxed her.

"We're going home," she whispered to him. "We're almost there."

They passed the mouth of Snowmass Valley, and whatever composure had remained to Erin fell away as she remembered the last time she had been here, slightly over a year ago. She could almost feel Matt's powerful arms around her, holding her in front of him on his horse, forcing her to the ground, taking her. She shivered at the memory. Why had it ever come to that? Why had she fought him so? It made no sense to her now. If only he gave her a chance to atone for the years of struggle between them. If only . . .

They entered a narrow, winding length of track—steep rock walls on the left, the chasm of the river on the right, the pale green branches of trees almost brushing the cars as they moved along the rails. Small waterfalls cascaded down the rock faces in streaks of silver wetness. Then the train crossed

Hunter Creek and the land opened up again. Erin could see Aspen Mountain looming ahead, curbing the town's runaway growth on one side, determining its shape and atmosphere. The morning sun struck the top of the mountain, while the valley still lay in shadow.

Erin lowered her eyes from the mountain to see the rapid approach of Aspen, her home. Then she gasped in shock. Everywhere she looked there were houses—wood-framed, small, large, several-storied. Matt had told her that the town had boomed since the railroad had arrived, but she had trouble believing her own eyes. The valley floor was covered with buildings. She could see the downtown section as the train drew closer; the tall brick structures crowded each other. The huge black mines squatted heavily over their tunnels like giant nesting birds. And the wagons, the carriages, the people crowding the streets! Dust, disturbed by the traffic, hung in a cloud over everything. As they approached the outskirts of the station, Erin saw a boy hawking newspapers. And the new train yard was filled with empty cars, freight cars, and railroad workers scurrying about.

She closed her eyes, recalling her first view of the valley nine years before—the dull November emptiness, the land rolling away in the distance, the white smoke rising from the chimneys of the few houses. And she remembered the vision she had had then. Yes, she thought, opening her eyes, it was just as she had seen it in her mind's eye. Aspen was a real city now, involved in its own business, impersonal, moving forward.

Then the train slowed, its brakes squealing as it pulled into the depot on the north side of town. For a moment her sight was obscured by a cloud of steam from the engine, but when it cleared, she could not see Matt's tall form anywhere in the throng that crowded the platform.

Erin turned from the window and busied herself with readying Patrick, smoothing her hair, and checking Abraham's traveling case. Her heart pounded heavily and her mouth felt as dry as dust. She closed her eyes and tried once more to calm herself, but she felt weak and lightheaded from so much nervous anticipation.

Hattie looked at her sympathetically and squeezed her hand. "It'll be all right," she said. "You'll see."

"Hattie, I hope you're right. I hope I did the right thing . . ."

"You did, Erin. And we're home now."

"Yes, home," Erin whispered, smiling shakily. Then, gathering her courage, she said more firmly, "Yes, we're home. Let's go."

Hattie carried the baby while Erin led the way, picking up Abraham's heavy case and edging out into the narrow corridor of the car. Her knees felt stiff, but she forced her feet, one in front of the other, down the passageway. At last she stood at the top of the steps, unable to move any farther. She searched the crowded platform but could not spot Matt at all; surely she would be able to see him if he were there. But the faces eddied and flowed below her, and Matt did not appear.

Erin's heart sank and her stomach knotted in despair. So he did not want her after all—his words had all been lies, her hopes were all destroyed, her decision made too late. She felt cold, as if her blood had turned to ice in her veins, but she lifted her skirt with one hand, got a better grip on Abraham's case, and began to climb slowly down the metal steps. As she stepped onto the platform she glanced up, and the crowd seemed to thin out for a moment.

A tall man was leaning with casual grace against the doorframe of the depot, his arms folded. The man's Stetson was pushed to the back of his dark head in a familiar fashion, and Erin could see a smile on his face—*his* old mocking smile, but filled with something else, something new. As he straightened up and walked toward her, she mouthed his name: *"Matt,"* and their eyes met across the platform in a look that said everything.

Erin knew that she had come home at last.

Dear Reader:

Would you take a few moments to fill out this questionnaire and mail it to:

Richard Gallen Books/Questionnaire
8-10 West 36th St., New York, N.Y. 10018

1. What rating would you give *The Silver Kiss?*
   ☐ excellent ☐ very good ☐ fair ☐ poor

2. What prompted you to buy this book? ☐ title
   ☐ front cover ☐ back cover ☐ friend's recommendation ☐ other (please specify) _____

3. Check off the elements you liked best:
   ☐ hero ☐ heroine ☐ other characters ☐ story
   ☐ setting ☐ ending ☐ love scenes

4. Were the love scenes ☐ too explicit
   ☐ not explicit enough ☐ just right

5. Any additional comments about the book?
   _____

6. Would you recommend this book to friends?
   ☐ yes ☐ no

7. Have you read other Richard Gallen
   romances? ☐ yes ☐ no

8. Do you plan to buy other Richard Gallen
   romances? ☐ yes ☐ no

9. What kind of romances do you enjoy reading?
   ☐ historical romance ☐ contemporary romance
   ☐ Regency romance ☐ light modern romance
   ☐ Gothic romance

10. Please check your general age group:
    ☐ under 25 ☐ 25-35 ☐ 35-45 ☐ 45-55 ☐ over 55

11. If you would like to receive a romance
    newsletter please fill in your name and
    address:
    _____
    _____
    _____